Their Property

THEIR PROPERTY

SONS OF ODIN MC

CRYSTAL ASH

To everyone who fights to be heard and taken seriously.

Keep giving them hell.

Their Property playlist

Survivor - Pop Evil
Dirty Thoughts - Chloe Adams
Afraid of Heights - Billy Talent
I'm Not Over - Carolina Liar
Turn The Page - Metallica
Red Eyes And Tears - Black Rebel Motorcycle Club
Virgo - Atmosphere
Gone Away - The Offspring
Ride Of The Valkyries - Brothers of Metal
Only Love Can Save Me Now - The Pretty Reckless
Thin Line - honey honey
The Heresy - Mushroomhead
Stand By Me - Ki:Theory
Heat Waves - Daniel Robinson
Ride - Lana Del Rey

Content Warning

This book takes place in a dystopian world. Our heroes never harm the heroine, but physical violence is a regular occurrence throughout the story.

This story also contains mentions of sexual assault, human trafficking, spousal and child abuse, murder, torture, sexism, and homophobia.

Chapter 38 contains references to past incidents of infanticide.

PROLOGUE

KYRIE

FOUR YEARS EARLIER

I paced the barren room, dragging my hand along the blank concrete walls. At first, I had been looking for cracks in the walls. Maybe a hidden door with a secret passage like in the books I read as a little girl.

But nothing was on the other side except for solid concrete. He made sure of that. He also made sure no one would be able to rescue me up here.

I stopped my pacing to lean my forehead against a patch of sunlight that hit the wall from one of the windows, too high for me to see out of.

"How could I have been so fucking stupid?" I whispered, not for the first time since being locked in here a week ago.

I pictured my father's disapproving frown in my head and hit the wall with the side of my fist. He'd chastise me for saying *fuck* first, because that was improper language, unbecoming of a governor's daughter, and *then* lecture me about sneaking off unchaperoned with a boy I barely knew.

A boy I thought I was in love with. Who'd said awful, cruel things to me once I was in his clutches, and then imprisoned me in this room.

"You'll stay here until you're my wife," Malcolm had said, his grin smug as his eyes raked over me. "And then you'll be moved to our room where you'll be…broken in."

I was blinded by his charm, his flirtations. His wit and arrestingly handsome face. Father said we were likely to get married at a later date, so what was the harm in spending more time with him? When Malcolm Blake, heir to the Blakeworth territory, asked me to sneak away so he could show me a surprise, I said yes without a second thought.

In hindsight, I realized what I wanted most of all was to get out from under my father's thumb. And that led me straight into a trap.

My eyelids fluttered closed as I rocked my forehead against that patch of sunlight on the wall. *Stupid, naive idiot. Even if I do make it back home, Dad won't ever let me step outside without a guard detail again.*

A flutter of wings had me blinking my eyes open. Hovering in the window, covered in glossy black feathers, was a raven. The bird was big enough to block the sunlight, and stared at me with dark, ominous eyes.

The raven cawed once before flying off, and my feet seemed to drag toward the window of their own volition. I wanted to follow that bird to freedom, to feel the sky and fresh air again.

I wondered if it was the same raven that came to me in my dreams. That caw soothed my nerves somehow. It was almost as comforting as a human voice telling me to wait, that help would come.

The sound of clanking metal across the room dashed that hope just as quickly as it arose. I turned to the door, my body already stiff as the series of locks clanked and slid. When it opened, a maid with a plain face and a simple dress walked in, her eyes downcast respectfully. My relief that it wasn't *him* was short-lived.

"Hello, Miss Vance. Mr. Blake would like you to attend the contractor's mixer in the gardens with him this afternoon," she said to the floor. "I'm here to help you prepare."

I blinked, momentarily confused. "He's...letting me out?"

"You are his fiancée. You are expected to make public appearances with him." This woman was so prim, so matter-of-fact, that I wanted to scream at her. His *fiancée?* Could she not see that I was his fucking prisoner?

"Ma'am, um." I wrapped my fingers around each other, my pulse quickening. "I'm not sure if you're aware of the situation, but he's keeping me against my will. I've been trapped in here for at least a week. Please, I'm begging you—"

"We need to get you washed and dressed, Miss Vance," she cut me off curtly as she opened the door wider and stepped aside. "Please follow me. If you try to run, you *will* be caught and reprimanded."

Her callousness hurt me almost as much as Malcolm's. I stared at her with my jaw hanging open. "How can you actually be loyal to him? To his family? When they treat people of your status so poorly? In my father's territory, you'd be making a livable wage, and no one would treat you like you're beneath them!"

The maid sneered at me, her first sign of emotion since walking in. "Don't act like you know me or my situation, rich girl."

I startled at the vitriol in her voice like she'd slapped me.

"You've been trapped here a week? Poor little thing," she mocked. "My family is indentured to the Blake family for three generations. If I help you, or even step a foot out of line, my son will be sent away to a labor camp. My daughter? Trafficked and used like an animal. And they'll add three more generations to my family's servitude." The woman took slow, measured steps closer to me as she spoke. "You? At least you'll lie back on a feathertop mattress, clad in silk and jewels, while only *one* man—your future husband—rapes you."

A choked gasp left my throat. The full weight of my reality hit me right then with the force of a collapsing building. No one in this territory was going to help me. I was never going to escape.

"Follow me now." The maid turned back to face the door. "The mixer starts in a few hours, and we need to prepare you to be seen by the public."

In a state of shock and numbness, I followed after her.

THE NEXT FEW hours passed by in a blur. I'd been washed, scrubbed, waxed, and tweezed by a team of maids, then manipulated like a doll into an expensive, floor-length gown. They put colored contact lenses in my eyes, some unnatural color like bright turquoise. They caked makeup on my face and put on fake lashes that were at least two inches long with feathers in them, which turned my thoughts to the raven hovering at my window. Would he see me out there, dressed like a ridiculous bird?

I looked flashy and rich, like a future member of the Blakeworth elite class. Inside, I felt numb. Dead. Hopelessly alone.

The staff walked me out to a foyer when they finished, and not even seeing Malcolm's face stirred anything in me. When he imprisoned me in that room, I sobbed like a heartbroken wreck for days. I pounded on the walls and door, begging and pleading for him not to treat me like this. He'd said he loved me.

Now, I gave a demure smile as I was presented to him, because it was expected of me. Be silent, agreeable, and pleasing to look at, *or else*. That was all the Blakeworth men wanted, a decorated prop at their sides.

Malcolm's cold appraisal of me from head to toe would have hurt my feelings, at one point. I would have wondered what I could do better to earn his approval. But now, I was only glad he looked bored, rather than in a mood to leave bruises on my arms and scream cruel obscenities in my face.

He spoke at me on the ride to the botanical gardens, and I answered when it was appropriate, but I wasn't really there. I used to marvel at all the rare, exotic plants in the gardens when I accompanied my father on diplomatic trips. Now I had tunnel vision and my other senses were numbed. No extinct flower or sweet scent could pull me out of the box I'd shut myself in.

At some point, Malcolm sat me down in a covered gazebo with his father, the governor of Blakeworth. His mother was there too, drinking herself into oblivion as usual. I used to wonder why she always appeared inebriated, and now I understood. I might as well have been looking into a mirror twenty years into the future.

Some woman joined us in the gazebo, likely some other man's wife that Malcolm and his father would take turns fucking just because they could. He certainly bragged about it often enough.

The woman sat next to me and oohed and ahhed over my engagement ring, some flashy rock that a maid had slipped onto my finger while dressing me. Malcolm wasn't even man enough to propose to me himself.

I sat there like the pretty, empty-headed doll I was supposed to be, fantasizing about when I'd be locked in my room again and away from these awful people. The woman then shoved a wadded-up tissue into my palm, and that curious thing was what brought me back to myself.

Carefully unfolding the tissue in my hand, I glanced at Malcolm and his father through my ridiculous lashes. Neither of them paid attention to me, so I returned to looking down in my lap while hiding the tissue as best I could. It took all my resolve not to change a single muscle in my posture or expression.

The woman had written in lipstick, *4C. Here 2 help.*

My heart kicked like a drum in my chest, but it wasn't entirely out of fear anymore. My father *did* send for my rescue. Of course they had to blend in with the Blakeworth elite to get near me. I took a careful glance at the woman, who smiled blankly at the governor. Even with her makeup, colored contacts, and crazy lashes like mine, I was certain I'd never seen her before. Who was she?

Out of nowhere, a sound like thunder clapped so hard that it made my ears ring. On instinct, I covered my head and doubled over. All around me were shouts, screams, and popping noises that could only be gunshots. Commotion flew around me, and I could hear the woman yelling something at the governor.

And then someone grabbed my wrist in a hold that was firm, but not painful like how Malcolm grabbed me. I looked up at the woman's face, her expression concerned and intense.

"You have to come with me." She pulled me to my feet, and I was too stunned to do anything but follow.

"Is it true?" I asked dumbly. "You're with my father?"

"Sort of." The woman's pace picked up, her head whipping around like she was looking for someone. "We're taking you home. You'll be safe."

We ran from the gazebo through a botanical garden that was now a war zone. The smoke in the air choked my throat and made my lungs feel frozen. A small part of me screamed to go back, to take cover with Malcolm and his family. It'd be better than the punishment I'd face after trying to escape and getting caught.

But the woman never released me as we ran across the lawn together. She was heading for the intersection at the edge of the block. Was she planning on running into traffic? Did she have a plan at all?

The *rat-tat-tat* of rapid gunfire sounded even louder. I didn't wonder if Blakeworth police would shoot me or not, I just ran faster. But my extra burst of speed was short-lived. Either I tripped or the woman did, but we flew through the air in the next moment and hit the ground hard.

No! No, I can't go back to him! I'd rather die…

Someone took hold of my arms and dragged me up to my feet. I would have cried out in despair if I could breathe easier. I didn't give a fuck about being a future governor's wife. I was not going to be trapped, used, and unloved…

A large palm pressed to the side of my face and then briefly on my neck and shoulders, as if to check for injuries. My eyes took a moment to focus on the face in front of me. It belonged to a man who looked vaguely familiar. Older than Malcolm by at least a decade, with crow's feet at the edges of his warm, brown eyes. Long, black hair framed his face and fell past his shoulders. His brows furrowed with concern as he checked me over. Even under his thick beard, I could see his full lips pressed together tightly.

More details filtered in, sending messages to my brain that I would later hold on to like precious mementos. I just didn't know it at the time.

A leather vest. A broad body covered in dense muscle. Leather boots and scuffed jeans. Large hands that were gentle when they touched me, but also carried a gun. One hand brought my gaze to his with light contact on my jaw. This man wasn't beautiful or classically handsome like Malcolm. He was all hard edges, a jagged exterior that was beautiful in the same way that mountains were.

My savior opened his mouth but didn't speak. He slowly mouthed the words, *You're safe.*

And I believed him.

CHAPTER 1

KYRIE

PRESENT DAY

I gripped the edge of my skirt and pulled the fabric down toward my knees for the hundredth time. My clothes were modest enough for the territory of Sevier. I just had to not psych myself out for when the governor and his cabinet would surely inspect me through a microscope.

The landscape raced by outside my car window, all craggy rock formations that looked like giants in the setting sun. Home was far behind me now, and getting farther with each rotation of the armored SUV's wheels.

Anxiety fluttered in my stomach, but most of it was excitement. I hadn't left my father's territory, Four Corners, in four long years. How poetic was that?

My feelings on that leaned more toward resentment than serendipitous, however. It took *this* long to convince my father that I wouldn't get kidnapped again if I stepped outside of his territory. Four years to make him see that I was a grown woman, not a helpless child. Four years of fighting and insisting that I could handle myself, within reason.

My captivity in Blakeworth had changed me, though my father was hard-pressed to believe it. I wasn't so naive, so blindly trusting anymore. In fact, I could count the number of people I trusted on one hand and still have fingers left over.

That didn't mean I wanted to be locked up and hidden away forever.

Months ago, I'd applied to be an ambassador in Sevier and jumped for joy when I was accepted. My father said nothing. He locked himself in his study and didn't come out for a full day. I feared the worst, like he might actually imprison me in my room as I had been in Blakeworth. But as overprotective as Governor Vance was, he loved me and wanted me to be happy.

Malcom Blake had only wanted to control me.

My father emerged from his study with tears in his eyes and held my hands. He said, "My biggest fear is losing you like I lost your mother. My second biggest fear is my child hating me because I crushed her dreams."

I left for my ambassadorship three months later. Poor Dad fretted and fussed like a mother hen the whole time leading up to my departure.

"You need to be closely guarded at all times. Things are still tense with Blakeworth," he'd said during a meeting. "General Bray, can we spare any of your best officers to be Kyrie's personal guard detail while she's in Sevier?"

"I'm afraid not, Governor," the general said regretfully. "We can certainly escort you there, Miss Vance, but I don't have the men to spare for a twenty-four seven job for the duration of her term."

"Sevier has a capable military, Dad," I said in an attempt to reassure him. "I've been communicating with the cabinet members. I'm sure they'll find people to watch me eat, sleep, and shit."

General Bray covered his mouth to hide his laugh while Dad blanched. His reactions to my profanity were always priceless.

"No, no. I need people I personally trust to guard you." Dad waved his hand dismissively. "No strangers. If we don't have the men here, then I need to make some calls."

I never did find out who he selected and, frankly, I didn't care. A fresh chapter of my life was starting in a brand new territory. I loved my father, but growing up as a politician's daughter in a post-Collapse world was stifling.

My gilded cage started feeling too small when I was around fifteen. At eighteen, Dad finally gave me a little leeway by allowing me to accompany him on diplomatic trips to other territories.

That was how I met Malcolm Blake, on a diplomatic tour of Blakeworth. Our fathers were clearly trying to set us up, but I didn't care then. Malcom was cute. Sweet, but devilish enough to not be bland. He charmed me and wrote me sweet letters after I returned home.

Then he kidnapped and imprisoned me at nineteen. I'd been rescued and returned home, but the damage was done. Dad locked his precious daughter in her gilded cage and threw away the key.

Until now.

I turned away from the car window to look at the man in the driver's seat. "How much farther to the capitol, Lieutenant?"

"Under half an hour, Miss Vance." Lieutenant Gonzalez's tone was clipped, but it didn't hamper my excitement in the least.

In a moment of boldness, I pressed the button on my door that lowered the window and stuck my head out into the rushing wind. A smile pulled at my lips unconsciously, my eyes falling shut at the cool blast of air. My hair whipped around me, getting tangled and out of control like a pile of straw, but did I care?

Not in the slightest. I could pretend I was on the back of a motorcycle like this. Instead of the armrest, I held the broad body of a man sitting in front of me, driving his iron steed with a mixture of brute strength and careful handling. For two days, it had been nothing but wind, the road, and us. It was pure freedom. *Real* freedom—the kind without any fear. My taste of it had been the smallest crumb, but it was enough to get me hooked.

Not a day went by that I didn't think of those men who'd saved me, with their loud guns and louder bikes. They sent the Blakeworth elites scattering like mice but never laid a hand on me. That motorcycle ride was a priceless gift and one of my most treasured memories.

But then my father never let me out of his sight. And the bikers who saved me? They left Four Corners and never came back.

"Miss Vance?"

A tap on my shoulder drew me out of my fantasy, and I pulled my head back inside the car to glare at the soldier in the backseat with me. Immediately, my window rolled up.

"Please keep the windows up and everything inside the vehicle," he said. "That's bulletproof glass, and we don't want to take any chances."

I resisted the urge to sigh and roll my eyes. "Duly

noted, thank you." I folded my hands in my lap and resumed looking straight ahead.

"Uh, miss?"

"Yes?" I cocked my head at the man next to me.

"You might want to brush your hair out before the Sevier dignitaries see you."

As tempting as it was to try my luck and ignore him, he had a point. Pushing buttons and seeing what I could get away with was a game I played with my father, not strangers. First impressions were important, and I *did* want to prove myself a capable, adult woman.

After handling most of my tangles with the small brush I carried in my purse, we drove into Sevier's most populated city, currently called Perrysville. A gleaming white structure stood tall in the distance, and my hands clenched into fists. It was a stark reminder of the tower where Malcolm kept me prisoned.

"Is that the capitol building?" I asked Gonzalez.

"Yes, Miss Vance. We'll be there shortly."

The road curved around, offering a wider view of the building. I breathed a little easier seeing that it wasn't only the lone tower I saw at first glance. It had several towers, the entire building resembling a stark white cathedral.

"It looks kind of like…a church."

"It was a Catholic church before the Collapse," said the soldier next to me. "Back when this was the state of Utah."

"I see."

The building seemed to expand as we approached, growing taller and wider until it blocked out the sun. By the time the SUV parked in front, the front tower loomed over us like a sheer white cliff face forged by nature.

The lieutenant got out of the driver's seat and came

around to open my door. "We'll stay with you until we have confirmation that your bodyguards have arrived."

"Thank you." I took his offered hand as I stepped out, the fluttering in my stomach expanding up to my chest and throat. This was really happening. Soon I'd be left alone in a new territory, without my father hovering.

My soldier escorts came to either side of me as we walked up the steps to the entrance. Three suited men waited for us in front of tall, intricately carved wooden doors.

"Welcome to Sevier, Miss Vance," said the oldest man. He was tall and thin with just a few wisps of white hair clinging to his scalp. "I'm Governor Kurtis Perry. It's an honor to have you as an ambassador in my territory."

"Thank you, Governor." I gave him my best charming smile. "I'm excited to work together so that both of our territories can flourish."

The older man tilted his head and huffed out a soft laugh, as if I'd made a joke. He recovered quickly and turned to his companions to make introductions. "This is Richard Willis, my Chief of Staff and closest adviser."

"It's a pleasure, Miss Vance." A middle-aged man with glasses extended his hand and gripped mine in a fast hand-shake before releasing me. "Your father and I have worked together for many years. Please give him my best."

"Of course, sir." I struggled to hold back my amuse-ment at both of his names. *Dick Willis.* "The pleasure is mine as well."

Governor Perry and I turned to his other companion and my heart sank. I tried not to let my disappointment color my face, but it took a hell of an effort. This cabinet member was young and handsome. Well-groomed with a charming, bright smile and a keenness in his eyes that made me want to shrink away.

I should have seen this coming. Dad probably knew about it all along too. Since my past kidnapping torpedoed any relationship with Blakeworth, Dad and Governor Perry wanted to set up a match in Sevier.

Fuck, that was probably the *only* reason Dad had allowed me to go. For all I knew, it was the only reason Perry accepted my ambassadorship. Why else would he laugh at the notion of *working together?*

In a post-Collapse society, territory and power was everything. It was the only way to ensure your survival. And just like the kings and queens of centuries past, the best way to secure power for future generations was through marriage arrangements.

Before Malcolm, I would have been thrilled at the idea of marrying a handsome man set to inherit a territory. Now? I wanted to scream my head off at these old fucking men who only wanted to use me.

"This is my nephew, Nathan, Treasury Secretary of Sevier." Governor Perry, oblivious to my inner rage, gave the younger man a not-so-subtle push in my direction.

"I've been eager to meet you, Miss Vance." Nathan held out his palm and when I made contact for a handshake, he turned my hand over and bent to kiss the back of my palm instead.

"It's…a pleasure." I regretted the words as soon as they left my mouth.

He looked up slowly from my hand, smirking as he straightened again. "The pleasure is entirely mine. I'm excited to see what we can do together."

I pulled my hand from his grasp, making a show of

demurely lacing my fingers in front of me even though my grip was like iron. "As am I."

"You must be exhausted from your journey," the governor said once Nathan stepped back into place. "We'll have the staff show you your temporary lodgings. If your ambassadorship works out long term," his eyes shifted to his nephew, "we'll add a housing stipend to your salary."

"Thank you, Governor." He turned toward the massive doors and I piped up again. "Um, only—"

"Yes?" He turned back to face me.

"These gentlemen have to return to Four Corners." I tilted my head to indicate the soldiers at my sides. "My father said he arranged for a personal guard detail for me. Do you know where they might be?"

"They were supposed to arrive with you." Already, the older man sounded cranky and in need of a nap.

"The lieutenant likes to drive fast." I elbowed the man next to me, prompting a grunt in protest. "We probably beat them here. Maybe we can wait in the lobby?"

"Yes, if you wish," the governor said dismissively. "I'm afraid I can't stay with you. I have business to attend to."

Yeah, nighty-night business with your pillow and blankie, old man.

"I'll be happy to stay with you, Miss Vance," Nathan announced. Before I could respond, he addressed my two soldier escorts. "You're dismissed, thank you."

Both men at my sides squared their shoulders. Lieutenant Gonzalez even touched the weapon in his holster. "We stay with the ambassador until her guards arrive. Those are our orders from Governor Vance."

The shocked expression on Nathan's face was priceless. *Not used to anyone telling you no, are you?* I was tempted to link arms with the soldiers to rub it in, maybe even kiss their cheeks.

"I appreciate the offer, Nathan." I struggled to keep the smugness out of my voice. "But my father considers my personal safety to be of the utmost importance."

"Of course. As a father should." He smiled, recovering quickly. "Especially after that *very* unfortunate incident in Blakeworth. That must have been a harrowing experience for you."

I held onto my practiced smile, refusing to let him see how my blood chilled. He really had no problems bringing it up in casual conversation like that? Was he that dense, or was he actively trying to insult me? And while he was supposedly *courting* me, no less.

"The lobby, then." Mr. Willis broke the tension, turning with the governor to open the doors. Nathan stepped aside to let me through first. Unfortunately for him, Lieutenant Gonzalez stepped in to march directly behind me and blocked his view of my ass.

Inside, the building felt just as massive as outside. Tall, domed ceilings stretched high above our heads. Our shoes echoed with each step over the polished tiles. The place felt cold. Solemn and church-like, which was the complete opposite of Four Corners' capitol building.

We had an expansive foyer with tall ceilings and tiled floors too, but it was always warm, even cozy, walking through that building. Dad supported local carpenters and artists by purchasing their furniture and paintings for the sitting areas. In the cold months, every fireplace was lit. Staff put out coffee, tea, and hot chocolate for anyone coming through the building for meetings or appointments.

As I turned in a slow circle, gazing up at the stark white

walls that stretched on forever, I wondered how Governor Perry would react to me cozying the place up. Maybe some comfortable couches instead of the stiff benches, or a rug to add some softness and color.

They might enjoy that too *much*, I thought bitterly. The young, female ambassador who cared more about decorating than actual policy. That would sure fit nicely into their expectations of me. Well, I didn't apply for the position and come all this way just to prove these stuffy old men right.

In a world with so much chaos and conflict, I was proud of what my father had accomplished in Four Corners. For all his faults, he was a true man of the people and kept those in his territory safe. I watched him closely, especially over the last four years when I had little other choice. I knew his policies, his visions for the future. And through my ambassadorship, I wanted to bring Four Corners' prosperity to other territories in need.

So what if the leaders of Sevier had already written me off as an empty-headed girl? I didn't give a fuck if I was just a prospective business contract with them. I would show them. I would earn my place. I would show all of them how seriously I took my position until they were forced to take *me* seriously.

With that resolute thought, I looked away from the architecture to find that Nathan had been staring at me the whole time. He'd been a respectful distance away, but edged closer when our eyes met.

"Remarkable, isn't it?" He turned a reverent gaze upward. "Feels like we've already reached heaven."

Lieutenant Gonzalez, still glued to my side, forced out a cough. I bit back my smile but couldn't suppress a smart remark.

"Yes. I'm sure the citizens of Sevier are just in awe when they walk through here."

Nathan looked at me with surprise, then barked out a laugh. "Oh, regular citizens aren't allowed through here. But can you imagine if they were? Scuffing up the floors and walls, my goodness."

I stared at him, forgetting all about schooling my features. "Not allowed? But where do people get building permits? Or marriage licenses?"

"Ah, she's so eager to start work already," he teased. "Sevier is a newly-formed territory, so we're still ironing things out, but don't worry. We'll show you how things are done here." I wanted to smack the patronizing look off his face, but he had already changed topics. "So, do you have any buildings like this in Four Corners?"

Thunder growled in the distance before I could reply. Everyone cocked their heads at the sound, looking toward the front doors.

"What an awful racket," Nathan muttered as the rumbling grew louder.

My skin prickled as if a ghost had touched me. I knew that sound. A motorcycle club had taken up residence in Four Corners years ago, and even helped my father protect the territory. I heard those roaring engines outside my window every day, taking me back to the brief, beautiful time when one of those machines had rumbled between my legs.

The motorcycles grew louder until the windowpanes and doors rattled in their frames. If this place was supposed to be heaven, then the devil was right outside. The thought brought a wild grin to my face. Thankfully, Nathan was looking out a window, not at me.

"What the hell are *they* doing here?" He whipped

around to face me, my expression now composed and blank. "Surely, they can't be…"

"My bodyguards?" I shrugged innocently. "My father has a good working relationship with a few biker clubs of the southwest. He trusts them."

The engines cut abruptly, rendering eerie silence in place of the noise. I wanted to squirm in anticipation, but Nathan was still staring at me. Who did my father send, some of the Steel Demons? If so, this would be *especially* fun.

Low male voices talked amongst themselves outside, but I couldn't make out the words. When one of the heavy doors creaked open, I pulled in a tight breath of excitement. Three tall, imposing figures strode into the foyer like they owned the place.

"Hey, what's up?" the biggest one said to Nathan. "We're the bodyguards for the new ambassador."

His voice was low, gravelly, and *so* familiar. But it didn't hit me until I saw the glossy black feathers of the raven sitting on his shoulder. Three pairs of eyes fell on me and I was *not* prepared. Everything in my body, even the air in my lungs, froze in utter disbelief.

Four years I had spent fantasizing about this moment, seeing the men who crashed into my life and then left without so much as a goodbye.

T-Bone, Dyno, and Grudge.

The Sons of Odin MC.

CHAPTER 2

DYNO

"Rise and shine, dick-fucks."

T-Bone gave no warning after that. The next thing I felt was the air whooshing from my lungs as he dropped his heavy ass on top of me.

"T, what the fuck?" I shoved at his shoulders, a futile effort due to being half-asleep and woefully under-caffeinated. Being a slim dude trapped under a giant hulk of a Viking certainly didn't help.

"New job starts tonight." T-Bone just wrapped his tree trunk arms and legs around me and snuggled me harder. He was like one of those dogs that are big enough to be a small horse but thought they were chihuahua-sized.

"I know, but I can't fucking breathe."

"Fuck you, then. Grudge?" He slid off me, thank *God*, and made his way across the bed to the third man in our triad. "At least you're always down for cuddles before we're up and at 'em."

Grudge hummed agreeably, even though he sounded more asleep than me.

I sat up in bed, rubbing my eyes while those two became a tangle of arms, legs, and lazy kisses. "What time is it?"

"Get-your-ass-up-o'clock." T-Bone's voice was muffled from being buried in Grudge's neck.

"Uh-huh." I leaned over and smacked his ass once before darting out of bed so he couldn't get me back.

"Put coffee on or give me more where that came from." T-Bone's mouth fell to Grudge's shoulder, his hips starting slow rolls against the other man's ass.

I chuckled while I started to get dressed. "For someone insisting it's time to get out of bed, you're being a shitty example."

"That's why I have you two fuckers." T-Bone grabbed a handful of Grudge's beard, angling his mouth for a kiss. "To keep me accountable."

"Accountable, right," I said dryly, watching the two of them make out.

Grudge turned in place, coming nose-to-nose with T-bone, and dragged a hand down his torso until it disappeared under the sheet. He smothered T-Bone's moan with another kiss, touching and teasing him without preamble. I couldn't see with the sheet bunched around their waists, but from T's hips kicking and his moans into Grudge's mouth, it seemed he'd forgotten all about the job he woke us up for.

Grudge kept him going for a few more seconds before stopping abruptly, jumping out of bed and narrowly dodging T-Bone's attempt to pull him back.

"Goddamn it." T-Bone rolled to his back, rubbing his

face as his half-hard cock twitched on his thigh. "I always fucking fall for that."

"'Cause you're always thinking with your dick."

"I'm sorry, is there some other organ I'm supposed to use in decision-making?"

Before I could answer, Grudge came up beside me and wrapped both arms around my waist. He dragged his lips from my shoulder to my neck, using just the edge of his teeth to make me shiver and melt into him. His lips moved over my skin as if he were speaking, even though no words came out.

The man wasn't mute by choice—he didn't have a tongue. But when it came to bedroom fun, he'd learned to use his lips and teeth in the best of ways. I never thought I'd enjoy the feeling of teeth on my dick, but Grudge somehow made it work.

Communication was no issue, either. After so many years together, T-Bone and I could read his body language like an open book. Grudge also kept pen and paper with him at all times to communicate more complex thoughts.

"See? I'm not the only one with cock for brains." T-Bone grinned at the sight of me leaning into Grudge's embrace.

"Yeah, whatever. Come on, *Pres.*" I grabbed T-Bone's ankle and dragged him a foot down the bed. "You've got to lead us and shit."

"Ugh, don't remind me." T-Bone finally rolled up, running fingers through his dark blond hair.

He didn't want the title of President, but after we lost everyone else in our original club, we needed a leader. T-Bone would have been next in line anyway, as the Sons of Odin Sergeant at Arms. But he and our former president,

Bash, were lovers too. He never expected to lose someone he loved, and then take his place.

It took many years of grieving and fighting for him to grudgingly accept that he was now president of the Sons of Odin MC.

The three of us were all that were left, and that was an issue. We needed bigger numbers, and T-Bone insisted that neither Grudge nor I take the Vice President position.

"If something happens to me, neither of you should be burdened with having to fill my shoes," he'd explained. "I wouldn't wish that on anybody. The VP needs to be someone I can trust, but not someone I'm in love with or fucking. That's my one rule."

Grudge had snorted derisively at that. T-Bone was the flirt of our trio and often facilitated bringing new bed partners for us to play with. Usually men, but sometimes women. The point was, there weren't many people we knew that T-Bone *hadn't* fucked.

Fortunately for us, that still left Chris and Tiff.

The three of us got dressed and decent enough to stumble out of the bedroom and into the clubhouse dining room, where Chris, our VP, was already nursing a cup of coffee at the bar.

"Please tell me you made a whole pot," T-Bone grumbled as he rounded the bar.

"Do I look like a prospect to you?" Chris shot back, smirking over the rim of his mug. "'Course I did, but we really should get a prospect or two."

A black man with a shaved head and short beard, Chris rivaled T-Bone and Grudge in terms of height and musculature. Like the two of them, he radiated pure masculinity, but to me, his most arresting features were the soft dusting of freckles over his nose and cheekbones and his long eyelashes. It was almost a shame we hadn't met him before his wife, Tiff, locked him down.

"You can look into prospects while we're on this body-guard job," T-Bone said, helping himself to the coffee pot. "Bring me a list when we're done, and we'll make selections from there." He took a deep swallow, sighing and smacking his lips. "Where's Tiff?"

"On a supply run," Chris said. "We're gonna stock up for a while and lay low while you guys are doing the job."

"You let her go by herself?" I asked.

Chris made a dismissive sound. "My wife, your treasurer, can handle herself. Worry about your own asses up in that creepy-ass building with a bunch of politicians lookin' down their noses at you." He paused for another sip of coffee. "Y'all really gotta, like, *stay* there?"

"The new ambassador needs 'round the clock protection, apparently." I shrugged and made my way behind the bar. "He's from our old stomping ground, Four Corners. So if he was a decorated soldier who fought against Blakeworth or New Ireland, it makes sense. Other territories aren't a big fan of Four Corners, and you never know who's secretly allied with who."

"Wait." Chris held up a hand. "Am I hearing right that he's from your old territory but you don't know *who* it is?"

"Mm-hm." Grudge nodded an affirmative, his mouth drawn into a tight frown. He'd been the least enthused about taking the job, and for good reason. During a battle with Blakeworth a few years back, he'd been captured by the enemy and subjected to nonstop torture and abuse for nearly two full days.

T-Bone almost went on a homicidal rampage over that. In his eyes, the Four Corners' governor didn't try hard enough to get Grudge back before he was seriously injured.

It was true, he wouldn't have lasted much longer and spent weeks in the hospital. Grudge was no stranger to torture and he recovered, emotionally even, relatively quickly. T-Bone, however, was broken up about it for nearly a year. He always felt personally responsible when he couldn't protect one of his own.

While I understood that hostage situations between warring territories needed to be handled delicately, that incident broke the camel's back for us. After years of being jerked around by Governor Vance, we'd had enough. We always came when he called, even risking our lives to save his daughter, and he still treated us like we were disposable. So we left with no regrets.

Well, maybe a few.

"Care to explain why, after insisting you'll never be Governor Vance's bitch again, you take another job from him, and you don't even know *who* you're protecting?" Chris' gaze swept across all three of us. "What if it's one of those dudes in his cabinet you told me about? The ones that were all scared you'd make them gay?"

"Then at least it'll be fun." T-Bone chuckled into his mug. "But the real answer is, we need the money."

"He's paying us in Sevier currency," I explained further. "Which, so far, is the only post-Collapse currency that's shown to be stable in the local economy. It's started being used in other territories as well."

"And we need a nest egg," T-Bone said. "Something to use for a rainy day, if our other ventures don't work out."

"He's paying that much, huh?" Chris mused.

"Yeah. What was it, Grudge? At least double what our old contracts paid?"

Grudge shook his head and held up three fingers.

"Triple! Yeah, that's right. So you see," T-Bone turned back to Chris, "it was too good to say no."

"Yeah. Watch it be too good to be true and you're stuck dealing with the nastiest piece of work in the territory."

"Already thought of that," I said. "So I made sure to add the stipulation that we'd do a month-long trial run first. If we can't stand this ambassador after thirty days, we'll cut loose and collect the money for the time we did serve."

"See, that's why you're the smart one." Chris pointed at me. "Always with a contingency plan. Oh yeah, also." He turned to T-Bone. "Get receipts. Tiff wants a paper trail."

"'Kay, Dad," T-Bone groaned into his coffee cup.

Grudge pulled out his pen and notepad, quickly scrawling a message before handing it to Chris. *Thank you and Tiff for holding down the fort while we're gone. Need anything else before we go?*

"My sanity. My soul. A beach house in the Bahamas. You know, nothing crazy."

We all had a good chuckle at that, then scarfed down our food and coffee before preparing to hit the road. Governor Vance said we'd have accommodations near the ambassador's quarters in the capitol building. All of our basic needs would be provided for, so we didn't need to pack much except our personal items.

And weapons, of course. For our own protection, as well as the ambassador's. The governor never mentioned weapons being against the law, but we weren't planning to announce it either. All three of us were proficient with a variety of weapons, slipping our hunting knives discreetly into boots and hidden sleeves inside our cuts. T-Bone liked his handguns. Grudge had an affinity for short-barreled rifles.

I liked guns okay, but my road name wasn't Dyno for no reason. My weapon of choice would always be explosives.

On my belt next to my gun holster, I had two small pouches to carry a couple of mini Molotov cocktails—my own handmade concoctions perfected after years of experimenting with flammable liquids. I distilled the recipe to be so potent that the bottles didn't need to be any bigger than airplane liquor bottles. It took a bit more experimentation to have my fuse and lighter ready when needed, and to minimize the risk of burning my hands or face off.

A half-hour later, we were all packed up and double-checking the cargo on the bikes. I turned my motorcycle on with a roar, the Indian Chief Dark Horse coming to life like a hungry beast.

"We all good?" T-Bone came up to me, his eyes and hair set aglow by the setting sun. Munin, his raven and spirit guide, sat on his broad shoulder, black feathers also taking on a golden sheen from the light.

"Ready when you are, President."

"Shut up," he growled, reaching up to grab the end of my braid. "Come here."

He pulled me in hard, his kiss hitting me with the force of a punch to the mouth. Which was just how I loved it from him.

I cupped a hand around T-Bone's neck, holding him in place for a moment to devour each other. It was the best way to kick off a ride together, no matter how brief. The Sevier capital of Perrysville was less than two hours away. T-Bone always kissed Grudge and me like we were riding off to war and might never see each other again. After everything we'd been through, it was a real enough possibility.

Only when Munin began cawing and nipping T-Bone's ear did our tongues untangle. Still, our faces didn't separate. Our foreheads rested against each other, noses bumping gently. His breath was warm on my lips, tickling the sensation of his beard that still lingered on my skin.

"Ride safe, Dylan." He whispered my given name like it was some secret he'd promised to keep.

"I'll be right behind you, Trav," I answered before stealing another lingering kiss for the road.

We released each other slowly, then he left to send Grudge off in the same way. I watched them from astride my bike, feeling my dick come to life at the sight of my two life partners groping and hungrily kissing each other. Already I couldn't wait for the ride to be over and to be in the privacy of our new lodgings. Who said we couldn't protect the ambassador while having a threesome at the same time? Governor Vance knew we were in a triad relationship, he must have considered that a possibility.

What if the ambassador wanted to join in? I snickered to myself. We'd definitely be keeping an eye on him then.

T-Bone and Grudge untangled just as reluctantly as we had, both of them adjusting the front of their pants before climbing on their bikes. I leaned forward to grip my handlebars, enjoying the gentle rumble of the machine on my dick and balls. We'd been together for over a decade and weren't spring chickens anymore, but no way this night was ending without getting sweaty and naked.

T-Bone peeled out first, hitting the throttle hard as Munin took off from his shoulder to fly overhead. I fell in line after him, and Grudge followed after me. It was a perfect, gorgeous ride. No mechanical issues for any of us, and a sunset across the landscape which made me feel like I rode through a painting. It was just turning dusk when we pulled up to the expansive white building, and that was when my sense of unease started.

I knew this wasn't a church anymore, but the pristine white building and all the cross motifs brought up disturbing memories for me. Christian missionaries tried to force my mother and other members of her tribe into assimilating to their religion. She told me about how they tried to erase her culture, from their hair and clothing to their daily spiritual practices. I didn't meet her until I was a teenager, and never fully felt like I was part of the Hopi people, but I treasured what she taught me before she passed.

We parked and shut our bikes off. The tall, white building loomed over us like a ghost in the eerie silence.

"Looks like the ambassador's already here." T-Bone nodded at the armored SUV we had parked next to. It definitely looked like one of Governor Vance's vehicles.

"Do we, like, knock on the door? Just go in?" I couldn't stop eyeballing the front doors with their intricate carvings and ornate handles. Government buildings in Four Corners were open to the public, but this place gave off a distinct *VIPs only, no peasants or bikers* vibe.

"Let's just go in." T-Bone was already ascending the steps. "We're gonna be working here. Shit, *living* here. Fuck them if they don't want us treating this place like we own it."

Munin resettled on his shoulder with a soft caw as he pulled one door open, moving aside to let me and Grudge through. My first step inside echoed all the way up to the high, vaulted ceiling. Yeah, definite creepy church vibes.

A couple of men in suits turned around when we

entered, taking us in like we were the mud they scraped off their shoes.

"Hey, what's up?" T-Bone said to one of them, which almost made me palm my forehead and groan. Formality and decorum were not his strong suits. "We're the body-guards for the new ambassador."

No one said anything as I turned to survey the rest of the open foyer. My eyes almost passed over the young woman, figuring she was someone's assistant. But recognition struck me hard, and I did a double-take. Then my eyes locked onto hers and I couldn't tear them away.

A feather could have knocked me over. This simply could not be. What was *she* doing here?

Those wide blue eyes, pouty lips that I'd fantasized too often about kissing, that windswept blonde hair that created such a beautiful, messy halo around her face. She was just as stunning as when I'd last seen her over four years ago.

Kyrie Vance, the daughter of the Four Corners' governor.

And the only woman I'd ever failed to get out of my mind.

CHAPTER 3

KYRIE

I didn't know how long we stood there staring at each other. I was too shocked to speak, and apparently so were the Sons.

"T-Bone," I finally breathed, then blurted out the first thing that came to mind. "You grew your hair out."

The tall Viking of a man dropped his gaze, huffing out a soft laugh as he ran a hand over his head. "Yeah, guess I did."

His head had been shaved the last time I saw him. I guess I never expected him to have a full head of hair, but the thick brownish-blond strands suited him. It made him look younger and contrasted with the dark brown beard peppering his jaw.

"It looks good." I swallowed, my tongue feeling thick and numb inside my mouth. "You all…look good."

Dyno stared at me with a dark gaze I couldn't interpret. He was just as tall as T-Bone, but slimmer with a graceful, willowy build. His warm medium-brown skin, prominent cheekbones, and long black hair hinted at the Indigenous ancestry he told me about all those years ago. He still shaved the sides of his head, but this time his hair was in a long braid over his shoulder rather than the topknot I'd seen before.

And Grudge. My eyes fell to the silent man who'd helped me to my feet and rushed me to safety back in Blakeworth. He was the shortest of the three, but was still imposing enough to tower over Nathan and Mr. Willis. Long, dark hair and a beard that touched the top of his chest, hid most of his face. But his dark brown eyes were the most expressive of the three bikers, wide and full of emotion at the sight of me.

The same emotion bloomed in my chest and sent fluttering sensations into my stomach. I recognized it as *longing*, as missing someone so much that even when you get used to being apart for years, seeing them again awakens a storm inside you.

"This has to be a mistake," Nathan's voice cut in, shattering the illusion that these bikers and I were in our own little world. "These…*men* cannot possibly be Miss Vance's bodyguards."

Grudge looked at him with a distasteful sneer, then reached into his cut to produce a folded letter. I recognized my father's seal stamped on the outside. He waved it in front of Nathan's face mockingly, but then T-Bone shocked everyone in the room.

"You're right. It has to be a mix-up."

Everyone turned to stare at him, Grudge and Dyno with disbelief, the other men with relief.

"Glad you agree Mr., uh, T-Bone." Nathan frowned at the road name patch on T-Bone's leather vest. "I'm glad we could settle this civilly. Now, if you would see yourselves out—"

"Wait!" I barely raised my voice, but it echoed off the floor and walls. Now all eyes were on me. "Can I have a word with the Sons in private, please?"

"The *who?*"

"Us." Dyno gestured to himself and his fellow bikers. "We're the Sons of Odin MC."

Mr. Willis, who had been silent until now, stepped up with a concerned expression. "Miss Vance, I don't think that would be proper."

I leveled him with my best stern look. "If they are to be my bodyguards, sir, it's only natural that I'll be in private with them regularly."

"Yeah, that," T-Bone shook his head, his face darkening, "is *not* going to happen." While his amber gaze had been locked on me a moment before, now he looked everywhere but at me. That hurt, especially combined with his sudden refusal to do the job.

He had been warm and jovial when we first met. Fun-loving and flirtatious without crossing any boundaries. But he'd done a one-eighty right before leaving Four Corners. He'd grown cold, distant. Stiff and formal, especially around my father. He never even said goodbye. None of them did.

After so much time had passed, I'd hoped he'd be a *little* happy to see me. But it was painfully clear, like back then, that he didn't want to be anywhere near me.

"Hold on." Dyno raised his hands. "We should talk about this before making any rash decisions."

"Decision's already been made," T-Bone argued. "We *can't* take this job, D."

"Are you saying that as president or as you?"

"Both."

The room fell silent again as the two men squared off to face each other, some unspoken battle waging between them. I didn't know if they'd start fighting or making out. Both options seemed equally likely. The Sons were always open about their love and affection for each other. I never got the courage to tell them how much I loved seeing them act that way.

Grudge stepped between them before anything could happen, teeth bared as he waved my father's letter in T-Bone's face. That broke the tension, at least temporarily, and I came back to my senses.

"You three have traveled all this way." I folded my hands and straightened my spine. "Maybe if we all sat down, had a bite to eat and a drink, we could come to a solution."

The tension bled out of T-Bone just a fraction, giving me a tiny shred of hope.

"I thought we just came to a solution?" Willis sputtered.

"*I* still have not made a decision, Mr. Willis." I shot him my best scathing look. "Don't I get a say in who my own bodyguards are?"

"With all due respect, Miss Vance, your father would not want his treasured daughter to be guided by…by a…"

"Come on, say it," T-Bone goaded him. "You're a big boy. You can do it."

"A…a *biker gang!*"

The bikers in question all snorted, and I had to stop myself from making a very similar noise.

"My father's decree is in that man's hand right now." I nodded at Grudge. "Which seems to contradict your statement, sir."

"But…but—"

"However, I am open to the possibility that this could be a misunderstanding." I released my hands and walked forward a few steps, my body growing warmer as I moved closer to the Sons. "Which is why I suggest sitting down and talking it out. Like civilized people."

T-Bone resumed looking at the ground, avoiding my gaze again, but looking like he was trying to hide a smile.

"As Sevier leadership, we are also hosts of this territory," I reminded the suited, shock-faced men. "What kind of leadership are we showing to not offer hospitality to weary travelers?"

Neither of the suited men seemed convinced, but all three Sons were full-on grinning.

"Have it your way, Miss Vance," Willis said, looking like he'd swallowed a sour melon. "Our dining area is this way. We'll have the kitchen staff prepare you something. But!" He held up an index finger, staring daggers at me. "We'll have soldiers posted at the doors, to keep an eye on you at all times."

I suppressed an eyeroll. Really, no one would believe I wasn't a child anymore.

"Um." Lieutenant Gonzalez cleared his throat. "Should we stay, Miss Vance?"

"No, you may go." I smiled at my soldier escorts. "I've kept you long enough. Thank you for coming this far with me."

"Best wishes, Miss Vance. And good luck." The soldiers nodded sharply and turned to leave, again to the stupefied faces of the Sevier officials. Lieutenant Gonzalez bumped fists with Dyno on his way out.

"Now." I turned to address the remaining men in the room with a smile. "Shall we?"

"YOU REALLY DIDN'T KNOW it would be me?" I scanned the letter from my father, which outlined the Sons' contract as my bodyguards. My name wasn't mentioned anywhere. I was only referred to as "The Ambassador".

"No," said Dyno. "And I take it you had no idea it would be us."

The three of them sat on the opposite side of a round banquet table. Except for the soldiers posted at the doors, we were the only ones in this massive dining hall. I had chosen a table in the center of the room for the most amount of privacy while we talked.

"No," I admitted, setting the letter down. "So it seems only my father would know both pieces of information. Why would he do that?"

"We assumed it was for extra security." T-Bone grabbed a handful of peanuts from one of the bowls on the table and shoved a few in his mouth. "If our orders were intercepted by a hostile territory, the ambassador could've become a target if they were named." He opened his palm, allowing the raven on his shoulder to peck at a few peanuts.

"That makes sense." I squirmed in my seat, unsure of how much of the past, if any, I should bring up. *Why did you leave?* I wanted to demand.

Like I even had a right to demand that. There was no history between us, not really. They rescued me on my father's orders. We had become friendly during and after the ride back. But that was it. There was nothing there.

I had a massive, out-of-control crush on them that

came roaring back with a vengeance after four years, but it certainly wasn't returned. They probably saw me as everyone else did—a naive, dimwitted, spoiled girl who knew nothing of the real world. Why would they ever want me? Besides, they had each other.

"Can I ask," I fingered the edge of the tablecloth, "why did you assume my father made a mistake?" I focused on Munin, T-Bone's raven, who was now preening his feathers. "And why do you feel unfit for the position?"

All three men shifted in their seats, sneaking glances at each other and looking highly uncomfortable with the question.

"Your father is…very protective of you," Dyno began.

"Please." I waved my hand and finally allowed my eyes to roll. "There's no need to remind me."

T-Bone chuckled, hiding another smile, while Munin cawed softly, as if echoing his laughter.

"*I* don't believe we're underqualified for the job." Dyno placed a hand on his chest. "We succeeded in getting you out of Blakeworth, after all." He looked to his right. "Grudge, what do you think?"

"Hm." Grudge jerked his chin down in a sharp nod and pointed across the table to my father's letter. He may have been a man of few words but his feelings were clear— he wanted to stay as well.

I gave him a grateful smile, warmth fluttering in my chest. He didn't return it, pulling his gaze away after catching my eye for a moment, and the flutters deflated. Well, he and Dyno were willing to stay, at least. The only holdout was T-Bone.

His peanuts now all gone, T-Bone crossed his arms over his broad chest and tipped his gaze up to the ceiling.

"No one is better qualified to protect Miss Vance than

we are," he said as if I weren't even in the room. "If you two still want to do the job, fine. I'm in."

"Then what was that all about earlier?" I blurted out, the hurt coloring my voice. "You said it *had* to be a mistake. That you *couldn't* take the job. Why?" I stopped myself from asking the question that I really wanted to know, *Do you really hate me so much?*

T-Bone rested his eyes on me for the first time, his expression blank. Even so, his gaze was arresting. I wanted him to always look at me. I wanted to poke cheeks and see that hidden smile shine full and bright, like it used to.

"I got defensive out of concern for you. Your, ah, reputation in this new territory."

"My reputation?" I repeated. "I just arrived today. I haven't had time to develop a reputation."

"A new ambassador, who's also the daughter of a prosperous governor, being guarded constantly by three roughneck bikers?" T-Bone cocked his head. "That's one hell of a way to start a reputation. You heard ol' Stick-Up-The-Ass out there. They don't even want you alone in the same room as us. By the way... Hey boys?" he yelled across the banquet room, holding up an empty bowl. "Can I get some more peanuts for my bird?"

None of the soldiers posted at the doors responded or moved a muscle.

"See? Fuckin' useless chaperones," T-Bone grumbled.

"I don't care what anyone thinks we're up to behind closed doors," I said. "I trust you three. My father trusts you. That's why he chose you."

"And we're grateful for that, but you *should* care about what people think," T-Bone retorted. "You're a representative. The people here have a lot of backwards ways of thinking. They're *years* behind Four Corners in terms of progress. How do you think they're gonna feel about the young, beautiful new ambassador being constantly surrounded by three outlaws who are twice her age?"

I opened my mouth to answer but my brain, heart, and stomach were stuck on the fact that he called me *beautiful*. T-Bone also seemed to realize that he said it because he was looking away from me again.

"I'm happy to represent Four Corners in such a way," I said, lifting my chin. "I will be proud to show them that our territory thrives due to its citizens, whether they love men, women, one person, or multiple people. No matter their age, ability, ethnicity, or background. Where we come from, everyone has a place and deserves basic respect and human rights. We'll show them how to do that here."

The table was silent for a few long moments. Dyno and Grudge stared at their partner the whole time, as if waiting for another argument.

Instead, T-Bone let out a heavy sigh and ran a hand through his hair. "Fine. Yee-fuckin'-haw. Let's do this."

CHAPTER 4

T-BONE

"Can't fuckin' believe you two, throwing me under the bus like that." It took everything in me not to slam the door. Kyrie was staying in the suite next to us and would likely hear it. So I settled for whipping off my cut and tossing it somewhere, then noisily took my boots off. I was moving around so much that Munin cawed irritably before flying from my shoulder to roost somewhere in the suite.

"I'm sorry, what happened to needing the money?" Dyno spread his hands out. "I thought we were willing to put up with any of the Four Corners dickheads for this job."

"That was before I realized it would be Kyrie *fucking* Vance!"

Grudge whacked me on the arm, gave me a stern look, then raised his hands up and down, palms facing the floor, in a *keep your fucking voice down* motion.

"Sorry, man. I didn't take into account that we'd be

working for Kyrie fucking Vance," I repeated at a normal volume.

Still looking for a way to take the edge off, I hunted through our suite for liquor. They set us up in a nice enough place, essentially a three-bedroom apartment. Of course, no one had bothered to ask if three dudes would be sleeping together. Thankfully, the biggest bed looked like it would fit all of us.

The housekeeping staff had pointed out a door that would lead directly to Kyrie's suite through a short corridor and another door on her end. I jerked my gaze away from that door as I stormed through our place. The last thing I needed on my mind was her, alone in her room. Probably getting undressed or—

Nope, nope. Not going there.

I ignored Dyno following me as I explored, then finally found my prize in one of the kitchen cabinets. I pulled down a dusty bottle of whiskey and three glasses, not turning to face him until my drink had been poured.

"What?" I demanded at his prying stare.

"It doesn't matter that it's her. We still need the job, and we're gonna do it." Dyno slapped my arm, nearly making me spill. "Right?"

"You two dicks already decided that for us, so yeah." I downed the whiskey and poured myself another. "Thanks, partners."

"Why are you being so dramatic about this?" Dyno crossed his arms and peered at me shrewdly.

"Dramatic?" I echoed. "Have you forgotten?"

I loved Dyno to the ends of the earth, but I swore to fuck he could be *too* unfeeling sometimes. Too even-keeled, too laser-focused on the end goal and not what we had to deal with before getting there. He was a good balance for me and Grudge, but I couldn't always understand how his mind worked.

"I haven't forgotten," Dyno said, reaching for the whiskey and one of the glasses. "I just know how to be a professional."

"Right," I huffed, going for my third drink. "Grudge, how do you feel about this?"

He let out a heavy sigh and then clutched a hand to his chest, curling his fingers and digging them in deep. The gesture and pained expression on his face illustrated exactly how I felt when I first saw her.

It hurts to be near her.

"Yeah." I nodded slowly.

Kyrie Vance. Just some rich girl we were tasked with rescuing who became a whole lot more, if only in our minds.

I'd never seen anyone look so happy, laugh so wildly, while on the back of a motorcycle as she did when we rescued her. Not even the dozens of other bikers I'd known for years, who lived and died for the love of the open road, held a candle to her. This girl had just spent a week in a hell that would traumatize anyone, and she still had enough joy left in her to let it all out.

We'd lost Bash, and our entire club, just a few months earlier. I knew how to look fine on the outside while the wound was still fresh, grief eating away at me like a cancer. That first day we rode back from Blakeworth, when I saw Kyrie release Grudge's waist to spread her arms out to the sky and lift her face up to the sunlight, I remembered for the first time in months why I loved to ride.

Her hair had streamed out behind her like a golden comet, and the pure elation, the pure freedom in her smile and laughter, were the first combatants of the dark, sickening grief that threatened to swallow me whole.

Kyrie Vance was curious, kind, and fearless. She made me want to *live* again, not just exist through life under a dark cloud. She even made me consider falling in love again.

And that was fucking dangerous.

That was why I distanced myself from her. While it wasn't the only reason, it was a big part of why we had left Four Corners for good.

It broke my heart to see such a beautiful, free-spirited person caged up again like an exotic pet. But at least Kyrie's father had good intentions, unlike that crusty cum-sock, Malcolm Blake.

She'd be safe. And she was smart enough to forge her own destiny when she was ready. I just never thought it would cross with ours again.

"Why would Vance pick *us*?" Dyno mused aloud. "You don't think he ever picked up that we were…*friendly* with his daughter?"

"The man's as dense as a box of bricks." I snorted. "I flirted with her hardcore at that dinner party when we got back, and he never batted an eye."

In hindsight, that would have gotten us out of our current situation. If I had made an actual pass at her, Daddy Dearest never would have considered us as bodyguards. Was it too late to write to him now? *Dear Governor Vance, I like your daughter very much. I would also like to fuck her stupid, if that's alright.*

Grudge came up to my side, wrapping an arm around my shoulders as he pressed against me. I was never one to deny affection, so I slid an arm around his back and went in for a kiss. He pecked me quickly and used his other arm to gesture to all three of us.

"That's a good point," Dyno said. "Vance also knew all three of us are together. I bet he figures we're not interested in women at all, which would make us the safest option to guard her."

"Of fucking course he would think that," I grumbled, untangling from Grudge. "Forgetting that bisexuals exist, again."

It wasn't just that. I hated how everyone had their fucking assumptions about us. Yes, we were crude, lewd bikers who had spent many a night with men, women, and every gender and identity that didn't fit into neat little categories. At least we were honest about it, even reveled in it. And while we flirted with straight men sometimes just to make them squirm, we never, *ever* coerced or assaulted anyone who didn't want to be part of our fun.

We were debaucherous horndogs, sure. But we weren't predators.

I couldn't say the same for the other men we met, though.

A growl rumbled through my chest before I realized it. I didn't trust those suits we met downstairs one bit. The younger guy *could* be harmless, just too eager. But that older guy, Dick Willie or whatever, was a definite wolf in sheep's clothing. He made my skin crawl, and I didn't want him alone in a room with our girl.

Our girl? What the fuck is wrong with you, T-Bone?

I scrubbed a hand down my face. This was why I needed to stay away from her. Just a few minutes of conversation and I was already getting obsessed again.

When Kyrie asked why I couldn't do the job, I couldn't

tell her the truth. I couldn't tell her I wanted to break the arms of every man who looked at her.

Dyno stepped forward, running his hands along my waist. Grudge was still clinging to my side, so I held both of them closer. Cuddle piles made everything a little easier.

"One day at a time," Dyno whispered as he inched closer to my lips. "I know it's gonna be hard to see her all the time, T. But we'll get through it. We've gotten through a lot worse than this."

"Yeah." I trailed my fingertips up his long braid. "We'll survive."

He kissed me deeply, tasting like a heady mixture of coffee and whiskey. I closed my eyes and tried to release the tension that had wound up my spine since stepping foot into this building. The touches from both of them seemed to be doing the trick.

Grudge dragged his lips across my neck, pulling the collar of my T-shirt down to suck on the muscle that ran to my shoulder. I made off with the shirt and turned to him, grasping his face and shoving my tongue in his mouth, even though he couldn't do the same. The man could fucking kiss though. His lack of tongue didn't hamper anything for his partners.

Dyno's teeth grazed my nipple and I grabbed the back of his head to hold him there. I was in the mood for pain tonight, maybe as some kind of atonement for my returned feelings for Kyrie. Dyno got the message and he bit down harder, at the same time squeezing my cock roughly through my jeans.

Grudge was starting to roll his hips against my side, groaning into my mouth while our lips scraped and sucked with the most delicious friction. I undid his belt one-handed and reached inside to cup and stroke him, palming the heat of his stiffening cock and massaging his heavy balls. While I played with him, Dyno started moving lower, biting rough kisses on my stomach until he reached the front of my pants, where he abruptly stopped.

"Oh, keep going," I begged, tearing my mouth away from Grudge. "Don't stop, D."

"Let's go to the bed, or a couch," he said.

"Why?" I cupped his face, running my thumb over his cheekbone. "You look so sexy on your knees for me."

He really was a gorgeous man, with sharp, beautiful angles to his face that were almost feminine. I wanted to thank the gods every day that he was attracted to men, and on top of that, wanted to be with *me*.

I was volatile. Temperamental. *Dramatic*, as he put it earlier. I was not an easy person to handle, but I loved hard. I loved for life. Dyno saw past all my issues and decided they were a small price to pay for loving me back.

He blushed prettily right then, dark eyes flicking up to me before focusing on the task in front of him—getting my dick out. I wondered if Kyrie would have that same cute, almost shy look if she ever—

For fuck's sake, we are not thinking about that.

"Ohh, yes…" I tipped my head back as Dyno stroked me from root to tip, squeezing on the upstroke, just how I loved it. "Taste me, you sexy fuck."

He teased me for a little longer, just licking my head as he stroked me. Dyno liked to test me, and I liked to put his pretty ass in its place, so I grabbed the back of his head and shoved him down the length of my cock until his nose touched my abs. He moaned around me, his free hand diving into his own pants. We'd take care of him soon, but first, Grudge needed more of my attention.

"You're sexy as fuck too," I whispered before sucking

his lower lip into my mouth. "Don't you ever fucking forget that."

Grudge moaned in response, caressing down my chest while I returned to handling his thick erection. He had one of the biggest dicks I'd ever seen, and I'd seen a *lot*. It pulsed in my hand, his slit leaking precum which I spread up and down his length. He bit my shoulder with a low growl, fucking through my hand with sloppy, wet sounds.

"Fuck, you're so hot." The rhythmic sliding of his length through my fist had me hypnotized. In Dyno's wet mouth, I was heavy and straining. For the millionth time, I wondered how a bastard like me had gotten so fucking lucky with these two.

I pulled Dyno off my cock and rested my swollen head on his lips. His ragged huffs of breath teased over my skin, his sweet, dark eyes pleading up at me for more. He would get more, in a minute.

"You." I released Grudge's cock and shoved him back roughly by the shoulder. "I want to suck you. Sit down."

He stumbled back, immediately heading for the long couch with an extended chaise attached and a wide, matching ottoman. Grudge sat in the center, kicking off his pants and boots before spreading his knees wide and fisting his thick base. I kicked the ottoman aside to kneel in front of him, first holding his sides and kissing him deeply.

"You're perfect," I murmured against his lips. "You're *ours*. You deserve this."

Dyno slid onto the couch next to him, now also gloriously naked. His skin looked golden in the warm lighting, shadows carving the shapes of his cheekbones and slender muscles as he leaned over to kiss Grudge's neck. Grudge writhed under the attention from both of us, tearing his mouth away from mine to kiss Dyno. He gripped Dyno's thigh next to his, groping and massaging before reaching for his cock.

The two of them now wrapped up in each other, I made a slow descent toward Grudge's cock. My skin slid against his, my lips falling indiscriminately to his many tattoos and scars on my way down.

Dyno and I had been through our fair share of shit, but our traumas were a drop in the bucket compared to Grudge's. Long before he met us, he'd lost so much more than just his tongue. For much of his life before the Sons, he'd lost his personhood.

That was why I got so hard every time I touched him, praised him, and pleased him to the point of release. I wasn't a doctor, I couldn't fix everything that fucked him up. But I'd never get tired of telling him how fucking hot he was. I'd never lose the thrill of hearing him moan or watching his hips buck because I made him feel so fucking good.

It turned me on so much to give him pleasure after a life of only knowing pain. To make him feel valued after being treated as disposable. I didn't know if there was a name for that kink, but it was at the top of my long list.

Grudge's decadent sigh, punctuated by Dyno's kisses, was like music to my ears as I drew his silky head into my mouth. He was wide, firm, and fucking delicious. From the corner of my eye, I saw him stroking Dyno's cock and copied the motion on him. My hand glided easily on Grudge's thick, meaty length, aided by spit and precum and his sexy fucking hip rolls. He shot through my fist like a piston, fucking roughly down my throat, which only made me harder.

I squeezed my woefully untouched cock with my free hand, running down the length to tug at my balls to ease some of the aching pressure. My lovers would get theirs first, and then they'd take care of me.

If only, the thought tickled the back of my brain, *if only another hand or mouth could be pleasing me right now. Maybe the soft touch of a woman to balance out all this testosterone—*

I took Grudge deeper down my throat with a loud moan to drown out those pesky thoughts. *Focus, T-Bone. You don't need anyone but them.*

Grudge leaned over to take Dyno in his mouth, pulling a hiss of pleasure from Dyno's teeth as he leaned his head back, eyelids heavy. Grudge ran those perfect lips up and down his length, rubbing and massaging his thighs while Dyno ran his hands through Grudge's hair and over his back. Dyno's mouth hung open in a soft, constant moan, his eyes closed and brows drawn tight. If blowjobs from Grudge could be a kink, that was Dyno's number one.

I pulled off of Grudge's cock for a quick breather and to just soak in the sight before me. Dyno's release was quickly approaching, evident by his fingers clasping Grudge's hair and neck, his soft whimpers growing desperate, and his needy thrusts up into Grudge's mouth.

"Oh, fuck, don't stop," Dyno begged. "No, don't slow down. I'm so close, fuck!" His whole body shook as Grudge brought him right to the edge and eased back, torturing the man in the best way. "F-f-fuck me, why do you always do that?" he panted, lips trembling from how tightly wound up he was.

I brought my free hand to the inside of his knee, caressing him there before leaning over to suck a few kisses on the warm, sensitive skin of his thighs. "Because you're so hot when you beg. Isn't he, Grudge?"

"Mm-hm." Grudge massaged his balls and planted kisses all around his hips and lower stomach, a wordless promise that the torture wouldn't last forever.

I chuckled at Dyno's groan of frustration while bringing two fingers to my mouth, wetting them thoroughly. My other hand teased Grudge's cockhead and made him squirm as he edged Dyno again. Once my fingers were slick, I returned my mouth to him, sucking his head while my fist worked his length, and my fingers made their way behind his balls.

I found his tight hole and pressed inside, earning a deep bellow of a moan as I curled my fingers and hit that spot that made all men come like geysers. It was a shame that so many guys would never entertain the idea of ass play. The male G-spot was back there, and Grudge was going crazy while I rubbed and sucked his fat cock down my throat.

He was having a hell of a time sucking Dyno, his once-precise movements now clumsy and frenzied as pleasure wrought through him. He was solid as iron on my tongue, balls drawn up and tight as he neared explosive release. I took him as far down as I could without legitimately suffo-cating, fucking his ass harder with my hand. I wasn't patient enough to edge my lovers like he was. I wanted his sweet, sticky cum filling my mouth *now*.

If Grudge's own mouth hadn't been filled with Dyno's cock, the sounds of his release would have filled the apart-ment. He came hard in my mouth, the rhythmic pulses of his cock shooting more cum down my throat with every squeeze. I kept playing with his ass and he kept coming, drowning in pleasure so intense that he just couldn't stop.

Dyno's shouts of release soon joined Grudge's, their combined chorus stroking over my skin like a touch. A small part of me secretly hoped that our lovely neighbor could hear us.

Grudge pushed at my shoulder when he couldn't take any more, and I savored one last drop of cum on my tongue before easing off of him. Panting and flushed, he gestured for me to stand, which I happily did.

The two of them went to their knees immediately, and what a gorgeous sight it was. Grudge took my cock first, sliding his lips over me in a way that made me see stars. He pulled away and let Dyno, who was also rubbing my balls and clutching my ass to drive me deeper into his mouth, take a few sucks of me.

"Was I mad at you before?" I asked in a strained voice, stroking over his neck and face. "I can't remember now."

"Hmph." The small noise he made was cute, eyes rolling up to mine as he released my dick with a pop of his lips. He passed my cock back to Grudge and chose to wrap his mouth around my balls instead of arguing with me.

I let out a soft laugh, tipping my head back and letting my eyes fall shut to their delicious sucks and slurps of me. My hands rested on their heads, fingers curling around Dyno's tight braid and Grudge's messy mane. We were so different, the three of us, but our jagged, broken pieces fit each other perfectly. We understood each other in ways few people did.

We're not right for her, I thought as pleasure coiled in the base of my spine. *This is enough. This is right. It always has been. We'd just hurt her.*

Someone's fingers nudged behind my balls and I planted my feet wider to give easier access. The thick digits penetrated me, ramping my pleasure up to where it was almost blinding.

"Fuck…" The curse dragged out of me with a heavy moan. "Gonna come so hard, boys. Be ready."

They just sucked, stroked, and fingered me harder, to the point of no return. The first convulsion nearly knocked me off my feet. I planted one knee on the couch and gripped the back of the couch as wave after wave of pleasure hit me. My dick lost the hot, wet suction of Grudge's mouth for a moment, only to be replaced by my other favorite mouth.

Dyno's tongue lapped and flicked at me, making me shudder between each pulse of my orgasm. He took every last drop, and then my strength really left. I collapsed on the couch, and my loves piled around me.

"Need anything else to make you forget about being upset?" Dyno teased, licking a stripe of sweat that trailed down my stomach.

"A pussy to eat," I said without thinking. *God fucking damn it. Just tell them you were thinking of her the whole time, why don't you?*

I had just been spent and satisfied by the two people I loved most, both of which I was wildly attracted to. Over the years, we had invited dozens of casual partners to our bed, just for fun and variety. None of them had stuck in my mind like this girl we had no chance with.

Dyno and Grudge went quiet for a moment, and I wondered if Kyrie had occupied their thoughts as much as she had mine.

"If you really want to go another round, I'm sure we could sneak a service girl up here," Dyno mused. "There's a brothel a couple streets down. I got enough to pay for one."

For the first time I could ever recall, the notion

sounded very unappealing. Not just any woman would do. I only wanted one. I had to get her out of my system somehow. Which I'd figure out after recovering from this orgasm that had left me feeling strangely empty.

"Nah, forget it." I smacked a kiss on both of them before rolling up from the couch. "Let's go to bed."

CHAPTER 5

KYRIE

I dreamed of a woman wearing a helmet with wings on the sides. She was tall and muscular, with blonde hair down to her waist, and she was dressed in leather, fur, and metal armor. Her face wasn't visible, but she had a circular shield strapped to one arm and a massive, two-headed battle axe in the other. She stood alone in a blank, empty landscape like it was covered in a soft fog.

The woman turned to face me, bringing her shield in front of her body. She struck the flat side of her axe against the shield, making a hard *thump* of metal on wood. Her face still hidden under her helmet, she thumped the axe against the shield again and again, until it became a steady drumbeat. A rhythm in time with my pulse, which quickened as the armored woman came closer to me.

Her drumming grew faster too, the beat becoming frenzied and vibrating through the air. It always kept time with my heart, now pounding wildly.

Right before I woke up, a raven landed on her shoulder and cawed to the same beat.

Unlike normal dreams, she didn't fade away immediately after waking. This strange, warrior woman remained imprinted on my mind as I got up and ready for the first day of my ambassadorship. Who was she? Ravens had been appearing in my dreams for years, but this was the first time the bird was a secondary character.

She looked kind of like me, I thought while scrubbing my hair in the shower. I was no warrior though. I'd never held a weapon in my life. General Bray had once offhandedly mentioned teaching me how to shoot a gun. He and my father were colleagues and friends, but after that comment, Dad was so incensed that I thought he might fire Bray and banish him from the territory.

Maybe she's a messenger. I tried to picture myself in armor and a winged helmet as I dried and brushed my hair, got dressed, and put on a light amount of makeup. *Whoever she is, I'll channel her strength for the day while I sit at this table full of men.*

A gentle knock came at my door just as I finished getting ready, the sound too soft to have been any of the Sons. "Come in," I called, my curiosity piqued.

A young, dark-haired woman in a long, business-casual dress entered my suite, clutching a book of some kind to her chest, her eyes downcast out of either shyness or respect. "Good morning, Miss Vance," she greeted softly. "I'm Anita, your personal assistant and secretary. I'm here to inform you of your schedule and appointments, plus help you with anything else you may need."

"Oh, lovely!" I approached her with a smile and extended my hand. "It's nice to meet you. Please call me Kyrie."

Anita stared down at my hand for a moment as though it would bite her. Finally, she took it in a soft, hesitant shake. "Lovely to meet you as well. I'd, ah, prefer to call you Miss Vance, if that's alright."

"Oh, sure. Whatever you're most comfortable with." Everyone back home was fairly casual with titles and formalities. I'd forgotten that some preferred not to blur those lines. "So, what do I have in store for my first day, Anita?"

Looking relieved, she opened the book she was clutching, which I now saw was an agenda. "You have a meeting to be introduced to the rest of Sevier's officials in half an hour. After that, you'll be shown to your office and will be taken on a tour through the capitol building. You'll have a one-hour lunch and then tour the rest of the territory."

That last part perked me up. I was eager to see the rest of Sevier, to meet its people and see what kind of potential this place had. Too bad it had to wait until the end while the boring stuff came first.

"Sounds great," I said. "Did you happen to see if my bodyguards were up yet?"

"Your…? Ah. No, Miss Vance. I don't believe so."

"Alright. We'll give them a minute before heading to this meeting. Shall we?" I gestured toward the door in offering that we leave together, but Anita remained rooted to her spot.

"Um." Anita fiddled with the edges of her agenda, her eyes sweeping over me. "Miss Vance, I don't mean any disrespect but…"

I turned to face her head-on. "Is something wrong?"

"Your clothes," she blurted out. "I think it would be best if you changed."

Confused, I looked down at myself. I was wearing

pressed, straight-legged slacks with a blouse tucked in. Everything fit properly and nothing was inappropriate. My accessories were minimal—a slim leather belt, a watch, and a ring from my father. I was even wearing loafers, nothing remotely sexy like heels. I figured today would be full of walking tours and had opted for the most comfortable footwear I owned.

"I'm sorry, I don't understand the problem," I confessed.

"They must not have told you the dress code." Anita frowned. "Women in Sevier are strongly encouraged to wear dresses or skirts. There is nothing *wrong* with your clothes, Miss Vance. They're just a bit…masculine."

I barely restrained myself from bursting out laughing but somehow managed. She was serious.

"You're saying this is a *law*?"

She fidgeted again. "No, just a strong preference by the territory's leaders."

Who are all men. It went without saying.

I scratched the base of my skull, considering my options for a moment. I could do as she suggested and change. It would be the peaceful, least disruptive thing to do. I'd be conforming to the standards of the territory, showing that I embraced and accepted this *strong preference*, as she put it.

The more I thought about it, the more uncomfortable I became. I wasn't a tomboy by any means. I *loved* putting on a dress and feeling pretty and feminine. But knowing it was *strongly encouraged* by my new colleagues and peers sucked all the fun out of the thought.

Plus, I decided last night that I wasn't going to be obedient and docile. I was here to make changes, to give these people ideas on how to make this territory successful.

And I wholeheartedly believed that personal choice was an integral part of that.

"Thank you for the heads-up, Anita," I said to her with a smile. "But I will not be changing. Shall we wait for my bodyguards now?"

My assistant blinked a few times, her mouth opening and closing with no sounds coming out. "Miss Vance?" she finally squeaked out.

"I'll deal with whatever fallout there may be," I said. "Now, the housekeeper last night told me there would be a light breakfast in the loft?"

Anita didn't answer, so I headed out my door, figuring she would follow. Staff were indeed setting up breakfast, and I made a beeline toward the food.

"Good morning, Miss Vance," greeted the friendly maid who had led the Sons and I to our suites last night. "I trust you had a restful evening?"

"I did, thank you. What was your name?"

She froze in the middle of unwrapping fruit on a tray. "Um, it's Marlene, Ambassador," she said, once recovered.

"Well, thank you for setting me and my bodyguards up so comfortably, Marlene. We appreciate it. And you're welcome to call me Kyrie, if you'd like."

The woman seemed confused again and snuck a glance past me to Anita, who had indeed followed me out. "Just doing my job, miss. But you're welcome. And I'll... consider that."

I took mental note of her and Anita's reactions while grabbing a jalapeño cheddar bagel. Was every person here so taken aback by simple thank-yous and common decency? Taking a seat in a comfortable armchair, I chewed on that thought and my bagel at the same time.

My eyes wandered as I ate, taking in the loft now that it was easier to see in full daylight.

It was a bright, open space, with three massive square windows that let natural light pour in. Aside from the table with the breakfast spread, there was little furniture aside from a few armchairs, couches, and desks. It made a nice spot for a study or sitting room, even a casual meeting. My and the Sons' suites were the only ones attached to this loft, which I was grateful for.

My gaze wandered to their door, no longer trying to fight the urge. I'd be late to my first meeting if they didn't come out soon. Should I knock? They were supposed to be accessible to me at *all* times, according to their contract.

If I *really* wanted them to follow their duties to the letter, I could have them move into my suite. I had a spare bedroom.

My throat suddenly went dry, and I suppressed a cough. I'd need a drink to wash this bagel down.

"We should get going, Miss Vance." Anita hovered by the table while I helped myself to a cup of grapefruit juice.

"Let's give them another minute," I said, feeling antsy as I glanced at their door again. "If they're not up soon, we'll—"

The knob turned and the door opened with a soft creak. My breath felt stuck in my chest as three imposing figures walked through and swallowed up all the remaining space in the loft.

"Mornin', ladies," T-Bone greeted. His eyes immediately went to the breakfast spread and lit up. "Oh, fuck yeah, cinnamon rolls."

On his shoulder, Munin let out an enthusiastic chirp, as if he shared the same feelings about cinnamon rolls.

"Ah, morning, guys," I said, my voice higher and breathier than I intended.

"Good morning, Kyrie. Did you sleep well?" Dyno hung back while T-Bone and Grudge went for the food, amusement dancing in his dark eyes. Dyno had two braids running back on each side of his head today, making him look even more like a Viking than normal.

"I did, thank you. How about you guys?"

He grinned like we shared a private joke. "Well enough."

"Oh, this is my assistant, Anita." I turned to the woman who now stared bug-eyed at the three men devouring half of the breakfast table. She clutched her agenda to her chest like a shield. "Anita, this is T-Bone, Dyno, and Grudge. The Sons of Odin MC."

"Hey," T-Bone said around a mouthful of cinnamon roll. "Nice t'meetcha." He picked up a bowl of some granola and trail-mix concoction and held it up to the raven at his shoulder, who pecked at the food.

The other two men grunted out greetings in between bites of food and slurps of coffee. To me, the scene was comical, if even endearing. Anita, on the other hand, looked horrified.

"These are your, um…bodyguards?" she asked in a small voice, eyes darting around.

"Yes!" I chirped, maybe a little too cheerily. "It's okay, they won't bite."

"I mean, if you want us to, all you have to do is a—" T-Bone's offer was quickly cut off by an elbow from Dyno.

"There will be no biting of my assistant!" I struggled to keep the laughter out of my voice, but couldn't hold back the grin or the heat running up my neck. Especially not as T-Bone took another massive bite out of a cinnamon roll, chewed it slowly, and licked the frosting from his lips. He also got a little bit on his finger and stuck the digit in his mouth to suck it off.

His whiskey-colored eyes then locked onto mine, catching my blatant staring, but I still couldn't look away. Not until Anita cleared her throat loudly. "*Ahem.* Should we get going, Miss Vance?"

"Ah, yes." I spun away from the Sons as if I could hide how red my face had already become. "Meetings, great! Let's get started."

CHAPTER 6

KYRIE

The morning meetings were just as boring as expected. Once my first-day jitters settled down, I struggled to keep my eyes open as a room full of fifty-plus year-old men told me their very forgettable names and mind-numbing stories of their positions and duties to Sevier. Thankfully, Anita stayed glued to my side and took copious notes. If I ever had smaller, more personal meetings with these men, at least I'd have a cheat sheet.

My *masculine* style of dress seemed to raise a few eyebrows as we walked in, but it was my bodyguards who stole the lion's share of the attention. Without a word, T-Bone took the seat to my right as if he had every right to be at that table. He and Munin swept their gazes over the room as if daring anyone to voice an objection. No one said a thing.

Every so often, I got a whiff of cinnamon, icing, and coffee when he swiveled in the chair. It made me want to lean into him, to nuzzle into the worn leather draped over his broad chest and find out if he smelled as good up close. But I kept my focus on the officials making their introductions, staying poised despite the desire to curl up against the man sitting next to me.

Dyno remained standing, posting himself at the door we'd come through. Grudge walked around the long conference table to the opposite side of the room, found a spot against the far wall where he could see all of us, and planted himself there. No matter how boring the introductions got, his eyes remained steadfast on me, T-Bone, and Dyno. Well, it was at least comforting to know they took the job seriously.

I wasn't the only one with bodyguards. Some of the higher-ranking officials had their own posted next to or behind them. Some guards were clearly military officers, sharply-dressed in camouflage uniforms with blank, stoic expressions. Others were rougher-looking with threadbare clothes and aged, dusty boots.

A stocky, brick house of man stood a few feet away from Grudge, directly behind his client's chair. His thick arms remained crossed over his chest during the whole meeting, eyes sweeping back and forth over the table with an occasional furrow from his bushy eyebrows. I didn't care for how long or often those eyes lingered on me.

When the tedious introductions were finally over, I smiled with relief. "Thank you all for the warm welcome. I'm excited for the coming months of working together and bringing Sevier to its full potential."

"Excellent." Governor Perry beamed. "On that topic," he flipped a few pages on the legal pad in front of him, "here are some of our goals for the territory over the next five years."

Everything he rattled off from the list sounded reasonable, from improving infrastructure to building new schools, hospitals, business districts, and residential neighborhoods. My father did all of that in the past decade and Four Corners was flourishing. The one thing I was waiting for, but didn't hear, was how he planned to improve the lives of citizens already in the territory and currently struggling. I wrote a note down in my own legal pad to bring up that topic later.

The governor finished reading off his goals and looked ready to move on, when T-Bone's hand shot into the air like a child waiting to be called on at school. Anita squeaked in surprise on my other side, and a low murmur of curiosity rose up from the men at the table.

Perry frowned in T-Bone's direction for a moment before huffing in annoyance. "Yes?"

"Forgive me if this is out of turn, Governor," T-Bone began, "but is Sevier currently in any conflicts with other territories? Or, to your knowledge, are there any hostile territories with their sights set here?"

"I'm sorry, wha—sir, that is *far* beyond the scope of this meeting." The governor's face darkened as he grew flustered. "Not to mention, that information is classified, to be discussed only with military personnel. Most of the people in this room don't have that clearance! What makes you think you can just ask something like that?"

Across the room, Grudge's lips twitched as he bit back a smile. Behind me, I was certain Dyno was doing the same.

"Because my duty is to keep Ambassador Vance safe." T-Bone angled his head toward me. "I'm trying to gauge whether I should consider foreign threats or just domestic ones."

"Our relations with other territories have nothing to do with your client's personal safety! There are *no* threats here."

"We'll be the judge of that." T-Bone leaned back far in his seat and for a moment, I thought he would put his feet on the table.

Every pair of eyes in the room then weighed heavily on me. I tried not to show any reaction, but didn't know whether to feel embarrassed, amused, or flattered. The question T-Bone asked was an important one, but I found myself agreeing with the governor that it wasn't the right setting for it.

Fortunately, the meeting was adjourned moments later and I was freed.

THE TOUR of the capitol building was nearly as boring as the meeting, but at least I was up and walking around. Just as I expected, there wasn't much to the building. White walls and tall ceilings. *Ooh, ahh.* There were small alcoves everywhere for altars and religious figurines from when the building served as a church during pre-Collapse times.

I was grateful my suite and loft area had some charm and personality at least. The rest of the building just felt too clean. Sterile, even. And I still hadn't figured out why only Sevier officials and staff were allowed in the building, aside from sheer elitism.

"This place gives me the creeps," Dyno muttered at one point.

I was inclined to agree.

After the tour, we had our lunch hour in the same

banquet room I had spoken with the Sons our first night here. The other officials quickly grouped up, grabbing tables and food together. I scanned the room for any friendly faces, hopefully female, but saw none.

"You'd think they'd put a little effort into being more welcoming," T-Bone scoffed, looking around the room as I had.

It's okay. I'm used to cold shoulders, I wanted to tell him, but didn't dare say the words out loud. I swallowed the thought as I grabbed an empty table for me and Anita, who let me pour over her notes from the meeting while we ate.

Finally, the time came for my tour of the territory. We'd be driving through some areas and walking in others, with the governor and another official to guide us. I had a sneaking suspicion as to who the other person would be, and my gut sank as Governor Perry and his nephew Nathan strode up to us at the end of lunch.

"I hope you're ready for some incredible views." Nathan beamed as we left the banquet room. "Some would even call them romantic."

One of the Sons snorted loudly behind me, but I resisted looking back to see who it was.

"I'm excited," I said, hoping I came off as polite but not over-enthusiastic. Someone touched my shoulder as we approached the governor's car, and I turned around to find myself face-to-face with T-Bone.

"Grudge is going to ride with you," he said. "D and I will get our bikes and keep an eye out from a distance. If we see anything fishy, Grudge will know. We have a system in place."

"Sounds great." I gave him my biggest, most genuine smile of the day. Jesus, he was just so *tall* and nice to look at. "Ride safe."

He gave a curt nod in return, eyes twinkling with playfulness before resuming stiff formality. "Enjoy the tour, Miss Vance."

T-Bone and Dyno left to get their bikes while the rest of us piled into the SUV, which was even bigger than the one I'd ridden in from Four Corners. Grudge sat directly behind Anita and I. Our row, thankfully, only had two seats, so Nathan and his uncle had to sit in front of us.

"So, if you don't mind me asking." Nathan turned to face me, casually draping an arm over the back of his seat as the driver pulled away from the capital.

Oh no, here we go, I thought.

"How old are you, Miss Vance?" he asked, flashing a charming smile.

"Twenty-three," I answered. "And you?"

"Twenty-five. So that would've made you thirteen when the Collapse happened, right? Because I was fifteen."

"Um, yes. I guess so." I swallowed, idly spinning the ring on my finger. "I don't remember, exactly."

"Don't remember?" Now the governor turned to look at me, his expression incredulous. "My dear, how could you not remember the most *devastating* event in recent history? A powerful, united country for hundreds of years, crumbled to dust overnight. My word, some days I still wake up and I can't believe it was real."

I looked down at my hands in my lap, my embarrassment rising and unsure of what to say. What would they think if I told them I didn't know it'd happened until almost a week later? That my father kept it from me, acting like everything was normal for several days. He wasn't a governor back then, but a mayor of a medium-sized city which was now in ruins. I remembered him looking more tired and stressed than usual, his hushed meetings with his staff that went late into the night, but thirteen-year-old me had *no* idea.

Not until my language tutor came in for our weekly sessions. She seemed tired too, and like she'd been crying a lot. Halfway through our lesson, she broke down completely. She sank to the floor, sobbing and wailing. I went to comfort her and she cried into my arms. She had tutored me for years and I wondered if something had happened to her sons or her husband.

"They killed everyone, destroyed everything," she had cried. "Senators, judges, hundreds of congressmen…all dead. DC is in ruins…I don't know what's going to happen, Kyrie, but I'm *so* scared. Women already have no rights, and girls are being kidnapped everywhere."

That was the moment I could never forget. Her grief and her utter terror at what was to come next.

When I confronted my father that evening, he didn't deny it. It happened a whole week earlier, the storming of the US capitol by an angry mob in the thousands. They murdered all nine Supreme Court justices in cold blood, trapped lawmakers in barricaded chambers and offices, to which they then set on fire. Thousands of documents were destroyed, monuments and statues blown up and defaced.

Tension and unrest in the country had boiled over to the point where people didn't just cripple the US government. They cut it off at the head, then watched it fall and bleed out. Everyone called it the Collapse.

With nothing to unify this now nameless, gigantic continent, there was chaos. People fought over territory, resources, power, everything. Nothing was against the law, because there were no laws. Eventually, territories arose from the skeletons of US states. Many were still volatile and dangerous, depending on who was in charge. But a few were safe, stable, and prosperous, like the one my father created—Four Corners.

One thing I still resented him for was that he staunchly defended his decision to keep me in the dark about the whole thing. *To protect me*, he said.

He didn't protect me. He made me ignorant. And now I looked like a fool in front of these two men who I would be working with in recovering from the Collapse. I'd bet anything Nathan's parents didn't feel the need to protect him from such a catastrophic event that literally affected everyone.

"Where were you when it happened, Uncle Kurtis?" Nathan asked. The conversation had moved on from me, thankfully.

"Ah, a decade ago, I worked for the mayor of Salt Lake City," Governor Perry said. "Truth be told, I hated that job. I always thought I would make a better mayor. He was far too outlandish with his ideas, wanted to do idiotic things with the budget, and what-have-you. Truth be told, the Collapse made a clean slate for this area. We can finally return to our original values and build a proper society from the ground up."

I didn't realize how hard my fists were clenched until the pain sliced through my palms. A clean slate? What a fucking callous thing to say, and from a governor, no less.

"The people who were robbed, kidnapped, and murdered in the chaos probably felt a bit differently," I said before I could stop myself.

The two men looked at me again. "Yes, the ensuing violence was unfortunate," Perry mused in a placating tone. "But consider this, Miss Vance. We've lost over fifteen percent of habitable land in the last hundred years due to the rising sea levels. With California and Florida underwater in a mere decade, it pushed more people inland. Everywhere, from major cities to small towns, ran out of housing for these people, most of whom turned out to be criminals anyway. And the population continued to boom, despite all this! Is a bit of population control to maintain order so bad?"

Nathan was nodding along as his uncle spoke, clearly in agreement, while every word made me want to throw up.

"If the goal was to prevent overpopulation and decrease criminal activity," I had to say every word slowly in order to not scream in their faces, "maybe sixty percent of US states shouldn't have outlawed birth control services or cut ninety percent of funding to public schools. Maybe then we wouldn't have needed the Collapse to create a *clean slate.*"

"Spoken like a true, idealistic young person." The governor smiled like he was trying to come off as teasing but I only felt patronized. "You weren't even a thought when the countdown to the Collapse began, my dear. Unrest had been building for decades, and there were many contributing factors to the country's demise. It's a very complicated situation with no clear solutions. We're just doing the best we can."

I slumped back in my seat, disbelief rendering me speechless. "Of course. You're right, governor."

My mind reeled as the two men resumed facing forward. Did they feel satisfied at putting the dumb little woman in her place? And did they really see the mass panic, the looting, rioting, displacement and trafficking of thousands, as necessary to justify their end goal?

So many people had suffered. The leader of my father's military, General Bray, and his wife had escaped from a labor camp and would have died if they hadn't reached Four Corners. Nearly every adult in my home territory had a similar story. For all of my father's faults, at least he never saw others' pain as a benefit to him. He rolled up his sleeves and helped his fellow man. I came to Sevier with the goal of doing the same, and I never imagined I'd see such nonchalance from my own colleagues.

The weight of a large hand came to rest briefly on my shoulder. Grudge. I'd forgotten about him for a moment, silently observing from the backseat. I reached up to touch his hand but he'd already taken it away.

Still, I recognized the gesture for what it was. Comfort, solidarity. He couldn't voice his opinion, but he knew where I was coming from. After feeling chastised and dismissed, I was grateful for that small reminder that I had someone on my side.

The driver parked at our first stop, immediately coming to my door to help me out. I was relieved that it was him and not Nathan or his uncle. After Anita and the others got out, Grudge came up next to me with an intense look in his eyes.

He touched my arm, then gestured to his ear with his other hand before bringing his palm over his heart. Anita stared at us, looking puzzled, but I understood his meaning perfectly. *You speak from the heart, and I hear you.*

"Thank you, Grudge," I said with a nod and forced smile. "I'm glad you're here, and I appreciate you saying that."

I went to touch his arm as he did with me, but he had already pulled away and resumed his guard position at my back. What I really wanted to do was hug him. He looked like he gave warm, wonderful hugs.

Who was I kidding? I wanted to burrow into the middle of a Sons of Odin cuddle pile and never come out.

Especially now that I had an even bigger uphill battle than I imagined with this job. I thought I'd found new opportunities but so far, I'd only been met with more barriers.

CHAPTER 7

KYRIE

I should have expected the tour around Sevier to only showcase the best spots, according to the governor and his nephew. They showed me the cliffs and mountains that were once famous national park sites, and they told me all about how they intended to build hotels and rental cabins to bring tourism back.

In another area, they showed me where they planned to build luxury homes for government officials and their associates, whom I suspected were just more privileged, rich people.

"Can you tell me, Governor," I asked after the third planned site, a golf resort, "do you have the contractors to build these projects?"

"Ah, yes, our architects are almost finished with the designs. Then we'll be posting jobs for the construction." His bushy white eyebrows raised as he leaned toward me. "Why? Does Four Corners have contractors they're willing to lend us?"

Son of a bitch, I saw that one coming. He knew Four Corners had some of the best tradesmen in the southwest, especially when it came to home builders.

"Perhaps," I answered with a coy smile. "Our contractors are used to being paid above-average wages. If you post competitive job offers, I'm sure they'll come. To boost your own economy though, might I suggest you offer it to Sevier locals first. Your people will jump for well-paying jobs, I'm sure."

The governor waved his hand dismissively as he turned away. "We'll look at the budget and see what we can afford for wages."

"Have you established a minimum wage yet?" I asked, following him back to the car.

"Don't worry your pretty little head about that."

I sucked in a deep breath as I returned to my seat, only releasing it when Grudge touched my shoulder on his way past me. I wished his touch would linger long enough for me to really acknowledge it.

On our way to the next stop, we drove through an area of rolling hills. It would have been scenic if everything wasn't burned to a blackened crisp. Several miles of charred landscape passed us on either side, looking desolate and alien.

"What happened here?" I asked with my nose pressed to the window. I'd never seen anything like it.

"Controlled burn," Nathan said, looking amused by my curiosity.

"Oh, like to prevent a bigger fire?"

"Not exactly," he murmured coyly. "This was a winegrowing area before the Collapse. Uncle Kurtis burned all the grapes when we took back the territory last year. See that there?" He pointed to the remains of a building in the distance, little more than a pile of burnt lumber. "That was where they harvested the grapes and made the wine."

"But…why?" I stared at him, trying to figure out the logic of it. "A winery could be great for the territory. It'll bring tourism and create more jobs. You can tax the product—"

"Alcohol should not be accessible to the common man," he said with a completely serious face. "People with no self-control abuse it, and that's how we get more crime and filthy vagrants wandering the streets. We made alcohol, tobacco, and marijuana illegal in Sevier on our first day back in power."

I kept waiting for him to laugh or smirk, but he was completely serious. Oh my God, what the actual *fuck* had I gotten myself into?

Did none of these people know what a black market was? It really never occurred to them that making things illegal increased the demand for said things? I had no experience as a diplomat, but Nathan must have had a similar education as me, if not better. This was basic economics.

How was I going to help their normal, struggling citizens with people like this in charge? I rubbed my forehead, tripping over my own thoughts until the car suddenly lurched forward.

"Watch out!" Perry yelled while tires squealed and the car spun. My lunch sloshed in my stomach as our surroundings whipped past the windows. I didn't even have time to think *what the fuck?* when it all stopped.

The car went still, but my pulse and stomach were still reeling from the spin-out. My chest felt heavy, and it was hard to breathe. I looked down and realized Grudge had wrapped an arm around me from behind, holding me pinned to the seat so I wouldn't get thrown around.

"Sorry, sir. Miss. Is everyone alright?" The driver turned in his seat to look back at us. "I'm so sorry, he just came out of nowhere."

"Who did?" Governor Perry demanded, aggressively removing his seatbelt before throwing his door open. "I don't see anyone."

The rumble of motorcycles drowned out the driver's reply as the other Sons caught up to us.

"What the fuck happened?" T-Bone yelled over his engine. "That was a crazy fuckin' spin-out."

Grudge came out from the backseat and kneeled next to me, lightly running a touch over my face, neck, and arms. My eyes fell closed at the gentle contact, savoring it. He had checked over me just like this four years ago in Blakeworth, right after Mari and I hit the dirt while running for our lives.

And behind my eyelids, just as vividly as in my dream, I saw the armored woman with blonde hair. She held her axe and shield in front of her, knees bent and teeth bared under her helmet like she was bracing for an attack.

"Kah." Grudge tapped my cheek lightly. "Hm?"

My eyes fluttered open, the woman only an echo in my vision as reality filtered in. I found Grudge staring at me with an intense frown of concern.

"I'm okay." I reached up to place my hand over his, lacing our fingers together without thinking. "I'm okay. Thank you."

He didn't look convinced and squeezed our fingers together.

"Are you okay?" I reached out to touch his shoulder,

but like before, he pulled away and only gave a curt nod in reply.

I turned in my seat, now only feeling awkwardness where there had been a sliver of intimacy the moment before. "Anita?"

"I'm okay, Miss Vance." My assistant rubbed her neck, wincing. "I might just be sore tomorrow."

With the motorcycles idling and T-Bone and Dyno investigating what had caused the near-accident, shouting voices alerted me to an argument in front of the SUV. I climbed out of the car and went to see for myself, Grudge right at my side.

"You almost hit a kid? What the fuck were you doing, jerking off behind the wheel?" T-Bone, of course.

"How dare you accuse my staff of such lewd behavior!" Governor Perry sputtered back.

"I swear, he just ran out into the road," the driver protested. "And now he won't leave!"

While the grown men argued, sitting in the middle of the road between them was a boy no older than ten. His face was dirty, with tear-tracks running down his cheeks. His clothes were threadbare and his hands were cupped palm-open in his lap. He stared blankly ahead, oblivious to the men arguing above him.

I felt, rather than saw, the armored woman from my dream beat her axe against the shield once. My gaze slid to the side because I *swore* she was right there in my peripheral vision. But the space was empty when I looked closer.

Nathan leaned down and wrapped a hand around the boy's arm. "Hey, kid, you gotta go." He started to move him physically, but the boy started screaming. A wordless wail erupted from his mouth, full of despair and frustration.

"Ah, what the—! You're gonna blow out my eardrums! Ungrateful little—"

The armored woman beat her shield again. I felt waves of aggression coming off her, the fierce urge to protect someone innocent from danger. T-Bone's raven was also cawing loudly, his beak stabbing in the direction of Nathan and the governor.

"What the fuck is wrong with you?" Dyno glared at Nathan, hands drifting to rest on his belt. "Manhandling a kid, really?"

The child yanked his arm back from Nathan and resumed his sitting position on the ground, sniffling quietly.

Do something, the armored woman seemed to urge me. *Protect him.*

"Have any of you tried asking him what he wants?" I piped up. "Or if he's okay?"

"He looks fine," Nathan sneered. "Just in desperate need of a bath. Hey." He leaned down and snapped his fingers in front of the boy's face. "Tell us what you want so we can make our way through this slum."

The boy ignored him, not reacting to the words or the snapping sound. I'd been fed up with Nathan and his uncle since the start of this tour, so I pushed my way forward with a sigh. "Leave him alone. Let me try."

I kneeled in front of the skinny boy, taking note of his downcast eyes and outward palms. "Hi there. Are you hurt? Do you need currency?" I asked, reaching into one of my pockets. "Or food?"

Again, he didn't react. Not until I placed a one-Sevier note in his hands and he looked up, making eye contact with me for the first time.

"Of course, a beggar," Nathan scoffed from somewhere behind me. "Just what we need more of."

I ignored him and smiled at the boy. "Is that all you needed? Just some money?"

He didn't respond, at least not with speech. His hand drifted up toward his chest, and he seemed to make the American Sign Language gesture for *hungry*.

A lightbulb flashed through my head right then, and I carefully signed with my hands as I spoke. "Are you hungry?"

The boy gasped in surprise, and he nodded before signing rapidly. *"The soup kitchen ran out of food, and the market is too far away to walk. Mom told me to wait by the road and make cars stop for money or food."*

A heavy pang cut through my chest at the sight of fresh tears in his eyes. How long had he been waiting? How many cars had refused to stop?

"Where do you live?" I asked him. *"Can you show me? My friends and I will bring you food."*

"Wait, are you communicating with him?" Governor Perry asked.

"Yes," I said, still speaking with my hands after the boy told me his address. "Sir, we need to supply the food bank in this neighborhood immediately."

My signing became more aggressive, my body language reflecting my emotions as I spoke. I could still feel and *almost* see the armored woman, and I channeled her strength while I addressed the governor and his nephew. "Before you build luxury homes or a golf resort, I suggest putting more affordable, accessible markets at the top of your list. No one in your territory should have to jump in front of cars to beg for food."

"Wow, impressive." Now Nathan smirked, leaning toward me. "How did you learn that?"

I faced him squarely, still using my hands to speak and

wishing I had a shield to beat him away. "Didn't you learn a foreign language growing up, Nathan?"

"Yeah, I picked German." He chuckled. "I'm pretty awful at it though."

"Well, I took two languages," I said. "Icelandic and American Sign Language. I'm fluent in both."

"Heh, overachiever." He smiled like he was teasing, but I saw the hostility he tried to keep buried.

"Why would he jump in front of the car for food?" Governor Perry asked, still staring at the boy like he was a curiosity.

"Because he had no other option," I said, my exasperation bleeding into my hand gestures.

"Okay, you can stop that now," the governor said, referring to my signing with a dismissive hand wave.

"No." My hands cut through the air aggressively. "He has a right to know what's going on."

The governor frowned at me, probably not accustomed to hearing the word *no* often. Dyno approached me before the older man could say anything else, resting a warm hand on my arm. In that moment, I felt the armored woman relax, her shield lowering a few inches.

"All three of us will help. Just tell us what we need." He flashed a smile at the boy, and my anger thawed just a fraction.

"Let's go back to the capital," I said, making sure the boy could understand. "We'll buy food from the main kitchen. There should be plenty to go around." I looked at Nathan and his uncle. "Unless there's a better place to get food from?"

Neither said a word for several seconds. Nathan looked blankly at his uncle for his decision, but I could see the wheels turning in the governor's head.

"That will suffice for now," he bit out before turning sharply back to the car.

UNSURPRISINGLY, my two tour guides had 'important matters to attend to' when we returned to the capitol. So it was me, Anita, our driver, and the Sons making trips back and forth with groceries for those who needed it. Word spread quickly in the neighborhood, and several more families came out of the woodwork, asking for rations. By the time we finished, it had been dark for hours, and I was dead on my feet.

"I can't thank you both enough," I said to Anita and our driver, whose name was Neil, as we prepared for our last trip home. "I'll make sure you're both compensated from my own budget for all the extra hours. I know this wasn't how you expected to spend your day."

"Thank you, Ambassador. I enjoyed this, actually." Neil smiled kindly at me in the rearview mirror. "It was certainly a break in the routine."

"Yes, Miss Vance. It felt good to do something nice for those families." Anita rubbed her eyes and yawned. "Um, if you don't need me for anything else, I might lie down in the backseat for the trip back. I'm exhausted."

"Of course, go ahead." I moved my legs to the side so she could get behind me. The Sons were just outside, talking among themselves. With only two bikes, I wondered if they would double-up or if someone would ride back with me.

I got my answer as the guys slapped each others' shoulders and broke away. T-Bone and Dyno headed for the bikes while Grudge came to join me. He started for the backseat, when I touched his forearm to stop him.

"Anita's resting back there. You can sit with me, if you'd like."

"Ah," he said, crouching and moving carefully to take the passenger-side window seat in my row, leaving a large space between us.

As Neil pulled onto the road heading back toward the capital, my thoughts drifted to wondering what I could get away with now that he was next to me. Nathan and the governor weren't here, and Anita was lying down. What would happen if I just reached over and tangled up my fingers with Grudge's again? Or let my weary head rest on that comfortable shoulder? Would it be so bad?

I was envious of how openly affectionate the Sons were with each other, especially in the small ways. Even today, as they unloaded the car and passed out crates of food, they snuck quick kisses and let touches linger on each other. They teased each other and laughed at private jokes.

I wanted that, but not just with anyone. Barely a full day had passed, and the old yearning from years ago was back with a vengeance. It was dawning on me that I wanted that *only* from them. I wanted to be included in their affection, part of their relationship.

Was that pathetic? Delusional? Probably.

I just didn't feel safe enough with any other men to cure my loneliness.

Before I could make up my mind about touching Grudge in any way, he did so first. I felt a nudge on my arm and looked to see a question written on a small notepad. *Why Icelandic?* he'd asked.

A laugh burst from my throat at the sudden question. "The short answer is because I wanted to annoy my dad."

Grudge smiled, laughing with soft huffs of breath. "Ah?"

He seemed interested in hearing the long answer, so I went on. "He was just being really overbearing and kept telling me to pick a 'useful' language, like Spanish. Which, in hindsight, I probably should have done. But when you're ten years old, always under someone's watch, and utterly bored with no way to rebel against your parent, you get creative. So I picked the most obscure language on the list to learn. And because I'm fueled by spite, I studied it for over ten years and became fluent."

Grudge nodded like he approved of my rebellion, still grinning and laughing quietly. I remembered the gesture he made earlier in the day, *I hear you.*

"Icelandic was the language I used to challenge myself," I said, now signing my words as well. "But ASL was my favorite of the two to learn. And it's been useful in more situations than I imagined, like today."

Grudge flipped to another page in his notepad. *Have you ever read the Eddas?*

"No, what are those?"

He smiled while writing down the answer. *Epic poems and stories written in Old Norse. They tell of the Norse gods, heroes, and legends of the medieval Viking age.*

"Oh, that's fascinating!" I said. "Have you read them?"

Only the English translations, he replied. *But I've heard Icelandic is very close to the Old Norse language. You may be able to read the Eddas in their original form. I have a book, if you would like to borrow it.*

"I would love to!" I exclaimed. "Thank you, Grudge. I promise I'll take good care of it."

He nodded again, his smile more shy, subdued. We had leaned closer to each other almost subconsciously. He, to show me his notepad, and me, eager to read what he wrote. Now there were only mere inches between us.

"Have you ever considered learning to sign?" I asked. "It may get things across easier for you. Faster, as well."

The mood shifted instantly, like a switch flipping. Grudge leaned away, his smile gone. He faced forward, body stiff. It was clear that my question struck a nerve. After a few seconds of tense stillness, he shook his head in a firm *no* gesture and looked out his window, away from me.

Shame and regret filled me, turning my stomach. Why did I have to open my big mouth? Dad always chastised me for asking too many questions at inappropriate times. I'd always been curious, perhaps to my detriment, but I never meant to be offensive. If I had taken just a second to think before speaking, it might have occurred to me that Grudge wasn't comfortable discussing his muteness.

My fingers skimmed over the seat between us, inching toward him before I pulled them back to my lap. He clearly didn't want to engage with me anymore, and I wasn't about to push those boundaries.

We rode the rest of the way home in uncomfortable silence.

CHAPTER 8
GRUDGE

"You don't impress girls with books, Grudge," T-Bone teased me with a playful nip to my earlobe. "You tell them your war stories, show off your scars and tattoos." His palm ran down the front of my pants. "Or just whip this bad boy out."

I snorted, knocking his hands away before closing the *Prose Edda* and sticking the book in an inner pocket of my cut. Something told me that Kyrie wasn't the type to be impressed by my cock, at least not that alone. I wasn't even trying to impress her, not really. She wanted to try reading Old Norse, and I happened to have a book in that language.

T-Bone saw everything as flirting. If someone attractive so much as breathed in his direction, he'd take it as an invitation to hit on them. But I already knew Kyrie would never see me with any kind of romantic interest. Yes, I had my own feelings to deal with now that we were guarding her all day every day, but that was on me to handle.

She wanted to do important things in this territory, and I admired her for that. I wouldn't let my own feelings get in the way of what she wanted to accomplish. But it didn't hurt to be friendly and share books, right?

"Here's what we got for today." T-Bone squinted at a piece of paper in front of him, Kyrie's schedule, given to us by her assistant.

"You need glasses," Dyno chuckled at him. "Let me see that."

"Fuck off. I do not."

"It's okay, T. We're all getting older."

"She didn't have to write this so fucking small. Jesus."

Just admit you can't read, T. The ribbing thought came to the forefront of my mind. It might have been funny, if I'd been able to say it. I loved hearing the guys laugh. Whenever they made jokes like that, they always included me. I could have written it down but the moment passed too quickly. Dyno had already snatched the paper from T-Bone and squinted at it himself.

"She has two meetings before lunch," Dyno reported. "First, with the infrastructure committee, then with the public housing board."

"What the fuck do those words even mean?" T-Bone groaned and scrubbed his hands down his face.

"I don't know, but they're in opposite wings of the capitol from each other." Dyno slapped the paper to T-Bone's chest with a quick glance at me. "How do you guys want to handle this?"

I made a few rough hand gestures with my idea, partially made-up and partially from the meager bits of ASL I did know. Usually the guys understood my meaning well enough, but I could always write it down if they didn't. They were patient with me and always listened.

They both watched me carefully, eyes fixated on my body language. It used to make me self-conscious. Now I just found their intense stares sexy.

"You saying one of us stay in the room with her, one posted outside at the exit, and the other keep a wider perimeter?"

I nodded and moved my hands around in an orbiting motion.

"Then we'll rotate positions for the second meeting," Dyno confirmed. "Works for me. Sound good to you, Pres?"

"Yes." T-Bone huffed in annoyance at the title, snapping his hand out to hit Dyno in the nipple. "Dyno-dick."

"Save the dirty pet names for tonight, *Pres.*" The other man goaded him with a smirk.

"You." T-Bone's hand slid up to grip the back of Dyno's head, fingers curling in his black hair as he pulled him close. They were a hair's breadth away from kissing and Dyno's breath hitched, as did mine.

"You can talk all the shit you want when you're riding my cock tonight." T-Bone grinned and closed the distance between them, planting a lingering kiss on Dyno's lips. He pulled away, still smiling. "At least, you can try."

I stifled a groan and adjusted my pants. I never could decide if it was hotter to watch them or to be positioned between them. Fortunately, I often had both.

We decided on our positions for the first guard rotation, then left the suite. I hung back at the end of the pack, as the perimeter lookout for the first meeting. Word had already gotten around that I was the mute bodyguard. No doubt that most of the officials here would assume I was stupid too. I was counting on it. The less guarded they were, the more I could learn about the people surrounding our pretty ambassador.

Kyrie looked over her shoulder and waved hello at me as our group followed her. I returned the gesture, my thoughts soured momentarily at the memory of last night. She had asked me if I ever learned to sign, and I acted like a dick.

Maybe I should have seen the question coming, but it was out of the blue for me. Except for T-Bone and Dyno, people didn't notice me. They didn't ask me questions or try to get to know me. People wrote me off as soon as they figured out I couldn't speak. It didn't bother me. I had gotten used to being invisible and often used it to my advantage. I was seen and valued by the only two people that mattered anyway.

But when I was treated like a normal person, it threw me off. I didn't always know how to respond. People tried, but they didn't know my body language and then got frustrated when I had to write things down. They usually wrote me off after that.

Kyrie didn't. I probably killed the conversation before it could get to that point. Still, I was rude, and she had always been nice to me. I owed her an apology, and hopefully the book in my pocket would earn me a smile.

And maybe I owed her an explanation for why I acted that way, which was the main reason why I wanted some distance from her first thing in the morning. I wasn't sure how to explain myself without prompting even more questions and possibly opening a massive can of worms.

But what worried me most was her not wanting to be my friend anymore if she knew. A perimeter walk would clear my head, help me find the right words. Keep me from being distracted. Not that she was distracting in a bad way. I just really liked listening to her speak and didn't want to miss a word. I enjoyed watching the shift of her moods and thoughts in her facial expressions. She was like T-Bone in that way, so openly expressive. It was beautiful and refreshing to see how someone felt just by looking at their face or listening to their voice. I was envious of people who could do that.

Dyno went into the meeting room with Kyrie while T-Bone posted himself outside the door. "I'll let you know if I see anything," he said, eyes already sweeping the corridor.

With a soft caw, Munin flew from his shoulder to one of the beams high in the ceiling. The raven was a treasured companion to all of us, but his bond with T-Bone was unique. T-Bone was the only one who could temporarily leave his body and see through the bird's eyes like they were his own.

We had no explanation for this ability, except that it was a gift from the Allfather, Odin himself. It was our secret weapon, how we had won battles and found each other when lost. It was how we were able to rescue Kyrie in Blakeworth.

Be careful, I mouthed to T-Bone. There were plenty of capitol employees still walking the halls, and we weren't exactly open about our gifts from the gods. T-Bone lost control of his body when looking through Munin. He would go limp like he was unconscious, and people would take notice.

"Cover me when you double back," he said. "Between you, me, and the bird, nothing should get past us."

I nodded and started off on my patrol, heading toward an outside exit. The windows from Kyrie's meeting room faced a small outdoor area, and I wanted to make sure nothing had a clear view of her or anyone in that room.

This area was a small courtyard with a stone fountain in the center, benches under drooping willow trees, and well-maintained greenery that was also lush and sweet-smelling. *She would like it out here*, was my first thought.

Kyrie hated being cooped up inside, I noticed. She grew bored and fidgety, and a blank look would cross her face as she daydreamed. Depending on what she was thinking about, sometimes her eyes would brighten or her lips twitched into a smile. I wondered what she thought about that brought out those reactions.

I should probably stop thinking about her so much.

She was the first and only woman to ride on the back of my bike. I wasn't the most sentimental man, but I never forgot how she'd held onto me when we got her out of that hellhole. How fearless she was and how she shrieked with laughter. I wanted to bottle that sound so I could hear it all the time.

It was only the second full day in Sevier, but she'd barely laughed once since we'd been here. Hopefully that would change once she found her footing.

I turned toward the windows of the building. The reflections of trees and blue sky made it difficult for anyone to see in, but that wasn't what caught my attention.

One of the bodyguards from Kyrie's first meeting stood just next to a windowpane, out of sight of the people inside. He was the mean, bulldog-looking motherfucker with a shaved head and permanent scowl. And he wasn't alone. Three other men huddled around him, one leaning against the wall, talking in low voices.

I didn't recognize the other three, but they looked just as shady as the bodyguard. Everyone's head swiveled from time to time, on the lookout for anyone eavesdropping. No one detected me, obscured by the fountain and the hanging leaves of a willow tree. The group was too far away for me to hear anything, but I kept eyes on them until they disbanded and walked away.

That's curious, I thought, waiting a few more minutes to continue my outside sweep before heading back inside. *The guys will want to know about it.*

"...SO you see, Ambassadors, we are asking for you to draw on your unique experiences when submitting proposals to the Treasury Secretary..."

Kyrie's lips parted and she released a soft sigh, eyes flicking in my direction once again. This was her second morning meeting, and the poor thing was utterly bored. We'd been catching each other's eye for the past half-hour, and everything I'd prepared to say in my first patrol went out the window. My mind was blank, and I was content to just watch her, to see her smile and blush.

The next time she glanced at me, I was ready. I stared at the tip of my nose until my eyes crossed, and sucked in my lower lip so it looked like I had a massive overbite.

Kyrie let out an impressive snort, then started to laugh, then began coughing to cover up her laughter. Every head turned in her direction, making her face grow even redder as she shrank down in her seat.

"Ambassador Vance, is everything alright?" asked the Chairman.

"Yes! Yes, I apologize." She composed herself quickly, but a hidden grin still pulled at her lips. "I, ah, had a sip of water and it went down the wrong pipe. Sorry for the interruption, everyone. Please continue."

The meeting went on as if nothing had happened, and I was grateful that no one took notice of me. Now I couldn't stop grinning victoriously at having made her laugh. It was even better than I expected and made my whole week.

Once the meeting ended and everyone filed out, I approached Kyrie with a note I had prepared.

"Is this an apology for embarrassing me?" she asked cheekily, taking the paper from me to read.

I chuckled with a shake of my head. I was proud of getting her to make those noises and would never apologize for it.

Her face sobered as she read over my brief note. "Oh, for last night in the car. Grudge, no." She lifted her eyes, shaking her head at me. "It's me who should be apologizing to you for that. I shouldn't ask invasive questions about—"

"Mugh." I waved my hand while making a sound of protest, then clenched my teeth and fist. Rarely did I hate my inability to speak. Usually I was at peace with it, but right now, I wished more than anything that I could just *say* what was on my mind.

There was nothing wrong with what you asked me in the car. It brought up painful memories, but you never could have known that. You are lovely and kind, and I shouldn't have been rude to you.

Kyrie stood still, waiting for me to elaborate in some way while I remained paralyzed by my frustration. Finally, I just cut my hand through the air again, huffing out a breath with a sheepish smile.

Kyrie smiled back, and my nerves eased just a little. "It's forgotten. We're good, Grudge."

I nodded, relieved that she understood. My apology note had been simple, without any long-winded explanation. My personal history wasn't something she needed to be burdened with.

"Well, I don't know about you, but I am *starving.*" Kyrie began gathering up documents and notes from her meeting. "I can't believe it's only lunchtime, and I have one more *long* meeting this afternoon." She pushed her hair behind her shoulder, looking up at me with a cheeky grin. "You should make more faces at me to help pass the time."

I returned her grin and tilted my head. It would be T-Bone's turn to be in the room with her next, but I got a kick out of amusing her. Would she think of my stupid face this afternoon and laugh to herself?

Nah, wishful thinking.

She started toward the door, and the *Prose Edda* was burning a hole in my pocket. Her assistant had stepped out to use the restroom earlier, so now was my only opportunity.

"Mm!" I moved quickly toward her, holding my arm out in a *stop* gesture.

Kyrie halted immediately and turned to me with a curious, if even hopeful, expression. "Is something wrong, Grudge?"

"Mm." I shook my head, my pulse pounding. Why the fuck was I so nervous? It wasn't like this was a surprise. I told her I'd give her the damn book.

I reached into my cut and withdrew it from the inner pocket, hoping she didn't notice how my hand shook when I held it out to her.

"Oh! Is this what you were talking about last night?" Kyrie took it from me with the utmost care, running a gentle hand over the worn-out, fabric cover.

"Mm-hm." I watched in fascination as she marveled over the book. She opened the cover and read the Old Norse title page, her lips and tongue moving around the ancient language in a way that I wanted to feel on my skin.

Read to me, I thought. *Better yet, read* on *me. Let me feel your voice on my skin.*

"This is beautiful, Grudge!" she cooed, turning the pages carefully. She whispered another line of prose in Old Norse, and I held back a sigh.

Not as beautiful as you—God, fuck! What is wrong with me?

"I'll take good care of this and return it to you soon." She hugged the book to her chest, and I tried not to think about my body heat transferring to her. "Thank you, I love it."

I fumbled for my notepad and quickly scrawled out a note. *You're welcome. Keep it for as long as you'd like.*

Kyrie grinned and hugged the book tighter, turning her body away from me. "You might have to wrestle it back from me then."

I held back the groan rising in my throat, hands clenching at the fantasy playing out in my head. *Sweet girl, you shouldn't joke about things like that.*

Her eyes dropped from my face, head tilting curiously. "Grudge, what's that?" She pointed at my arm, stepping closer and reaching all the way until her finger touched my shoulder.

"Ah." She was looking at one of my tattoos, and I pulled my sleeve up to show her the full piece. Maybe there was something to T-Bone's advice about impressing girls with tattoos.

Kyrie's eyebrows raised, her face paling as her expression turned to shock. "Who is she? I mean, I'm sorry, it's beautiful! But can you tell me about her?"

Her reaction puzzled me, and I glanced down at my shoulder piece again before releasing my sleeve. Kyrie leaned over eagerly as I wrote my explanation.

She's a valkyrie. A mythical warrior woman from the Norse sagas. They choose who lives or dies in battle and take slain warriors to the afterlife. There are stories of them in that book, the Prose Edda.

"A valkyrie," Kyrie whispered reverently just as I wrote the word down. "So they're like angels?"

Sort of, I wrote. *Warriors thought of them as guardians, protectors. Some say valkyries were the fiercest of women during their mortal lives. Warriors themselves, protectors of their family, or mothers who sacrificed themselves for their children.*

Kyrie's expression grew even more bewildered as I wrote out my explanation. I was still confused by her reaction but unsure of the right question to ask her.

"Does it mean anything if…if a valkyrie visits someone in a dream?" she asked.

I stared at her for another few moments before writing a response. *I've never heard of that. Maybe she is protecting you.*

"It felt like a warning," Kyrie said, her brows furrowing. "She kept beating an ax against a shield, making this drumbeat that went faster and faster." Kyrie pulled her lower lip between her teeth. "And a raven landed on her shoulder and started cawing."

Now it was my turn to look shocked. A valkyrie alone was one thing, but a raven accompanying her, a guardian of the fallen? That couldn't be a coincidence.

Kyrie wasn't even done yet. "And—shit, I'm sorry. This is stupid."

I shook my head and rolled my hand in her direction, urging her to go on. I needed to hear everything, down to the last detail.

She appeared hesitant, but humored my request. "I saw her, or more like felt her, yesterday. When we ran into that boy on the road." A smile pulled at one corner of her lips. "She almost felt like a fourth bodyguard. It was like I could sense her standing near me. I felt how badly she wanted to use her axe and shield to protect that boy. But she wasn't *really* there, almost like a ghost. So I stepped up and did it in her stead."

Kyrie gave a small shake of her head and stepped away, her cheeks flushing again and her smile sheepish. "Sounds crazy, right?"

I shook my head and quickly wrote down, *No! Absolutely not.* But I couldn't articulate my thoughts more than that and spun the pen in my fingers as I searched for the right words. I'd read the Eddas several times and never once read of a valkyrie guarding a living woman. And the raven…that had to be some kind of link to us. Or was that just wishful thinking again? The guys would know better than me.

In the time I was taking to think, Kyrie seemed ready to move on from the subject. "It's probably nothing," she mused, fiddling with her purse strap. "My father says dreams don't mean anything. That it's just your brain filtering through random information in your head. And this one was especially vivid, so maybe it just stuck with me."

I pressed my lips together in a frown. I couldn't disagree more. Dreams were messages from the gods. And they were telling her something, I was sure of it.

"Thank you again for the book, Grudge. I'm excited to read it." Finished with our conversation, she headed for the door, and I dutifully followed after her.

"SO, WAIT." T-Bone rubbed his forehead with a sigh, swirling his whiskey with the other hand. "What exactly are you saying, Grudge?"

I growled in frustration and stabbed my finger at my notepad where I'd written, *She dreams of valkyries and ravens. A valkyrie was guarding her yesterday.*

"I understand, but what does it mean?"

My hands went up in the air in an *I don't know* gesture, then I turned to Dyno for help. He leaned against the side of the couch in our suite, solemn and thoughtful.

"It's something to do with us," he said finally. "The imagery is too specific *not* to."

Grateful for the support, I walked over and kissed him. Dyno smiled against my lips and ran his fingers through my beard, holding me close with his other arm.

"Mm, I dunno." T-Bone's voice grew low and husky at the sight of us.

"You don't know?" Dyno turned his head to face him, leaving his neck open for me to kiss and suck. "The only guy who can see through the eyes of a raven is skeptical of dreams being a message from the gods? Mm, fuck. Hold that thought, Grudge. You're distracting me." He placated me with a peck on the lips, and I eased away. I couldn't help myself, he was too fucking delicious.

"The gods have never spoken to me through dreams," T-Bone argued.

"Alright, well, newsflash, you're not the only one here," Dyno said. "Dreams are a huge part of indigenous cultures. I have absolutely received messages from dreams.

Who's to say Kyrie can't? And the fact that she sensed the valkyrie while awake? That's no dream. That's a spirit who's attached itself to her."

"But what does it mean?" T-Bone repeated tiredly. "A valkyrie and a raven. Okay, so what?"

I grabbed my pen and paper, then paused. Spinning the pen idly in my hand, I tried to think of the best way to articulate not just my thoughts, but how I felt. How to explain this sensation in my gut that had never left me since Kyrie and I last spoke?

Finally, I just thought, *fuck it*, and wrote out the biggest question gnawing at my mind. *What if she is meant to be ours?*

"Grudge, that's a little—" Dyno started.

"Are you out of your fucking mind?" T-Bone cut in angrily. I expected him to have the most explosive reaction. He was smitten with Kyrie and in complete denial about it.

I cut my hand aggressively through the air so they would let me finish. *Not just the dreams, but consider everything. How did we end up working for her now, after avoiding 4C for years? In a new territory outside of her father's watch, no less? This can't all be coincidences. All four of us have been steered toward each other by forces outside of our control.*

The guys went silent for a while, staring at my words on the notepad.

"I hear what you're saying," Dyno said softly. "And I'm not disagreeing, Grudge. Not entirely. It's just..." He trailed off, looking at T-Bone for support.

"She has everything to lose and nothing to gain by being with us, that's what," T-Bone spat. "It's what I tried to warn her and you dicks about the first night we got here. She gets involved with us, her life is ruined. All the good she's trying to do will be for nothing." He looked at me and gave a sad shake of his head. "We're no good for her, guys.

We can't...*pursue* anything with her. Not if we care about her, which I think goes without saying."

I brought my hands to my knees and closed them into fists. Logically, I knew what he was saying. But I still didn't understand it. If she wanted us like we wanted her, who cared what anyone else thought? Why did reputation and her father and all this other shit really matter?

My hands opened with a sigh. I was getting ahead of myself anyway. She probably didn't see us that way, especially not me. And yet...

She kept glancing at me during her meetings, and I saw her look at T-Bone and Dyno the same way. I made her laugh, and she always seemed to wander close to me when I wrote things down.

"So, we're actually admitting this to ourselves now?" Dyno's gaze slid between T-Bone and me.

"Admitting what?" T-Bone growled.

"Don't pretend you're a dumbass, T."

"You want me to just say it then?" T-Bone shot back. "That I fucking want her? That if only she wasn't a governor's daughter, and a rising political figure herself, she'd be perfect for us?" He poured another generous helping of whiskey and confessed under his breath, "I've thought of her while we're fucking."

Dyno smirked. "I have too. Haven't stopped, to be honest."

"Mm," I confirmed with a nod. I still wasn't convinced she'd want *me*, but I imagined watching her with them. Just the thought of her soft curves between all their hard edges was enough to make me swell in my jeans. No other woman we'd brought to bed held a candle to the effect she had on me.

"But T's right." Dyno looked at me with an almost

apologetic expression. "Even if she's interested, getting with us would only be a bad move for her. These crusty old politicians will drag her through the mud if she so much as hops on our bikes again."

"I told you fuckers." T-Bone pointed at us as he took another swallow of whiskey. "We shouldn't have taken the job. We should have stayed the fuck away from Kyrie Vance like we agreed to the first time we left."

"Maybe," Dyno admitted. "But if we're being honest, there was no way we could leave. Not while she's surrounded by a bunch of small-dicked egos in suits."

"Yeah," T-Bone sighed, rubbing his eyes. "So, what? We just keep doing nothing? Business as usual?"

Dyno lifted one shoulder in a shrug. "I think that's all we can do."

"This is going to be a *long* fucking month."

I sighed and lazily scrawled out the summation of our collective thoughts.

We are so fucked.

CHAPTER 9

KYRIE

"I'm sorry, Mr. Chairman, but I disagree with these points." I underlined several bullet points of the proposal laid out in front of me. "I think Sevier would benefit more by having a family planning clinic in the inner neighborhoods than a stronger military presence. The people in the poorer areas need access to those services more than those in wealthier areas. And a clinic would attract professionals like doctors and nurses to the territory, as long as the wages were competitive. In Four Corners, we——"

The Chairman of the Budget Committee took his glasses off and rubbed his eyes. "Miss Vance——"

"Ambassador Vance," I corrected.

"Miss Ambassador, the budget allocations have already been approved by the committee. You are welcome to submit your suggestions for next quarter's budget."

I blinked at him from across the table. "But Ambassador Heim was able to submit his proposal this morning. Is there a deadline that I wasn't aware of?"

"Well, not exactly. But we generally finalize the budget on the afternoon of the quarterly meeting. Everything runs smoother that way, and we can move on to other business."

"I understand but *running smoother* means a good chunk of your citizens are going without essential needs, like food and medical care." I tapped my finger on the bullet-pointed list in front of me. "I poured over this entire budget during my lunch hour, Mr. Chairman, and it's concerning to me how unbalanced it is."

"Unbalanced?" another committee member scoffed. "Young lady, how many budget proposals for an entire territory have you seen in your lifetime?"

"About a dozen, give or take a few," I answered. "I sat in on a few of my father's cabinet meetings. You're all aware, I'm sure, of Four Corners' military prowess. Defending a territory *is* important, I'm not denying that. But investing in your citizens is just as, if not more, impor-tant than a strong military."

"Something you don't understand, Miss," another man leaned forward, lip curling distastefully at me, "is that Four Corners has had time to establish itself. We *just* won this territory back last year after devastating losses. Other terri-tories still have eyes on us and may be planning to topple us as we speak. So I object to you, young lady, coming in here and trying to change everything when you don't know what you're talking about!"

The man grew louder, his gesticulations almost aggres-sive as he spoke, to the point that my bodyguards moved in closer to surround me. My cheeks flamed, the embarrass-ment flooding me at being chastised like a child. No one, not a single person, spoke up in my defense. Everyone was either staring down at their documents or openly watching me and the older gentleman who spoke. I didn't remember his name but knew he was a senior member of the governor's cabinet. Even so, was no one going to back me up?

"Sir." I swallowed down the lump in my throat and folded my hands on the table. "I was invited to this committee meeting based on my knowledge of Four Corners' government spending. I'm open to discourse, but I assure you I *do* know what I'm talking about. I only want to help—"

"Four Corners doesn't need to meddle in our affairs," the man hissed. "You don't see us interfering in your father's business, do you?"

"He's hosting three representatives from Sevier currently," I said. "I'm sure they're involved in many meetings and discussions. This is all I'm trying to do, sir. Open a dialogue and share with you what has worked in our territory."

"I'm sure you could share plenty of what goes on in Four Corners." It could have been my imagination, but I swore his gaze slid disapprovingly over my bodyguards. "But I believe the quarterly budget should be left up to the officials of Sevier only."

Again, no one spoke up in my defense. Not even Ambassador Heim, who was a new appointee himself and had invited me to this meeting. He was currently looking very busy shuffling papers around in front of him. The only sound was a soft murmuring of voices agreeing with the cranky old man who argued with me.

Don't cry. Don't look sad. Don't look defeated. Don't be weak. You'll just be proving them right.

I forced a smile past my erratic pulse and flustered nerves as I gathered up my documents. "Well then," I said with false cheer, head high. "If my presence isn't needed at this meeting, I'll take my leave. Good afternoon, gentlemen."

I left as quickly as I could, while trying to not look like I was. My mind was so frazzled, I barely took notice of Anita hurrying to stay next to me and the Sons falling in line behind me.

"You can go, Anita," I said, my voice tight. "I don't have anything else today, right?"

"Um, no, Ambassador. But are you sure?"

"Yes." I turned to her, forcing another smile. "Take the rest of the day off. We'll catch up tomorrow morning."

"Oh, okay! Don't hesitate to send for me if you need anything."

She finally hurried away, giving me just a fraction more breathing room. I still had my three hulking shadows to deal with.

I headed for the nearest exit, which led out to a beautiful courtyard with a fountain, walking paths, and lots of trees. Heavy footsteps followed me dutifully, but I needed a fucking moment and didn't want to break down in front of them.

"I'd like to be alone, please," I said without turning around.

"No can do, little lady." T-Bone's voice floated over me like a caress, the sound somehow both comforting and invasive.

"Then just…stand further away. I need a little bit of fucking privacy." My voice wobbled, and I clenched my fists.

"Kyrie." Dyno sounded closer, his footsteps crunching over the gravel path. "We have to stay near you to protect you."

"I just—fuck." A tear escaped my eye and I hurried to wipe it away, but then another one came. And when I inhaled, my nose sniffled. God fucking damn it. How was I supposed to be taken seriously when I ran out of a meeting and started crying like a baby? In front of my three hot bodyguards, no less.

"Hey." A gentle touch came to my shoulder, and I turned to find Dyno next to me, concern drawn deeply into his face. "It's okay, Kyrie. That crotchety old man was fucking out of line." Dyno wiped a tear from my cheekbone with his thumb, the touch trailing down my face a few inches before falling away.

"Fuck, I wanted to throw that wrinkly old ballsack out the window," T-Bone grumbled. He sat down on the edge of the water fountain a few feet away. "And every one of those dumb shits who were too cowardly to say anything. Politicians can choke on a dick." He winced, then looked up at me. "No offense."

I laughed, despite feeling shitty. "None taken." Sniffling carefully, I wiped the remaining tears from my eyes. "Thank you for saying that, actually. I felt…really alone in there."

T-Bone surprised me by taking one of my hands, his rough fingers massaging the inside of my palm. "I wish we could speak up for you. Fuck, I was so close to breaking protocol." He sighed and gave me a sympathetic look. "You're never alone, Kyrie. Not when you have us."

On his shoulder, Munin made a soft cawing sound like he was agreeing.

My fingers closed around T-Bone's hand like I never wanted to let go. His hand was so large I could barely get a grip, but he squeezed back.

"It means a lot to hear you say that, thank you. I

just…" A big sigh left my chest as Grudge came around to join the other two, his expression just as concerned. "I was so excited to come here and do something meaningful. Now I just feel…defeated. Like I'm roadblocked at every turn."

"Mm-mm." Grudge shook his head, his expression now determined. He pointed at me, then curled that hand into fist before hitting it with his opposite palm.

"He's right." Dyno sat next to T-Bone on edge of the fountain and leaned his head on the other man's shoulder. "You gotta keep going, Kyrie. Meaningful change never happens without a ton of resistance."

"You're right," I sighed. "You all are. It's an uphill battle, but I can't stop. Not when there's people in need."

"For what it's worth, we support you." T-Bone rested his temple on Dyno's head, the two of them looking relaxed and adorable. "We can't speak out on your behalf in meetings, but we'll do what we can."

"If it was my father in the room, or any male ambassador instead of me, no one would've talked to me like that." I crossed my arms, suddenly feeling homesick. Dad had a fair amount of crotchety old men working for him, but at least they were always respectful to me. Then again, I'd never spoken up against their ideas before. It was easy enough to be pleasant when no one challenged them. As soon as I stopped letting things slide, the claws came out.

"Oh, I have an idea!" T-Bone perked up.

"What?"

"Cut your hair really short, dye it gray, then shave the top so it looks like male pattern baldness—I'm serious, why are you laughing?" His smirk grew into a full-on grin as I fought to keep my giggling contained. "Get creative with some makeup or some shit, I dunno. Walk into that meeting all stooped over like this." He got up to demonstrate, and I almost started crying again, but from laughing this time.

"She should get a cane," Dyno added, chuckling.

"No, she needs one of those fucking walker things. With the little tennis balls on the bottom. She's gotta look *ancient.*"

Grudge patted Dyno's hip, then stuck a finger into the waistband of his jeans. Dyno leaned back, cackling so wildly he almost fell into the fountain. While he was incapacitated, T-Bone explained it for me. "Yes, excellent point, Grudge. She needs a whole pack of them adult diapers."

"Oh my God, stop!" I cried, holding my stomach because I was laughing so hard. These guys accomplished their mission, and I already felt lighter. Not *better* necessarily, but not so alone.

It wasn't until I recovered and composed myself that I saw Grudge holding a note out to me. *That's better. The world is much brighter when you laugh.*

"Oh, Grudge." My hand flew to my chest, speechless. He looked panicked for a moment, like he might have said the wrong thing. But there simply weren't any words for how touched I felt. "Can I hug you?"

He blinked and only dipped his head in a nod before I rushed toward him, wrapping my arms around his waist. Grudge was solidly built, but there was a softness about him too. His arms came around my back, pressing me gently into his barreled chest where I just wanted to nestle and hide forever. He was so warm, and I felt safe and supported to the point where a small sigh escaped me. His beard tickled the top of my head and he smelled like fresh, clean sheets.

I was right. He gave great hugs.

"Let her go, man. You're making us jealous," T-Bone cracked.

Grudge responded by holding me tighter and turning us away. The ensuing laughter and jokes from the others were short-lived as I saw a very determined Nathan storming toward us over Grudge's shoulder.

Oh please, no. He's not going to try some knight-rescuing-a-damsel bullshit, is he?

I pulled out of Grudge's embrace, but the damage was already done.

"Miss Vance, are you alright?" Nathan stopped short a few feet away, nostrils flaring as he looked over at Grudge distastefully. "Is there a reason why this man was touching you?"

"Yes! Yes, everything's fine." I stepped between him and Grudge while T-Bone and Dyno stood from the fountain to flank me on either side. The intimidation tactic worked, and Nathan took a step back from my looming bodyguards. "Thank you for your concern, but all is well," I said, offering him a smile.

"You're sure?" Nathan stared at the two men sandwiching me. "I heard you were…distressed enough to leave a meeting early. So I wanted to check on you."

I barely suppressed the urge to roll my eyes. "I'm fine, as I said. But thank you for being thoughtful."

He didn't seem satisfied with that and continued to size up my bodyguards. All three of them stared back, stone-faced and unflinching.

"Miss Vance," he tried again. "Might I have a word with you in private?"

"No."

The single word came from T-Bone, making Nathan startle while sending a delighted thrill up my spine.

"I wasn't asking *you*," Nathan scoffed.

"Our orders are to stay with Ambassador Vance at all times," Dyno said, his tone oozing politeness in a way that was clearly mocking. "Unless she dismisses us."

Nathan returned his gaze to me, eyebrows lifting with a clear expectation. I'd already had enough with men pushing me around for the day, and that one facial expression was the straw that broke the camel's back.

Fuck. You.

"I'm sorry, Mr. Treasury Secretary, but my guards will stay beside me. If there's something you'd like to discuss with me, you're welcome to leave a message with my assistant and we can set up a meeting."

Behind me, Grudge laughed softly at the shock on Nathan's face. I struggled to keep my own expression blankly pleasant.

"Furthermore," I went on. "I'd appreciate it if you'd address my guards with respect. They're performing an important duty and are risking their own lives to protect me. Please don't speak down to them or insinuate that they're behaving inappropriately."

Nathan's mouth flopped open, eyes blinking in disbelief. "I…what…"

"I think the words you're looking for are *'I'm sorry'*." Dyno smirked.

Nathan's gaze snapped to him, lips curling before thinking better of it, then pressed his mouth tightly closed.

"I apologize if I caused any offense," he said stiffly, inclining his head toward me. "It wasn't my intention."

"Here's a tip for future reference." T-Bone leaned

forward, towering over the younger man, and I held my breath. "The ambassador isn't a helpless damsel who needs a hero to save her. We'll do our job. Her safety is not your concern. Give her, and us, the same respect you would give anyone else in your workplace, and we'll get along just fine."

Nathan's Adam's apple bobbed as he swallowed, head craning back to meet T-Bone's eyes. "Understood. Sir." He looked at me once more and jerked his chin down in a nod. "Have a nice day, Miss Vance."

With that, he turned and hurried in the opposite direction. His gait was just short of running, and it was almost comical. At least the Sons waited until he was out of earshot before they burst out laughing.

"Always scaring off the poor little bitch boys, T." Dyno sighed as he leaned into his partner affectionately.

"Good." T-Bone draped an arm around Dyno's shoulders. "We don't need any of them around us, or the little lady. Although…" Grinning, he stroked his short beard, and I wondered what it would feel like if I did the same thing. "No one's called me *sir* in a long time. I might be into that."

Grudge huffed and poked his side in a playful, chiding gesture.

"What? I won't go into pornographic detail in front of the lady, I'm just saying."

"Well, thank you, *sir.*" I laughed, enjoying the sight of their eyes widening. "For coming to my defense anyway. That was brilliant."

T-Bone sucked on his teeth. "Not exactly the context I was referring to, but you're welcome. And Kyrie, listen."

"Yes?" I realized he used my given name instead of

calling me *Miss Vance*, and I breathed the word out like a sigh.

T-Bone's face darkened. "If *anyone* bothers you, tell us. Suit or servant, it doesn't matter. I don't care if it's the fucking governor himself. We'll do the best we can to be vigilant, but it's possible your instincts will pick up something we miss."

I nodded and took a deep breath, glancing around before I spoke again. "This territory is fucking weird, isn't it?"

"Mm-hm." Grudge nodded while the other two looked seconds away from laughing again.

"What?"

"Nothing." T-Bone suddenly looked very interested in the water pouring from the fountain. "You're right, though. This territory is bonkers."

I frowned, confused, until Dyno said, "The way you say *fuck* is adorable, that's all."

T-Bone made a disapproving sound, while Grudge only nodded in agreement.

"It is not." I bit the inside of my cheek as I crossed my arms. "I say the word *fuck* with serious *fucking* authority, okay?"

All three of them laughed, and Grudge motioned for me to do it again.

"Don't encourage her to start talking with a foul mouth." T-Bone smacked his arm.

"Aw, why not?" Dyno asked. He and T-Bone stared at each other with serious expressions, like something unspoken had passed between them.

"Yeah, why the fuck not?" I piped up.

T-Bone finally smiled and chuckled again, his gaze dipping away from me like the first day here.

But unlike that day, when I was filled with shock and uncertainty, my chest was now alight with a blaze that could no longer be extinguished.

CHAPTER 10

KYRIE

"Anita, can you find me the minutes from the housing committee meeting yesterday morning?"

"Oh, of course! I put them in the filing cabinet, let me grab them." My assistant put down her armful of paperwork on a corner of my desk, then produced an envelope from her cardigan pocket. "The Treasury Secretary's assistant handed me this to give to you."

I stared at the envelope like it would bite me before reluctantly taking it from her. *Well, I did tell him this was how he should reach me.* I had just assumed Nathan wouldn't put forth the effort.

My office was quiet this afternoon, with only me, Anita, and two of my bodyguards in the room. Dyno was posted at the door, leaning casually where he stood with his booted feet crossed at the ankles. Today, his hair was pulled back in a half ponytail with several braids running through it. Across the room was T-Bone, lounging on a chaise under a window as he petted his raven. The bird's eyes would close and it would make soft chirps whenever T-Bone scratched a certain spot on his head.

The guys were relaxed today, as I had cleared my schedule of meetings to work in my office. Grudge was just outside my office door and would come in when they rotated posts every hour.

At first, I was grateful for a quiet, easygoing workday, but now the silence made the envelope in my hands feel heavy. I wanted to throw it into the trash bin without opening it, but Nathan was nothing if not persistent. He would make sure I got it and expect a response.

Anita's stare only added to heaviness as she thumbed through documents in the filing cabinet. "What do you think it says? Are you going to open it?" She smiled excitedly as she returned with the documents I asked for.

Of course. Most people would be excited by the prospect of a young, handsome man showing interest in them. Especially one who was wealthy, powerful, and set to rise in the political ranks. But only a sinking sense of dread filled me as I stared at the envelope. Nathan might not have been as predatory as Malcolm Blake. He might even be angelic in comparison, but they shared enough characteristics to make me deeply uncomfortable.

The persistence, the charm, the sense of entitlement. I never wanted to be with a man who felt like I owed him anything.

"Well?" Anita pressed, oblivious to my discomfort.

She wasn't going to leave it alone, so I gave her a tight smile and grabbed my letter opener. I might as well get it over with. Dyno and T-Bone didn't comment or look my way, their faces carefully neutral as I opened the envelope.

"Ooh!" Anita cooed as I pulled out an embossed invitation made of thick cardstock. "He wants you to go to the Sevier Day Ball with him!"

"Sevier Day Ball?" I repeated, scanning the information on the card. It appeared to be a high-end, black tie affair, with an elaborate ten-course meal and dancing in one of the banquet rooms here in the capitol.

"Yes, it's on Sevier Independence Day, the most important holiday in the territory," Anita said excitedly. "Everyone has the day off to celebrate, and officials have an exclusive dinner party."

Well, obviously cooks and wait staff won't have the day off, I thought. "Everyone working in the capitol goes to this?"

"Yes! I mean, last year was the first one, but it was a huge hit. We, support staff, threw our own party in the kitchen with all the leftover food and wine."

"So," I set the card down on my desk. "I don't *have* to go as Nathan's plus-one? I can just show up?"

Anita blinked, her smile faltering. "Well, yes, you can go alone, but why would you want to? Anyone would love to be his date for a night like this!"

I'd rather go with anyone but *him.*

A thought crossed my mind of being escorted into a grand ballroom by my handsome bodyguards. One man on each arm, the third behind me, or even arms linked with one of the other two. They wouldn't wear tuxes or suits, no, not these bikers. But I'd be in my floor-length gown, and they'd be in crisp shirts that would cling to every broad muscle. I would be the envy of every woman and the ego-killer of every man.

I wondered if any of them could dance. Dyno seemed graceful and coordinated enough.

"I'll think about it," I said to Anita's waiting stare. "Either way, I'll need to order a dress, won't I?"

"Yes, Ambassador." Anita flipped open her agenda. "Should I schedule an appointment at a dress shop?"

"Yes, please." The event was in three weeks. Hopefully, Nathan wouldn't be too pressed for an answer right away.

The hours crawled by after that. I wished Anita hadn't given me that invitation until the end of the day. Now my mind was occupied with rejecting Nathan as delicately as possible, and nothing seemed good enough.

You don't have to let him down gently. Your bodyguards will keep him in line, one part of my brain whispered.

Yes, but you are a public figure and have an image to maintain, said another part. *Grace and poise at all times, just like your father said.*

I sighed in annoyance, leaning back in my seat. My father would think I was crazy to turn Nathan down, even after everything that happened with Malcolm. He thought Malcolm was a one-off and would never understand it from my view. If a man wasn't abusive or adulterous to his wife, it was enough, in his eyes.

I don't want that. I don't want to just tolerate a man who isn't awful.

My gaze drifted up Dyno's long legs, taking in his casual slouch by the door. He was looking across the room at T-Bone, who caught his eye and made a lewd gesture with his fist and tongue. Dyno laughed softly, flipped him the middle finger, and then slowly stuck that finger in his mouth and closed his lips around it.

I jerked my eyes to my desk again before they caught me staring.

I want that, I realized. Playfulness and passion. A sense of ease and trust. The ability to turn the public persona off and just be myself around my partner. Or *partners.*

Because I didn't just want what the Sons had. I wanted *them.*

I have wanted them since the moment they freed me from Blakeworth. That was *real* freedom, and I couldn't ignore the persistent ache that told me only *they* could make me feel this way.

It hurt so badly when they had left. Since being near them again, I felt glimpses of that beautiful sense of freedom again. It felt like I could jump out of a window, and I knew they'd be there to catch me. I could walk into battle like the valkyrie in my dream, and they would be my sword, shield, and wings.

Speaking of the valkyrie, I kept seeing her at the edges of my vision while awake and vividly when I slept. She stood in the corner of my office then, always disappearing when I tried to look at her straight on. But I felt her constantly, a calming source of strength. When she moved slightly, I saw sunlight reflecting off her armor. The guys never noticed her, but I swore Munin looked in her direction and cawed softly once in a while, as if speaking to her.

Grudge never brought it up again after I told him about her the first time, so I figured he had written it off as nothing. Personally, I still didn't know what to think. The valkyrie only started coming to me after taking this job and seeing the Sons again. Their connection to Norse myths was undeniable, so what did this valkyrie want with me? Was she even anything besides my own brain responding to a new environment? Or my territory-sized crush on the Sons?

Did I need to see a doctor? Ugh, the Sevier officials would have a field day with that. *The poor little female ambassador was so overwhelmed, she started hallucinating and needed her head checked.*

I felt fine in every other way, though. The valkyrie's presence was honestly just as comforting as it was mysterious. And I couldn't shake the feeling that she was some kind of tether from me to the Sons, which brought me back to my original train of thought.

If I had been born into an average, everyday girl's life, maybe the Sons and I could have had a chance. But our circumstances made it so that we could never happen.

Those three men were always nearby to listen, cheer me up, and, of course, physically protect me, but that was as far as it could go. Grudge was lucky that Nathan only saw him hug me. If he'd done anything else, even a kiss on the cheek, I just knew Sevier officials would throw them in jail at the first chance. Even just a hug was skirting a dangerous line.

In Four Corners, it would be frowned upon too. Maybe my father wouldn't treat them like criminals, but anything closer than a platonic friendship would be highly frowned upon. I didn't want to test how overprotective Dad would be if three bikers showed any sign of interest in me. All because we were born into completely different lives.

"I need a drink," I groaned, slouching further in my chair.

"Miss Ambassador!" Anita squeaked. "That's illegal."

"I know, I haven't forgotten." I really missed winding down with a glass of champagne in the evenings. Even the smell of a cigar would do right about now. I always found a reason to hang around when Dad had cigar nights on the back patio.

But I couldn't have that either. The best I could get was a walk down the street, and this office felt far too cramped now.

"Go ahead and take the rest of the day off, 'Nita." I

stood from my chair and stretched, then reached for my coat on a nearby hook.

"…Off? Again?" Okay, the incident by the fountain was three days ago, but she didn't have to put it like *that*. "Miss Vance, is everything alright?"

"Yes, perfectly." I smiled at her. "I just need to stretch my legs. If I come back today, I'll take care of everything."

"*If* you come back?"

"I'm going down the street, I'll probably check out some shops and see what's going on. Would you like to come? Just as a companion, not my assistant."

"You mean *leave* the capitol?! Alone?"

"Not alone, the Sons will be with us." I angled my head toward Dyno, who was no longer leaning against the door but standing upright and alert.

Anita looked out the window nervously before shaking her head. "It's getting dark, and it's dangerous to leave the capitol at night, Ambassador. I think you should reconsider."

"The ambassador will be perfectly safe." T-Bone swung his legs down from the chaise and jumped to his feet. "I think a night out on the town sounds fucking great."

"I have been wanting to explore the territory," I mused. "And I mean the *actual* territory, where the people are and not all the construction sites they showed me."

"Well, if you insist." Anita wrung her hands. "But please don't stay out too late, Ambassador."

"Yes, *Mom.*" I grinned at her but a pang clutched my chest. My mother died when I was an infant. The only mothering I ever got was from nannies and tutors.

Dad hardly ever talked about her, and it was clearly a painful subject whenever he did. I refused to believe she was *just* a wife to him. He wouldn't be so choked up all these years later, never remarrying, if their marriage had only been a political move. So I couldn't understand why he would want me to settle for that, instead of holding out for someone I was deeply in love with.

"I'll let Grudge know what we're doing." Dyno stepped outside the office while Anita finished gathering her things.

"Anywhere in particular you'd like to go?" T-Bone asked me, idly petting Munin who was now cradled against his chest.

"Not really. I'd just like to see what the locals are up to." Excitement ran through me. It felt like I was doing something bad, like when I used to sneak out my window back home, but I couldn't figure out why.

"It'll be dinnertime soon. Have you ever had dive-y restaurant food?" T-Bone grinned like he was divulging a secret.

"No!" I gasped. My food had always been prepared for me by chefs. While convenient, it was predictable and boring. "Do you think I could get a burger somewhere? With fries?"

"Sure. Or fish and chips if you want. Maybe even chicken and waffles."

"Chicken and…excuse me? That's a thing?"

T-Bone laughed, a low rough sound that was pleasing to my ears. I wanted to listen to it again with my ear against his chest. "Get ready for a bit of culture shock, little lady."

"THESE ARE BEAUTIFUL!" I said to the shop owner who

kept staring at me, wide-eyed. "Can I buy two pairs? Oh, no, wait, I love this design too…"

I was in a jewelry shop no bigger than my closet, but the earrings on display drew me in like a magnet. At first, it was the delicate hoops made of silver, but then I saw another pair with textured, hammered details in bronze. There were no precious stones here, but the jewelry was beautifully crafted metal, and I had to stop myself from touching everything.

"These three, please," I said, laying my selections down on the counter. "And then I'll be out of your hair for the night."

"You honor me, Ambassador," said the flustered shop owner as he wrapped up my order. "No one from the capitol comes here."

"That's a shame." My fingers drummed on my elbow while the gears turned in my head. "I wonder if we could set up a fair at the capitol so everyone can browse and see what talented artisans we have right in our backyard."

"You would do that?" The shop owner carefully placed my items in small jewelry boxes before tying them together with a ribbon.

"I can certainly try. The tricky part is getting other people on board." I accepted the bundle from him with a smile. "But I'll wear these every day and tell everyone where I got them."

"Thank you. Thank you, Miss. Please come back anytime. Oh, and if you need something custom-made, please let me know! I can create something to your exact specifications."

"Thank you so much." I gave a small wave as I turned to leave, Grudge following after me. "Have a good evening."

We met up with T-Bone and Dyno who were waiting on the sidewalk, the two of them sharing a slim cigar.

"Did you buy up the whole place?" T-Bone teased with an exhale of smoke before handing the cigar back to Dyno.

"Not today," I said. "Where did you get that?"

"Bought it up the street." The cherried end lit up Dyno's face as he puffed.

"How? I thought they were illegal here?"

"They are. You just have to ask the right people." Smoke curled around Dyno's grin. "And the right questions."

He passed it to Grudge, who shook his head at me with an, "Mm-mm," before taking a drag.

"Aww, why not?"

"Just doin' our job." T-Bone started down the street first, and the rest of us followed.

"Keeping my precious reputation safe from doing illegal drugs?" I asked with an eye roll.

"The smell will cling to you," Dyno said. "And people will notice, so yes." He playfully bumped into my side. "We also don't need questions about why the ambassador is hacking up a lung."

"I know how to smoke a cigar," I huffed.

"Your father let you?" T-Bone asked in surprise.

"Well, no," I said. "But he doesn't know I know how."

"Naughty," he teased, and the word seemed to stroke right between my legs. "Who taught you?"

"Reaper," I admitted. "He broke out some special ones at a party when Mari announced her pregnancy. My dad couldn't make it, but they invited me."

"Mari's pregnant?" Dyno gasped.

"She already had the babies. Twins," I said. "A boy and

a girl, born about six months ago." Along with the Sons, Mari and one of her now-husbands had helped to get me out of Blakeworth. She had been the woman in the gazebo with me. Now, she was settled in Four Corners with her four biker men and their children.

She has exactly what I want, I realized.

"Aww, mah." Grudge cooed, placing a hand over his chest. The thought of that big, burly man holding an infant in his arms kicked my heart into high speed.

"Guess we've missed out on some things while we've been away," T-Bone said softly.

I caught up to him and poked him in the side. "You'll have to tell me what you've been up to over the last four years. Over dinner."

"Dinner?" Dyno repeated. "Are you taking us out on a date, Ambassador?"

"Sure, why not?" I waved a hand in the air. "But I want real food, dripping in grease and calories."

Grudge made a hum of approval while Dyno clicked his tongue. "We can arrange that, but it's *our* treat. Not yours."

"I thought you guys were working." I grinned. "Can you take a girl out to eat and perform your guard duties at the same time?"

Dyno had the cigar again, smoke blowing from his nostrils and curling around his lips as he smiled. "I can assure you we're very good at multitasking."

His tone and that sentence dripped with innuendo. If he kept talking like that, it wouldn't be the only thing dripping.

T-Bone had turned around, glancing back at us from the head of the pack. "You know, if you still want that drink, Miss Vance," he said carefully. "We can arrange for that too."

"Really?" I grabbed his forearm before I could think better of it. "And it'll be like a normal-person drink, not champagne?"

"Probably," he chuckled. "It'll be a flat cask ale or liquor, most likely."

I hesitated. "And no one will get in trouble?"

"It's a risk." He shrugged. "But all good things are worth the risk."

Those words seemed to have a double-meaning too, but that might have been my wishful thinking.

"Okay," I said with a nod. "So how do we get some?"

All three of them chuckled.

"Just like with this," T-Bone took the nearly-finished cigar from Dyno, "you've got to go to the right places and say the right things. Talk to the right people." He took a heavy drag then tossed it, eyes locked on me as smoke blew past his parted lips.

My heart drummed with anticipation, my stomach fluttering with nerves that were more excited than anything else. I loved this feeling, even lived for it. Any other time, there would have been a healthy dose of fear riding behind my excitement. Fear of getting caught, of the melodramatic lecture from my father that would surely follow. But I had no fear with these men. None at all.

"Lead the way," I told T-Bone.

CHAPTER 11

DYNO

We all followed T-Bone's lead to a building situated on a hill two blocks away. Darkness had fallen now, a persistent chill in the air that reddened the tip of Kyrie's nose. I pushed away the thought of kissing her there until the redness went away.

I thought we weren't going to do this, was what I chose to focus on instead. We weren't supposed to be anything but bodyguards to her, no matter the dreams or feelings that cropped up.

Technically, we weren't crossing any lines, but ambassadors didn't typically go for evening strolls in run-down neighborhoods. And bodyguards definitely didn't take their VIP clients to dive-y establishments with secret booze lairs.

The four of us went up a flight of stairs to the building's front door, which indicated there was a basement or *something else* underneath the main floor.

T-Bone opened the door for Kyrie and stepped aside to

let her in first. I hovered next to him as Grudge went in after her.

"You sure about this?" I said low next to his ear.

He shook his head. "I'm not sure about anything."

"Well, as long as we're in agreement there," I muttered, sliding past him.

The floorboards creaked under my boots. The tables, chairs, and front counter all looked equally creaky, but the place was warm, clean, and well-maintained. T-Bone and I joined Kyrie and Grudge, who waited for us up front.

"Table for four?" asked the grizzled older man behind the counter, gathering paper menus in his hands.

"Yeah, actually." T-Bone leaned forward, placing his forearm on the counter. "We'd like to check out the antique collection."

A heavy pause hung in the air as the man narrowed his eyes. "Don't know what you're talking about."

T-Bone smiled good-naturedly, leaning closer to the man. "I think you do."

"Nah." The man shook his head. "You're at the wrong place."

I was just about to tug T-Bone's sleeve and head back out when he said, "We'll put a deposit down on a grandfather clock."

Now the man leaned his forearm on the counter and angled his head toward T-Bone. "All four of ya?"

T-Bone nodded. "All of us."

The man's gaze slid over each of us, as if he could tell by a look if we'd run our mouths or not. His eyes lingered on Kyrie. Not in a creepy way, but I could tell he questioned what a pretty, well-dressed girl in her twenties was doing with the likes of us.

"Let's see it," he said finally.

T-Bone reached into his cut pocket and pulled out a wad of Sevier currency. Kyrie started reaching for her coat pocket, and I grabbed her wrist to stop her.

The man counted out the bills, then jerked his head to the side as he shoved the money in his shirt pocket. "Side door, then follow me."

"The Sons of Odin are grateful," I said under my breath as we moved away from the counter.

The man startled at that, his eyes widening for a moment before letting out a dry chuckle. "You should have just said that."

We went through the side door, meeting him next to the kitchen in a dark corridor. "You run an honest business," T-Bone told him with a slap on the shoulder. "We're honest customers."

Kyrie followed him and the restaurant owner through the corridor and down a flight of stairs. I reached forward and placed a hand on her shoulder, leaning close to her ear. "You alright?" Her hair tickled my cheek, the sweet smell of it a reprieve from this musty stairwell.

She squeezed my hand on her shoulder in reply, so I kept it there until we reached the bottom of the stairs and entered a wide room.

The ceiling was low, nearly brushing my head as I stood to full height. Some vinyl jazz album spun on an ancient record player in the corner next to the bar, which had every seat filled and was backed by an impressive collection of liquor bottles.

Couches, armchairs, and low tables were spread out throughout the rest of the room, roughly half of them occupied. A few people glanced up at our arrival, but most kept their eyes away. It was an unspoken rule at establishments like this—if you saw anyone you recognized… no, you didn't.

The patrons were mostly men, rough-looking sorts like us, but a few had women sitting with them. Long legs in short dresses stretched over men's laps. Their partners'—or customers'—rough hands held possessively onto exposed knees and thighs. The women smoked thin cigarettes and peered through fake eyelashes to regard Kyrie with curiosity.

"Enjoy your stay." The restaurant owner held his arm out toward a few empty couches clustered around a low table, then immediately headed back upstairs.

Grudge and I guided Kyrie in that direction while T-Bone headed for the bar.

"Culture-shocked, yet?" I asked in a low whisper as we sat down. The loveseat cushions were soft and well-worn. Kyrie nearly tumbled into my chest as we sank into them, and I had half a mind to put an arm around her and keep her there.

"This is so much fun!" she whispered back excitedly, eying every light fixture and detail of the room. "How many places like this are out there?"

"No one knows for sure." I looked toward T-Bone, talking to the bartender in a low voice, before scanning the rest of the room. No one looked like trouble, and I didn't get a bad vibe. You could never be sure in places like this where the drinking and smoking had to be kept underground. But tonight, it seemed like everyone in attendance was only trying to wind down for the evening.

"Hm." Grudge tapped Kyrie's thigh to get her attention, then pointed at T-Bone. Our president was gathering up a set of glasses and a whiskey bottle, while the bartender pulled up and down on a lever mounted next to the bar.

"The bartender's pouring you a cask ale," I said to Kyrie. "Hope it's a good one."

"What's that?" She got up to watch him hand-pump the beer from the couch across from me.

Before answering, I toyed with the idea of pulling her back to me and never letting her go. "Beer at cellar-temperature, conditioned inside of a wooden barrel. It's how they drank it before refrigeration. Or if a place doesn't have reliable electricity since the Collapse."

"Well, the lights are staying on," she noted, glancing at the bare bulbs on the walls.

"They could be trying to conserve electricity too," I said. "Or cask ale might even be some people's preference."

T-Bone returned and set the pint glass in front of her. It didn't look bad for a cask. Natural carbonation had given the pale, golden beer a creamy head of foam on top.

"He told me what it was, but I'm gonna make you guess." T-Bone smirked as he set out the glasses and poured whiskey for us.

"Oh, that's not fair. I've never had beer before." Kyrie took the glass and smelled it before taking a careful sip.

T-Bone openly stared like he wished he was the beer she was drinking from, so I whacked him on the arm. "Did you order food?"

"Yeah," he muttered distractedly, returning to pouring. "It's gonna take a while though. They're short on meat, so he's gotta run to the butcher."

"Oh, wow!" Kyrie smacked her lips adorably and sniffed the beer again. "That's really good, but it's…a little spicy?"

All eyes went to T-Bone. "Wha?" Grudge demanded, spreading his hands wide.

"It's infused with habanero peppers." Our president grinned. "Brewer's special."

"Sneaky dog," Kyrie chided, but smiled as she took another sip. "I have to take this slowly, but it's really good! Just enough to warm me up."

"Can I try it?"

She passed me the pint, our fingers brushing as the glass transferred hands. I didn't normally care for cask ale, but she was right, it was good.

"I might have to get one with dinner," I said, handing it back to her.

"Can I try yours?"

All three of us chuckled, but it was Grudge who handed his whiskey tumbler to her. He pinched his thumb and forefinger close together, indicating she should take a small sip. Kyrie nodded and did so, but apparently it wasn't small enough.

She coughed and shuddered, her face reddening through the grimace she made.

"Aw, poor thing. Take it easy." T-Bone rubbed her arm for a moment before pulling his hand away quickly. "I'll get you some water." He stood and headed straight for the bar.

"How can you guys—ugh—drink that?" Kyrie handed the glass back to Grudge and went for her beer.

"It's an acquired taste," I said. "Are you okay?" T-Bone returned with a glass of water and she nodded while gulping it down gratefully.

"It's much more palatable with a cigar," T-Bone laughed sympathetically.

Kyrie's eyes brightened. "Do you have another one?"

"No! Down girl, that was my only one." He laughed,

claiming the spot next to her on the couch. "You've gotta ease into these illicit substances, little lady. Can't go diving in headfirst."

"Hm, if you insist." Kyrie kicked off her shoes, then curled her feet underneath her on the couch, sinking into the cushions. Her upper body leaned slightly toward T-Bone, but there was nothing subtle about how they eye-fucked each other.

"So, what has the Sons of Odin MC been up to these last few years?" She propped her elbow up on the back of the couch, leaning her cheek on her fist. "Spending much time in the politician's bodyguard field?"

"Huh, no," I scoffed, swirling my drink. "Protecting people is a new field for us."

"That's an interesting choice of words." She narrowed her eyes. "You've been protecting something else then?"

"Oh, she's good." T-Bone leaned back, bringing an arm behind his head. "You try to be sly, D, but she sees right through it."

"What, then?" Kyrie looked at Grudge, but he grinned and shrugged, playing coy. "Come on, you guys know I won't say anything."

"What we're imbibing right now." T-Bone gently clinked his glass against hers.

Kyrie looked at him. "Protecting alcohol?"

"Among other things. How do you think it gets here without being stolen?"

"I figured it was just made here, I guess."

"Some of it is, but that's more risky," I said. "It takes weeks, if not longer, for good alcohol to be made drinkable. It'll sell in a fraction of that time."

"And because it's illegal," Kyrie said carefully. "It's in high demand and goes for a high price."

"Mm-hm." Grudge nodded at her observation and reached over the arm of our couch to touch his glass to hers.

"So, we've made a decent living in the past couple of years escorting precious cargo, such as this, into backward-ass territories like these." T-Bone tilted his head to the side, looking at Kyrie with a familiar smile. He made that face when he wanted to cuddle and kiss. His fist clenched on his knee, the only sign of tension in his relaxed body language. It was like he had to physically restrain himself from drawing her into his lap so they could melt into each other.

If he had any sense, he'd get up from that couch and move away to the armchair next to her. But all three of us seemed to have lost our common sense with her, and fuck, I really didn't mind. Hanging out with her like this felt natural and good. It felt *right*.

"Isn't that dangerous?" Kyrie asked, looking at all three of us. "Is the Sons of Odin still just you three?"

"It is dangerous, but that's our life," T-Bone said. "That's just MC life."

"We've expanded a little," I said to answer her second question. "We have a married couple as our VP and trea-surer. But the core of the club is still us three. We almost never do anything separately."

Kyrie was now halfway done with her habanero beer, looking flushed, cozy, and too fucking adorable. Grudge had started to lean against me, his hand on my thigh, and I ran my fingers through his hair while we talked. The whiskey buzz was trying to convince me to bring her to our couch. She could curl up all cozy and warm between the two of us, instead of being hogged by T-Bone over there.

"You guys are so…" She curled up even smaller and sighed wistfully, a dreamy smile coming to her face.

"We're dickheads, you can just say it." T-Bone's grin never faded, his eyes relaxed but drinking in every detail of her face.

"No!" She whacked him on his chest, which made Grudge snort with laughter. "I was going to say you guys are like a fairytale."

Now I nearly choked on my drink. "What? Where did you get that notion?"

"It's just how the three of you are together." She wrapped her arms around her knees, making herself smaller, with a tinge of embarrassment on her face. "You're always together. You've been through so much. It's just admirable, that's all. Nothing has driven you apart, and you remain deeply in love. That seems so rare, like a fairytale kind of love."

Silence fell around our table, the ambiance of the bar filtering through our little bubble. T-Bone glanced at Grudge and I for the first time since we sat down. His expression was full of emotion, full of *want*, but he still looked conflicted.

"I'm sorry if I—"

"No, Kyrie." T-Bone stopped her gently. His hand wrapped around hers at some point, fingers rubbing her palm. "We're just speechless, because you're right. You get it. We're just…devoted to each other. And it just so happens that we're all men, and there's three of us. People see guys like us together and make all kinds of assumptions. But the way you summed it up just now, you get it better than anyone else does."

Their gazes locked together, and I felt Grudge's squeeze on my knee, his body stiffening. We stared at them and wondered the same thing—*are they about to kiss right now?* Throughout their whole time sitting there,

Kyrie and T-Bone had gradually moved closer together. Now they were inches away from touching, faces leaning in.

Some small alarm rang in my head, but it was far away. It warned me to say something, to stop T-Bone before he did something he couldn't undo. But a bigger part of me asked, *Why? Who the fuck cares?*

We were just four people having a good time. None of us were drunk, we were all in control of ourselves. So what if Kyrie and T-Bone wanted to kiss? They liked each other. We all did. Why did social status or anything else have to matter?

Ring ring ring ring!

"I got two bison burgers and two chicken and waffles here!" yelled the bartender after ringing an obnoxiously loud bell.

"Shit, that's us." T-Bone practically jumped away from Kyrie up to the bar. I slid out from under Grudge so I could follow him.

"What's happening?" I said in T-Bone's ear when we reached the bar.

"Nothin'."

"Nothin'? You're telling me what almost just happened was nothin'?"

"Nothing. Happened," he repeated staunchly.

"T." I grabbed his chin and made him look at me to show how serious I was. "We're getting in too deep, man."

"No, we're not. It's fine. Grab those." He took a plate of food in each hand, and I went for the other two. "I lost my head for a second," he admitted as we turned to head back to our seats. "But I got it under control. Nothing's gonna happen."

"Are you sure?" I pressed. "Because I'd bet that whole

whiskey bottle she wouldn't stop you. What if she makes a move and you're the one who has to slam on the brakes?"

"I said it's under fuckin' control," he barked under his breath before approaching Kyrie with a flirtatious grin. "Check this out, little lady."

"This is chicken and waffles?" She leaned curiously over the plate.

"Well, it's not shrimp and grits."

"I've never had that either."

T-Bone leaned into her with a laugh, and I held my breath for a second, thinking again that he might kiss her. But he just scooted the plate toward her. "Try it. If you like it, that's yours, and I'll have the burger."

She didn't just like it, she went nuts over it. "Oh my God, this is magical!" she moaned, carving into the fried chicken thigh and smothering her forkful in maple syrup. "Why didn't anyone tell me this combination of flavors was so good?"

"We can't let the rich folks have all the good food," T-Bone teased her while wiping a crumb from the corner of her mouth.

Of course that didn't stop her from sampling his bison burger and fries too. We all got another round of drinks, and I struggled to focus on my food instead of watching T-Bone and Kyrie's constant flirting. It felt like the more I drank, the more it got under my skin. But it wasn't just because T-Bone brushed me off with his 'I got it under control' bullshit. Grudge summed it up with a single word that he sneakily wrote on his notepad.

Jealous.

"Yeah," I sighed, leaning away from the table. The alcohol had warmed my blood, and my hunger was sated.

Well, one type of hunger was. The other kind gnawed and ached. It lit up the nerve endings under my skin and made me crave touch and heat. If I had to be honest with myself, this feeling never truly went away. Not even when the guys made me come so hard that stars dotted my vision. This ache was for something specific, a type of intimacy and connection that was different from the two men I'd made my life with. And I couldn't shake the feeling that it could only be soothed by the woman sitting on the couch across from me.

The woman we had to guard constantly but could never, *ever* touch. That was what I had to keep reminding myself of. It could never be as simple as just four people who wanted to spend time together. That wasn't the kind of world we lived in.

Kyrie got up to use the restroom at some point, and T-Bone patted the space where she'd been. Grudge slid into it a moment later, his mouth connecting hungrily with T-Bone's. Yeah, it seemed I wasn't the only one who was worked up.

"You just gonna watch?" T-Bone asked when his lips were free for a moment. "Get over here."

"And make her feel weird when she gets back?" I scoffed. "Nah, later."

"Just for a sec. You've been in a mood all night." T-Bone sighed, limbs tangling with Grudge's in a full-body embrace. "You've got that look on your face like you're gonna stew on something for hours."

"I won't. I'm just trying to be considerate of the company we have." He didn't look like the type, but T-Bone got insecure if one of us wasn't cuddled up to him after a certain amount of time. I'd want a few hours alone to ride or think, and he stuck to me like a barnacle when I got back. "I'll suck your dick 'til you fall asleep tonight, alright?"

Kyrie returned before he could reply. "Oh, no, don't move!" she said when he and Grudge started to separate. "You two look comfortable, stay there."

"Sit here, Ky." I scooted over and patted the seat next to me, realizing too late I'd shortened her name. Shit, what was it about just being near her that made me want to treat her like she was mine?

"Thanks, *Dy*." She smirked and plopped down next to me.

Again, she kicked off her shoes and curled her feet underneath her, leaning slightly toward me. And I couldn't bring myself to move away.

"Dyno's not your real name, is it?" she asked, reaching to cradle her third beer in her hands.

"No, it's a road name," I said. "All of us use road names."

She pursed her lips. "Are your real names top secret?"

"Not really. Sometimes we refer to each other by name in private. Every MC is different, but for us, it's just an intimacy thing. Like a pet name."

"Aw, that's sweet."

"Yo, I'm Travis." T-Bone saluted her from the couch. "But in public, I prefer T-Bone."

Kyrie smiled as she took a sip of beer, and I thought she might ask what my name was, but she pivoted instead. "Can you tell me how you got your road name?"

"It's short for dynamite. I just like to blow shit up sometimes." I downed the rest of my whiskey, smiling at her surprised expression behind my glass. "There's not much to it, really."

"I wasn't expecting *that*," she breathed. "You seem so

calm and collected. I'd expect someone who enjoys explosives to…have more of an explosive personality, I guess."

"What, like T-Bone?"

"The fuck you sayin' about me?" he drawled with a lazy smile. His eyes were hooded, his whole body relaxed and leaning back with Grudge reclined against his chest.

"Tell her how you got your road name," I told him.

"Oh, I T-boned a supposedly armored SUV with my bike back when I was just a prospect. It was some protest riot like twenty years go, I don't remember. But the dumbass inside kept yelling that it was armored and he'd turn me into roadkill." T-Bone shrugged, bringing his hands together on Grudge's chest. "I called him out. Turned out, he was bluffing. Long story short, I survived and he didn't."

"Oh my God, how did you know it wasn't armored?" Kyrie demanded.

"I didn't." T-Bone stroked over Grudge's chest and stomach, a motion that Kyrie followed with her eyes. "See, that's what happens when you have *no* supervision when you're young. You don't care if you die or not, and you do stupid shit." He rested his cheek on top of Grudge's head. "That is, until you find people that make you care about living."

"Aw," Grudge said, reaching up to scratch the back of T-Bone's head.

Kyrie smiled at the affection, then her head tilted with a puzzled expression. "How old were you twenty years ago?"

"Eighteen, I think." T-Bone smirked at her then pointed at his temple. "Things have gotten scrambled up in here over the years, so don't quote me."

Her eyes widened. "So you're…thirty-eight?"

"That's right, little lady."

"All of you?"

"Grudge *might* be forty," I said. "He doesn't know his exact birth date, and he's got more gray than any of us."

"Meh." Grudge rolled his eyes and raised his middle finger at me.

"The gray's sexy," T-Bone assured him, stroking a hand through the salt and pepper of his beard.

"And you?" Kyrie asked me.

"I'm thirty-nine," I told her, unable to resist adding a wink. "Had me for younger, didn't you?"

"Oh my God, I figured you for late twenties." She scrubbed her hands down her face, cheeks reddening.

"Most people do," T-Bone said. "It's his Indigenous side. He doesn't fuckin' age."

"Remember that time Chris thought I was your son?" I laughed.

T-Bone nodded, grinning. "And I told him, 'Well he *does* call me Daddy'."

"Except I don't," I snorted.

"Yes, you do. I just make you come so hard that you black out and don't remember."

Grudge slapped at T-Bone's arm then, giving him a disapproving look and gesturing to Kyrie, who was holding back adorable snorts of laughter.

"What? She thinks it's funny."

"Please." Kyrie held up a hand, swallowing another laugh. "I hate it when people act like I'm a delicate fucking flower." She lowered her hand to her lap, eyes taking in all three of us. "I like seeing you guys as yourselves. It's refreshing. Please don't feel like you have to watch what you say around me."

"Be careful what you wish for." I gave her a playful nudge. "Uncensored Sons of Odin tend to get in trouble."

Her smile went a little wobbly. "Does it bother you guys that I'm only twenty-three?"

"Why would it bother us?" T-Bone demanded, his tone bordering on aggressive.

I wanted to smack him for that response. It sounded reactionary, defensive. A foolish denial of the *something* that existed here between the three of us and this woman nearly twenty years younger. Perhaps it was good to remind everyone that we could never indulge in that something, but not at the cost of her crestfallen face.

"What T-Bone means is," I said carefully. "You're very driven and accomplished for someone your age. None of us did a fraction of what you've done by twenty-three. You're a remarkable person, regardless of how old you are."

"Aww. Thanks, Dyno." She leaned closer toward me, and damn if I didn't stop myself from going for a kiss. Thankfully, T was there to ruin the moment.

"Hey, I resent that! I T-boned a whole truck when I was younger than her."

"Yeah, and look where it got you," I scoffed, straightening.

Kyrie smiled into her drink. "I don't think T-boning a truck will be going on my bucket list."

"What is on that list?" I wanted to know everything. Her hopes, dreams, fears, and all that she wanted to accomplish in her lifetime. "What's the number one thing you want to do before you leave this earth?"

Kyrie stared intently at her beer. "You don't want to know. It's silly."

"Have you met our stupid asses?" T-Bone spread his arms wide. "We are nothing if not silly."

Grudge made a face, crossing his eyes and screwing up his features until Kyrie snorted with laughter.

"Tell us," I urged when she composed herself. "I promise you, it's nothing worse than anything we've done or said."

She took a deep drink of her beer and set it down before speaking. "I want to make decisions. Important ones, whether they're for me or other people. And I want that feeling of *knowing* it was the right thing to do. That *I* decided this and not someone whispering in my ear, trying to influence me for their own gain." Her expression wobbled, embarrassment creeping into her features. "Does that make any sense? It's hard to put into words."

"We get it, little lady," T-Bone told her gently. "It's a beautiful thing, being able to throw yourself completely behind what you stand for. It's scary as fuck too. Takes a whole lot of gonads sometimes."

She wants the freedom to be her own person, I realized but couldn't bring myself to say. Because I knew the next words out of my mouth would be, *Stay with us. Don't go back to the capitol, it's a viper's den. They want to use you, but we would only free you.*

Of course, the rational part of me remembered that she would have to make that choice on her own too. And choosing us was definitely the wrong one.

CHAPTER 12

KYRIE

"The governor would like to see you in his office first thing this morning."

Anita wore a tight-lipped frown and seemed even more uptight than usual. The Sons and I were enjoying our breakfast spread in our loft the next morning, after getting home from the bar much later than I had anticipated.

"Thank you, Anita." I suppressed a yawn and swallowed another gulp of tea.

"Someone's been a bad girl." T-Bone smirked at me from where he was casually draped in an armchair, finishing off another cinnamon roll.

He started acting like his old self last night, and it thankfully continued this morning. Flirtatious and crass, but in a harmless, endearing way.

"What else is new?" I said with a melodramatic sigh.

He chuckled but didn't comment further. I had a feeling he was still holding back, but at least he wasn't completely icing me out like before.

Something between the four of us had definitely shifted last night. We talked in the underground bar for hours, but it felt like no time passed at all. I wasn't an ambassador while out with them, and they weren't my bodyguards. We were just spending time together, like friends.

Or lovers.

T-Bone had fed me French fries and wiped crumbs from my mouth. Dyno talked to me like no one else existed. And it could have been the beer I drank but I swore both of them almost kissed me.

Their attention seemed split equally between me and Grudge, who I wished I could have gotten to know better last night. I never did find out how he got his road name, or why he didn't know his exact date of birth.

No amount of time with these men ever seemed to be enough. And I couldn't ignore the feeling that some people didn't seem too happy about that. I'd bet my big toe that was exactly what this "urgent meeting" with the governor was about.

"Shall we get this over with?" I finished my tea and stood, with T-Bone right behind me.

"After you, little lady."

The soft words were like a caress in my ear, making me stop in my tracks just so I could absorb them. *Tell me more. Touch me for real,* I thought.

He did touch me, but barely. A light brush of his hand against the back of my arm. All of them had touched me in some small manner like this, and it was the worst kind of foreplay. It wasn't enough. I ached for a kiss, the press of a body, or even a possessive hold that said, *you're ours.*

"You alright, Kyrie?" T-Bone hovered behind me, his voice near my ear but nowhere close enough.

"Yes." I walked forward, putting distance between us instead of leaning back into his chest like I wanted to.

GOVERNOR PERRY HAD his nephew Nathan in his office with him, unsurprisingly, along with two other higher-ranking officials.

"Miss Vance, please." Perry gestured to the armchair in front of his desk. "Take a seat."

He still wasn't addressing me by my title, Ambassador, but now didn't seem like the best time to correct him.

"What can I do for you, Governor?" I eased into the chair, taking note of the leering gazes of the other men in the room.

The governor's gaze hovered above my head on the bodyguards who stood dutifully around me. "Might I have some privacy to speak with the ambassador, gentlemen?"

"You may not, Governor," T-Bone said with a surprising amount of calm.

Perry huffed, his bushy eyebrows drawing together. "We will be discussing matters concerning the territory. Matters of security—"

"The ambassador's security is our concern," Dyno broke in. "We're not interested in matters of the territory. We're just doing our job."

"Oh, for fuck's sake," Nathan blurted out. "Nothing's going to happen while we speak to her for ten goddamn minutes. You act like someone's going to snatch her away if you're not hovering every waking second."

"We don't know if that'll happen or not." Dyno shrugged. "We're here to mitigate that risk."

One of the governor's cabinet members spoke up. "Are you insinuating that the ambassador would be less safe in a room with us than with the likes of *you*?" The insult was clear, and it was one that my bodyguards would not take lying down.

"Are you insinuating that we harm women, *sir?*" T-Bone fired back.

"Please!" I shot to my feet, desperate to get this under control before it got uglier. "Stop." The room went ominously silent as I turned to face my bodyguards. "Wait for me outside," I said in a low whisper. "I'll be there soon."

"Mm-mm," Grudge said with an emphatic shake of his head.

"No," T-Bone echoed, eyes blazing.

"I don't like this, Kyrie." Dyno's scrutinizing gaze flicked to the faces behind me.

"I don't either," I admitted. "But I need to keep the peace in my work place. If I'm not out in ten minutes, feel free to barge back in."

Seconds ticked by and the guys didn't budge.

"Please," I said again. "I know you guys don't care about appeasing them, but do this because I'm asking you to."

I was almost going to plead a third time when T-Bone jerked his head toward the door. "Go."

Dyno and Grudge looked at him for only a moment before following the order, leaving the office.

"You're absolutely sure?" T-Bone's gaze bore into me, heating my blood. His lips remained parted after speaking, and I couldn't stop staring at them.

Getting turned on by my bodyguard in front of

onlooking politicians was probably not the right reaction, but I found myself caring less with each passing second.

"Yes," I whispered.

If only I could be answering a completely different question, such as, *Can I kiss you, Kyrie?*

But T-Bone was already leaning away, heading for the door. "Ten minutes," he said before joining the other two outside.

I turned back around, dreading the disappointment and disapproval I would see on the faces of the governor and his cohorts. Their expressions were just as I expected, frowning and tight-lipped.

But in the corner of the room, I caught a familiar silhouette holding an axe and a circular shield.

I returned my focus to the panel of men, drawing on the unwavering strength of my valkyrie watching over me. "I apologize, gentlemen. My guards can be…zealous when it comes to my personal protection."

"Thank you, Miss Vance. Have a seat," Governor Perry told me tersely. "Do you know why I asked to meet with you this morning?"

"No, sir. My assistant didn't receive any information regarding that." I kept my tone neutral, my demeanor calm. But inside, I felt as quiet as a wasp's nest. The valkyrie stood silent, weapon and shield poised in front of her body.

"That," he pointed at the door the Sons had just gone through, "is quite a large part of it, I'm afraid."

I blinked but otherwise kept my face carefully blank. "You requested a meeting about my bodyguards, and then asked them to leave?"

"It's not about your bodyguards themselves, Miss

Vance. But we've had some concerns about how you...conduct yourself with them."

"I'm afraid I don't follow," I said innocently.

"Those three men in particular have been rumored to have, well, participated in lewd acts with each other. Sometimes with other men and women."

I already knew the Sons were in a relationship with each other. But it was the implication that they also slept with women that made me burn with jealousy.

"It's none of my business what my bodyguards do in their personal lives," I said stiffly. "Assuming everyone involved is a consenting adult."

"Unfortunately, their chosen lifestyle does reflect on you, Miss Vance," Nathan chimed in. "Especially if they insist on being around you at all times. And in turn, you seem, well...overly familiar."

I stared at him. What a little shit. Did *he* arrange this meeting because he was sour about what happened in the courtyard? I had figured he would complain, but I didn't expect him to take it *this* far.

"Is it true that you went to an establishment in the Porter neighborhood with them last night?" asked the governor.

My gaze snapped to him, my pulse thundering. "Governor, if I may ask, why is that even a question? Their job is to guard me, and what I do in my free time is my own business."

"Because a young woman spending her time in the company of three..." He trailed off, gesticulating with his hands while I narrowed my eyes, waiting for him go on. Fuck maintaining appearances if he was going to insult those men, *my* men. I didn't care if they sent me packing back to Four Corners. The Sons did nothing wrong, and I wouldn't let them be insulted.

"...Three men of their ilk," he decided on, "is not appropriate for a woman in leadership, especially in such a seedy area of the city."

I didn't know which to address first, the fact I hardly felt like I was leadership because he and his cabinet steamrolled me at every turn, or the sheer hypocrisy that he had someone, probably another capitol employee, go to this exact same neighborhood to keep fucking tabs on me. If I were a man, no one would bat an eye. Hell, these same cabinet members probably spent most of their free time in hidden dive bars as well.

Pulling in a deep breath, I straightened my spine and ignored it all. I couldn't let all the petty insults sidetrack me, and I went for the heart of the matter instead.

"I won't deny that my bodyguards and I are close." Four sets of eyebrows shot up at that. "We're friendly," I amended. "There is familiarity between us because I trust them. My father trusts them and has known them for years." I sat up straighter. "It's frankly rather insulting to hear you question another governor's judgment, as well as my own."

"Miss Vance," said a cabinet member. "We understand that Four Corners is...tolerant of different lifestyles, but that isn't how we do things here."

I released a tense breath while looking at him. "Then why did you request an ambassador from Four Corners, if not to learn how we do things?"

"Please." The governor raised a palm. "There's no need to be combative. Our peaceful, prosperous relationship with your territory is paramount to our success. We *want* to continue working with you, Miss Vance. But you must understand, our territory is in its infancy. Our reputation, our public image, is everything. To rise up as united and strong, we can't have rumors of deviancy running through our leadership."

I wanted to roll my eyes so many times while they talked, but I forced my expression into one of agreeableness. It was clear they'd never be willing to hear me out anyway. Arguing would only take us around in circles.

"Is there something you'd like me to do in order to...rectify this situation?" I asked demurely.

Nathan didn't miss a beat. "Attend the Sevier Day ball with me, as my date."

Son of a bitch. I should have seen that coming.

"I haven't decided whether or not I'll attend," I lied.

"It would be pertinent if you did," said the governor. "All Sevier officials are expected to."

Well, fuck. That sure backed me into a corner. If I was trying to be agreeable, at least on the surface, I couldn't outright refuse.

"My bodyguards will still have to attend as well," I said. "To see to my personal safety."

"Of course." Satisfied, the governor waved his hand dismissively. "But they will have to give you a bit more breathing room. Other officials will want to meet you. And it's important that everyone sees you on Nathan's arm. Not constantly surrounded by those three."

Fuck.

The valkyrie thumped her axe against her shield in time to my racing heart. A warning beat if I ever heard one.

"Understood," I said grimly.

CHAPTER 13

KYRIE

"You don't think this is too much?" I looked over my shoulder and into the mirror, staring at the expanse of my bare back in the floor-length evening gown.

"It's *stunning*, Ambassador," Anita said in a breathless whisper. "*You* make it look stunning."

My face grew warm at her compliment, and I turned to look at the dress from a few more angles. The dark blue, backless gown had been my favorite design at the dress shop but now that the state dinner was here, the endless warnings of not soiling my reputation rang loudly in my head.

My dress had sleeves and a high neckline, but was an open back too scandalous for such a conservative territory? Anita didn't warn me like she had with my 'masculine' work clothes, so it seemed I was safe.

"Nathan better appreciate his arm candy," I muttered, securing my earrings.

After finishing touches on hair, makeup, and accessories, I was as ready as I'd ever be. The low voices of the Sons murmured out in the loft, waiting to escort me to the ballroom.

My heart pounded harder at the thought of them seeing me, then it jumped into my throat when Anita opened my suite door.

The conversation between them stopped abruptly, their mouths hanging open as I stepped out.

"Holy *fuck*." T-Bone spoke first, making Anita gasp at the curse.

"Kyrie..." Dyno breathed my name reverently, like a prayer. I only ever wanted to hear him say my name like that from now on.

With Grudge, I could only imagine what was going through his mind. He stared at me like I was the only person who existed.

The attention was more gratifying than I could have imagined. I wanted to soak in it like a hot bath. Why couldn't I stay up here in the loft with them, instead of going to a party with a bunch of people whose attention I *didn't* want?

Dyno sobered first, elbowing T-Bone, who cleared his throat loudly. "Uh, you look fu—uh, ravishing. I mean, not like that. I mean..." He swallowed thickly. "Great. You look really good."

"Beautiful," Dyno corrected, shooting him a scathing look. "The word he's looking for is beautiful."

The clumsy compliment soothed my nerves, and I was smiling before I realized it. "Thank you. You guys look good too." They still wore leather vests and looked ready to ride off at any moment, but their boots were polished and their white shirts were crisp and tailored.

And they smelled incredible. Whoever chose their

cologne and managed to dab it on deserved a raise. The warm, masculine scent only amplified the desire to hide away from everyone else and stay right here with them. Anita fidgeted next to me all too soon.

"Shall we?" she asked.

I tore my gaze away from the three men I wanted to stare at and talk to all night, then headed for the stairs. Nathan would likely be waiting for me at the bottom, and each step felt like walking through concrete. Feeling the Sons' footsteps echoing my own, knowing they were near, was the only thing that kept me going.

"Miss Vance!" a voice called brightly before I'd even reached the bottom. "You are an absolute vision."

I forced my lips into a smile as I continued down to the floor. "Thank you. You look very dashing."

Nathan wore a charcoal gray three-piece suit with accents of gold thread embroidered at the cuffs and collar. He did look good, but I could only wonder about the people who'd likely slaved over making his suit. My dressmaker had started crying when I insisted on giving her a tip on top of my dress's cost.

Nathan's eyes flickered over the men behind me, but it was short-lived as he offered me his elbow. "Shall we?"

I accepted, keeping a loose hold around his bicep and my body several inches away.

"This is where I leave you, Ambassador." Anita smiled, heading for a side door. "Have an excellent time."

"Oh, we will," Nathan called after her.

We started a walk toward the banquet room that felt too stiff, too formal. In the quietness echoing up to the high ceilings, it felt too much like walking down a wedding aisle.

"What was the state dinner like last year?" I asked, mainly just to break the tense atmosphere.

"Oh, it was incredible." Nathan smiled and covered my hand that rested on his arm. "We didn't decide until after the fact to make it an annual thing. But it made sense, you know? The first official Sevier holiday, celebrating our independence. Must have been what the founding fathers of the US felt like so long ago."

"Yes." I bit my tongue on the rest of what I wanted to say. *When they weren't killing the people who were already here.*

"We've been looking forward to this all year." He gave my hand a small squeeze and I resisted the urge to pull it away. "Once you see it, you'll see why." He leaned to speak into my ear and I stiffened. "And you'll never want to go back home."

T-Bone cleared his throat loudly from a few feet behind us, the rough sound echoing, and I bit back a laugh.

Conversely, Nathan glanced behind him in annoyance. "I do hope your overgrown babysitters keep a bit of distance tonight. It's hard to get to know someone when there's always a shadow hovering."

"It's hard to kidnap, stab, or poison someone too, which is what I'm banking on," I said pleasantly.

Nathan let out an indignant scoff. "If there was going to be an assassination or kidnapping attempt on anyone in the ballroom tonight, believe me, the target won't be some ambassador from Four Corners."

"Well, you sure know how to make a girl feel special," I said without thinking.

One of the Sons behind us snorted while Nathan gave me a hard look, one that turned my spine to ice because I recognized it. Malcolm gave me that look a few times. The one that came right before his anger unleashed and sent me into a spiral of confusion and heartache.

I began to pull away from Nathan, releasing his arm,

but he clasped my hand firmer. In the next moment, the look was gone. His features smoothed over, brow now pinching either out of concern or like a puppy that had been scolded.

"You know I didn't mean it like that," he said. "Please don't misinterpret my words."

It took a few breaths for me to calm down and respond. "Please don't belittle my personal safety."

"I didn't. But I'm sorry you saw it that way. Your safety is of utmost importance to me." He brought my hand to his lips and brushed a kiss over my knuckles, sad puppy eyes still locked onto me. "Can we go in now?"

"Yes," I said stiffly.

He reached toward my face and I forced myself to stay put instead of flinching away. Thankfully, it was only a stroke of his thumb on my jaw. "You're a feisty girl. You don't need as much protection as you think." His hand dropped and he angled his head toward the ballroom entrance. "Let's show everyone how good we look together."

I nodded tightly and resumed hold of his arm, standing even further away than before. He pulled me closer, bringing his mouth to my ear. "And give me that smile again."

I closed my eyes and counted my breaths. *Fuck, this is going to be such a long night.*

We had just reached the wide double-doors when T-Bone jumped in front of us. "I need a word with Miss Vance before y'all go in."

"Seriously?" Nathan huffed. "We need to go in together. With you three far away."

"It will just be a moment, *sir*," T-Bone sneered. "We have some logistical questions, that's all."

"I'll be with the doorman," Nathan grumbled, stomping ahead to the entrance.

"What is it?" I turned to T-Bone and stepped in close to him. It gave the illusion of wanting privacy, but I really just wanted *him*—that scent, those large hands he kept infuriatingly to himself, and the sense of feeling truly safe. He was everything Nathan wasn't.

"I just wanted to make sure you're okay." A muscle ticked in his jaw, his gaze flickering up and then back down to me. "I don't like how he's touching you."

"I don't either," I admitted in a whisper.

That rallied the other two to surround me.

"Do you want us to do anything?" Dyno asked. "We can make up an excuse for you to not go in."

"Mm-hm." Grudge nodded emphatically, his expression pleading for me to say yes.

And as much as I wanted to, I couldn't.

"Thank you guys, but no." I sighed. "I don't like it, but it'll be better when other people are around. He'll try to show off, but he won't be inappropriate."

"I just hate to think what he'd be trying if we weren't here," T-Bone growled through his teeth. "Fuck, I hate that slimy piece of shit."

"I know." I touched his arm, and the corded muscles jumped beneath my fingers. "But I do have to maintain my image here, and that means tolerating him."

"He better not touch you again," T-Bone said, and I knew the threat in his eyes was sincere.

Dyno clapped a hand on his shoulder. "Maybe you and Grudge should do a perimeter sweep first. I'll go in with Kyrie."

"Yeah?" T-Bone challenged. "You're kicking me back?"

"You need to cool off," the other man told him. "There's going to be dancing and shit. You can't be getting all territorial over every guy that talks to her."

T-Bone groaned out a protest, the sound nothing short of sexual. Combined with the notion that he might actually be jealous of Nathan, I felt an aching heat build up in my body.

"Fine." He barked out the word like he felt anything but fine, but he and Grudge headed in opposite directions for the side exits. "We'll be back."

Now alone with Dyno, the beautiful man faced me with a gently inquisitive expression. "Okay to go in?"

"Yes." I gave a small smile, one that actually wasn't forced. "Thank you, all of you, for checking in with me."

"T was gonna dropkick that dude in the kidneys if we didn't take a time-out." He offered me his elbow with a grin, and I looped my arm around it without a second thought.

"Oh no, we wouldn't want that." I earned a soft, breathy laugh in reply as we walked toward the entrance together. "Do you ever dance, Dyno?"

He angled his head and raised his eyebrows suggestively. "It's been known to happen a time or two."

"Really?" I couldn't hide my delight at that answer. "I might have to steal you for one then."

He chuckled lightly. "That'll be a surefire way to make T want to dropkick *me* in my kidneys."

"Why would he do that?"

Dyno hesitated like he wasn't sure if he should answer. "He's a bit...possessive of you."

"Possessive?" Why did that word fire up the ache in my body, especially the one concentrating between my legs?

"Let me put it this way," Dyno said, turning to face me.

"All of us would happily handle Nathan for you. But T-Bone would enjoy hurting him the most."

I shouldn't have felt bubbling giddiness at that information. I should have been horrified, should have pulled away from the tall, gorgeous biker immediately and reprimanded him for saying such a thing. I definitely shouldn't have held my head higher and bit back a smug grin as we headed for the ballroom.

But oh, I did.

CHAPTER 14

KYRIE

Dyno handed me off to Nathan at the ballroom entrance, stepping back with a quick bow that could have been respectful, but I interpreted it as mocking. Especially when he caught my eye and winked, smirking as he straightened up.

The sense of flattery was short-lived. Nathan placed his hand on my lower back, *on my bare skin*, as he led me into the ballroom. I was forced to turn away from Dyno, skin crawling, while making our way through the crowd at Nathan's side.

"I like this dress on you," he said, mouth too close to my ear again.

"Thank you, so do I." Like hell I was going to compliment him in return. My gaze swept around the room, eying the decor instead of him.

Three massive, glittering chandeliers had been mounted to the ceiling. Tables had been moved toward the edges of the room to open up the space for a dance floor. A small cluster of musicians played gentle background music as everyone filed in and got settled. The floor had been polished to a brilliant shine, and everything was draped in swaths of gold. With the chandeliers as the only light source, the room was dimmer than before. If it had been anyone else at my side, it would have felt romantic.

"This way." Nathan's fingers dug into my skin as he directed me to a table. I was stiff as a board but allowed him to guide me. Knowing that Dyno was nearby offered some small comfort.

Nathan finally released me to pull a high-backed chair out for me, which I accepted with my best gracious smile. He took the seat next to me and held a hand out toward the center of the table. "Champagne?"

I blinked, surprised to see the bottle sitting in a metal bucket filled with ice. "I thought alcohol was illegal?"

He grinned. "Not for those who have the right connections."

It shouldn't have surprised me, but it turned my stomach regardless. People of this territory had to pay premiums, find underground cellars, and risk jail time to enjoy a drink, but government officials could do the exact same thing without a care in the world.

Nathan didn't ask me again but snapped his fingers. A white-gloved waiter hurried over to open and pour the bottle for the two of us.

"Thank you," I murmured to the young man who looked roughly my age and held out a 5-Sevier note to him for a tip.

He startled for a moment before accepting it quickly with a bow of his head. "Thank you, ma'am. Please wave me down if I can do anything else for you."

"Have another bottle ready for when this one's done," Nathan said, slouching in his seat. When the waiter disappeared, his attention returned to me. "Charitable little thing, aren't you?"

I took my champagne flute and downed half of it, not giving one fuck if it wasn't ladylike. "Everyone deserves to earn a living wage. As things are now, he probably works three jobs to make ends meet."

"Let's not talk politics tonight," Nathan groaned. "But I hope he's incentivized to be quick with the service. The first course should be coming out once everyone is settled."

Our generously-sized table seated four, so thankfully I wouldn't be stuck with only his company all evening. An older gentleman and his wife joined us a few moments later, and the first course, a small plate of green salad, was brought out shortly after.

I leaned all the way into my governor's daughter role throughout the meal, keeping the topic of conversation polite and eating my courses as I'd been taught in etiquette lessons. All the while, I remained aware of Dyno standing behind me and wished I could relax into a couch next to him while sipping beer and eating French fries.

Halfway through our ten-course meal, Governor Perry went out to the empty floor to deliver a speech about Sevier independence and the future of the territory. I barely listened and just clapped and toasted along when prompted to.

"We'll now have an hour for dancing before the rest of the meal is served," Perry said at the end of his speech. "Move around and make room in there, people! Or sit back and digest, whichever suits you."

He had barely finished talking before Nathan reached across the table and clasped my hand. "Dance with me." It wasn't a question, or an invitation, but a command. The next thing I knew, he was standing and pulling me along with him.

I had enough sense to know that I couldn't refuse him, but our table had made it through the second bottle of champagne and it was getting harder to keep up my mask of politeness and poise. I glanced at Dyno while Nathan practically dragged me out to the dance floor and made an obvious show of rolling my eyes.

I turned back around before I could see his reaction. Some sleepy part of me, buried under the champagne bubbles, scolded myself for doing that. Multiple people probably saw. But I couldn't bring myself to care anymore. I was fucking tired of projecting a certain image for the so-called greater good.

"What's going on with you? Two left feet?" Nathan whipped around to face me, pressing his palms unashamedly to my bare back as he drew me close.

"I'm in four-inch heels, in case you didn't notice." I yanked my hand from his hold and braced both hands against his chest. "And stop touching me like that. You're doing too much."

He removed his hands from my back, transferring his grip to my upper arms instead. My breath stilled as he brought his face down even closer, forehead brushing mine. No way. He wouldn't kiss me here, would he?

"I like your fire, Miss Vance. I really do," he whispered, breath ghosting over my lips. "But there is a time and a place. And right now, while every important figure in the territory is watching, you *will* let me lead."

"I have no problem with that," I answered. "But you will not drag me around like a pet and put your hands all over me like you own me. I'm not your property."

Nathan huffed and rolled his eyes, like what I just said was the most ridiculous notion in the world and not exactly how he saw me. "Fine. Can we just dance?"

"Yes," I said in the exact same tone, like I didn't want to be there at all.

We placed our hands at the proper positions, but that was as far as it went. Nathan saw something over my shoulder and did a double-take, his hands dropping and body going stiff. I turned around and could have jumped for joy at the sight of a smug Dyno behind me.

"Mind if I cut in?"

I could have kissed him. *Saved by the biker!*

Nathan let out an indignant huff, then turned and walked away without another word. He couldn't even be bothered to fight for the dance when threatened by a better man. Dyno and I looked at each other and I could feel how hard it was for both of us to not burst out laughing.

"Now that was a little mean," I said, my body instinctively swaying toward him.

He shrugged nonchalantly and held out his hand. "Dance with me?"

The room and everyone in it fell away the moment our hands touched. Dyno drew me into him with a calm assuredness while still allowing plenty of slack for me to stay distant. Which was the absolute last thing I wanted.

My free hand rested on his shoulder while his hand found gentle placement on my waist. He didn't go anywhere near the bare skin of my back, and I wanted to lean in and arch until he touched me there, until he completely erased the sensation of Nathan's hand.

Dyno timed the music perfectly and started spinning us slowly at the right beat. Just as I suspected, he was graceful in his movement and easy to follow.

"Where did you learn to dance?" I loved that his handsome face was my only focus while everything else blurred.

"Places," he answered coyly, lips pulling up in a half-smile. His smile deepened the lines around his eyes, and I wanted to kiss every one.

"Is that how it's gonna be?" I teased. My hand slipped from his shoulder, running to his upper back in a movement that drew us closer together. "I ask you questions and you give me one-word answers?"

"It doesn't have to be." His forearm now braced securely against my lower back, and I knew we had to be the most intimate-looking couple on the dance floor. None of these old pearl-clutchers would dance so scandalously, not even the ones who'd been married for decades. "I'm a little surprised you agreed to dance with me."

"Why?" My fingers brushed one of the braids through his silky hair.

"Because everyone can see us." Dyno didn't appear deterred by that. If anything, he seemed emboldened and drew me flush to his body. "After that intervention they gave you too." He clicked his tongue in joking disapproval. "You really are a bad girl, Kyrie."

"I've always been bad," I sighed. "Never quiet enough. Never obedient enough. Always getting involved in affairs I should stay out of. People find it charming until they realize they can't control me."

"You weren't born to be controlled." Dyno pressed his cheek to mine, his face so warm and smooth and *close* that it made me gasp. "You were born to make noise, to bring changes. The valkyrie you see isn't an accident. I believe she's a guide to you. And she's telling you to strike your axe on your shield until everyone pays attention. Don't ever let anyone silence you."

"Wow," I breathed. Stunned was the only way I could describe the effect his words had on me. "Grudge told you about that, huh?"

Dyno pulled away, regret in his face. "I'm sorry if that was meant to be in confidence. The three of us tend to share everything." He made another expression that I couldn't interpret.

What else do you share? I wanted to know. They shared each other, obviously, in a committed albeit unconventional relationship. One that I fantasized about and was endlessly curious about. I never did like conventional things in general.

"No, it's fine," I reassured him with a smile. "I'm just glad you don't think the valkyrie is ridiculous. My father or anyone else would have written it off as nothing. Or worse, a sign of a mental breakdown."

"You seem mentally sound to me. And messengers from the gods are never nothing." His fingers teased the edge of my dress on my back. "Your feelings are never nothing."

I was feeling emboldened right then and brought my hand closer to his neck, brushing his shirt collar with the edge of my finger. "Thank you, Dyno."

"Dylan," he said softly. "My given name is Dylan."

Sparks and flutters burst in my chest. It felt like I'd been given a precious gift. "Is that what you'd prefer me to call you?"

"In private, maybe." His eyes were bright with affection, his smile warm. "If you would like to."

I remembered him saying how they used each other's given names as a form of intimacy. They weren't secrets exactly, but the significance was different enough that I was moved to be included. As we flew across the dance floor in our small world of just the two of us, I couldn't imagine anything more private and intimate.

"I think I will," I said. "Dylan."

CHAPTER 15

T-BONE

Dyno was right, as usual. I did need a walk outside to cool down. By the time I headed back to the ballroom, I felt adequately calm and like I didn't need to snap Nathan's neck with my bare hands. Once I stepped inside that overly-glitzed room though, my temper soared back up for completely different reasons.

Kyrie was dancing.

With Dyno.

"What…the fuck?"

The curse tumbled from my lips as I watched them move and spin across the open floor. He held her close. Very close. People still sitting at tables or watching from the edge of the dance floor watched them as well and whispered to each other.

Shit, shit, shit. This is not fucking good.

What the hell did I miss on my walk? As much as I hated Nathan's little bitch face, I thought Kyrie had planned on being his arm candy the whole night. We were supposed to keep our distance and not act so *familiar* with her. What the fuck happened in the last hour that all of that went out the window?

Grudge was still patrolling outside, so I couldn't even share my confusion with him. On top of being completely blindsided, I was also jealous as fuck. And helpless to do anything about it.

Kyrie was safe in Dyno's arms, yes. But she could be even safer in mine.

The music faded as the song came to a slow, gradual end, and the dancers' movements slowed with it. I couldn't tell you what kind of music it was, some kind of high-brow classical shit that rich people listened to. Kyrie and Dyno's eyes remained locked on each other, their expressions dreamy, even as they left the dance floor side by side. She leaned toward his ear to say something, and his lips grazed so fucking close to her cheek. Fuck me, if he kissed her *now*, my head would actually fucking explode.

Whether that rage was a result of jealousy or the sheer recklessness of it, I couldn't be sure.

They parted from each other a moment later, with Kyrie heading down a corridor to what I assumed was the ladies' room. Once Dyno slid through the throng of people to wait for her at the hall's entryway, I went straight for him and didn't hold back.

He was completely relaxed when I brought a hand down on his shoulder and spun him around to face me, which meant he knew I was coming.

"What," I snarled, "the *fuck* was that?"

His expression betrayed nothing but cool indifference. "It's called dancing. You should try it sometime."

"Dylan." I growled out his given name to show how serious I was. "I am not in the fucking mood for your smartass mouth. As your president, I'll ask again. Why the fuck were *you* dancing with her?"

His eyes narrowed, the only shift in his face. "Nathan was manhandling her. She was getting upset and pushed him away. So I stepped in."

A tiny amount of my anger drained away, relieved that he had been there. But it quickly refilled once my system registered that Nathan had tried to push her around *again*. If the prick couldn't control his hands, I'd be happy to remove them for him.

"But why did *you* have to dance with her?" I repeated. "We're supposed to be hanging back, remember?"

Dyno's lip curled. "He's stubborn as a fucking cockroach. He would've come right back and tried again if I stepped away. If not him, some other rich piece of shit would."

That wasn't all. The emotion was finally bleeding out of him, cutting through his words and his clenched fists. Not many things got under Dyno's skin, but Kyrie did. She dug her way deep inside years ago and made a home in all of us.

And I didn't have to ask Dyno or Grudge to know that none of us wanted her to leave that place she occupied.

"Also because I wanted to," Dyno finally admitted. "I told myself she would be safest if I stayed close to her, but I also just...*wanted* to be closer to her."

All the air in my chest left with a big sigh. Not because I was disappointed in him, but because I knew exactly how he felt.

"What are we doing, D?" I whispered, not expecting an answer.

"I don't know," he said, rubbing his jaw. "We kept

telling ourselves not to, and it's not working. Would it really be so bad if we just—"

"Stop," I warned him. "Do not say what I think you're about to say."

He gave me a heavy look. "I think it's too late to stop, Trav."

I shook my head and then looked down the empty corridor to the washrooms. I wasn't sure how much time had passed, but surely enough for a woman to do her business and come back?

"She's been gone awhile," Dyno echoed my thoughts.

"I'll check on her." I slapped his chest and gave him a gentle push in the opposite direction. "Grudge should be getting back from checking the outside. Go switch with him to *cool your head.*"

Dyno snorted. "Yes, President."

Like my blood wasn't already hot enough, then he had to go and call me that. I wanted to shove him to his knees and make him take my cock in that smartass mouth until he choked on it. I wanted to fuck him so deep in his ass until he babbled apologies for not sticking to the plan.

And I want Kyrie to watch.

I forced the thought from my head with a frustrated growl as I stormed down the hallway. That was the last place my mind needed to be, although Dyno had a point. The more I fought how much I craved her, the deeper and more gnawing the ache became.

"Kyrie?" I pounded the side of my fist on the first door I found. "You in there?"

No answer came and I moved on to the next one, which was a swinging door that opened easily when I pushed it. Inside was a powder room of sorts—no toilets, only a long vanity counter with a wall of mirrors and plush couches along the far walls.

My eyes swept the room, barely acknowledging the two women who had been kissing on the couch and were now frozen in shock at my intrusion. I only looked around enough to confirm that Kyrie was not there either.

"Sorry, ladies," I muttered before backing out of the room.

"Come on, Kyrie," I said, thundering down the hallway. "Where the fuck are you?"

"Looking for me?"

I whipped around, realizing that in my tunnel-vision, I'd missed a small alcove in the wall, barely more than an indent with a small bench to sit. Kyrie leaned her upper back against the wall, her face flushed and a near-empty champagne flute in her hand.

Relief whooshed out of me. "There you are. Let's go."

"Mm." Kyrie drained the rest of her glass and set it on the bench. "Nah, I'm good."

My hands flexed at my sides, and some distant warning bell sounded in my head. "Your absence from the ballroom will be noticed, *Ambassador.* Let's get you back now."

"No thank you, T-Bone." Her speech was clear, not at all slurred as she crossed her arms in front of her dark, glittery dress.

"Kyrie," I tried again, firmer. "I wasn't asking. We *need* to go back."

She put on a bored expression. "The world is not going to collapse again if I ditch a stupid dinner party. I'm tired of putting on a fake persona for *them.*" She jerked her chin down the hallway before casting a smile in my direction. "I like talking to you one-on-one a lot better."

"Yeah?" I bit out. "Did you like dancing with Dyno?"

I didn't mean to ask that question. I was supposed to say a snappy comeback but *that* was burning on my tongue.

"I did," she said proudly, lifting her chin. "Are you jealous, T-Bone? Think I'm gonna steal your man?"

"Stop being a brat," I ordered, lifting a finger and stepping closer to her. "Drop the attitude, put your big girl panties back on, and come back to the fucking party."

"I said no." Kyrie leaned forward, arms still crossed. "I'm not being a brat. I'm being an adult, making my own fucking decisions because I'm tired of being told how to act!"

"Okay, okay." I lowered my hands, looking both ways down the hall to make sure we didn't attract any unwanted attention. She had practically yelled, all the frustration bleeding out of her. I sympathized with her, I really did. But now was a bad time to unload about how unfair life was.

When my eyes landed on Kyrie again, she was smirking.

"What?" I barked.

"You like it when I'm a brat, don't you?"

"Kyrie." I dropped my voice low, full of warning. "Don't go there."

Of course I liked it. My cock wouldn't be rock-hard and pulsing right now if her rebellious nature wasn't a huge fucking turn-on. It was my favorite thing about her, how she dared to rattle the bars of her cage no matter where she was placed.

"You do." Kyrie grinned victoriously. "Do you want to turn me around and spank me right now, T-Bone?"

"What the fuck has gotten into you?" Yes, I wanted to spank her, soothe her, hold her, and support her. I wanted to watch her ass turn red and see the faces she made when she came. I wanted everything.

"Is that what you do?" she pressed on. "When you three have wild, crazy orgies, sleeping with other men *and* women?"

"What are you talk—just…*what?*" She was giving me such whiplash with this shit, I didn't know which direction was up.

It took me a moment, but a lightbulb went on when I figured it out. I wasn't the only one who was jealous. The thing was, we hadn't played with others in over a year. Those fucking snake politicians must have put this in her ear at that meeting. The one we weren't allowed to stay in.

Fucking dumbshits. It was some stupid attempt to make her turn against us, but it only hurt her instead. The insecurity was written clearly on her face, and I hated it more than anything.

"We haven't done that in a long time." Fuck, it sounded like such a lame excuse. "For the past year, it's only been the three of us. It's…it's not a huge part of our lives, to be honest. We're committed to each other, you know that."

I shouldn't have been reassuring her about that. A few weeks ago, I never would have touched this topic with her, but now I wanted to. She didn't deserve to have our past exploits thrown in her face, cutting down her self-worth. Her feelings for all of us were becoming clearer by the day, and I could only speculate that whatever sexual experience she had was limited.

"I don't want to do this anymore." Kyrie's lower lip was now trembling and a deep, pleading sadness was in her eyes.

"Kyrie…" My resolve was leaving me, draining quickly

as a bleeding wound. I wasn't exactly sure what she meant by *this*, but I became overwhelmed with the need to take her sadness away.

"You can drag me back out there, if you want." Kyrie took in a shaky breath and lifted her chin, always poised and strong. "Drag me down this hallway, yell at me, humiliate me. Do whatever you need to do." She blinked and then the tears fell. "Just don't ever leave me again."

All my instincts fired at once, and I moved without thinking. Somehow, I still knew to cradle the back of her head, shielding her from the wall before I kissed her.

Kyrie's mouth opened against mine, probably in shock, but there was no stopping me as my tongue swept inside. I pulled her against my chest, a hand splayed on the bare skin of her back.

This fucking backless dress. It undid me the moment she stepped out of her suite. It was a miracle I didn't rage sooner while Nathan tried to put his filthy hands all over her.

Kyrie responded to me after a moment, pressing her tongue against mine and kissing me back. I held the nape of her neck, my other hand stroking in light passes up and down her back. She shivered but didn't pull away. Instead, she grabbed the edges of my cut to pull me closer, mouth widening to kiss me deeper.

She tasted sweeter than I ever could have imagined. Bubbly and with a hint of fruit, like the champagne she drank. Lips so soft and kisses like whispers, nothing like the rough claiming that came with kissing men. It had been so long since I kissed a woman, but even so, none of my previous encounters had been like this. Kissing had always been part of foreplay, a simple means of getting the fun started. I had never kissed a woman just because I wanted to. Until now, I had only kissed Dyno and Grudge like that.

Until now, I had believed they were enough for me.

This woman—no, this *girl* who was almost twenty years younger than me—had no business tasting this good. She had no right to mold her body to mine so perfectly that I never wanted us to separate. The little breaths and moans she made shouldn't have made me so weak-kneed. But every swipe of each other's tongues, every sip from her mouth had me returning for more, like a sailor to a siren's call.

Every one of my senses filled so much with *her* that it took me a moment to realize that the wall vibrated behind her.

I tore my mouth from Kyrie's, my pulse thrumming and breaths ragged as I tuned back into my surroundings.

"T-Bone?" My name was a whisper on her lips, which were flushed, swollen, and parted softly to breathe in soft pants.

I brought a finger to my lips and her mouth clamped shut, dilated eyes widening as alertness returned to her. Pressing my opposite palm against the wall next to her head, I waited for that vibrating sensation again. This time, the floor shook too, and Kyrie nearly stumbled.

"What's happening?" she whispered.

"Don't know yet, just stay close."

She held onto my arm while I drew my gun and slowly peeked around the wall. I could see into the banquet room where everyone seemed to be gathered at a bank of windows, staring at something outside. Was there a fireworks display or something? I didn't remember hearing about it.

"Hey, Kyrie?"

"Yeah?"

"Don't freak out, but I'm about to go limp and look really weird. I'll explain later, but trust that I'm fine, okay? It'll only be for a few seconds."

She looked confused but gave me a solemn nod. "I trust you."

I leaned against the wall for support, then closed my eyes. Leaving my body was always a trip, more exhilarating than any drug. Nothing else in the world mirrored the sensation of my consciousness hurtling through space before finding home in another body that was not my own.

Munin was on a road outside the capitol building, stacking a collection of bottle caps for fun. He knew the moment my consciousness occupied him, and he let out an annoyed caw.

Something's happening at the capitol, bird brain. Let's see it.

He turned and flew toward the building. Right away, I spotted the corridor Kyrie and I were in. Through a window, I saw her looking at me worriedly. Somehow, my body was still upright and leaning against the wall. At least I wasn't laid out on the floor. And hopefully I wasn't drooling, that'd be embarrassing.

Closer, I instructed Munin. *What's happening on the other side of the ballroom?*

He flew us overhead, and I used his eyes to scan the ground below. A steady stream of people seemed to be leaving the building through a side door. I recognized the white shirts and black pants of the waiters' uniforms and thought I spotted Kyrie's assistant, Anita, filing out with them.

The staff is walking out? What the fuck is going on?

Someone dressed in all black lobbed an object at the

window and that was when Munin forced me out and sent me back to my own body.

I felt Kyrie's hand on my arm while my head swam. I needed a moment to get my bearings, but there was no time. I heard glass breaking, then screams, while a loud booming sound rattled the walls, floors, and chandeliers.

"Come on." I sprung into action, pulling Kyrie in the opposite direction. "We gotta go."

She tried to follow but teetered precariously on her heels. "Wait." In seconds, she flung the ridiculous shoes off and ran barefoot alongside me. She wouldn't last long like that, but I'd throw her over my shoulder like a caveman if I needed to. "What's happening, T-Bone—oh my God!" We'd only run a few dozen yards when she stopped in her tracks, bringing her hands to her mouth at the sight through the window.

Across the courtyard, the southern wing of the capitol was on fire. Smoke and flames filled the air in the distance too. The night sky was alight with orange and panicked screams.

I tugged at Kyrie to keep us moving. "Looks like someone's attacking the city, so we need to *go*."

She broke into a run again without any more coaxing. "What about Dyno and Grudge?"

I gritted my teeth. My mind was in the exact same place, but those two could handle themselves. I had to get her to safety first.

"We'll meet up with them soon. They'll be fine."

Those dick-fucks better be.

CHAPTER 16

GRUDGE

I was surprised to see Dyno looking *heated* on my perimeter walk and frowned. He usually had a cool, easygoing demeanor, but now he was tense, agitated. He was also fifteen minutes early to switch spots with me, and I was not at all eager to go inside a crowded ballroom. Seeing Kyrie would be a plus, but crowds and enclosed spaces sent my heart racing with anxiety.

I spread my hands at Dyno as he approached to ask what was wrong.

"T tried to chew me out for dancing with Kyrie, then he stalked after her down a hallway like he planned to fuck her in a dark corner." Dyno crossed his arms, looking everywhere but at me. "Hypocrite."

I chuckled and scrawled out a note. *Is he going to?*

"No. I mean, I'm pretty sure he won't."

I cocked my head, lifting an eyebrow at him.

"We're a package deal, Grudge. Same as always. He wouldn't unless the two of us were there." Dyno rubbed his jaw thoughtfully. "He might kiss her though. I almost did when I danced with her and…I think he saw."

I groaned and quickly scratched out another message. *We're too far gone to resist anymore, aren't we?*

Dyno laughed wryly and nodded. "Not a day's gone by in the last few years where I haven't thought of her and wished things could be different." He tilted his head toward me. "Be careful what you wish for, as they say."

I hesitated a long while before writing out my next thought. *What if things work out, but she doesn't want one of us?*

"Then she gets none of us." Dyno gave me a hard look. "I don't think that's likely to happen, but what we agreed upon years ago still remains."

I frowned, uneasy at that idea. He and T-Bone were smitten with Kyrie. So was I, but if they were happy with her and she found me lacking…

"We're a package deal," Dyno repeated. "No one gets between the three of us, Grudge. That's the same shit Lacey tried to pull with me way back when. If Kyrie's right for us, she gets all of us. She'll *want* all of us."

He moved directly in front of me and wrapped a hand around the back of my neck, his nose nearly touching mine. "What do T and I tell you all the time, huh?"

"Hmm…" I couldn't say the words, but I touched my forehead to his and gripped the edges of his cut, nodding that I understood.

"You're ours." His warm breath fanned over my lips, fingers curling into the back of my neck. "And you're perfect."

I shook my head, closing my eyes. They always tried to tell me that, but I was the furthest thing from perfect. My failures were imprinted in my DNA, beaten into my head, and permanently carved into me. What little muscle remained in my mouth, the removal of my speech, was a constant reminder of that.

"Hey." Dyno clapped both hands to the sides of my neck. "Stop that. Yes, you are. T and I will keep telling you until you believe it. Shit, maybe Kyrie will too."

I huffed out an incredulous laugh. Kyrie could have her choice of men. Despite her dreams and the signs, I still wasn't convinced it would be us in the end. Dyno and T-Bone were better choices than me, but they still didn't have much to offer a governor's daughter.

Dyno kissed me roughly, sucking hard at my lips until I opened them for him. Trying to distract me, of course. His tongue swept inside and I wished I could do the same to him. It was so hot watching his and T-Bone's tongues thrusting against each other, mimicking sex when they tried to dominate each other's mouths.

I was grateful that they did everything possible to not exclude me. I *believed* that they loved me. But even within our happy trio, I still had moments of feeling like a complete outsider.

"Do I need to suck your cock to make you feel better?" Dyno kissed me again, groping the front of my jeans. His lips dragged to my ear. "Or should I talk about how much I want Kyrie sandwiched between us right now?"

That got a groan out of me, and I clutched his shoulders, my cock springing to life at the thought of him touching me *and* her.

"Knew it." He bit playfully on my earlobe. "She'd be riding you, getting you all slick and hot so that you can take me next. I'd be in her ass, feeling you through her while she takes us both."

"Mm?" I cocked my head, and he knew from my expression what I was asking.

"T-Bone's bossy ass will be directing the show, of course." Dyno's laugh tickled my neck and made me pulse against his hand. "Kissing each of us when he feels like it, letting all of us suck him like he's a king."

I groaned at the thought and bucked my hips into Dyno's hand. Nothing would be better than sharing them with her—seeing the pleasure on her face, teasing T-Bone into oblivion while we both sucked him—*what was that?*

A distant sound had me putting a hand on Dyno's chest and a finger to my lips. He immediately pulled back and listened too, hands drifting over his belt. We were on a walkway near the capitol grounds, so everything was well-lit. But lights also created deep shadows at night, thus plenty of hiding places.

We should have been more alert, not messing around. But Kyrie had never been in any immediate danger, except possibly from Nathan, so our dumbasses had gotten lax with our security. Fuck, we should have been better than this. I clenched my teeth and hovered my hand over the gun at my hip.

"Grudge!" Dyno hissed, gaze pinned over my shoulder.

I whipped around, drawing my gun to point it at the man who seemed to appear out of thin air. The other bodyguard. I recognized his pitbull-like scowl as he took a few fearless steps toward me.

"Hah!" I warned him, cocking my gun and pointing it at his chest.

"He won't hesitate," Dyno added. "I suggest you stop where you are if you enjoy breathing."

The man's steps slowed to a halt a few feet away from me. Aside from that, he looked utterly nonplussed at Dyno's threat.

"If you care about your little ambassador girl," he said

softly, "you'll get her out of that building within the next five minutes."

"Why? What's happening?" Dyno demanded.

The man's chin lifted. "We're taking our fucking city back from these rich pricks. That's what's happening."

Oh. Fuck.

Rebellions and uprisings were a regular occurrence after the Collapse. The fights for territory and control were never-ending, so it shouldn't have been all that surprising. But now couldn't have been a worse time.

Or the perfect time, from the rebellion's point of view. All the cabinet members, officials, and dignitaries gathered together in the ballroom made them an easy target.

"You're making a mistake. A bigger army will hear of this by tomorrow and crush you by the end of the week. Don't put your people's lives at risk." Dyno was trying to dissuade the man, but I saw the hard determination in his eyes.

"Oh, the big army's coming. But they're on my side." The man was eerily calm. "And you have no idea how big our resistance is. The territory is already ours. The rich pricks just don't know it yet." He tilted his head, eying us warily. "You're normal folk, like us. And your ambassador seems like she'd be willing to stand with us. So consider this a courtesy; get her out before it's too late."

He raised his arm in the air, extending two fingers as some kind of signal. Moments later, we heard a high-pitched whistle, then turned to the sound of a boom and crackle in the night sky, which lit up with streams of color and smoke.

Fireworks—an apt distraction for people who couldn't resist marveling over shiny things.

"Come on!" Dyno slapped at my arm and then we were off, running to the nearest entrance to the ballroom.

We didn't make it twenty feet before the first explosion hit, knocking us to the ground with a blast of heat. My ears rang painfully, and I could still hear the *oohs* and *ahhs* morphing into screams of terror.

"Fuck! Courtesy, my ass, he barely gave us any fucking warning." Dyno rolled over and groped at me. "You okay?"

I nodded and returned to my feet. The air felt hot and when I looked up, flames licked out of a broken window directly above us. Through a long entryway just ahead of us, a set of doors groaned and buckled with the force of people on the other side, desperate to make it out.

Dyno and I headed straight for those doors without another word. Upon closer inspection, we saw that they had been barred with a long two-by-four drilled directly into the doors. Holy shit, they fucking barricaded everyone inside!

Prying and pulling at the bar did nothing. They had screwed this thing in in multiple places. Panic flooded me as I redrew my gun, but Dyno shoved my hands away. "You could hit someone if they're all shoved up against it."

He was right, but that gave me another idea.

I pointed at the mini molotovs on his belt, then cupped my hands around my mouth to mimic yelling, and then throwing the explosives. A slow smile came to his face as he understood my meaning, then he kissed me quickly.

"You're a genius, you sexy fuck."

He pressed his hands and forehead to the door, then proceeded to yell at the top of his lungs. "Hey! Can anyone hear me in there?"

The screams and pounding from the other side intensified, reaching a fever pitch. "Help us!" they cried. "Everything is burning, and we can't get out!"

I tried to listen for Kyrie and T-Bone in the chaotic mass of voices but couldn't pick them out.

"You all need to listen to me!" Dyno hollered through the wood. "Step as far away as you can from the door! I'm going to blow it up!"

"Everything's on fire!" someone answered. "We're trapped! We can't go anywhere!"

"Get as far away from the door as you can!" Dyno pulled one of the small explosives from his belt. "I'm going to count to five, and you all *need* to back away!"

"Help us! Let us out!"

The cries on the other side only seem to grow louder, more desperate and panicked, but Dyno stuffed the bottle with a fuse and then lit it, counting down loudly as he set the bomb in front of the door. As soon as it touched the ground we took off, hurrying away as Dyno screamed his last ferocious warning for everyone to back away. And it blew.

For the second time in five minutes, I was thrown off my feet by the blast. My hands, knees, and forearms were scraped raw, and now I couldn't hear anything past the ringing in my ears. Dyno must have distilled his recipe even more, because I couldn't remember those little bombs being that strong.

My mind immediately turned to Kyrie and I forced myself to move, rolling out of the path of stampeding people escaping the building. Once I righted myself, I searched desperately in the sea of faces rushing out. *Where were they?*

"Kyrie!" Dyno called, his voice growing hoarse from all the yelling he'd already done. "T-Bone! Are you here?" He stuck his fingers in his mouth and whistled loudly, our distress signal for each other. Some people turned their heads, curious at the sound, but none of the faces were familiar.

The smoke spilling out of the doorway was thick, stinging my eyes and throat. Dyno and I approached the doorway once the rush of people thinned out, and I grabbed the back of his cut to prevent him from rushing inside. He turned to look at me and I shook my head, then jerked my chin away. Kyrie and T-Bone weren't with those people, and we'd suffocate or be burned alive if we went in that way.

"They were, uh, in a hallway before I came out." He turned and coughed, the smoke already fucking up his lungs. "They must not have gone back to the ballroom."

Another blast went off somewhere, shaking the walls of the building. I tugged him away from the door and we took off running again, following the long exterior wall.

"This way!" Dyno turned sharply, cutting across one of the smaller courtyards, and I followed him. After patrolling inside and outside the capitol for weeks, we knew the layout of the building well. I trusted he knew exactly where T-Bone and Kyrie had last been.

Fires were everywhere now, flickering in windows that I knew were offices and conference rooms. Across the street, a smaller building used as a smoking lounge by many in the governor's cabinet was also ablaze. We'd heard rumors that officials bribed women from poorer families to come out there for better job opportunities or to pick up donated items, then they were actually solicited, and often coerced, for sex.

The rumors were never substantiated, and so we never brought it up to Kyrie, but I felt no small amount of pleasure at seeing the place burn. Not all violent conflicts came from wanting better, but this one probably was.

Kyrie had been trying to help these people the peaceful way, through her political channels, but she might as well have been screaming into a void. Sometimes the only way to implement change was to do it forcefully, and by setting fire to the ones who pushed your face into the mud.

"Kyrie!" Dyno yelled, his voice getting weaker from running and the smoke inhalation. "T-Bone!"

His footsteps slowed as we approached another entrance up ahead. The doors were open at this end of the building, but they weren't without damage. The wood was buckled and splintered in some areas and hung crookedly on its hinges. Whoever had been trapped on the other side had managed to force their way out.

Clouds of smoke billowed out of windows and the gaps in the doors. Here there wasn't much fire, as the floor and walls were made of some kind of stone tile. But we'd still get cooked alive if we tried to go in.

And anyone still inside probably already was.

"They were right here." Dyno's breaths were labored, ragged. His lungs seized up into a coughing fit before he could speak again. "In this hallway. The ballroom's through there." He pointed to the far end of the corridor where it connected to the main building. "She came down this hall. T-Bone went to go find her. Fuck! Where are they?"

His voice was full of frustration and worry. If I could speak, I would have sounded the same. I grabbed his shoulder and squeezed in an attempt to be comforting, but the clench of my grip only betrayed how worried I was.

"They had to have made it out, right?" Dyno said

more to himself than me, his face pale. "The door wouldn't be like that if they didn't make it."

I clenched my jaw, empathizing with his pain. Not knowing was the worst. They weren't here now, and until the fire died back so we could investigate, we didn't know if their bodies were in that corridor or not.

Dyno's eyes remained fixed on the beat-up doors, and I tugged at his sleeve to get his attention. When he looked at me, I jerked my head to the side, pulling him in that direction. He nodded slowly, understanding. We had to keep looking. Kyrie and T-Bone might be in there, or they might have gotten out. Since we couldn't run inside yet, we had to check everywhere else.

"I don't…" Dyno blinked, scanning the now smoky, fiery horizon as if in a daze. "I don't know where else to look. They—"

"Hm!" I grabbed the sides of his neck, much like he did to me earlier. I slapped his cheek lightly and grabbed his jaw, making him look directly at me. If he didn't know what I was trying to say, he'd figure it out soon enough. *You're a fucking Son of Odin. Get it together.*

He blinked at me in surprise right before I saw movement over his shoulder. Without warning, I shoved him aside and drew my gun. "Hah!" I shouted a warning at the figure obscured by smoke and shadows.

Dyno turned around and followed suit, aiming his gun next to me. But the figure continued toward us, its silhouette distorted and strange.

"Stop!" Dyno called out. "Identify yourself!"

"It's me, you dick-fuck!"

We lowered our guns and sighed out our relief together, but it was short-lived. T-Bone limped as he came closer, a grimace of pain on his face and blood coating his entire right side from his neck down to his hip. All at once, I saw why his figure had looked distorted from far away.

He carried a woman-sized bundle in his arms, limp and lifeless. Kyrie's hand hung free, waving only from T-Bone's agonized steps. Her head lolled on his shoulder, nearly flopping back as a dead weight.

"Kah?" Her name burst from my lips as I ran toward them, cold fear sealing my chest in a block of ice.

"She's not breathing," T-Bone said in an agonized voice. "I think she inhaled too much smoke."

I touched her face, running my thumb along her cold cheekbone in hopes of rousing her. *Wake up, sweet girl. We need you.* She was so eerily still, and her lips were turning blue.

"Lay her down on the ground." Dyno's voice was a sharp command, and T-Bone pulled her away from me to do as he instructed.

"What are you going to do?" T-Bone laid our girl gingerly on her back, supporting her head the whole time as if she were a baby.

"Mari taught me CPR before we left." Dyno ran his hands up and down Kyrie's bloodstained arm. "Does she have any other injuries?"

"No, that's all my blood." With his arms now free, T-Bone winced and held his bloody shoulder. "Had to hit that door a hundred fucking times before we could get out."

Dyno set to work quickly, breathing into Kyrie's mouth and doing compressions on her chest. "How long since she's been out?" He brought his ear to her mouth, listening for breath.

T-Bone shook his head, his expression heartbroken. "I

don't know, a couple minutes. She passed out right when I got the door open."

Time seemed to stretch on forever as Dyno tried to revive Kyrie and we watched helplessly. He was exhausting himself, his own breaths weak from his own smoke inhalation.

"Let me." T-Bone rolled forward when Dyno nearly collapsed on top of Kyrie. "Just tell me what to do."

Dyno shook his head wearily. "You can't do compressions with a busted shoulder."

"Hm!" I moved up, hovering over the woman we'd all found ourselves obsessed with, and Dyno nodded.

"I'll do compressions," he said. "You breathe into her mouth. Two breaths."

I nodded and tilted Kyrie's chin up slightly as he had. Pinching her nose shut, I leaned down to seal my lips over hers. Ironically, I was certain this would be the only time our mouths would ever touch. She'd never want to kiss a defective one like mine under any other circumstances.

I forced all the air from my lungs into hers and on the second breath, I felt movement.

Dyno froze, his hands still flat on her chest. "Did she—
"

Kyrie sucked in a harsh, ragged breath, and then started coughing. Dyno and I rolled her up to a sitting position, rubbing her back and encouraging her to breathe. The weight of the world lifted from all of us in that moment, and we huddled around her protectively, touching her arms and her back. We stared at her eyes, finally awake and open, her chest heaving as she took in more fresh air.

"Ohh fucking Odin, thank you." T-Bone was beside himself, nearly weeping as he leaned in to touch her face, his forehead leaning intimately on hers. "Thank them all, you're alive."

"Guys?" Kyrie's voice was a weak rasp, eyes glancing at all of us. "What's happening?"

We'd forgotten about everything but her for a moment, but reality hit us again. We were sitting on the ground in the middle of a fucking war zone.

T-Bone's face hardened and he pulled Kyrie to him with his good arm, cradling her against his chest as he returned to his feet.

"Get the bikes ready," he growled to Dyno and me. "We're leaving."

CHAPTER 17

KYRIE

The valkyrie looked to be in a pensive mood.

She was relaxed, sitting on top of a boulder in the same foggy landscape I'd seen in this dream before. For once, her hands were free. Her shield and axe leaned against the rock while she looked off somewhere in the distance.

The raven was there too, preening his feathers and making soft vocalizations rather than his intense cawing sounds.

"I'm somewhere safe," I heard myself say. "And you know this. You know when I'm in danger or not."

The woman's head tilted just a fraction, the corner of her mouth lifting like she was pleased with my observation.

"Can you speak?" I asked her. "Do you understand me?" She didn't respond, and I repeated the questions in Icelandic. If she was a figure of ancient Norse legends, maybe she needed to hear a language close to her own.

Again, I got no answer from her. But I wouldn't be deterred that easily.

"Who are you?" When she didn't react to that, I tried, "Who am *I* to you?"

That got her attention. Her head turned slowly until she looked at me straight on. I still couldn't see her eyes or the top half of her face. Only her nose, mouth, and chin were visible under her winged helmet.

The valkyrie laid her forearms on top of each other, hands near her elbows. Then she gently swung her arms from side to side, as if rocking a baby.

I WOKE UP ACHING EVERYWHERE. My feet, arms, legs, even inside my lungs and throat. Turning over in bed, I was beyond relieved to find a glass of water on the nightstand and gulped it down greedily.

Once my thirst was sated, it took me a moment to get my bearings and figure out where I was. This wasn't my suite at the Sevier capitol. The room was much smaller, barely bigger than the futon I had just slept on. Wood paneling covered the walls—a dated design choice, but the tiny bedroom was cozy and my bed had been piled high with blankets. I wrapped one around my shoulders as I slid my feet to the floor.

I winced at the ache shooting up my legs the moment I put weight on them. Why did everything hurt so much? I sat back down and leaned forward over my lap, rubbing my pounding head as the night before returned to me in disjointed flashes.

Running barefoot over a stone floor, my hand clenched

in T-Bone's. Coughing endlessly, fighting to breathe while he slammed his fists, shoulder, and foot into the door over and over. And then staring up at a fiery sky with the three Sons of Odin huddled closely around me. My head shot up with a gasp as it hit me all at once. Explosions. Screaming.

T-Bone kissing me.

How messed up was it that the capitol had been attacked but my mind latched onto that kiss above all else? I brought my bruised fingers to my lips, remembering the friction and press of him against me, his tongue invading and claiming my mouth. It had completely overwhelmed me but in the best way. A familiar heat rushed between my legs, concentrating there now just as it did last night.

I stole another nervous glance at the bed, walls, and simple furniture in the small bedroom. Was this…his house? *Their* house? It dawned on me that I knew so little about the Sons outside of their work life. Did they all live together, as married partners would?

Only one way to find out.

My second attempt at getting out of bed was more successful than my first, despite my feet still killing me. Pulling the blanket tighter around my shoulders, I made my way to the door and slipped out of the room.

A much larger, open room greeted me on the other side. It reminded me of our shared loft in the capitol, with a couple of couches and armchairs around a stone fireplace. There was a bar and open-concept kitchen at the far end and a dining table where someone was using a sewing machine.

The machine whirred softly, the sound accompanied by a soft humming from the person bent over it in concentration. I walked toward them, my steps light on my tender feet. "Um, hello?"

The machine stopped and its user looked up. A black woman, probably in her thirties, blinked at me in surprise, her long eyelashes sweeping over her cheeks. "Sleeping Beauty finally awakens," she said by way of greeting. Her voice was low and warm, with a soft rasp to it that made me feel immediately at ease.

I certainly didn't feel beautiful though, and I ran a self-conscious hand through my tangled mess of hair. "Guess I've been out a while, huh?"

"Almost a full day." She tossed a long braid over her shoulder as she got up from her chair. "Have a seat. You hungry?"

"Yes, thank you." I nodded and slid into the chair next to hers at the sewing machine. Up close, I could see that she'd been sewing a patch of a black fist onto a leather Sons of Odin cut. I glanced up at her putzing through the kitchen.

"I'm Tiff." She pulled items from the fridge as she spoke, turning a dial on the stove until it clicked three times and blue flames appeared on a burner.

"Kyrie," I answered, mouth watering at the eggs and bacon she set out.

Tiff smiled and let out a soft, knowing chuckle as she cracked eggs into a bowl. "I've heard a lot about you, Miss Kyrie."

"Are you, um…" I hesitated, unsure if my question would be overstepping. "Are you with the Sons?"

"Aha!" Laughter spilled out of her and her amusement was infectious. "*With them,* with them? Like they are with each other? No, but I'm the club treasurer. My man's the VP, you'll meet him soon." Her eyes slid toward a closed door where male voices murmured. "Whenever they finish up in there."

I leaned back with relief. I didn't *think* T-Bone would kiss me, nor would Dyno dance so close to me if they had someone else, but it was nice to have that confirmed.

The door opened just as I wolfed down my food and a tall black man with a shaved head and short beard strode out into the dining room. He was so strikingly handsome that I hitched in a breath, nearly choking on my bacon at the sight of him. But he took no notice of me and went straight for Tiff.

"Fix my patch, baby?" His hands went around her waist, drawing her into him as he leaned down for a kiss.

My eyes immediately took in the silver wedding band on his left hand, and the matching one accompanied by an impressive diamond on hers, as she placed her fingers against his lips, halting his kiss.

"Yes." Tiff's expression was a mixture of amused and annoyed. "Next time, you're fixing it your-damn-self."

Unfazed, he moved her hand aside and took the kiss he wanted. "Thank you, my queen," he added in a low murmur.

The room heated by a few degrees, but Tiff still managed to pull away with a soft chuckle. "Chris, baby, meet our guest, Kyrie Vance."

Chris drew a reluctant gaze away from his wife, noticing me for the first time. He had gorgeous eyelashes for a man—combined with Tiff's, any children they had would win the genetic lottery there—a light dusting of freckles over his cheeks, and an easy, teasing smile.

"You don't look like a crusty old politician," he said by way of greeting.

I lifted one shoulder in a shrug. "Sorry to disappoint?"

He laughed softly, snatching a piece of bacon from the platter on the counter. "You're not disappointing at all, Kyrie."

"No flirting, Chris." The gruff voice came from the same doorway Chris had emerged from, and T-Bone's lumbering steps quickly followed. He stopped at the sight of me, and then came forward and dropped his knees to the floor in front of me, taking one of my hands. "How are you feeling, little lady?"

Well, right then I was short on fucking breath because this massive, gorgeous Viking of a man was literally *kneeling* at my feet.

"Little rough, but okay." I licked my lips, realizing that the salty bacon and eggs had dried out my sore throat again. "I could go for some water."

While Tiff got me a drink, T-Bone examined my hand with a frown. My nails and fingers were still covered in dried blood. *His blood,* I realized, from throwing himself against a barricaded door to get us out. Under my blanket, I still wore the gown from the dinner party. Not even when I was unconscious did they touch me or undress me. I couldn't decide if that was endearing or frustrating.

"How are you?" I asked, taking in T-Bone's appearance. He'd cleaned up, but I noticed his shoulder was bandaged and he kept his arm close to his body.

"None of these fucks are competent at popping a dislocated shoulder back into place, so I pretty much did it myself," he grumbled before flashing me a smile. "But I'll live."

"I got some clothes you can borrow," Tiff said, placing the water in front of me. "You're a teeny little thing, so they might be a bit big on you."

"Thank you." I looked up at her gratefully. Feeding *and*

clothing me? She might have been a decade older than me, if that, but I felt a motherly warmth from her as surely as this blanket around my shoulders. "I'll return them to you and pay you back for the food once I can get my things from my suite."

T-Bone hissed in a breath, his hand tightening around mine. "Yeah, about that." He gave me a sorrowful look. "There's no going back to Sevier, little lady. Not anytime soon."

"What do you mean?" I squinted at him, trying to read the concern in his face. "The attacks on the city will be handled soon, won't they?"

He pulled his bottom lip between his teeth, chewing it as his gaze slid away from me. "This wasn't anything like an attempt on Four Corners. The capital was attacked by Sevier citizens."

"What?" Now I was the one squeezing his hand, silently demanding he look at me again. "Why would they do that?"

"It was an uprising," he said. "The people were fed up with the leadership and took the capitol for themselves." His thumb rubbed over the back of my palm. "They'd been planning it, probably since the beginning."

"Planning it since…wait, what?" I rubbed my forehead, trying to get timelines straightened out in my shock-ridden brain. "Sevier had only been an established territory for two years. It barely had a chance!"

"Some territories only last a few months." T-Bone's tone was apologetic. "Someone else might come in and topple the new leaders soon, we don't know. That's just how the world is right now."

My hands went limp, falling to my lap. His hands continued to surround them—gentle, soothing, and heavy on my thighs. My mind wasn't on his touch for once, but several weeks into the past. I thought back to my first days as an ambassador, when I was so hopeful and full of optimism. I had ideas and plans. I had wanted to give those people a better life, but they took it themselves with violence.

The bone-deep aches in my body were a potent reminder of that.

"T-Bone." My gaze snapped back to him, hands clutching his again. "All those people trapped inside! Did they…did any of them…" I couldn't bring myself to say it. I hadn't exactly made friends in the capitol, but I didn't wish for them to be trapped and burned to death either.

"Some got out. Not everyone, but some." He gave my hands a reassuring squeeze.

"Anita? She told me the staff threw their own party in the kitchens. Oh my God, all the waiters and cooks—"

"Shhh." T-Bone's lips pursed as he made the noise and my mind went back to our kiss. "I'm not certain, but I'm pretty sure I saw Anita and a bunch of staff evacuating out a side door before it got really bad. Maybe they were given a heads up, I don't know. Don't lose hope yet, little lady."

My brain felt like a scrambled hopscotch game, jumping from one thought to the next. All those people. The kiss. The Sons. The valkyrie in my dream. The aches in my body. Why couldn't I focus?

"What about the governor?" I asked next. "His cabinet members and his nephew? Did you see them?"

T-Bone shook his head. "No. I don't know if they made it out."

"Fuck," I breathed, looking up helplessly. "What a waste. They were out of touch with the people, but they didn't deserve to *die*. If I had more time, if I could've just had a year to get them to *listen* to me—"

"An uprising was inevitable with people like *that* in charge." T-Bone's jaw clenched. "Your heart was in the right place, Kyrie, but you couldn't have made them see reason on your own. Violence would have come for them regardless of how long you'd been there."

I hated that he was right. Getting the cabinet to shift their priorities would have been as effective as banging my head against the wall. The best I could have hoped for was incremental change, and even that probably would've taken years. But fire, guns, and explosives? That changed everything overnight.

"Dyno and Grudge are scouting the area now, checking out what the aftermath looks like," T-Bone said. "That'll determine our next move."

I frowned at him. "How so?"

He got up from the floor and took the seat next to me in front of Tiff's sewing machine. I distantly noticed that she and Chris had made themselves scarce, leaving T-Bone and I alone to talk. I also realized I preferred T-Bone closer than far away, and I wished he'd kneel in front of me again. Or pull me into his lap and kiss me like he did in the corridor.

So far, he was making it seem like nothing happened between us at all, and that bothered me more than I wanted to admit.

"We don't know what the rebels' plans are," he explained. "Whether they only intend to take the territory that was Sevier, or expand into other regions." He drummed his fingers on the table. "If it's the latter situation, it wouldn't be safe to take you back to Four Corners right away. They'll be watching the roads for more challengers to their little kingdom. You'd have to lie low with us for a while."

"Who said I wanted to go back to Four Corners?" I huffed without thinking.

T-Bone's lips twitched as though he was hiding a smile. "Your father will learn about the uprising soon, if he hasn't already. He'll be sick with worry and want you safely back at home."

"You mean he'll want to lock me up in my room and never let me out again," I groaned, rubbing my face.

"You would be safe," T-Bone pointed out.

"I'd be a *prisoner*," I shot back, then regretted how melodramatic and whiny that sounded. There were probably survivors of last night's attack who were *actual* prisoners. Maybe even the governor and his nephew.

But T-Bone only gave me a sympathetic look, and it sent an ache of longing through my chest. He and the others never treated me like I was some spoiled, selfish brat. They were some of the few that didn't, and I appreciated that beyond words.

"We don't have to make any decisions right away," he said, getting up from the table. "You're our property now, so you'll be safe here. Try to get some rest for the next few days."

"Sorry, I'm…what?" He definitely did not say what I thought he just said.

T-Bone grinned, rubbing his jaw sheepishly. "Our property. It's just an MC term that means you're under our protection." He dropped his hand, his expression turning serious. "We won't let anything happen to you, Kyrie. Even if your father demands your immediate return." He shook his head, eyes burning with determination. "If you're safer with us, we'll refuse."

All at once, his whole demeanor changed. His shoulders softened and that playful, teasing smile returned. "Get cleaned up and rested, little lady. I'll let you know when the other two are back."

He turned and left then, and I returned to the bedroom I woke up in to find a folded pair of leggings, a sweater, and a towel on the bed. Picking up the towel, I headed for the small, adjoining bathroom. It was tiny, little more than a standing shower and a toilet, but once I stepped under the hot spray, the water pressure and temperature were *divine*.

I didn't realize how filthy and smoky my dress and skin were until I stood under that showerhead. I just stood there, leaning against the wall when my feet ached too much, letting the water wash away everything from the night before.

Except that kiss. I wanted to keep it and hold on to it like the most precious of treasures. Actually, fuck that, I wanted to collect more kisses and build a dragon's hoard worth of them. Not just from T-Bone, but from all three of them.

My mind turned to moments ago when he said I was *their property*. It was jarring in the moment, evoking a reaction I didn't know how to process. What a strange term to signal that I was under protection.

But thinking of it again, it felt possessive. Even primal. And I liked it.

CHAPTER 18

DYNO

Grudge and I returned to the clubhouse in the evening, my ears immediately pricking up at the sound of Kyrie's voice in the kitchen, along with Chris' and Tiff's. *So she's up, and in decent spirits, it sounds like.*

I smiled to myself while I removed my gloves and scraped my boots on the mat in the mudroom. Nothing could ever keep her down—not being kidnapped and definitely not escaping a burning building by the skin of her teeth.

No sooner had I entered the house than T-Bone's form approached with heavy, lumbering steps down the hallway. Munin took off from his shoulder, flying the short distance to land in front of Kyrie at the kitchen table.

His gaze fell to Kyrie, who was petting the raven's head as she listened to Tiff, before landing on me. "You're back." He greeted me with a kiss.

"Yeah, wasn't that much to see, honestly."

T-Bone nudged another kiss at my temple, his hands

going to my shoulder and my waist. "How'd it go? Where's Grudge?"

"Tell you in a minute. He's cleaning a bunch of ash and shit off the bikes." I put my hand over his, turning my head to kiss him again. It never mattered if we were apart for a few hours or weeks, he was always affectionate to the point of clinginess when we came back together.

After spending a childhood as my father's favorite punching bag, I would gladly take being kissed every time I came home instead.

"See that?" I overheard Tiff say to Kyrie. "Since *day one* they've been like that. Smooching like a bunch of teenagers."

Kyrie made a sound that I couldn't quite discern, something like a polite laugh that was also embarrassed. I pulled away from T-Bone to see that her face was red, and she was very intently looking at Munin and not us. Her thighs were also clamped together in her borrowed leggings from Tiff, and she kept chewing on her lip.

She was either uncomfortable, which, considering she'd seen us kiss before, didn't make a lot of sense. That, or she was turned on by it.

Oh, it's definitely that second one. She barely moved, but I saw the subtle shifting of her legs rubbing together.

The blood rushed to my cock in a surge of heat. She was completely off-limits before, but now? She was our property, staying in our home and under our protection. The barriers between had literally crumbled and gone up in flames.

And yet, she was still the daughter of a governor, who would certainly lose his shit if he found out she was shacking up with us.

Fuck, as if it wasn't already hard enough to not fall for

her while at the capitol. Now, while she sat at our breakfast bar? Ate our food? Slept under blankets that my mother and grandmother made? How could she be anything but ours?

Grudge walked in then, grunting a greeting to everyone as he headed for the sink to wash his hands, which were coated in ash and dust. The moment he finished, T-Bone assaulted him with kisses too.

"Alright, we're all here." T-Bone slid behind Grudge and wrapped his arms around the other man's neck. "Time for church." He smacked a kiss on Grudge's cheek before moving them both that way.

"You coming?" I asked Kyrie, who remained seated at the breakfast bar.

"Me?" Her eyes widened. "But I thought church was only for club members."

"That includes club property." I held my hand out to her.

Her teeth sank into her lip again as she slid down from the stool. Another hot pulse hit my cock when she took my hand. *You like being owned by us, don't you?*

I adjusted myself subtly as I led her down the hall. "And anyway," I cleared my throat, "this situation involves you, regardless of your status with the club."

The room we held church in was the home's den, with double doors leading in. It was sparsely furnished, the focal point was just the large dining table we all sat around to discuss club business.

We never closed the doors. T-Bone didn't have a gavel or any official markings of an MC president, except the patch on his cut. After the club was massacred and it was down to just the three of us, it felt silly to keep doing all those little formalities. If our numbers kept growing, maybe we'd pick them up again.

"Have a seat anywhere, little lady. Make yourself comfortable." T-Bone took his spot at the head of the table, with Chris to his right. I took his left, and Kyrie sat next to me. Tiff took the seat next to her husband, and Grudge sat on Kyrie's other side.

"Alright." T-Bone put his palms together on top of the table and looked at me. "What's the damage?"

"A whole fucking lot," I said, with Grudge grunting in agreement. "The capitol building has been razed to the ground."

Kyrie let out a soft gasp. "You mean it's…gone?"

I nodded slowly. "There's nothing left, just rubble where it once stood. What wasn't burnable was likely destroyed by explosives. These people didn't want to just take over the territory, they wanted to completely erase those who came before them."

"A clean slate," Kyrie muttered to herself.

"Was anything else destroyed?" T-Bone asked. "Homes or businesses? Construction sites?"

"See, that's the thing," I said. "We couldn't get close enough to check. Every entry point into the city had an armed guard posted. They didn't tell us who they were with, and obviously we didn't have names of anyone who'd let us in. Best we could do was circle around, go offroad, and climb some hills, but we couldn't see much beyond the smoking ruin where the capitol was."

Grudge raised his arms in the air before lowering his hands slowly to eye level, then made a motion of brush off his shoulders and arms.

"Smoke and ash still pretty bad?" T-Bone asked, to which Grudge nodded.

"Visibility was shit," I added. "The smoke started clearing when we left, but there's ash falling everywhere for miles. Looked like fucking snow right outside of the city. If neighboring territories didn't see the blaze last night, they'll figure out what happened soon."

"Kyrie." T-Bone rubbed the beard on his jaw. "Did you ever find out what Sevier's relationship was with neighboring territories? If they had allies or enemies nearby?"

"I don't know." She shook her head apologetically. "I was never given clearance to attend the foreign relations meetings. Aside from me, they also had ambassadors from Blakeworth, Cascadia, New Jerriton, Texahoma." She pursed her lips. "I think that's all. So it's probably safe to assume relations with those territories were good."

"If they've got guards controlling who comes in and out of the city," Chris mused, "then this can't be a simple uprising of the people, right? There's gotta be a bigger power play here."

"I think you're right," I said. "Those guards had nice, shiny rifles. Clean, matching uniforms, and armored cars. The regular folk of Sevier were struggling badly. They could scrape together an uprising, sure, but the guys we met today were professionals."

"So someone is helping them out, either another territory or a group that's hoping to make its own territory." T-Bone rubbed his forehead. "Can't we all just fuckin' get along? Jesus."

"There is another thing to consider," Tiff said. "If we can't get into Sevier, we can't oversee the alcohol deliveries." Her eyes slid to Kyrie. "I'm assuming you know about that little side business of ours?"

"Oh yeah," Kyrie piped up. "They took me to an underground bar. I had a great time."

"Aw, look at them." Chris grabbed his wife's hand and leaned back as he smiled at her. "They're just like us when we were young."

"If I had to guess, there will be no deliveries coming in and out at all," T-Bone said, ignoring Chris' remark. "Only what's approved by whoever's in charge, I guess."

"So are there any other backward-ass territories that could use our services?"

"That's for you two to find out." T-Bone aimed a big grin at Chris and Tiff. "As for us." His smile faded as his gaze swept to our side of the table. "We have to decide what's safest for our little lady here."

The fact that he called her *ours* sent a delicious thrill through me.

"I don't want to go back to Four Corners," Kyrie announced. "At least, not permanently."

"I understand—"

"No, you don't." She cut T-Bone off with a sharpness I'd never heard from her before. Grudge and I both stared at her. Fuck, the whole table stared. One thing we kept sacred about church was that the president's word was final. No one had ever spoken to Bash like that, and certainly not to T-Bone. But he just looked at her, eyebrows raised imploringly as he waited for her to continue.

Now Kyrie seemed nervous at all the eyes on her and the silence that followed. She placed her hands on the table, gaze focused on her fingers.

"After the three of you saved me the first time," she began softly, "I couldn't go anywhere without a guard. My dad had eyes on me twenty-four seven. Do you have any idea how smothering that is? Never having a minute of privacy, not to eat, sleep, shit, or just… I don't know, stare out a window. Or read a book, or pick at my nail polish. I literally never had a moment to myself. Every time I complained to my dad, he told me it was for my own safety." She pulled in a deep, shuddering breath. "I'm an adult woman with a world-class education. I'm fluent in three languages. And he insisted on treating me like an unruly child because I made the mistake of trusting the wrong guy. You'd think I was the first woman in history to ever do that."

Kyrie's voice grew louder, stronger as she spoke. She looked up from her hands and stared directly at T-Bone. "It took four years before I could even *suggest* leaving Four Corners. So what do you think he'll do when he finds out my former workplace is now a smoking ruin?"

A few beats of silence passed before T-Bone answered. "He'll never let you leave."

"Yes, exactly. So, please, if you care about me at all—" T-Bone inhaled sharply "—you won't take me back there." Her gaze fluttered back down to the table, her insecurity showing once again. "That—that doesn't mean I'll overstay my welcome here. I'll figure something out. I can—"

"You're safest with us," T-Bone growled out. "So here is where you'll stay."

That wasn't entirely true. Objectively speaking, she'd be safest within her father's borders, under the watchful eye of the best military in any territory. But she would be miserable, the joy in her eyes snuffed out for good. And none of us could bear to see her so deeply unhappy.

Kyrie blew out a breath, folding her hands together. "I can keep paying your personal protection fee—"

"Forget that." T-Bone cut a hand through the air. "That fucking contract is dust in a million fuckin' places now. We're not protecting you for a paycheck."

"Well then, give me a role in the club. I don't want to sit around being useless."

A smirk pulled at T-Bone's mouth. "We'll find something for you, little lady."

"While I agree it's best for Kyrie to stay with us," I said. "We should still let her father know she's alive and well."

T-Bone rubbed his jaw. "I agree, but should we say where? And with who?"

"My father trusts you all," Kyrie pointed out.

"He would want us to deliver you straight back to him," I told her. "And if we don't, he might not think so highly of us anymore."

"It's *my* choice," Kyrie huffed. "It's not like you're keeping me here against my will."

Oh, but how we'd like to. An image of her flashed through my head, naked and bound by the soft rope I kept stashed in our drawer. It would make a gorgeous contrast against her skin.

"Hm." Grudge snapped his fingers to get our attention, then made the sign for the letter S.

"S?" Kyrie repeated. "What's S?"

"You talking about Shadow?" I asked.

Grudge nodded and mimed writing out a letter.

"That's perfect, let's do that," T-Bone said. Then, for everyone else to understand, "Grudge will write a coded message to Shadow, in case it gets intercepted. Shadow will let the governor know that Kyrie is safe and well, without revealing too many details."

"Are you talking about Mari's husband?" Kyrie asked. "Big and scarred, but a total sweetheart? That Shadow?"

"That's the one." I elbowed her. "Did you know he and Grudge are brothers?"

Her mouth dropped open in surprise. "No! I can see the resemblance though." She leaned back in her chair, smiling at the man to her right. "Grudge is obviously the cuter one."

He barked out a laugh of surprise, shaking his head as his cheeks flamed red. "Nahhh." His grin was hidden under his beard, but I saw how it lit up his eyes.

"No flirting in church," T-Bone teased with a slap of his palm on the table.

"So Kyrie stays with us," I said, counting off the business items on my fingers. "We lay low and keep an eye out on the activity in Sevier. We have Shadow deliver a message to her father for us. Anything else we need to discuss?"

"There is one thing, yeah." T-Bone went solemn, an odd look for him. "It's in three days."

"What is?"

"You *know* what, Dyno," he growled.

It took me a second but hit me quickly. "Oh, right. The anniversary."

"Yeah, the fuckin' anniversary of our whole club getting fuckin' massacred."

"Easy, T." I raised a calming hand toward him, but I wasn't surprised in the least. He was always in a cantankerous mood when the date came around.

"I'm going to the memorial," he said. "No one else has to come, but I'm leaving tomorrow."

"Dude. You think that's a good idea? With everything else we have going on?"

"It doesn't matter what kind of idea it is, Dyno, or what else there is going on. I will not skip paying my respects to the ones who brought us up just because the timing is inconvenient."

"You don't *have* to go right on the anniversary. We can—"

"Yes, I do."

I released a sigh. It was exhausting arguing with him about any topic, but this one always took the cake. "Well, you shouldn't go alone."

He shook his head. "You guys need to stay here with Kyrie."

"And what if you get ambushed out there? No one rides alone, that's one of our few laws, T."

"Well, I'm not skipping out on this. I don't know what else to tell you guys."

"Uh." Chris spoke up for the first time in several minutes. "There seems to be a pretty simple solution here. What if we all go?"

Tiff nodded her agreement. "Been a while since I've been on a good, long ride. We'll lock this place up tight, keep watch over y'all and the little lady."

The tension in T-Bone's shoulders eased a fraction, his gaze sliding to Kyrie's. "What do you say, Kyrie? Up for a *real* ride?"

She straightened, the excitement already lighting up her face. "I'd love to."

"We'll be closer to Four Corners too," Chris added. "So just in case you want to pay your dear ol' dad a visit, we can probably manage."

Kyrie grumbled something that sounded like, "Don't count on it."

T-Bone thumped his palm on the table. "Alright then. It's a family road trip. We leave first thing tomorrow morning."

CHAPTER 19

KYRIE

T-Bone was in a sullen mood for the rest of the evening and the next day when we set out on our ride. I knew some tragedy had befallen his club a few months before they came for me in Blakeworth, but I didn't know the full extent of it.

The Sons of Odin were once numerous. As a teenager, I remembered seeing a dozen bikers, maybe more, roaring down the streets of Four Corners, all wearing the Sons of Odin patch on their backs. Their faces, hidden under helmets, beards, sunglasses, or balaclavas, whipped past me in a blur. T-Bone, Dyno, and Grudge were once in that sea of leather, muscle, and machinery, completely unknown to me.

And one day, it was only the three of them. A plaque was created and displayed in the foyer of our capitol building. It was made to honor all of the fallen bikers who had helped defend Four Corners in a war against New Ireland, a neighboring territory that was once extremely hostile.

But what exactly had happened to the other Sons of Odin? I had no idea, and none of them seemed eager to talk about it.

I rode with Dyno for the first leg of the journey, then with Grudge for the later part. T-Bone rode some distance ahead of us, while Tiff and Chris guarded the rear. I had naively thought the two of them would double up, but Tiff had her own motorcycle, which she handled and maneuvered with ease. It made me a little envious. Dad would have a heart attack on the spot if I asked him, but I wondered if the Sons would teach me to ride.

We avoided the main roads on the slight chance that hostile troops were en route to Sevier. Instead, we took longer, more scenic routes, and I was ecstatic that we did. Our elevation was high, the air chilly as a result, but the sun was bright. The sky was an endless blue. Gorgeous rock formations stood out like monuments, their stunning orange-reddish hues illuminated by the sun.

Years ago as a child, I learned about the US national parks and that Utah was home to some of the most beautiful natural formations in the world. As I got older, Dad was more and more hesitant to leave home, except for work trips, of course. I had lost hope and then forgotten about wanting to visit all the national parks in person.

There was no longer a government agency protecting these areas, but the striped canyons and the towering rock pillars looked as untouched as ever. Like they'd been here for thousands of years and would keep standing until humans were just a distant memory. I couldn't imagine a better way to experience it all than on the back of a motorcycle. We drove through one canyon so narrow that I could have released Grudge's waist with one arm and touched that smooth wall formed by millions of years of wind and rain.

It felt too soon when we came to a stop. The only evidence that we'd been riding all day was the sun dipping to touch the horizon and the persistent soreness in my thighs. T-Bone pulled over at the mouth of another canyon, this one a shorter distance through, maybe the length of ten motorcycles, but a wider distance between the two walls.

"We'll stop here for the night," T-Bone said when everyone cut their engines. "It'll shelter us from the elements and get nice and cozy once we build a fire." He cocked his head and shot me a grin, apparently in better spirits after the ride. "Hope you don't mind roughin' it, little lady."

"If it's anything like that night after Blakeworth, I'm sure I'll live." Excitement thrummed through me. I liked modern comforts, sure. But I'd never been camping before. Not *actual* camping. And I was never one to turn down a new adventure.

Dyno snorted out a laugh at my response while he dismounted. "It'll be far more comfortable than that."

After I was rescued, the guys drove Mari and me in a stolen Hummer to the middle of nowhere to escape the armed police in the city. Mari and I slept in the car, while the guys kept watch outside. It was cramped but not totally uncomfortable.

I hopped down from behind Grudge, the solid ground a bit disorienting to my feet. "What can I help with?" I asked him.

"Mm-mm." He shook his head and made a shooing motion at me before unbuckling his saddlebags.

"Aw, come on! Let me help." I grabbed hold of his

forearm and looked directly up at him, my best pouty lip and wide, innocent eyes on display. "Please?"

The corded muscles jumped under his tattooed skin. My fingers itched to explore up the length of that arm, to his bicep and shoulder where the valkyrie tattoo was hidden under his sleeve.

Grudge smiled bashfully while looking away from me, huffing out a soft laugh. When he met my eyes again, it was with a look that said, *Oh, alright.*

"Yes!" I fist-pumped the air with my victory, and he laughed again before handing me a stack of folded tarps from his saddlebag.

Once Chris and T-Bone checked out the canyon and made sure it was clear of critters, I spread out the tarps where we'd set up tents and sleeping bags. I hunted down a few heavy rocks to hold down the corners while Tiff set up a cooking fire in the center. The guys got tents set up with sleeping bags inside, and once night fell, the six of us were cozy around a roaring fire.

Chicken thighs sizzled on a cast-iron cooking grate over the flame. Next to the meat, a pot of rice bubbled as it cooked. It was a simple dinner, but perfect. A collection of seasonings and sauces stood off to the side for when the food was ready. The logs crackled, and in the distance, coyotes sang their song.

I pulled the blanket tighter around my shoulders and couldn't stop grinning. It was just us and the open, wild wilderness. Everything about this was so unlike anything I'd ever experienced. I was among friends, safe while also free. And there was just enough danger, just enough wild and unknown in that endless darkness beyond our campfire to send a thrill up my spine.

"Hey, Dyno," Chris called across the fire from where

he cuddled up with Tiff. "You bring your thing?" He wiggled his fingers in a motion that suggested some kind of musical instrument.

Dyno smiled as he poked the fire with a long tree branch. "Never go anywhere without it."

"Has Kyrie heard you play?"

"Nah."

"Play what?" I asked. "I want to hear."

T-Bone finished turning over the chicken thighs and plopped down next to me. "He acts like a shy motherfucker but he loves it, and he's actually really good." Then louder, "Just play the damn thing, D."

Dyno set aside his branch and scooted back to sit next to Grudge, folding his legs in front of him as he reached into his cut. "Kyrie, have you heard of Kokopelli?"

"No, I don't think so."

He produced a slim, wooden flute from his cut, long fingers automatically placing over a few of the holes. "Kokopelli is a fertility deity of my mother's people, the Hopi tribe. He presides over agriculture and childbirth." Dyno raised the flute toward his mouth, still smiling. "He's also the spirit of music and is always depicted playing a flute."

"He also used to be depicted with a big ol' boner," T-Bone added informatively.

I nearly spat out the water I'd been drinking. "Seriously?"

"Yeah, because of the whole fertility thing. That is, until his image was cleaned up by the prudes that colonized this area. I always did find interesting that the Hopi had a male fertility god, because it's usually a female—"

"Will you let the man play some damn music?" Tiff threw a pebble at T-Bone.

"Anyway," Dyno said with a laugh. "I hope you enjoy, and if Kokopelli moves you to join in, feel free."

Silence fell over the camp as Dyno brought the mouth-piece to his lips. There was a beat of silence as he took a breath, and then the music began.

The flute sounds were lower-pitched than I expected, warm and with a rough texture to the sound that had to be a result of grooves in the wood. It sounded like a wind whistling through trees and canyons, wild and ancient, but controlled by Dyno's breaths and his fingers moving over the air holes.

I didn't realize I started swaying to the music until my shoulder bumped into T-Bone's chest. I looked up at him to apologize, but he just smiled and started moving with me, the heat of his broad chest sliding gently against my back.

Chris and Tiff moved too, their bodies shifting every time Dyno hit a different beat. Chris started drumming a matching beat on his knees while Tiff hummed along with the song. Their eyes closed as they swayed, letting the music take them.

I couldn't find words to describe it. The music was beautiful, yes, but also passionate as the notes rose and fell. It had started gently but I could feel the intensity of the song as it went on, and Dyno's concentration as he played. Someone started clapping along, I didn't know who because my eyes had fallen shut too. I clapped too, the strike of my palms against each other adding to the vibrations thrumming against my skin. The air felt almost solid, tangible, like it was a living thing.

It felt magical.

The song hit its climax, the notes transitioning faster than ever before. Somewhere distantly, I swore I could hear the valkyrie from my dream drumming against her shield to the music too. Everything was connected and alive, so why shouldn't she join in? If I let my eyes slit open, I would not have been surprised to see Kokopelli himself dancing around the fire as he played his flute along with Dyno.

As the music slowed, gently nearing the song's end, the vibrations through the air only became more prominent. My skin buzzed with awareness, and my pulse thrummed in every sensitive point in my body—my chest, my lips, my neck.

Between my legs.

T-Bone's chest was a pulsing wall against my back, his heart beating in time with mine. When my eyes fluttered open, I became aware of his hand resting on the side of my hip. The weight and heat of him so close to me registered all at once, and that only amplified my senses more.

I looked through half-hooded eyes across the fire, curious about the state of the others. Chris and Tiff were wrapped up in each other, kissing aggressively while scooting toward their tent. The song had ended mere moments ago, and Dyno's mouth was now in a firm lock with Grudge's. The two men pawed and groped at each other, kissing like they needed the other one for air.

A soft groan rumbled out of the chest behind me. T-Bone and I were watching them both, a pair of voyeurs. My core throbbed harder, the sensation near overwhelming now. I was frozen in place but was desperate to move, to slide against T-Bone and feel more of him. To see if he'd soothe this pulsing ache between my legs, if he'd call the other two over here to help. Or they could just keep playing with each other and let us watch. I didn't care, I needed it all.

I straightened, tilting my gaze up to T-Bone's face. He

was honestly so handsome up close, in a rough, brutal way. His beard was peppered with gray in some areas, and there was a bare spot under his chin that indicated some kind of scar. His mouth was relaxed in a soft smile, but his eyes were sharp and alert as a hunter's. Firelight danced in his irises and made his skin glow. He was looking straight ahead, gaze fixated on his two lovers manhandling each other.

My pulse hammered as I leaned into him, focusing on a spot just under his beard on his neck. I was just as terrified as I was emboldened. He had already kissed me, so what was the big deal?

He might not want to stop at kissing. That was what scared me most. Dyno and Grudge were already running hands under clothing, grasping at bare skin and other areas they knew and had plenty of practice with. Unlike me.

But these men were the *only* people I felt safe with. If I couldn't take a leap of faith with them, I couldn't with anyone.

I leaned in until my lips connected to T-Bone's neck. His skin was so warm and surprisingly soft there. He stilled as his pulse thrummed under my mouth.

"Kyrie." His voice was so rough, I swore I felt it caress over my skin.

"Travis," I murmured back before placing another kiss, this time darting my tongue out to give a small lick to his skin. He tasted a little smoky and salty.

"What are you doing, little lady?" He brought a hand to my shoulder and gently pushed me away. His head dipped and he was staring at me now, but not with the heated desire from watching his men moments ago. It looked like confusion, his brows furrowed and mouth frowning.

"I...I thought..." The rejection hit me like a kick to the chest. I struggled to regain my breath, my mind reeling as I tried to figure out what the fuck I'd gotten so wrong. "You kissed me at the capitol, so I thought..."

T-Bone edged away from me until no parts of us were touching. He couldn't look at me again, his expression sorrowful as he focused on the fire. "I'm sorry. I shouldn't have done that."

My body refused to accept it. I ached for his warmth and his touch so much that it *hurt*. It felt so cruel of him to just tear that away. I curled my fingers into a fist to avoid reaching out for him again. And my mind couldn't make heads or tails of any of his behavior since that kiss.

"But just now..." I knew it was stupid to keep talking, keep fighting this after he made himself clear, but it just poured out of me. "During the song, you were so close. You were...*holding* me."

"I'm sorry, Kyrie," he repeated. "You don't want someone like me. Like us." He lifted his chin to refer to the other two. "We're no good for a woman like you." He rose to his feet and awkwardly dusted off his pants. "Goodnight. Sleep well."

With that, he walked over to the next tent and left me alone in front of mine.

CHAPTER 20

T-BONE

"What the fuck did you say to her?" Dyno hissed in my face. Not the way I liked to be greeted first thing in the morning, but understandable.

"What we all should have said weeks ago," I muttered, stuffing my folded up tent and sleeping bag into the saddlebag of my bike.

It was the next morning, everyone noticed the shift in Kyrie's mood, no matter how much she smiled and tried to shove down the hurt that was written so clearly on her face. She clearly didn't sleep either, her eyes exhausted and swollen with redness.

And it's all your fucking fault, you piece of shit.

A hard shove pressed to my shoulder, making me stumble back a few steps. Grudge had taken Dyno's place, scowling and getting in my face. Clearly, he wasn't satisfied with my answer.

"Can we handle this later?" I grumbled irritably.

"When we're not on our way to visit the site of our entire dead club?"

Grudge shook his head disapprovingly, his jaw clenched, but he got out of my way to pack up his own stuff. I sighed heavily, ignoring all the glares in my direction as I secured my belongings.

I knew I'd been a grumpy fucking bastard since church yesterday. Kyrie and the others didn't deserve that. The guys were rightfully treating me like an asshole. This fucking day, the event that marked this day, they just haunted me, and I didn't know how to make it stop.

The original Sons of Odin were our family, and we'd failed them. Dyno and Grudge grieved in their own ways and, for the most part, seemed to come to terms with it. Five years had passed since it happened, after all. But for some reason, I just couldn't fucking let go.

Bash, our former president, was the first man I fell in love with. I owed him everything for making me the man I was. With years of patience and guidance, he helped me unlearn every toxic belief about myself. He even gave me his blessing to pursue relationships with Dyno and Grudge when I developed feelings for them as well.

Toward the end, Bash and I were more platonic than romantic, but it never felt like our relationship had *ended*. It just changed as time went on and we grew older. He wanted to dote on his children before they got too old, but I never felt ready for a settled-down family life. I fell head over heels for Dyno and Grudge, and because of my foundation with Bash, I was able to be a good partner to them, not a vile piece of shit like I'd been in the past. Bash saved my life, saved the people I would've hurt if I didn't change, and I'd always love him deeply for that.

And then he was just gone.

How was I supposed to move on? Become president in his stead? Fall in love with someone else? A woman, no less?

I hated hurting Kyrie, but I had to turn her down last night. Not only did she deserve better than an outlaw nearly twice her age, she didn't deserve to compete with a dead man. I could do casual sex, no problem. I could tease and flirt with her. I could love the two men Bash had already known and approved of, but my heart was too twisted, too complicated of a place for her. She deserved an equal share, and I longed to give that to her, but I didn't know if I was capable of giving any more.

Munin sat perched on my handlebars, making soft vocalizations and tilting his head as he watched me violently pack my shit.

"You know what's coming," I said, stroking his chest feathers. "Are you ready to say hello to your brother?"

The raven cooed like a dove and hopped higher up my handlebars, bobbing his head up and down in a humanlike *yes* motion.

I chuckled softly. "Yeah, I miss him too."

Just like in the Norse sagas, Munin had been one of a pair. His brother, Hugin, had been Bash's raven. Like me, Bash could see through Hugin's eyes. Our ravens and this unique ability was just another thread that tied us together, another festering wound that refused to heal.

Dyno, Grudge, and I had been away reporting to Governor Vance in Four Corners when the fire hit our clubhouse. I regretted going on that ride every moment of every day. When everyone inside perished, I assumed the same had happened to Hugin. We never saw him again.

Once done packing, I started up my bike and headed out of the canyon, not bothering to see if the others were following. They'd catch up soon enough. I couldn't be their president right now and they knew that. I was a grieving mess, and every year, they allowed me to be just that.

It was only a few hours of riding before we reached the spot. It was easy to miss these days, with most of the charred ruins disintegrating with time. Some shrubs and grasses had sprouted at the site of our old clubhouse, with only hints of the black scar on the ground poking through. Saguaro cacti stood tall like guardians of this resting place. Mountains rose in the distance, striped with oranges and reds. I once considered this desert my home. I realized too late that my home had been the people who were taken from me. All except for two.

I cut my engine and was only distantly aware of the others riding up behind me. They turned off their bikes and silence fell over our surroundings. Everyone knew better than to talk to me while I was here.

It felt…peaceful here. I knew our friends the Steel Demons MC came out here and paid their respects not long after the massacre had happened. Maybe that had been enough to lay everyone to rest. If only I could take some of that peace for myself and not feel so damn guilty for being alive.

Munin flew from my handlebars as I dismounted my bike and started toward the burn site. He landed on one of the smaller cacti and cawed, gesturing down with his beak. I frowned. This was new.

"What is it, Munin?" I knelt down in front of the cactus, touching my fingers to the gravelly soil in front of it.

He cawed louder, flapping his wings excitedly, and hopped up and down on the cactus.

Curious, I began a shallow dig with my fingers. I didn't have to go far before I touched something smooth, dragged my finger along it, and felt a sharp corner. Digging with both hands now, it was just a few minutes before I found all four edges of a picture frame. My digging became frantic, which had to make me look like a maniac to everyone else, but fuck if I cared.

I lifted the picture frame from the ground and got hit with an intense wave of memories once I wiped the glass clean.

"Fuck," I choked out through my closed-up throat.

It was of Bash and I, taken on some disposable camera nearly fifteen years ago. We were hugging each other, grinning like idiots. I remembered the tight squeeze of his arms, the smell of his cigarettes. Despite how drunk I must have been, I remembered that party clearly and how happy everyone was.

I rubbed my finger over the glass, staring at that immortalized moment, now damaged by years of dirt, sun, wind, and rain. My chest squeezed with the yearning to go back to that time, when club life was nothing but a fun adrenaline rush. Racing through the desert, chasing highs, and chasing the people I wanted to fuck. Life was so much simpler back then, and it sure as shit didn't hurt as much as now.

"I don't know what to do," I confessed to the photograph. "I don't know how to let you go."

Munin let out a soft series of caws and clicks then, almost like he was chiding me.

I looked up, angrily meeting the eyes set in the inky black feathers. "Do you even know what this is like? Hugin isn't here anymore, either. Do you know what it means to miss someone, you stupid fucking bird?"

Yes.

That single world knocked me flat on my ass. It was in my head but also in the breeze. I heard stories of gods communicating to people, but never their messengers. Munin had lent me his eyes for years, but I never heard him speak a word to me.

"What's happening?" I whispered, keeping my eyes locked on the raven. "Why are you talking to me *now*?"

You have made yourself lost, Travis. No one is meant to live in the past, but you have kept yourself there.

"Well, can you fucking blame me? I lost everything! I lost *him*." I stabbed a finger at the protective glass covering the photo.

And yet you have everything in those five people standing over there. Munin turned his head, pointing his beak to where Grudge, Dyno, Kyrie, Chris, and Tiff stood by the bikes, watching me with tense expressions. *You can't have lost everything while still having something. It's impossible.*

"Well, shit, thanks for the fucking lesson." I looked down at the photo, running my finger over Bash's face again. "I just...I don't ever want to forget him."

Then remember him.

"But what if I don't?" I returned my gaze to the raven, my throat tight just as I found the ability to voice my fears for the first time. "What if I go days and weeks without thinking about him? What if I start to forget what he looked like?" My eyes dropped to the photo again, as if I was in danger of losing Bash's face from my mind at that very moment.

You won't.

"But how do you know?" I demanded. "People are forgotten all the time, and Bash deserves better."

Because I have been with you this whole time.

I narrowed my eyes, not understanding, then my heart jumped into my throat. "Bash?"

No, Travis. The bird cocked his head from left to right as he looked at me. *I am Memory.*

A scene played out in my head right then, one of my many conversations with Bash from years ago that I thought I'd forgotten.

"Odin had two ravens he would send out into the world for information," Bash had said, the details of his face obscured by cigar smoke. "They were Hugin and Munin, thought and memory. Through these ravens was how he obtained his wisdom."

"Did the birds talk?" I had asked, just to humor him. "Or did he see through them?"

"Both. He gave them the gift of speech and also went into trance-like states when his mind journeyed with them." Bash had gone quiet then, carefully ashing his cigar before puffing it back to life. "There's a poem in the Poetic Edda, I'm sure Grudge knows it, where Odin is worried about his ravens returning. Interestingly, he seems to be more worried about Munin returning than Hugin."

"Why's that?"

Bash went quiet again, almost meditatively still, while wisps of smoke drifted around his head and shoulders. "Because if Munin doesn't return, his memories are lost forever."

The very next day, we happened upon two raven chicks that appeared to have fallen out of a nest. Neither one of us had understood the compulsion to take care of the screaming baby birds, but we didn't fight it either. Their names had come to us effortlessly, with barely a thought. Hugin had bonded to Bash. Munin chose me.

I stared at the adult raven now, on the precipice of

some greater understanding that was just out of reach. When it finally hit me, it felt like stepping off the edge of a cliff.

"Did you know he would become a memory to me? And that's why you've stayed?"

Munin cawed softly. *All things become memories in time. Some are painful, but you are not honoring Bash's memory by remaining embroiled in the pain of his loss. He does not want this for you.*

The fact that he referred to Bash in the present tense made my heart stop. "How…? Is he…?" I didn't even know what I was trying to ask.

He is at peace. Beyond that, I do not know.

That knowledge made me feel lighter, like a boulder sitting on my chest for years had been lifted. I looked at the photo of us one more time and the cutting ache of seeing his face eased slightly.

"Can I keep this?" I wondered aloud.

Memories are meant to be kept. Bash desires nothing of this world, except for your happiness.

"Why does it feel wrong though? I feel…guilty about feeling happy."

You feel guilty because you believe it should have been you instead. You've ventured so far into your pain and grief that its familiarity is comforting. To release your pain and step fully into the present takes courage, Travis. The bird stretched his wings out to the sides before resettling them against his body. *That is why I am here. To guide you out of the past so your memories can be just that, memories.*

I always knew, to some extent, that it wasn't fair to Dyno and Grudge that I remained so stuck on losing Bash. They never complained about my years-long grieving process, but that wasn't an excuse to not be fully present with them. They deserved more of me. And now with Kyrie potentially in the mix, all three of them deserved a better me. I just wasn't sure if I had it in me to be that man.

Bash believed I could be.

My grip tightened on the picture frame. "And you, well, my memory of him, won't ever leave me?"

Munin made a series of noises that sounded like chuckling. *I am bound to you for this purpose, among others.*

"Others? Like what?"

He fluffed up his feathers and smoothed them down again, beak open with more of that odd laughter. *What fun is going through life already knowing all of its mysteries?*

"It's gonna be like that, huh?"

I looked to the side, taking in the others who had started walking through the burn site. Kyrie stood before a pile of charred logs, hands shoved in the pockets of the oversized jacket she had borrowed, probably mine. She met my eyes, brow furrowed with concern, before looking away quickly.

The pang of rejecting her cut through me again. That was not how Bash wanted me to be, not the person he saw me as. If he were here, I could tell him all about the beautiful girl who occupied so many of my thoughts. He'd listen to me ramble without any jealousy, grinning through cigar smoke as I went on and on about how she was so vibrant and sweet and fearless. Then he'd tell me to get off my ass and go after her.

But first, I had to own up to being a dick and apologize.

I slid the photo into a pocket as I stood up, when a thought occurred to me.

"Does *she* have anything to do with these other purposes?" I asked Munin.

The raven spread his wings and flew the short distance to my shoulder, then playfully nipped my ear with his beak.

She may.

CHAPTER 21

KYRIE

We left the burn site not long after T-Bone finished kneeling in front of a cactus. He looked to be talking to Munin for part of it while holding something in his hands, but I couldn't be sure.

T-Bone said a quick word to Chris, then headed directly to his bike without saying anything else. He straddled the machine and started it up, while I looked confusedly to the others.

Was that it? I wondered. He had seemed so insistent about coming here, I was surprised he wanted to leave so quickly.

"We'll be staying at a service center in friendly territory," Chris told the rest of us. "We'll lay low there and see if we hear anything else about Sevier."

"Is T-Bone okay?" I asked Dyno when we all made ready to follow their president.

"Your guess is as good as mine." He squeezed my locked hands on his flat stomach and threw a smile at me over his shoulder. "After what he did to you last night, I'm surprised you're asking."

"Well, I still care about him." The statement came out easily, despite still reeling from the rejection last night.

Dyno squeezed my hands once more before returning his grip to the handlebars. "He'll be fine. We'll make sure of it."

We rode a couple hours south and parked in front of a sprawling building that was clearly pre-Collapse. The exterior was old with peeling paint, but was otherwise well-kept. The windows of the many rooms were clean and the surrounding landscaping was trimmed back and maintained.

T-Bone cut his engine and immediately went to the front door, the rest of us following. Chris held the door open for the rest of us while muttering about what the hell was T's problem. We spilled into a spacious lobby with low couches in front of coffee tables and a long bar on the opposite side.

Surprisingly, the place appeared to be staffed entirely by women. From what I'd heard, it was usually pimps who ran service centers and pushed women to sell their bodies to travelers passing through. But these women didn't look like sex workers. They were fully dressed, for one thing. And even more surprisingly, they were armed.

One woman who looked to be in her late thirties held a rifle across her body. She planted her booted feet wide at T-Bone's approach, a clear sign for him not to go any further.

"Y'all look like trouble," she remarked, eying each one of us. "And we don't take kindly to trouble around here."

"No trouble, you can relax," T-Bone said. She didn't

look convinced until he added, "we're friends with the Demons."

The woman's eyebrows lifted just a fraction. "Name one."

"Reaper."

The woman scoffed. "Everybody knows *him*."

"Jandro, then."

She scoffed again and rolled her eyes.

"Mariposa," I piped up with Mari's full name.

The woman's eyebrows shot up at that, her gaze landing heavily on me. "I haven't heard that name in a long-ass time." She released the barrel of her rifle to touch low on her stomach, her fingers drifting out toward her hip.

"Gretchen!" she barked, slinging her weapon over her shoulder. "Get these folks set up with food and somethin' to drink." She held up an index finger and hovered it in front of T-Bone's nose. "The girls aren't for sale. You get one chance to keep your hands to yourself. That goes for all of you."

"Got it."

"I'm Kitty. Come to me if you need anything." She was more relaxed from moments before but kept her eyes sharply on us as she turned away. "I'll show you to your rooms. Then you can come back down to eat."

"Thank you, Kitty," I said as we all moved to follow her.

Her eyes lingered on me before facing forward to lead us up a set of stairs. She looked curious, maybe even a little judgmental about someone like me hanging out with bikers. But whatever thoughts she had, she kept to herself.

We took up three rooms—Chris and Tiff together, the trio in another room, and I had a room to myself. It was sweet of them to consider my privacy, but I couldn't fully ignore the stab of loneliness. Everyone had a bed partner, except me. I'd slept alone in big bedrooms my whole life, and I was sick of it.

Still, I accepted the room key from Kitty with a smile and no complaints. I had only been in my room for a few minutes, putting away my borrowed changes of clothes into dresser drawers, when a gentle knock came to my door.

"Come in," I called, smoothing out one of Tiff's shirts on the bed so it wouldn't wrinkle. My door creaked open, and I froze in shock at seeing T-Bone on the other side.

"Hey," he said softly. "Can we talk for a minute?"

"Uh, yeah! Yeah, of course." I moved my things off the bed and smoothed out the duvet cover while my heart raced and I tried to compose myself. *What does he want? Oh shit, this talk is gonna suck.*

T-Bone closed my door and sat a few feet away from me on the edge of the bed. He moved slowly, as though he didn't want to spook me. He looked thoughtful for a few moments before opening his mouth to speak, but my flustered nerves beat him to the punch.

"I'm really sorry I misunderstood things. It won't happen again." I stuck my hands between my thighs so I wouldn't wring them. "I'd love to keep you on as my bodyguard. If you want to, that is. Fuck, I'm rambling. I'm sorry, I didn't mean to make this weird."

I stared down at my legs, my face burning while wishing I could hide under the bed. T-Bone only laughed that soft, dry chuckle of his.

"I swear, hearing you say *fuck* is the cutest fuckin' thing I've ever heard."

My confusion only mounted, and I slid a wary glance

toward him. He scratched his beard with a soft smile, whiskey-colored eyes bright from the window light. The bed was big and he was just sitting on the edge, but he looked big enough to take over the whole thing. He didn't look angry, but I'd never seen T-Bone so quiet before.

"You didn't misunderstand anything, Kyrie," he said with a thick swallow. "I was just a dick, and I'm sorry."

"You…you don't have to say that to make me feel better." I was still confused, but I offered a strained smile. "It's okay."

"No, it's not okay." His mouth hardened with the firmness of his tone. "I was pushing down my own feelings and I hurt you in the process."

My stupid heart dared to lift with hope. "Your…feelings?"

T-Bone nodded. "When the guys and I first met you years ago, it was a few months after Bash died. After," he paused to swallow again, "*everyone* died."

I scooted closer to him on instinct, my hand reaching for his forearm. "T-Bone, you don't have to—"

"Yes, I do." His hand covered mine, eyes blazing with intensity. "I'm not good with words, but please let me get this out, Kyrie."

It was painful for him, I could see that plainly. I wondered for a second if the kiss wasn't a misunderstanding after all, if I should kiss him now as a distraction. But my confidence was still bruised from my first attempt, and telling me this story was clearly important to him. So I nodded and squeezed his forearm in support, running my thumb over the tattoos there.

"So, obviously, I was still in a dark place when we went out to get you. Externally, I was running on autopilot, just going through the motions. But inside, I was a fucking mess. All of us were, but mostly me because…"

"You and Bash were lovers," I said softly. No one had told me that explicitly, but I gathered it from how important visiting the burn site was to T-Bone.

"We were, and more," he affirmed with a nod. "He was…like a mentor and best friend too. He taught me how to be a better person. A better lover to them." T-Bone angled his head toward the door, referring to Dyno and Grudge. "Bash and I weren't sexually or even emotionally exclusive. His primary partner was the mother of his children. I never slept with her though." T-Bone coughed, his face reddening. "Shit, this is probably too much information, but what I'm getting at is that Bash and I had a closeness that was beyond romantic or sexual." He smiled, sheepish and adorable. "Am I making a lick of sense?"

"You are." I smiled back. "That sounds really beautiful, what you two had. Bash sounds like he was an amazing person." Another pang of envy hit me. His relationship with Dyno and Grudge seemed so warm, wholesome, and supportive. And he'd had another relationship like that before them. It all seemed so romantic and like something out of a fairytale. Something I never had the chance to experience.

"He really was. He would have adored you." T-Bone sighed, pausing for another few moments. "When we got you out of Blakeworth and were riding back home, it was like…I was seeing the sun for the first time in months. I felt the wind and the warmth on my skin like I was finally remembering how to be alive." He met my eyes again. "All because of this beautiful girl who was having the time of her life on a motorcycle after spending a week locked up in a tower."

My heart thundered in my chest and I found myself scooting closer, until my leg nearly brushed his. The pull to be near him, to be curled up in the safety of that broad chest, was nearly impossible to fight now. "That ride *was* the best time of my life. I felt alive too. It was…" I forced a shuddering, nervous breath from my chest. "It was the first and only time I felt actually free."

"Kyrie…"

The way he said my name brought a rushing pulse of heat between my legs. I was so taken aback by how quickly I was aroused that I barely processed his arm sliding around my back, pulling me closer. Our legs were firmly in contact now, outer thighs pressed together while his hand stroked gently toward my far hip. It wasn't until his rough cheek nudged against mine, lips barely grazing my face, that my mouth decided to ruin the moment.

"It hurt so badly when you guys left," I confessed in a rushed whisper. "I thought I'd never see you again. And now that you're here, I'm so scared you're going to drop me off in Four Corners and leave me alone again."

T-Bone pulled away, and I hated how the warmth of him dissipated. His face hovered in front of me, every beautifully rugged feature in crisp detail. He had a pale scar on his forehead and small tinges of green in his eyes that I'd never noticed before.

"Little lady, we never wanted to leave you." His voice was rough. "We probably could have handled it better, but we felt like our hand was forced." He rubbed a knuckle over my cheekbone. I didn't even realize a tear had fallen until he wiped it away. He then kissed the same spot so tenderly, I felt another rush of moisture to my eyes. "Will you let me explain?"

I nodded, sitting a bit further away and sniffling to

compose myself. Both of our hands became intertwined, resting on our legs between us.

"I won't presume to know how you feel about the three of us," T-Bone began. "But we all felt something for you back then. Speaking only for myself, it felt wrong to start falling for someone new so soon after Bash died. It felt wrong to feel…happy. And I've never…" His fingers squeezed around mine when he paused. "I've never developed feelings for a woman before. I didn't know that I could. I was just…very confused about everything I was feeling and didn't know how to handle it all."

"I never imagined you guys thought twice about me," I admitted with a sheepish laugh. "I was crushing madly on all three of you. I had no idea what any of you were going through, I just wished you noticed me more."

"We absolutely did, little lady. We still do." T-Bone looked down at our hands, his forehead almost touching mine. "The other reason we left was more for, let's say, business reasons."

"My father wasn't fair to you when you worked for him," I said flatly.

T-Bone lifted his gaze to me with an affectionate smile. "Should've known you'd read between the lines. I never wanted to talk shit about him to you."

"It's fine. I understand," I sighed. "My whole life is defined by my father being unfair."

"That's not true," T-Bone chided gently. "You are so smart and driven to do good. You can do anything you want."

"Not if my dad gets his way."

T-Bone growled, another sound I felt directly between my legs. "You are your own person, Kyrie. Only you get to decide what defines your life."

"I just wish people would take me seriously," I sighed. "Just because I'm a girl, or that I was sheltered my whole life, and not by my own choice, doesn't mean I'm stupid."

"I don't think that," T-Bone said. "None of us do."

I frowned at him. "But you make fun of me when I say *fuck.*"

His smile widened. "I do not. I just tell you it's cute because it is." I grunted in protest and he laughed, his smile turning sympathetic. "I'm sorry you didn't get much of a chance to make waves in Sevier. Your time will come, little lady."

"Thank you, T-Bone."

I looked down at our joined hands and felt him brush a kiss on my forehead. He was being so sweet, making it so easy to melt into him, that it was overwhelming. If I tipped forward, he would surely catch me and hold me. As much as I wanted that, hesitation still pulled me back.

"So, at the memorial today…"

"Oh, right. Yeah." T-Bone cleared his throat and took a deep breath. "I think it finally clicked for me that Bash is at peace, and he would want me to be happy. I have our memories. I'm the person I am because of him. But I can't stay stuck in the past, can't keep dwelling on how much losing him hurts." He gave me a wobbly smile. "Not when I have three amazing people who are right here with me."

"Still, I'm so sorry for what happened." My hand itched to touch his face, to offer what little comfort I could to this man. "Can I ask, the fire… Was it an accident?"

His eyes closed, head shaking slowly from side to side. "No."

A small gasp escaped me, and my hands squeezed tighter around his as if I could protect him from such a loss. "Fuck, I'm so sorry, T-Bone."

"The people responsible were dealt with." His tone hardened, making it clear he didn't want to talk about it further. "But it didn't help, you know. It didn't make me feel better. Nothing did." A crooked smile returned to his face. "Besides time, a little chat with Memory, and realizing I was a damned fool to turn down a kiss from a beautiful girl."

"I'm glad you're healing. I can't imagine what it must have been like." I wasn't ignoring the last part of what he said, I just didn't know how to address it. Did he just want to kiss me? Or more? And did he still want to play with others like he mentioned back at the party?

"You said you weren't…exclusive with Bash?" My voice trembled with nerves, eyes fixed on our laced fingers.

He cleared his throat uncomfortably. "Uh, yeah. That's correct. With everyone's knowledge, of course."

"…And it's the same with Dyno and Grudge?"

"No, it's not the same," he said quickly. "The three of us have been emotionally committed to each other for years. Physically, we've been…open to bringing others in, to spice things up on occasion. But we have rules."

"Oh." My face burned. "Such as?"

T-Bone's smile went wider, amusement lighting up his eyes. "It doesn't matter. I don't think any of us want casual fucking anymore. We've all got it bad for a certain girl."

He drew my gaze up with a finger under my chin, looking at me with such warmth and affection. And still I could only squeak out, "Me?"

"Yes, you. What have I been saying this whole time?" he huffed out with laughter. "It's taken four years and running into you again, but we've all pretty much admitted we're crazy about you." His hand dropped from my face, smile wilting. "We just didn't want to overwhelm you with our own wants. And, you know…"

"The fact that I'm an ambassador-slash-governor's daughter and you're hired muscle who are all outlaw bikers?" I ventured.

"Yeah, that," T-Bone sighed. "Not to mention that we're old farts, you're young and beautiful, and there's three of us." He swallowed. "Your father, shit, any government you work with, would clutch all the pearls in the sea at just *one* of those things."

"You're right." I finally reached for his face, my palm finding the warmth and texture of his bearded cheek. "So fuck what they think."

There was a beat of silence as T-Bone's gaze dropped to my lips, his head leaning into my hand for a moment. The next thing I knew, I was tasting him.

His lips slid over mine, warm and pulsing. We opened up and our tongues met in the middle, more than ready to continue the erotic dance they'd started back in that corridor. T-Bone slid an arm around my back, holding my hip and turning me to face him. I reacted instinctively, spreading my legs open and straddling his thighs. My hands went to his shoulders, his neck, then dragged through his hair. It was so freeing to finally touch him, taste him, explore him.

I felt frenzied, kissing him desperately and running my hands all over him like I was trying to make up for years in these mere moments. I wanted to inhale him like a drug, to feel him everywhere at once. T-Bone, on the other hand, was the epitome of calm. He made each kiss linger for several seconds, hands moving in slow, sensual passes from my waist to the nape of my neck.

"Take it easy, little lady," he chuckled, kissing the

corner of my jaw. "We don't have to rush nothin'." His beard sent the most delicious shivers over my skin, and that only made me clutch at him harder.

"I want to." My core throbbed with a greedy ache, and I ground myself against the hardening erection in his jeans. "Please. I don't want to wait. I just want you."

"Hold on, beautiful. Let's time out real quick." He took gentle hold of my arms, putting a few inches of space between us. "Have you had sex before?"

My face burned. I must have turned red enough, because he gave me a skeptical look and I knew it wouldn't be worth lying. "No."

T-Bone's shoulder's deflated with a sigh of breath.

"You're relieved," I noted.

"Yeah, I am," he admitted.

"Because no other man has touched me before?"

He snorted out a laugh before catching himself. "What? No, I don't give a fuck about that." Leaning in, he kissed me so tenderly that my chest erupted in flutters. His arms came around me again, bringing me toward his chest until his lips touched down to my shoulder. "I'm just relieved that the Blakeworth prick never got a chance to hurt you."

Touched beyond words, I wrapped an arm around his neck and let my other hand drift down his back. "It was hard to trust men for a while," I admitted, nuzzling his ear. "I still don't, not really. You three are the only ones I trust."

"Men are dirtbags, especially to women." He kissed my cheek, palms running up my back with such delicious pressure, I wanted to moan. "But you're safe with us, Kyrie. I give you my word as president, we'll never harm you or make you feel unsafe."

I pulled back just enough to hold his face, nudging my

nose against his. "The Sons of Odin are the only ones who've ever made me feel that way."

Our mouths connected in an intense kiss, the momentum sending my back flat on the bed. My legs locked around T-Bone's waist, the weight of him hovering over me, so satisfying and frustrating at the same time. The urgency to bring him inside me returned. I may not have had sexual experience, but I took anatomy classes and knew how it worked.

My back arched off the bed, hands roaming, and mouth devouring. I wanted him so badly that it was painful. But he remained infuriatingly calm, his movements slow, and his tenting erection away from my pussy. When I reached for his belt, he stopped me with a hand on my wrist.

"Am I…doing something wrong?" The old feeling of rejection rang painfully through my chest.

"No, gorgeous. Not at all." He kissed me again, pressing me down onto the mattress. "It's just, I think we'll have more fun if we take our time exploring." He dragged a kiss to my neck, where I felt his smile against my skin. "There's more to me than just my dick, you know."

My laugh morphed into a moan when he cupped my breast, thumb stroking over my nipple, which was already stiff and aching through my bra and shirt. He kneaded and molded my flesh, his touch gentle while being so firm and assured. He treated each breast to the same thorough massage, all the while kissing my mouth, face, and neck until I was panting.

"I think you just really like to tease," I accused, only somewhat playfully.

T-Bone chuckled darkly, his lips against my collarbone. "Wait until Dyno and Grudge get a taste of you."

The thought of two more men with their hands and mouths on me was enough to make me shiver, when a thought hit me. "Do they know about this, right now?"

"I'm sure they have some idea." T-Bone didn't seem fazed as he lifted the hem of my shirt and placed a kiss next to my belly button.

"This doesn't go against any of your rules?"

He paused to look up at me. "Our main rule is that we're always together for penetrative sex. But when it comes to kissing, exploring, things like this," he ran a light touch along my waist, "we're a little less strict about always being present."

I chewed on that information while digging my teeth into my lip. "So, if we do, um…"

"Have sex." He smirked helpfully.

"All three of you will be there?"

His expression turned thoughtful, fingers still gently caressing my waist. "Sex can be intense. With multiple people, it can be overwhelming. If you're not comfortable, I'm sure we can—"

"No, you misunderstand me." I couldn't help grinning, despite my shyness. "I *want* all of you. Together."

T-Bone's eyebrows lifted in clear surprise. "You do?"

"Yes." I nodded. "When I've seen you all, with each other, I…I like it. I've wondered what the three of you do and how I would, you know…" I was absolutely on fire with equal parts embarrassment and arousal, but it was too late to stop now. "How I would…fit in."

"Holy—fuck me." He scrubbed a hand down his face.

"I mean, I would if you'd let me."

T-Bone laughed, leaning down to kiss me again. "You're the dirtiest, sexiest virgin I've ever met."

"I'm still very much willing to scrub that last little detail off my record."

He continued to kiss me, raining them down generously over my lips, face, and neck. "And I still want to take my time savoring you. But if you're frustrated, maybe I can help."

"Help? I like the sound of that."

His grin was slow, wolfish. "Have you ever touched yourself before?"

Oh.

Oh! That was what he meant by *help*.

"Um, a little."

"Hm." His eyebrow quirked up, hand dragging slowly from my waist and heading down over my leggings. "Have you ever made yourself come?"

"I…don't think so."

"I see."

He went lower until his palm cupped the entire space between my legs. I nearly flew off the bed at the contact. Holy fuck, I thought kissing him blew my mind, but *this* was something else.

"That good, little lady?" he growled in my ear, hand pressing and rubbing in tiny movements that had me wanting to climb all over him until I reached God.

"Yes! Oh fuck, yes."

He didn't laugh at me saying fuck then. He moaned against my neck, tongue licking out to add intensity to his kisses. I clutched at his wide shoulders, bucking and writhing against his hand for more friction. I could barely speak, barely *breathe*. It was an itch I desperately needed scratched, but the more I chased his hand, the hotter the need burned. Holy shit, was it supposed to feel this good?

"T-Bone, I'm…I can't stop," I whimpered. My whole

lower body arched off the bed, one foot pressed into the mattress, the other wrapped around T-Bone's hip. He supported my lower back with his hand that wasn't working magic between my legs. And holy hell, he never stopped kissing me. I would have been swooning if I wasn't a panting, desperate mess.

"Then don't stop. Take what you need." His lips hovered over mine, just out of reach for a kiss. "Ride my hand all the way to your peak, little lady. You're so close."

I did feel close to *something*. The pressure under my skin, in all my nerve endings, had built up to a point that had me trembling in his arms. It felt so unspeakably good, but I needed *more*, some kind of release.

T-Bone rubbed the heel of his palm against the top of my pussy, where all my sensitivity seemed to concentrate in one spot. Lightning struck through me at the contact while some distant part of my brain recalled that spot from an anatomy lesson. *The clitoris, whose sole purpose is to provide pleasure.*

Pleasure was too dull of a word for the shock waves licking through me, for the sounds escaping my mouth as I climbed even higher, and then the explosive release that broke me apart in the best way, before floating gently back down.

I fell limply to the bed, utterly spent yet strangely invigorated. My pulse thrummed throughout my whole body, chest heaving with my ragged breaths. I was still fully clothed and entirely too hot. T-Bone eased down to his side next to me, his expression smug and his hands annoyingly to himself.

"How do you feel?" That cocky grin told me he already knew and that he'd made others feel that way probably countless times before.

Instead of jealousy, I only felt gratitude, ease, and contentment. He used his experience to guide me, to make me feel not only physically incredible, but safe and cared for. He could have been a bully like Malcolm, who threatened to make me bleed and only use me for his own pleasure. I had expected some amount of pain along with a healthy dose of shame, but there was none of that.

Everything I always knew about the Sons just solidified in my mind even more. They were trustworthy. They cared about *me*, not what my family or political connections could do for them. And I was safer with them than anywhere else.

"Is it always that good?" I said in answer to T-Bone's question.

He laughed and clamped a hand on my waist to roll me toward him for a kiss. "Little lady, we've barely gotten started on how good it can be."

CHAPTER 22

DYNO

After getting our rooms, Chris and Tiff went to rest up after the ride. T-Bone went into Kyrie's room, presumably to apologize, but neither of them came out after ten minutes.

"Screw him." I knocked my shoulder into Grudge's. "Let's go down to eat. I'm starving."

"Mm," he agreed, following me down the stairs. I couldn't help but notice how he kept looking back at Kyrie's door as we headed down.

"Jealous?" I teased him.

Grudge shook his head, pulling out his pen and paper to elaborate when we reached the bar. *No, worried. And pissed. He made her cry. I heard her all night.*

"I know. Hopefully, she's making him cry. Wait, actually no. If he's crying, it's probably over Bash, and that would just be awkward."

Grudge frowned, stroking over his beard while he

wrote with the other hand. *What happened at the burn site? He's acting differently than all the times before.*

"Your guess is as good as mine," I muttered. "I know what it looked like, but only T really knows."

Grudge elbowed me and made a rolling motion with his hand, asking me to talk more.

"He was talking to the raven," I said, lowering my voice. The bar was mostly empty, but I still didn't want eavesdroppers. "Communicating with…something. That's never happened before, so something has definitely changed."

Odin, you think? Grudge underlined the question on his notepad.

"I don't know. I just hope the guy's finally getting some closure."

"Mm-hm." Grudge wrote slowly, his thoughts relaxed and unhurried. *He's blamed himself for too long already.*

"I know. Bash's spirit probably came through the raven and told him to quit wallowing."

Grudge chuckled and used quotes around the next sentence he wrote. *"Martyrs are fuckin' useless. You want to stand for something? Live your fuckin' life."*

I smiled down at the quote. "I do miss hearing him say that."

Grudge raised his eyebrows and tapped a finger to one of the many tattoos on his forearm.

"That would be a good tattoo idea. I think T-Bone needs it more than either of us though. Oh, speaking of tattoos," I lowered my voice again, "have you heard from Shadow yet?"

Grudge shook his head and flipped to a fresh page. *I sent a coded message the same morning we left. He'll leave a reply by next week at the Kokopelli rock.*

"You think he'll take that long to reply?"

I dunno, he's a dad now. He's busy and shit.

One of the service center employees, a young woman in her late teens or *very* early twenties, walked out from the kitchen right then. Her blonde hair was thrown up in a messy ponytail, and she openly carried a handgun holstered to her hip.

"You guys good with chicken tortilla soup?" she called to us.

"Works for us. Could we get some whiskey?"

She disappeared through the kitchen doors without an answer but reappeared through another set of doors behind the bar moments later, some generic whiskey bottle in her hand. "I'll find you some glasses." She set the bottle in front of us, remaining an arm's length away before running off again.

"Five of them, please. Our friends might come down to join us. Do you have any beer?" I remembered Kyrie's face when she tasted our drinks at dinner that night, which felt like years ago.

"Yeah, we got a lager or something. Just let me know when you want it." The girl set the glasses down and immediately hurried to the doors.

"Miss! Wait, hold on," I hollered after her.

She turned slowly to face us, stiff as a board. "Yes?" The poor thing clearly didn't want to spend a moment alone with us any longer than necessary, and I could only imagine what made her so jumpy around men.

"Have you heard anything about the territory a few hours north of here? Sevier?"

She shook her head. "We're in a neutral zone here. We don't get involved in any territory's business."

"Have you seen armies heading up that way? Or heard any guests talking about it?"

"No. I'll get your soup, if you guys don't need anything else."

I offered my best non-threatening smile. "We're good, thank you."

She turned to leave before I finished speaking, but I noticed her posture had relaxed slightly, so at least that was something. Grudge had poured our drinks while we'd been talking. The moment she was gone, he wrote down, *Maybe let Kyrie ask them questions. They must've heard something down this way. Rumors, at least.*

"Yeah, that's a good idea. Letting us stay don't mean they trust us."

Seems like they have their reasons.

"I know. I'm not mad." I fidgeted in my seat, spinning my whiskey glass on the bar without taking a drink. Grudge noticed my antsiness and frowned but didn't ask a question. "If we lay low here a few more days," I mused, circling the rim of my glass, "you think T would be alright if I took off for a day, maybe two?"

Grudge glared at me then, grunting as he spread his palms out and shrugged his shoulders.

"You know where, man."

He groaned in annoyance and downed his drink, shaking his head when he slapped the empty glass down on the bar.

"I have to. It's been almost six months since I've seen him."

Grudge wrote aggressively on his notepad. *I don't see why you can't just steal him away.*

"We've talked about this. I can't just take my son from his mother."

It's what she did to you!

"I know, but he's happy down there," I sighed. "Her family spoils him, and he's got no struggles. I'm just the absent dad that rolls in every once in a while."

Don't say that about yourself. You'd raise him good if she gave you the chance to. Grudge paused to take another drink, then stopped with the glass halfway to his mouth. He set it down quickly and scribbled out, *Have you told Kyrie about him?*

I finally took a drink and winced as the cheap whiskey burned its way down. "No. It hasn't really come up. But still shitty of me, I know." *Especially if we actually give this a shot with her.*

Despite the current circumstances, I couldn't express how good it felt to have her riding with us again. The way she wrapped around me on the road, how she moved to my flute music by the campfire. She fit in with us so seamlessly, like she was the balm to the wound left behind when we lost everyone else.

I realized right then how much I wanted her to meet my son, Isaac. The only way his mother would allow him to spend more time with me was if I had a stable female figure in his life. But I didn't want Kyrie just for that reason, nor did I want to thrust her into a situation she might not want.

Sharing three romantic partners was more than a handful for most people. Sharing one of them with a child and another woman as a co-parent just might be too much.

That's exactly why *you haven't told her, coward,* I thought. *You want to have your cake and eat it too.*

Grudge whacked me on the arm to get my attention, then gestured behind us to the stairs. I turned to see Kyrie and T-Bone walking down together.

Holding hands.

Other details became clearer as they got closer. His dopey smile. Her flushed cheeks and kiss-swollen lips. So *that's* what they were up to in there. I didn't know whether to be annoyed, jealous, or just…happy for them. T didn't look like he was carrying Bash's memory like a heavy sack anymore. He stood a little taller, even looked a little younger. And Kyrie at least didn't look sad anymore.

Grudge and I openly stared as they walked up to us, while the two of them acted like newlyweds floating on clouds. Attached at the hip and grinning like they got away with murder.

Okay, I was definitely jealous.

"Hey, guys." T-Bone put his free hand on the back of my barstool while draping the other over Kyrie's shoulders, their fingers still laced. "Food coming out?"

"Yeah. It's chicken tortilla soup." I pointed at their linked hands and made a circular motion with my finger. "So, when did *this* happen?"

"What are you talking about, D?" T-Bone straightened his fingers. "You like my nails?"

Kyrie snorted and smacked the back of her palm on his chest. "It happened just now. He apologized, we talked about stuff, and we…connected."

"Mmm-hmm." Grudge watched them while stroking his beard pensively.

"That better have been a hell of an apology," I mused, even though I had no right to talk.

T-Bone was open to the point of being an oversharer. He would have told her about his history with Bash at some point. Me, on the other hand? My instinct was to keep things locked away. It was years until I truly had no secrets with the guys. Now with Kyrie, I wanted to do this right from the get-go. But what would she think if she knew I had a son that I barely got to see?

"I'd say it was an adequate amount of groveling." Kyrie's eyes were glued to T-Bone.

"Adequate, huh?" He grinned back at her, leaning down until his forehead touched hers.

"So this means what?" I asked right before Grudge kicked my barstool with a grunt. "Don't kick me, man. It's a fair question. What does this mean for all of us, and what are we going to tell Governor Vance?"

"What's got into you? I'm supposed to be the cranky one." T-Bone rubbed my upper back and the nape of my neck. "Let's have some food, drink some whiskey, and talk this out after we wind down."

"I would love to go just one day without someone wondering what my father will think." Kyrie smiled, but her words were serious.

"I'm sure you would, but the fact is there could be serious consequences for *us* once he finds out about this." I gestured to their joined hands again. "I'm talking jail time. Exile, if we're lucky."

"What the fuck else is new?" T-Bone scoffed. "We're outlaws, and he knows this. He hires us to keep his own hands clean."

"She's his *daughter.*"

"I hear you, D, but is now really the time? I thought you'd be happy about this. I'm finally living my fuckin' life, like Bash said."

Easy for him to say. He never had a woman threaten to run off with his child.

Kyrie's brows drew together, her lips turning into a

frown. "This is exactly what I didn't want. To drive a wedge between you guys."

"You're not." T-Bone squeezed her shoulder before fixing me with a glare. "Since when do you give a fuck what others think about us?"

"I don't. I'm just trying to keep our necks *and* hers out of a noose. You *know* there are people who would do that, T."

"Why?" Kyrie demanded. "Who would do that? Who would care, if this is what we all want?"

I sighed and pinched the bridge of my nose. Our food still hadn't come out and I imagined our waitress peeking through the kitchen doors, watching the drama unfold. I didn't want to be having this discussion here or now, but it was already happening, and I wasn't about to sugarcoat things for Kyrie. If she really wanted to be with us, this was our reality.

"You know what happens when homophobes see two men acting more than friendly with each other?" I took Kyrie's silence as an answer. "They beat them to death. Sometimes rape them too, because all that hatred is a projection of shame toward themselves." Kyrie paled but didn't interrupt, so I went on. "If it's two women, same deal. Usually a lot more rape though, to 'teach them a lesson'."

T-Bone clenched his teeth. "Dyno—"

"No, it's okay." Kyrie silenced him with a raised hand. "I didn't know it was that bad. And I need to know."

"Those suits you worked with? The ones who politely warned you not to become too *familiar* with men like us? I guarantee you, some of them got queer mens' blood on their hands. And those who don't have no problem looking the other way."

"I…suspected, but never imagined they could actually…" Kyrie drew in a shaky breath but otherwise stood strong. "I'm sorry, Dyno."

I slumped back with a mixture of exhaustion and relief. Kyrie might not have been exposed to the uglier sides of life as we had, but she was smart enough to acknowledge that it existed.

"It hasn't been as bad in recent years," I admitted. "After the Collapse, everyone suffered. Now, people like us are down in the dirt where we belong." I nodded at Kyrie and T-Bone's linked hands again. "But what do you think will happen if guys like us act like we're worthy of a governor's daughter? If someone of *your* upbringing stoops to *our* level? It won't be just us they target. They'll want to punish you too."

"Dyno," Kyrie breathed softly. "There's a chance, a small chance, I'll admit, that my father could support us."

"Even if that does happen, it doesn't undo generations of disdain toward us. I'm not ashamed of who I love, but I'm sorry, I'm not willing to get us all executed for it." I finished off my glass of whiskey and slid from the barstool, in sudden need of the open road and fresh air. "I'm hitting the road. See you all in a couple of days."

"Days?" T-Bone repeated. "Where the fuck you goin'?"

"Gonna clear my head and see Isaac." I turned to face T-Bone, daring him to tell me otherwise. I knew he wouldn't because he had a soft spot for my kid. All three of us wished we could raise him, but it was T-Bone that seemed really attached to the idea of becoming a dad.

"Tell Isaac I miss him," was all that he muttered.

"Hm." Grudge tapped his chest to say, *me too.*

"Who's Isaac?" Kyrie asked in a small voice, almost fearful.

"My son," I told her, fully embracing the feeling of my stomach dropping. "Who I barely see because he lives far away with his mother." Apparently, I didn't know when to stop because I added, "That's another thing to consider before you get with three bisexual men much older than you. We've got hordes of skeletons in our closets."

Without another word, I turned and left the bar.

CHAPTER 23

GRUDGE

"I want you to ignore everything he said for the past half-hour." T-Bone kissed Kyrie's temple when her glum expression didn't change. "You hear me, little lady? He's just in a mood that has nothing to do with you."

He's right, I added, sliding my notepad closer so she could see it. *We were talking about Isaac before you came down. His mind was already in a negative place.*

Kyrie had taken Dyno's seat at the bar, now sandwiched between T-Bone and me. Her tortilla soup was barely touched, but she had downed a couple beers already. Her face had been practically glowing when she came down the stairs with T-Bone. Now it was like a permanent cloud had settled over her, and I wanted to pop Dyno across the jaw for putting it there.

"He's not wrong though." She scratched a nail idly over the worn bartop. "I could put you guys in danger."

T-Bone dismissed that with a wave of his hand. "We're in danger all the time. It's part of our life."

Kyrie didn't seem comforted by the fact. Her face was still drawn into a frown, eyes focused on nothing in front of her. "Why are Dyno and his son's mother no longer together?"

I snorted, the sound echoed by T-Bone. "They were never together to begin with."

There was no relationship, I wrote down to clarify. *Just fucking.*

"Oh." Kyrie's frown only deepened as I saw the wheels turning in her head.

T-Bone caught on before I did. "Neither of us got with her. She only wanted Dyno." He elbowed Kyrie playfully. "We're not *that* slutty."

It worked. Her lips tilted in a half-smile. "So, how did that work out? I thought you all had to be together when you brought in…extra partners."

"Mm!" I held up a hand to pause T-Bone before he started talking. *Do you really want to know details?* I underlined *really* on my notepad. Some people got weirded out by colorful sexual history and regretted their curiosity, especially if they were less experienced.

"She can handle it, Grudge," T-Bone said. "I told her about Bash and me."

I shrugged and leaned back, ready to let him tell the story, which Kyrie did seem eager to hear.

"So Isaac's mom, Lacey, and a few of her friends, came upon our clubhouse a few years back. They were just looking for fun, you know? Wanted to let loose and hook up with some bikers." T-Bone took a sip of whiskey, settling into storyteller mode. "Well, Lacey took a liking to Dyno, and only him. He told her what was up, that we're a package deal. Well, they kept going back and forth, because she wanted him *bad* but wasn't interested in

Grudge or me."

"That was her loss." Kyrie tossed her hair over her shoulder and shot me a grin that nearly made my heart stop.

"Eh, the disinterest was mutual. Wasn't it, Grudge?"

"Mm-hm." I barely remembered what Lacey looked like, except for the fact that she was loud, couldn't hold her drink, and her perfume was too strong.

"So we worked out a compromise. She could fuck Dyno as long as Grudge and I could play in the same room while it was happening." T-Bone started laughing at the memory. "And let me tell you, little lady. I've had a lot of sex in my day, but *that* was fucking awkward."

"Awkward why?" Kyrie's face had darkened to a deep shade of red, tongue darting out to wet her lips. Fuck, was she *excited* at the thought of T-Bone and me together?

"Because Dyno was fucking her across the room, trying to make us feel included, while she was trying to ignore the fact that we were there at all." He chuckled and drank more whiskey. "It was just not a great time for anybody."

That wasn't even the worst part, I wrote on the notepad corner closest to Kyrie.

She read it and looked up at me with wide eyes. "What was the worst part?"

"When she and her friends were done partying and ready to move on, she tried to get Dyno to leave us and be with her." T-Bone's tone sobered. "Told him all kinds of bullshit like she saw us fucking other girls behind his back. Just trying to stir shit up and break us apart so she could take him home like a souvenir. Good thing D's not a dumbass and told her to get fucked. By someone else. So they all left."

"Hm." I held up an index finger.

"Right," T-Bone sighed. "That was the first time they left."

"They came back?" Kyrie asked.

"Lacey did." He nodded. "A year-and-a-half later, with a dark-haired baby strapped to her chest."

"Oh no."

"Yeah. Said he was Dyno's and that he needed to be in his son's life. AKA with *her.* Again, D's not dumb. So he grabbed one of the kid's teething toys and went to the hospital in Four Corners for a paternity test." T-Bone shrugged and opened his palms toward Kyrie. "You can probably guess what the results were."

"His," she said softly.

"Yeah. So he tried talking to Lacey to work something out, because he *did* want to be there for the boy. Still does. But she wasn't having any of it. She didn't want Isaac raised near the clubhouse or by any of us, not even part-time. The only thing she wanted was for Dyno to leave us for good and be with her."

D gave it serious thought, and we don't blame him, I wrote down. *He loves that boy, and after the fallout with* his *dad, he wanted to do the right thing.*

"What happened with Dyno's dad?" Kyrie asked.

T-Bone rested a large hand on her shoulder. "As much as I love blabbering, that's Dyno's story to tell, not ours. But to sum up this story, he stayed with us and Lacey left again. Now Dyno sees Isaac whenever he can, but Lacey intentionally makes it difficult because her ego can't handle that he chose us over her."

I flipped to a fresh page. *I think D regrets it sometimes. Not that he chose us, but that he's not more present in Isaac's life.*

"That's awful for Dyno, he just couldn't win." Kyrie

leaned over the bar, her chin nearly touching her hands. "And poor Isaac is just caught in the middle."

"Yeah, that's the worst part," T-Bone said. "When she couldn't hook him the first time, she tried to use their son as leverage. Thank all the gods he didn't fall for that shit." He drained the rest of his whiskey and pushed the glass away. "We're hoping in a few years, when Isaac's older and more independent, he can spend some extended time with us, if he chooses."

Kyrie propped her elbows on the bar and drove her fingers through her hair. "I wonder why he didn't say anything sooner. I had no idea he had a son before tonight."

I clicked my pen a few times while I thought of the right words. *I think he's embarrassed,* I wrote. *Not of his son, but the situation. He doesn't want you to think of him as a bad or absent father.*

"I would never!" Kyrie exclaimed. "Not if he just explained it to me like you two did."

T-Bone leaned into her, his hand sliding along the back of her barstool until his thumb brushed her arm. "Dyno's not easily shaken by a lot of things. He's good at keeping it together, but the one thing that threatens to unravel him is worrying about his son." T-Bone leaned away, still smirking at her. "And you, come to think of it."

"Me?" Kyrie brought a hand to her chest. "Why me?"

I huffed out a breath in disbelief. She really didn't know?

"Isn't it obvious? We're all crazy about you, little lady."

The room temperature heated by a few noticeable degrees. Over the course of our conversation, T-Bone and I seemed to have gradually moved in closer to Kyrie. Only now I realized how close. She couldn't turn in her chair without brushing up against either of us. And she didn't seem to mind.

T had been touching her face, her legs, and back—whatever barrier between them was now broken. Kyrie had hugged me, had always been friendly and affectionate, but so far, not like *that*. Whenever the guys and I played with others, I was never anyone's first choice. I was too quiet. Too weird, as I'd overheard Lacey say once. I was just the opportunity cost for a chance at T-Bone and Dyno.

Kyrie's eyes were full of T-Bone now, the two of them lost in their own little world. The guys never made me feel excluded, but it was always a delicate balance when we brought others in. All these years later, I still wasn't sure what those two saw in me. We'd had enough casual partners for me to see a pattern.

I wasn't anyone's preference, and that usually didn't bother me. But when Kyrie and T-Bone shared a kiss and smiled over some whispered words, it was impossible to ignore the stab of jealousy. She was the only woman that I wished would see *me*.

"What should we do until Dyno gets back?" Kyrie turned in her seat to flash me a warm smile, and I forced my mouth to make one back at her.

"I can think of a few things." T-Bone swept the hair off her shoulder, fingers digging in to massage her nape.

I held back a snort. Always a horndog, that one.

"While he's gone?" Kyrie tried to give him a skeptical look, but her face was too blissed out from the neck massage. "Isn't that breaking your rules?"

"Like I told you upstairs, we can just keep exploring." His other hand went to her leg, repeating the massage just above her knee. "You can watch me and Grudge, if you'd like." He looked up at me, eyes already dark with all the fantasies playing out in his head. "You good with that, man?"

I stroked my beard, watching Kyrie's face before I answered. Her pupils were almost as blown out as T-Bone's, her slight body melting into the barstool as he rubbed into her muscles. She looked so at ease, open and inviting, like she would try anything we suggested. Her legs had even spread open, maybe subconsciously, so that her other knee rested against my leg.

And she was looking at me. Both of them were, expressions openly lustful and waiting for my response. I could almost fool myself into thinking she did want me, that she would look at me like that even if T-Bone wasn't there.

I waved my hand in a noncommittal gesture. Whatever happened, I would be fine. I'd be satisfied and enjoy it. I just shouldn't let myself think too much.

"He's leaving it up to you, little lady." T-Bone nuzzled the side of her face. "I have plenty of suggestions, but you're an equal player here. If there's something you'd like to try, let us know."

Kyrie slid further down in her seat, blushing darker, and biting her lips to hide a smile. When it didn't work, she covered her face. Fuck me, it was cute.

"You going shy on us?" T-Bone chuckled and pinched her waist. "Need some whiskey to loosen up, Miss Ambassador?"

"Don't call me that!" Kyrie shrieked with laughter and leaned away from him, which brought her closer to me. I wasn't sure if she lost balance or if maybe it was the beer she already drank, but she rested the full weight of her head and upper back against my chest. "Hi, Grudge." She tilted her face up at me, smiling broadly. "You're comfy."

"He is. He's the best pillow." T-Bone didn't seem at all

bothered to have lost her attention, but he never was the jealous type. He only looked amused as he helped himself to another glass of whiskey. "She's halfway off that chair, man. She'll be on the floor soon if you don't do something."

I glared at him over Kyrie's head, knowing exactly what he was trying to make me do. Trying my best to ignore my thundering pulse, I braced my arms along Kyrie's sides, hands resting just past her hips so she wouldn't fall.

I'd never held anyone this small before. She felt nice in my arms.

One of Kyrie's hands drifted up like she was going to touch my face. She paused at the edge of my beard, fingertips lightly stroking the coarse hair.

"Can I ask you something, Grudge?"

"Mm-hm." I might have sounded calm but I was dreading having to answer. Not because of anything she might ask me. I just didn't want to stop holding her to write something down.

"How did you get your road name?" She angled her head to look up at me. "And what's your given name? If you don't mind me asking."

Ah, that was easy enough to answer. I jerked my chin at T-Bone, indicating he should talk for me.

"They are one and the same," he said solemnly. "Grudge didn't have a legal name before the Sons found him. Obviously, he didn't say a word when we brought him in. One of the prospects was unnerved by this and said something like, 'Damn, that guy holds a hell of a grudge.' And the name stuck."

"Well, that just begs more questions." Kyrie grew bolder as she played with my beard, her fingers running lightly over my cheek now. "Did you *want* to be called Grudge?"

"Eh." I shrugged. It made our enemies fear me and was too late to change now. And it was better than no name at all. Joining the Sons and receiving my name made me a person for the first time. A *someone*, worthy of an identity.

"I take it your life before the Sons wasn't a very happy one," Kyrie mused, her brow furrowing slightly as she looked at me.

Understatement of the century, I thought. Outwardly, I scoffed and shook my head.

Her fingers danced on my cheek some more, running lightly toward my neck and jaw. "I'll ask about it another day then." Her head turned on my chest to look at T-Bone. "Right now, I'm more interested in what you were saying earlier."

His eyes lit up, a grin spreading over his face. "Oh yeah? Name it, little lady." He reached for her legs that were still on the chair between us, running a touch up her calf muscle. "What do you want to play?"

She lifted up from my chest, and I hated the loss of warmth and slight pressure of her resting on me. Still, I dropped my arms from her sides to let her move. She pulled her legs from the middle chair and my heart completely stopped when she sat on my thigh, her legs draping between mine.

I could only stare at her in shock. *She's sitting in my lap.*
She's sitting in my *fucking lap.*
And she was looking back at me. And so *so* close.

"Don't have a heart attack now, Grudge," T-Bone cracked. "I don't know that CPR shit like D does."

Kyrie must have mistook my shock for discomfort. She

brought a hand to my cheek, where she had been touching me earlier. "Is this okay, Grudge?"

My limited voice refused to work, so I just nodded stiffly.

"You're sure?"

"Mmm," was all I could get out. I leaned my cheek into her palm, seeking more of that softness I craved. I realized too late that it brought my forehead close to nudging hers.

She brought both hands to my face then, fingers stroking lightly over my beard. As if on instinct, my arms went around her. I told myself it was to keep her from falling again but really, the crook of my arm just felt right nestled into the curve of her waist.

"Can I kiss you, Grudge?" She was so close, I felt her breath fan over my mouth. Her lips were so pink and pretty. Yes, I absolutely wanted to taste them…

My brain processed her question a beat too slow, and everything shut down in an instant. *No, she can't!*

I grabbed her wrists and pushed her hands away from my face, panic sending my pulse into overdrive. My chest felt tight, and I struggled to breathe.

But none of it was worse than the shock of hurt flashing across her face.

You stupid son of a bitch, look what you did.

Kyrie was gone, no longer in my lap but several feet away. T-Bone's hands wrapped around her shoulders while he tried to soothe her.

"Hey, it's okay. He wasn't rejecting you, alright? Grudge isn't a dumbass like me." His hands ran up and down her arms. "Kissing someone new is just…tricky for him. I'm sorry, I should have mentioned it earlier. My bad, Grudge. I didn't tell her about…"

I turned away, fully facing the bar now and wishing I could tune them out. If she wasn't put off by me before, she definitely was now. I never should have bothered getting my hopes up. Dyno was right about one thing. What right did I have to think I was good enough for her?

A hand came to my shoulder, smaller and lighter than T-Bone's. "I'm sorry, Grudge," Kyrie said. "I didn't mean to make you uncomfortable."

I shook my head at nothing, an indignant huff of air leaving my mouth. *Why* did she have to be so good, so sweet? Why was she so insistent on making me believe she could want me? The sooner she realized how fucked up I was, the better off she'd be.

Except not having her around would make T-Bone and Dyno mope like sad sacks. And dropping her off at her father's place would guarantee her misery. At least with us, she had fun.

Fuck, why did everything have to be intertwined and complicated?

"Hey, what's going on?"

I lifted my head and looked around, realizing the women of the service center were barricading windows and doors. Kitty, the one who stopped us at the door, was handing out rifles and boxes of ammo to the other employees.

"Nothin' to worry about, boys," she said in answer to T-Bone's question. "Just our monthly visitors."

He cocked his head, squinting as he stared at her. "Your monthly…what now?"

Rapid footsteps thundered down the stairs, Chris and Tiff appearing at the bottom moments later, each with armloads of guns.

"Kyrie, can you shoot?" Tiff approached her quickly, holding out the handle of a 9mm.

"Uh, no?" Kyrie stared wide-eyed at the weapon.

"Then you better hide, because there's a horde of bikers coming in hot from the southeast. They don't look friendly." Tiff held the weapon out to me and I took it, tucking it into the waistband of my jeans before accepting another gun from her.

"Y'all helping?" Kitty didn't seem displeased by the idea as she cocked her shotgun. "These pricks come once a month or so, trying to steal this place from us. It's just routine pest control, but if you wanna join in, we don't mind cleaning them up early."

"Hell yeah, we're in." T-Bone accepted a pair of handguns from Chris, who shared a grin with him. "Been too long since we've been in a good ol' gunfight, huh, VP?"

"You know it, Pres." Chris sounded downright cheerful.

"Your girl should get behind the bar," Kitty advised.

The young blonde who had served us food took Kyrie's elbow and began to lead her away, but Kyrie resisted, her face torn. "Are you guys going to be okay?"

"Just fine, little lady. You get to where it's safe." T-Bone was almost jittery with excitement. The only thing he liked better than a good fuck was a good fight. "We'll play when we're done here," he added, his voice husky.

Kyrie allowed the other girl to lead her away, and T-Bone bumped his shoulder into me. "Dyno's gonna be sore when he finds out he missed this."

I wasn't sure if he was talking about the gunfight or messing around with Kyrie.

CHAPTER 24

KYRIE

My chest felt like it would explode from holding my breath as I huddled behind the bar with Gretchen, the kitchen server. When the first shot rang out, it didn't make breathing any easier.

"Oh my God..." I slapped my hands over my ears at gunfire emanating from all around me. It felt like escaping Blakeworth again, everything from the fear gripping my chest in a tight squeeze to the shouting and smell of gunpowder in the air. I didn't even realize I was trembling until Gretchen slid her arms around me.

"It's pretty loud, but you get used to it," she said, rubbing my back.

"This happens once a month?" I was cowering in her embrace while she radiated absolute calm. She looked about my age and was probably even younger. How could she be used to this?

"Roughly, yeah. Depends on how bad Kitty and the

others fuck 'em up. With your guys helping, hopefully they don't come back for several months."

A stray shot hit a stack of glasses just above us, and I screamed. Gretchen covered my head while the shards rained down on us.

Where the fuck is my valkyrie now?

"You girls alright?" someone yelled. My ears were ringing too hard to know, but it sounded like T-Bone.

"We're good!" Gretchen answered, carefully brushing glass out of my hair. Then to me, "Here, I got an idea." She started crawling away, and I almost cried out and held onto her so she wouldn't leave me.

She only went a few feet away though, to poke through a set of drawers set in the bar. Gretchen snatched something just as a series of bullet holes dotted the wall above us. She spun around on her butt and held it up victoriously as she came back to me.

A...tablecloth?

"So you don't get cut up by glass," she explained, unfolding the cloth and carefully draping it over my head and shoulders.

I held the fabric up with a shaking hand so she could slide under it too. With some fiddling, we tucked the edges into the shelves of the bar and weighed it down with dishes so it served more as a canopy than a head covering. It reminded me of the blanket forts I made with my dad when I was little.

Once settled under our makeshift canopy, Gretchen reached for my hand and squeezed. "You doin' okay?"

I was shaking less, but I wasn't sure if I was truly calmer or just numb. My ears rang and felt like they were plugged up with cotton. I could still smell gunpowder and hear muffled voices and shots ringing out.

"How long will this take?" I asked.

Gretchen shrugged. "Couple hours, maybe. They probably brought backup 'cause last time, Kitty and the crew cleaned 'em up pretty quick with homemade stink bombs." She snickered. "It almost wasn't worth cleaning up all the puke outside."

"Have they ever gotten close to…?"

"Making it inside? Yeah, we had a couple close calls. Some of the girls had bullet wounds, but we won out in the end. It's amazing how hard you'll fight when your only alternative is under the boots of *men*." She sneered at that final word. "Anyway, we found ourselves a lady doctor after that. Self-preservation can't save you all the time."

"Yeah." I flinched at the sound of glass shattering. It was nowhere near us, but I thought I heard a masculine groan of pain. That sound unfroze me, and my hands clenched into fists. All at once, I had forgotten my fear. Now I fought the urge to jump to my feet and run into the fray to check on T-Bone and Grudge.

Gretchen watched me carefully as I responded to the chaotic sounds all around us. "Your guys are alright, huh?"

"More than that," I said. "They're great. I mean, they have their issues, but they've always been really good to me." I swallowed, my throat as parched as a bone. "But I have dealt with bad men too. If I could fight, I would be up there with them."

"Yeah, I'm still learning." Gretchen gestured to the gun still holstered on her hip. "Just carrying one around makes you feel a little stronger. And men tend to keep their distance when they see you packin'."

"I'll have to borrow one." My forced smile was cut short by another groan of pain directly after a gunshot. "Fuck! Is there anything we can do?"

"Just wait it out," Gretchen said sympathetically. "Let them handle it and give them less bodies to worry about. Priya, the doctor, is out there too. She won't let anything happen to your guys."

"But what if the doctor gets shot?" I demanded.

Gretchen shrugged. "Then we're kinda screwed, I guess."

The maelstrom continued for an immeasurable amount of time. Glass rained down on us, bullet holes decorated the far wall, and indecipherable shouts rang out among the gunshots. I couldn't tell if we were any closer to winning or losing. The women and the guys seemed optimistic at first, even excited for this fight. But what if it turned out to be way more than they bargained for?

All the while, my legs burned with the need to jump up. To stop cowering back here and *do* something.

"Where you from?" Gretchen asked after a long stretch of silence between us.

"Four Corners," I said. "But the guys and I came from Sevier. I was working up there."

Her eyebrows raised. "Oh, they're letting women work now? That's a good sign, I guess."

"Well, there was an uprising, so who knows what'll happen now," I said. "But Four Corners is safe and full of opportunities. Women can do whatever they want there."

Gretchen nodded. "Heard about it. That's where that lady medic ended up, right? Mari?"

"Yes, exactly! She's settled down there now with her husbands and kids."

"Sounds nice, but I couldn't leave this place. Kitty might leave it to me and her daughter one day."

"Well, I hope a day comes where you don't have to defend it with guns."

Gretchen snorted. "Yeah, that'll be a while." She perked up, as if suddenly remembering something. "You trust those guys you're with?"

"Yes," I said without hesitating. "With my life."

But with my heart? I wondered. I felt a little less sure about that. I was reeling from Grudge abruptly pushing me away from kissing him, despite trying not to take it personally. And it hurt that Dyno never said a word about his son, that he assumed I would write him off because of it.

"Even the pretty, long-haired guy that took off?"

I nodded firmly at Gretchen. There was a lot to unpack with Dyno, with all three of them, really. But one thing I knew for certain was that they were trustworthy and would never let any harm come to me.

"He asked about armies riding north to Sevier before you came downstairs. I told him I didn't see anything, because, frankly, I don't trust any men that come through here." Her eyes met mine. "But if they treat you good, and *you* trust them, then…"

"What did you see?" I all but demanded of her. "How many, Gretchen?"

"About thirty hired guns stopped here three days ago. They weren't soldiers, but they were…professionals, you know? All matching uniforms, shiny weapons. Clean cut and in great shape. I served them food and they all stayed hands off, thank fuck. But they were focused, and I heard them talking."

"About?"

"Securing Perrysville. Is that in Sevier?"

I leaned back against the bar, the wind knocked out of me. "Yeah, that's the capital."

Gretchen's eyebrows lifted. "Guess you got your answer."

"What else did you hear? What about where they came from or whose orders they were under?"

She shook her head regretfully. "They were a quiet bunch. Like I said, focused. Only stayed for a night and then left early."

"Maybe one of the other girls heard something? Can you ask around?"

"I can try, but I'm telling you, these guys stayed really tight-lipped. Everyone thought it was weird, because it's the opposite of most men who can't keep it shut."

We both laughed a little at that. At some point, I started to feel more at ease while we talked. I was still tense and scared, but no longer in full-blown panic mode.

"Thank you, Gretchen."

She squeezed my hands affectionately. "Girls gotta help each other, you know?"

"You're absolutely right about that."

Another series of shots fired, close and loud enough that I felt the bar shift as it absorbed the impact.

"Fuck, they're getting around my cover!" one of the women yelled.

"Hold on!" a man's voice answered, but more gunfire drowned him out.

The situation seemed to be getting worse. More shots from the other side were hitting their marks, if the panicked shouts were anything to go by. My feet felt like they were actually on fire now. Hiding while the others risked their lives was literally paining me.

"I can't stay here."

"Wait!" Gretchen grabbed my arm as I began to stand, her blue eyes massive. "You can't go out there!"

"You don't understand, I have to do something!"

"Don't give your men a body to bury!"

"I won't! I'm going to shield them."

The words left my mouth before they registered in my head, like someone else had used my lips to speak. All at once, I became aware of the circular shield strapped to my forearm, my fingers wrapped around the smooth, wooden handle of an axe, and the weight of a metal helmet on my head.

Shield them, daughter, and I will shield you.

That omniscient voice in my head spurred me into movement like a shot of adrenaline. All my fear was replaced by a pressing need to *protect* at all costs, to block the carnage coming for my men and those who hosted us here.

If Gretchen noticed my valkyrie garb, she didn't mention it. She tried to keep me from walking out from behind the bar, pulling and pleading at me to stop, but I shook her off easily. Nothing would touch me. Somehow I *knew* this.

She, and everything else, sounded far away and garbled, like I was underwater. Multiple people yelled my name, but it was all white noise. Some kind of barrier surrounded me, I could tell that much. Shots continued to fire, but none of them came within feet of me. I felt like the sharp side of an axe, cold and impervious as I cut through the room.

Kitty and two other women hid behind an overturned table that was moments away from becoming splinters. One woman's hands shook as she reloaded her gun while Kitty had taken off her T-shirt and was wrapping it around the other woman's bloodied arm. All three of them opened their mouths and yelled as I walked past them, but the sound didn't reach me. I ignored them and stood in front of their table to face our attackers instead.

No glass remained in the window, and the men outside all pointed their guns in my direction. The one in front, their apparent leader, started laughing at the sight of me. The others quickly followed, making obscene gestures at me while they laughed.

The leader's mouth moved, asking me a question that looked like, *so desperate to die?*

I clapped the flat side of my axe against my shield, the sound ringing out clear and beautiful in my challenge to him.

His grin faded. Then he pointed his gun directly at my chest and fired.

Distantly, I heard the roars of, *No!* and, *Kyrie!* But nothing rang as clear as the bullet clattering harmlessly to the ground in front of my feet.

A smile curved along my mouth at the shooter's expression. Shock, disbelief, and utter *fear.*

They all started firing, their shots rapid, desperate, and wild, but the shield around me stopped it all. Our attackers became so concentrated on me, they didn't notice their own men falling until it was too late.

The last two men standing ran for their bikes, but a clean shot to each had them slumped over and lifeless on the ground before they could touch the handlebars.

All at once, the world came into focus like a bubble bursting. Sounds were clear, every detail sharp. The first person I noticed was Tiff, her arms still stretched out in front of her and her gun smoking from those last two shots. Sweat dotted her brow, and her chest rose and fell with ragged breaths. Someone touched her shoulder and then her posture finally relaxed, though her eyes cut sharply to me.

I looked down at myself to see that everything was

gone—no shield on my arm or axe in my hand. I touched my head and felt sharp bits of glass in my hair, no winged helmet to speak of.

It felt like I had just woken from a dream in the middle of a warzone.

Glass covered the floor like glittering snow. Every piece of furniture had been turned over and shot to pieces. I spun around in a slow circle, realizing for the first time what I had actually walked out into, unarmed and un-barricaded.

And not a single bullet had touched me.

People emerged from their hiding places slowly. Some stared at me, while others were more preoccupied with their injuries and the state of the place. But everyone was moving, which meant no one had died.

"What the fuck was that?" demanded the woman who had been next to Kitty behind the table. She stared at me with a heated mix of confusion and fear.

"Kyrie!" Gretchen ran to me and clasped me in a tight, panicked hug. "Oh my God, why did you do that?" She pulled away, hands running down my arms. "How did you not get hurt?"

"I don't…I…" No words could explain it. I was just as confused as everyone else.

"She saved our asses, that's what happened."

I whipped around, my heart in my throat as I searched the room. Chris came out from behind his cover and rose to his full height, blood dripping down his arm. Tiff was right there, grabbing his wrist to pull him closer and examine the wound.

"Is that glass or did you get grazed?" she asked.

"I hope it's a fuckin' graze. We're already gonna find glass everywhere. Hang on, baby. You got some here." He carefully picked shards from her braids while she stemmed the flow of blood from his arm.

"T-Bone?" I called, wandering out to the center of the room. "Grudge? Where'd they go?"

"Pres!" Chris barked. "Don't tell me you ran."

"Over here." I heard T-Bone's voice from a far corner of the room. "Is there a doctor? We could use some help."

I hurried in the direction of his voice, driven by the pressing need to just *see* him, to know that they were both alive. Of course, I was completely unprepared for the sight before me.

Behind an overturned table, T-Bone had Grudge sitting on the floor and propped up against a wall. His blood-soaked hand pressed over Grudge's forehead and eyes. Blood streamed down Grudge's face, so much that he was constantly spitting out the blood that got into his mouth. His teeth clenched and his fists shook, either from shock or pain, or probably a mixture of both.

I froze again, stunned into stillness while the doctor brushed past me and knelt at the man's side. "What happened?" she asked.

"Got an explosion of glass in his face." T-Bone's voice was heavy with worry. "I don't know if it got *in* his eyes or…"

"Let me see."

T-Bone carefully peeled his hand away, and Grudge sucked in a pained hiss of breath. I couldn't bring myself to look at the gore on his face, but that sound he made spurred me into movement again.

I went to his opposite side, out of the doctor's way, and grabbed his hand, ignoring that it too was slick with blood.

"You're going to be fine, Grudge." It was probably a

useless, stupid sentiment, but I didn't know what else to do. "We're all here. You're going to be okay."

His hand squeezed around mine as the doctor examined him. I brought his knuckles to my lips and brushed a kiss over them before I remembered and abruptly stopped. *Jesus fucking Christ, you idiot. He doesn't need any more trauma right now.*

But Grudge only squeezed my hand even harder, then his trembling index finger reached to touch the edge of my face.

CHAPTER 25

KYRIE

After the long, painstaking process of having glass shards removed from in and around his eyes, Grudge thankfully suffered no loss to his vision.

Due to the bleeding and swelling however, Doctor Priya recommended his eyes remain bandaged for a few days. He was not happy about that but begrudgingly allowed T-Bone and I to lead him upstairs to rest and get cleaned up.

"What can I help with?" I hovered as T-Bone led his partner to the shower, directing Grudge's hand to the towel rack for support.

"I got it from here, little lady. Go on and rest." He threw a weary smile in my direction. "Unless you're dying to be in the middle of two naked men in the shower?"

I mean, yeah, kind of?

The longer I stood there, hesitating, the humor slowly drained from T-Bone's face. His gaze grew openly inviting as he peeled off Grudge's cut and then his own. Carefully, he took off Grudge's bloodstained shirt next, revealing an expanse of dense muscle, more dark tattoos, and *scars*. So many scars.

I was completely still, but not frozen this time. Just entranced. My stomach flipped as T-Bone turned to face me, not saying a word as he gripped the bottom of his shirt and pulled it over his head in one swift, fluid movement. Some dried blood still coated his shoulders and chest, but at the sight of him, a familiar throb hit like a drum between my legs.

He looked like he was cut from marble, every muscle and contour with clearly defined lines. A massive raven with its wings spread was the centerpiece of his chest, feathers stretching out to his shoulders where smaller, more intricate tattoos ran down his arms. This was the man who kissed me into a limp puddle of need and brought me to ecstasy with just his hand. *Over* my clothes, no less.

And he was inviting me to shower with the two of them?

The room suddenly felt too hot and too small. I needed air and space.

"Um, I'll go take a shower and come back?" I squeaked, cringing at the sound of my own voice. "I… yeah, I don't want to be alone, but…"

T-Bone's expression changed quickly, flashing me an easy smile. "Sure thing, Kyrie. Just knock before you come in."

I nodded before hurrying from the room, not releasing the breath in my chest until I was in my own room down the hall. My back pressed against my door and I let it all out in a big *whoosh*.

What a day.

Shit, what a *week*.

Everything seemed to hit me all at once right then. Sevier, a promising new territory, had fallen. My father was likely frantic with worry. He had to know I was missing by now and would scour the continent to search for me.

I was overwhelmed by my intense feelings for the Sons and the emotional whiplash they all gave me. T-Bone had not only kissed me stupid, but gave me an orgasm. Dyno had a *child*, and Grudge would likely never allow me to kiss him.

We'd been attacked mere hours ago, and I'd walked in front of gunfire to make it out without a scratch.

Yeah, that last one was something I couldn't quite wrap my head around. In that moment, the valkyrie was…me? Or had possessed me? Nothing about it made sense.

Once I caught my breath, I leaned away from the door and headed for the shower. Maybe I could process all this better under hot water and with less dried blood caked under my nails.

No such luck. My thoughts went round and round in circles as I stood under the spray. The only thing I was certain of? I wanted those three men more than anything else. They were my freedom, my sense of adventure, and my safe place. Nothing else mattered.

The water ran cold by the time I stepped out. After drying off with a towel and changing into fresh clothes, I stopped in front of the mirror. My face looked different, with a warm glow and light freckles thanks to sun exposure from the rides. I was stalling, still a bit nervous about returning to their room, but I wanted to take note of these changes in myself.

Would my father even recognize me when I saw him again? Or was I shedding my old, naive self like a snake's skin?

I marched out of my door and down the hall before I could chicken out and softly knocked at the Sons' door. T-Bone opened it quickly. He had changed into a clean T-shirt and soft lounge pants and gave me that easy, heart-flipping smile.

"Started to wonder if you'd changed your mind." He stepped aside to let me through.

"Never." I walked in, stopping directly in front of him and lifted to my tiptoes to kiss him. "How's Grudge?"

His kiss was warm and lingering, tasting slightly of whiskey while his fingers caressed my neck. "He's alright," he murmured, running his touch lightly over my cheek. "Mostly calmed down and resting."

He turned aside, giving me a view of Grudge laid up in bed while he closed the door. Grudge was still shirtless, the sheet pulled up to his waist and white gauze wrapped around his head, covering his eyes.

Munin was perched on the headboard, preening his feathers and vocalizing softly.

"Hey, Grudge," I called softly, heading to his bedside. "It's me."

At the sound of my voice, his head turned abruptly, facing away from me. His fists clenched at his sides, gripping the sheet as his mouth curled into a snarl.

T-Bone gave him a chiding look. "Don't be like that, man. It's just Kyrie." He sat down and scooted toward his partner in the middle of the wide, king-sized mattress. "He doesn't like being seen as weak," T-Bone said to me. "Especially by people he likes."

Grudge growled and swung his arm out blindly, whacking T-Bone in the chest.

"Oh, Grudge, are you kidding me?" I climbed on the bed and crawled toward the two of them, prompting

Grudge's head to swivel back in my direction. "You're one of the strongest men I know." I took his hand, lacing my fingers with his and squeezing like how we did after the shootout. "You're in the top three, for sure."

"Huh." A smile twitched at his lips before he went stone-faced again.

Moving slowly, I took my chances getting closer to him. Stretching my legs out over the sheet next to him, I scooted in until my temple rested lightly on Grudge's shoulder. Across from me, T-Bone copied my position and rested his head on the opposite shoulder, his expression warm and amused.

"I'm really glad you're okay, Grudge." I stroked my thumb over our combined fingers. "It could have been so much worse. Thank God it wasn't."

He pulled in a long breath and sighed it out, along with a soft groan of frustration from his throat. T-Bone lifted his head, resting his chin on Grudge's shoulder. "What's the matter? You're still hot as fuck, if that's what's bothering you."

Grudge snorted, then pantomimed writing before cutting his hand sharply through the air.

"Oh, I get it." My heart ached painfully with the realization. "You can't write like this. It's even harder to communicate when you can't see."

Grudge nodded and T-Bone pushed aside his hair to kiss his neck. "It's just until your eyes heal. A couple of days, maybe even sooner."

"Hrmmm." The rumble from Grudge's throat was frustrated, dissatisfied. I could only imagine how slowly two days would go by when you couldn't communicate your needs.

An idea struck me when I looked down at our hands

clasped together. It could work, but considering how he reacted when I first brought it up, I'd have to tread carefully.

"Hey, Grudge?"

"Mm, Kah?" His face turned toward me, and he must not have realized how close I was, because his lips just barely brushed my forehead.

"We could try signing, if you'd like," I said. "Not anything complex, but we could finger spell into each other's hands. It would just take learning the alphabet."

T-Bone sat up excitedly. "That's a great idea."

"Hmm." Grudge didn't sound convinced.

"Aw, come on, man. You know D and I have wanted to learn it. Kyrie can teach us. I mean, why the fuck not?"

Grudge made another disgruntled noise, and T-Bone rolled his eyes. "He does know some words and most of the alphabet already. He's just…got some bad memories associated with it."

"That's okay, we don't have to. Instead, we can keep it simple to yes or no questions, or—"

Grudge pulled his hand from my grasp and clumsily splayed my fingers open. He used his opposite hand to sign into my palm, *"O-K."*

"Okay?" I repeated. "You're sure you want to do this, Grudge?"

He nodded and spelled another word into my hand. *"V-E-S."*

I stifled my giggle as I turned his palm to face up. "Good! This is the letter Y, you use your pinky and thumb." I signed the letter into his palm then spelled out, *"Y-E-S."*

"Ah, meh," he groaned, but another smile pulled at his lips. This time, it stayed there.

I wanted to kiss his cheek or forehead so badly, but settled for squeezing his hand instead. "It's okay. You'll pick it up quickly."

"Can you show me, little lady?" T-Bone's eyes brightened eagerly.

Maybe it was silly but I loved so much that he asked. None of us mentioned a thing about the attack or my apparent ability to shield bullets, and I preferred it that way. Teaching the ASL alphabet was the perfect distraction, at least for now.

"Sure. We'll start from the beginning." I placed my left hand in Grudge's palm and brought my other hand next to my face so T-Bone could see and follow along. "Ready? This is A, B, C…"

CHAPTER 26

KYRIE

My eyes blinked open, heavy with sleep but also refreshed. I barely remembered falling asleep, so I must have passed out hard. The bed was warm and *so* comfortable, I curled up smaller against my pillow despite all my senses waking up.

The pillow, I quickly realized, was actually a man's chest. And the heavy, warm blanket around me? His arm. Grudge's arm.

And I'd been sleeping on Grudge's chest.

Wide awake now, I lifted my head, feeling curious but also cautious. Grudge lie flat on his back, the bandages still over his eyes as he breathed deeply, completely asleep. The hand that wasn't wrapped around me rested on his stomach, lifting and falling gently with his breaths.

He looked so much bigger like this. I only now took note of how big his hands were, the spanning width of his chest and shoulders. Not to mention the sight of all of his tattoos in clear detail. If he were anyone else, I'd be trying my damnedest not to wake up. But this was Grudge, and the sight of him just made me want to return to that warmth and cuddle him. So I did.

He stirred with a soft groan as I returned my head to his chest but didn't wake. His arm around my back tightened, fingers curling into my shirt at the waist.

Moments before drifting off again, the scent of leather and whiskey surrounded me, and then T-Bone's solid form pressed to my back. A light kiss fell to my shoulder. "Sleep well, little lady?"

"Mm-hm." He felt so snug and perfectly aligned with my body, I knew we had to have slept like this throughout most of the night. The thought of spending the whole night between their two bodies sent warmth pooling in my belly.

"Good." He peppered more kisses on my cheek and the back of my neck, then captured my mouth as I turned to face him.

I rolled to my back, sinking into the weight of T-Bone's kiss. My legs slid apart and his solid body settled into the cradle between them. He was hard and warm everywhere, the fabric between us itchy and stifling. Our lips and tongues danced lazily while I explored the width of his shoulders. I went to deepen our kisses, clutched him tighter to pull more of his warm, delicious body on top of me, but he resisted when I tried.

"Do you want to talk about what happened yesterday?" He lifted away and rolled to his side, only keeping his arm around my waist, and I tried not to sigh out my disappointment.

"You mean you've never seen a girl just walk into the direct path of a bunch of guns and block all the bullets before?"

T-Bone humored me with a chuckle. "No, I can't say that I have."

Munin then hopped down from the headboard, cawing softly as he approached T-Bone.

"I know you're hungry. We'll get breakfast in a minute." He scratched the bird's head as he looked at me again. "Grudge told us about your valkyrie."

I stole a glance at the other man in bed with me, still fast asleep. "I've been seeing her sometimes when I'm awake. She's like a ghost, only visible in the corner of my vision. But yesterday was different." Looking back at T-Bone, I was relieved to see that he was raptly listening. "You don't think I'm nuts?"

His mouth quirked up in the smile that always put me at ease. "We're all a little nuts, but no, not because you can see a valkyrie. That's a gift, not an illness." He looked at the raven, who returned his gaze. "Munin is a gift too. One that I don't deserve but is mine all the same." The bird closed his eyes, trilling softly as T-Bone rubbed a certain spot on his neck. "I can leave my body and see through him. We're connected in a way that's unexplainable."

"That time in the hallway," I said, recalling how he went eerily still and his eyes had rolled back until only the whites were visible.

"Correct. I saw through him to find out what was happening outside." He scratched under the bird's beak. "And when we went to the memorial, Munin spoke to me for the first time. He made me realize that I needed to let go of my guilt from the past." Whiskey-colored eyes flicked up to me. "And make room for new memories."

"The valkyrie said to me," I swallowed at the memory of that heavy, omnipresent voice. "'Shield them, daughter, and I will shield you.' Then I looked down and I saw her shield on my arm. I felt her helmet on my head, and I just knew I had to protect everyone and wouldn't get hit."

"Well, I didn't see a valkyrie out there. Just my favorite little lady." T-Bone squeezed my waist, but his smile faded. "And I was scared to fucking death because I thought you were a goner. Grudge was about to jump in front of you."

"Sorry I worried you." I went to touch his face and got my finger lightly bitten instead. "I didn't really know what was happening. It felt like I was in a bubble."

T-Bone released my finger. "You saved Kitty and her friends. And let us take out the rest. That's no small thing." He picked up my hand and kissed the finger he had just bitten, his gaze turning thoughtful. "The valkyrie called you 'daughter'?"

"Yeah. And she did this in a dream I had." I put my forearms together and rocked them back and forth like a baby.

T-Bone's eyebrows lifted. "Kyrie, if you don't mind me asking, what happened to your mother?"

"She passed away a few weeks after I was born. I was told the pregnancy was rough on her, but that wasn't what did it. She got an infection while in recovery and her body couldn't fight it."

"I'm sorry." T-Bone's face fell in sympathy.

"It's okay. I never got to know her, though I would like to think she would've kept my dad off my back." I pushed my hair back, wondering what she would have thought of me falling for three men. "That's why he's so overprotective of me, I think. She was the love of his life, and I'm all he's got left. It's also why he pushed so hard for setting up the hospital in Four Corners with the best doctors and medics he could find."

"Makes sense," T-Bone mused. "Not an excuse to keep you locked up like a prized show pony though."

"No, I guess not." I played with my hair some more, unsure of how to broach the elephant in the room. "So, are you thinking the valkyrie is…?"

"I don't know. Honestly, for being able to see through a bird, I'm not very knowledgeable about this stuff." T-Bone rested a hand on my hip. "But I think it's okay to not know everything. If this valkyrie is helping you, guiding you and not freaking you out, that's all that really matters, right?" His fingers drummed on me thoughtfully. "Knowing the connection is there, that someone's looking out for you, is enough." He leaned in and tickled my neck with his beard before kissing me there. "Or I could just be talking out my ass, as usual."

"You do not." I laughed and squirmed against him.

He chuckled, low and throaty as he kissed me some more. I was just getting ready to wedge myself underneath him again when he abruptly got up from bed and headed for the connected bathroom. When he came out he was, sadly, fully dressed in his jeans, T-shirt, and cut.

"You going somewhere?" I asked while he sat at the foot of the bed to put his boots on.

"Just gonna talk to Chris for a bit. Won't take long, then I'll grab some breakfast from downstairs." He leaned over the bed and kissed me again. "Stay with Grudge for me? The doc will come by later to check him out."

I wished he'd stay, but I also really wanted breakfast, so I said, "Yeah, of course."

"That's our girl," T-Bone said with a soft growl before he kissed me once more, long and lingering. It was near-torture feeling him pull away. Munin flew to his shoulder with a loud caw, nipping at his ear and clearly just as eager for breakfast as me.

I watched T-Bone leave the room, then rolled toward Grudge, who had roused in the last few moments. He stretched long with a groan, making those sexy tattoos expand on his torso, then went to rub his eyes before remembering they were bandaged up.

"Fuhhh meh," he grumbled, letting his arms fall. One of which inevitably fell on me.

"Hey, Grudge," I said quietly, so as to not spook him.

He startled anyway, sitting up in bed in a fumbled rush. "Kah?"

"Yeah, it's me. You're okay. T-Bone just went down to get food."

"Mmm." He calmed slightly, releasing a big breath and signing, *"OK."*

"How did you sleep? Do you need anything? Water?"

"Mm-mm." He shook his head and reached his hand in my direction. I gave him my palm, into which he finger-spelled a brief sentence, letter by letter. *"How are you? Ok?"*

I smiled, touched both by his thoughtfulness and how fast he'd picked up the letters after a quick practice last night.

"I'm, ah, well…"

No one had asked me that question and genuinely wanted to know the answer in a really long time. How was I supposed to sum up my emotional and mental state in just a few words? Nothing could come close to describing the overwhelm roiling inside me. I loved being closer to the Sons, but everything else tightened my gut with anxiety. Plus, there was still Dyno throwing a wrench into things. I missed him, despite his pushback.

"Kah?" Grudge squeezed my hand, lips thinning as he waited for my answer.

"Sorry, I just started thinking about…everything." I laughed sheepishly. "I'm doing okay, Grudge. Hanging in and taking it one day at a time. Thank you for asking." I returned his hand-squeeze, wishing once again that I could kiss him. "Being with you guys makes it easier though."

"Hmm." He tilted his head, opening my palm so he could finger-spell to me again. *"Here for you."*

Well damn, if that didn't make me melt like an ice cube on the sidewalk.

"I'm here for you too," I said. "How do your eyes feel?"

"Eh." He wobbled his hand in the air, then elaborated into my palm. *"Less pain."*

"Less pain is good. T-Bone said the doctor will be by to check you out today."

"Hm." Grudge released my hands and stretched again, groaning. I was glad he couldn't see my gaze roving over his body. He was built like an oak tree, so solid and strong, but moved with a fluid confidence that was almost graceful. His fingers dug through his thick hair to scratch over his scalp, then he scratched at his beard, wincing like it was uncomfortable.

"Kah?" He reached for my hand again and spelled out, *"Help."*

"Yes?" My voice went a little high and breathy. "What can I help you with?"

"Comb my rat's nest," he answered.

"Sure," I said with a light laugh. "Do you know where your comb is?"

I found it after a bit of rummaging through his saddle bags, then had him scoot forward on the bed so I could sit behind him and comb his hair. After a few minutes, I was genuinely surprised he owned a comb. The man had gorgeous hair, but it was tangled within tangles. I held a section of strands in my fist while attacking the clumps with the comb, trying my best not to pull on his scalp.

"Let me know if I'm pulling on you," I said.

"Hm," was his only reply.

Grudge sat between my legs, my knees bent at his sides. His hands remained in his lap when we began but after a few minutes, he draped his arms over my thighs, fingers brushing gently over the tops of my feet.

"OK?" He signed the two letters against the side of my leg.

"Yes, Grudge. I don't mind. Actually, I…" Nerves clammed up my chest, but I pushed through them anyway. "I really like it when you touch me."

He stilled for a moment before rumbling a low, "Mm-hm." His large hands circled my ankles, fingertips touching easily. Just as quickly as he gripped them, he opened his hands and continued a light touch up my calf muscle. What a shame that I wore leggings. I wanted that light, playful touch exploring my bare skin.

Should've just hopped in the shower with them last night.

"OK?" Grudge asked again.

"More than okay, that feels really nice." I released the section of hair I was combing, to give my hands a rest. "How about you? Feeling okay?"

"Heh." He made a scissoring motion in the air with his index and middle finger, then threw his hands up as if in frustration.

"You want to cut all this off?" I ran my fingers over his scalp to his answering shrug. "I can do that, if you want."

"Eh?" He turned in the direction of my voice.

"I'm a little rusty, but I took some barbering classes a while back. I can cut these tangles out and try to shape it so it's not so in your face. Would you like that?"

"Hm?" He stroked the length of his coarse beard, the end of it reaching the top of his chest.

"A beard trim too? I can do that." I patted his arm, letting my fingers drag over the thick muscle and lines in his tattoos. "We'll have to get out of bed though."

"Meh," he huffed.

Meh indeed. The bed was so much more comfortable.

Twenty minutes later, I had Grudge seated in a chair with a towel around his shoulders and the first clumps of tangled hair had hit the floor. I had to ask around, but one of the service center women found a pair of scissors to loan me. They weren't anywhere near as sharp as barbering shears, but they would do the job well enough.

I walked in circles around him, carefully measuring, combing, and trimming his hair into a style that was hopefully even on both sides, on top of not looking terrible. He raised a hand to finger-spell a question to me about halfway through.

"Why barbering?"

"Why not?" I answered with a laugh. "I was cooped up at home and bored out of my skull. There was nothing for me to do but wander the halls of the capitol or take lessons to learn new things. Plus, learning weird stuff always got funny reactions from my dad."

"What was the weirdest?" Grudge was getting more comfortable with signing already, his hand moving fluidly between the letters and pausing for a beat between each word.

"Hmm." I paused to think, tapping the comb against my cheek. "I think silkworm propagation wins that one."

"Huh?" Even without seeing his eyes, Grudge's look of bewilderment was adorable.

"Yeah, it's where the material silk comes from. They're actually a type of caterpillar that weaves their cocoons from silk. It's fascinating to watch them do it. Then they emerge as moths and only live for a few days before they have to mate and lay eggs. I raised several generations before my dad said it was enough. My few pet caterpillars kind of exploded into a whole colony."

Grudge's lips pulled into a smile, soft laughter huffing from his mouth. He probably couldn't picture me bent over my silkworm containers, content to watch them munch leaves and crawl on sticks for hours. I fell asleep to them sometimes, their constant eating a gentle white noise, like rain.

"That is weird," he said with his hand. *"But cute."*

I snorted, returning my attention to his hair. "I'll take that as a compliment, thank you."

"It is," he signed. *"Normal is boring."*

"We're in agreement there."

Once I got his hair to a point that looked decent and I didn't want to mess with it further, I started trimming his beard.

"Your beard is softer than I thought it would be," I said, carefully holding sections as I trimmed and shaped it closer to his face. I never wanted to stop running my fingers through it.

Grudge said nothing for a while, then lifted his hand to sign slowly. *"Not as soft as you."* My stomach flipped, heart pitter-pattering as he added, *"Glad you stayed the night."*

"Me too," I said, reluctantly dropping my hands from his face. He'd have nothing but a five-o'clock shadow left if

I kept going. "Whenever I'm around you guys, it's easy to be myself."

Grudge held out his palm and I gave him my hand, thinking he wanted to sign. But instead, he returned my hand to his face, leaning his cheek into my palm. The pounding in my chest accelerated, my breath stuck in my throat as he turned his face and tenderly kissed my wrist.

"Grudge…" I smoothed my fingers over his rough cheek, unsure of what I was asking for, if anything. His mouth was off-limits for kissing, but were other places?

With impeccable timing, the door swung open then with a loud creak, startling me into jumping away.

"Whoa, didn't mean to spook you." T-Bone carried a large tray stacked with pancakes, fruit, scrambled eggs, and some kind of sausage. He set everything on top of a chest of drawers before peering more closely at us. "Grudge, is that you?"

"Mm-hm." Grudge nodded in his direction, reaching up to touch his newly trimmed beard.

"Holy shit, you look like a new man." T-Bone grinned appreciatively, coming over to run his fingers through Grudge's hair. "Fuckin' sexy. You did this?" he asked with a curious look.

"Yeah." I stood to the side, a little self-conscious, with the comb and scissors in my hands. "He asked to be cleaned up, and I took some barbering classes a while ago, so…"

"I don't know shit about haircuts, but he looks great, little lady."

"Thank you." I mentally preened at the praise. "He was handsome before, but I agree. It's nice to see more of his face now."

"Heh." Grudge smirked and playfully bit at T-Bone's fingers.

T-Bone's smile faltered when he spotted something outside the window. He moved behind Grudge to look closer, then crossed his arms with a click of his tongue.

"Well. Someone's back awfully early."

My breath stuttered in my chest. "Is it…?"

I went to stand next to him, barely aware of the reassuring hand he placed on my back at the sight Dyno's long black braid, his form hugging around his motorcycle as he pulled up to the service center.

CHAPTER 27

DYNO

What a shitshow I missed.

I would have taken a defensive shootout over dealing with my son's mother any day of the week. The spiteful bitch didn't even let me see him, so the long ride wasn't even worth it.

I hadn't eaten anything since yesterday, so T-Bone and Grudge filled me in while I wolfed down some breakfast. Guilt gnawed at my gut as they told me what happened. If I had been here instead of on the road with my tail between my legs, maybe I could have prevented Grudge's eye injury.

"That wasn't the only notable thing that happened." T-Bone looked at Kyrie and gave her an encouraging nod.

I paused with a fork halfway to my mouth and set it down, watching the subtle tells between the three of them. Kyrie had been quiet, barely touching her food and stealing glances at me while sandwiched between the two guys. T-Bone took every opportunity to touch her and feed her small morsels. Even Grudge was sitting close to her, his hair and beard all nicely trimmed and signing to communicate, a rarity for him.

Seemed like a shootout wasn't the only thing I missed out on, but I didn't like the implication that Kyrie was somehow involved in the fight.

"What's he talking about?" I asked her.

She swallowed heavily and set her plate to the side. "My valkyrie showed up and…I shielded everyone from getting shot."

If there was food in my mouth, it would have fallen out. "You…what?"

I had seen my fair share of miraculous things, and I could see it play out vividly in my head as she described it to me. But, fuck, what I would give to see that happen in real time, knowing she didn't get hurt.

The awe was clear in T-Bone's face as he watched her speak. Even though Grudge's eyes were wrapped up, his posture leaned toward her. The valkyrie on his arm even nudged against the woman who walked out into battle like a shield maiden of the old legends.

The shift since yesterday was clear. The signs were clear. This woman had been touched by gods, *our* gods, and there was no letting her go.

But first, I had to swallow my pride and set things right.

"That's incredible," I said, at a loss for any other words. "But stopping bullets or not, I'm glad nothing worse happened."

"Yeah, me too." Kyrie looked down at her folded hands in her lap, and that tugged at my chest hard. I had to fix this now.

I shoved my plate away and stood. "Can I talk to you for a second, Kyrie?"

All three of them looked up at me—well, Grudge lifted his head in my direction. T-Bone stared me down with a look of warning, while Kyrie was visibly surprised.

"Sure, Dyno," she said lightly. She accepted a cheek kiss and something murmured in her ear from T-Bone before sliding off the bed.

"Let's go up to the roof," I suggested, already bouncing on the balls of my feet with nervous energy.

"I'll get my shoes. They're in my room."

T-Bone stood the moment she left our room, walking up to me until his chest brushed mine. "What're you gonna talk about?" He sounded calm but the demand was clear in his expression.

"Everything."

He rocked back, eyebrows lifted in surprise. "Yeah?"

"It's not like I didn't have time to think." I hadn't slept since we camped and rubbed my eyes, feeling the exhaustion settling in deep in my bones. This conversation needed to happen though, and I didn't dare put it off even longer.

"Riding tends to do that." T-Bone's lips quirked up, his close stance no longer aggressively protective of his *little lady*. He knew what I meant by *everything*, and proceeded to wrap an arm around my shoulders, pulling me in for a quick kiss. "We love you, you know."

"I know," I sighed against his mouth. "Thanks."

The three of us were always more affectionate with actions than words. Love was a shared laugh over drinks, a rough kiss before a ride, or an emotionally charged fuck. But when he said *we*, the first person that popped into my mind was her.

"Ready when you are," Kyrie said with forced cheer outside our door.

I turned, shooting her a smile that seemed to ease her nerves slightly. "Follow me."

We took the stairs to the roof, which was little more than a barren platform now, but looked as though it could have been a bar or lounge before the Collapse. Rickety furniture, sun-damaged and caked in dust, had been shoved off to the side. Nothing was really comfortable to sit on, so I stood at the railing at the edge of the building, looking out at the surrounding desert.

Arizona, this place was once called.

"How is your son?" Kyrie asked. She stood next to me, watching the landscape as I was, slender forearms propped on the railing.

"Dunno," I answered. "They didn't let me into the house to see him. I know he was there though. I heard him crying out for me."

"I'm so sorry, Dyno. That's awful."

"I need to ask you two things, Kyrie. And I need straight answers."

She visibly flinched at my shift in tone. "Okay."

"Does it bother you that I have a son?"

"No!" She said it with such conviction that I wanted to pull her against my chest and devour her in a kiss right then. "I would have liked to have known sooner, but I understand the situation is…complicated."

"Right. Second question."

She straightened. "Yes?"

"Do you want T-Bone all to yourself? Or Grudge, for that matter."

"No." She placed a hand on my forearm and squeezed until I looked at her, taken aback by the sheer determination on her stunningly pretty face. "I would never, ever try to break apart the three of you. The relationship you all have, it's beautiful. You're all so devoted to each other. I can see in every interaction how much the three of you love one another. To try to take one of you for myself would be so selfish, I couldn't. I actually, um…" She pulled her hand back, eyes flicking away shyly. "I'm a little envious, to be honest. I would like to have what the three of you have."

Oh, sweetheart, you already have us.

I reined in the urge to sweep her up and carry her back to the bedroom, where she could have the three of us in any which way she wanted. Instead, I looked back out to the desert, intent on saying everything I needed to. She deserved to hear it all and decide for herself if she still wanted us.

"My son's mother tried to split us up. She tried to use my son to do so."

"T-Bone told me." Kyrie turned to look at the horizon as well. "I'm sorry that happened. It's cruel, what she did."

"So, you wouldn't have a problem with…" I hesitated, choosing my next words carefully. "A child being raised among men. Who, you know, sleep with each other." I looked at her intently. "Because I would like to get full custody of my son one day."

"Not at all." Kyrie returned my gaze, no longer nervous, but the epitome of calm. "I would love to meet your son one day, if that's okay with you."

The words tumbled out of me before I could stop them. "I would love nothing more."

Kyrie smiled. "How old is he?"

"He's six."

"What does he like?"

I thought for a moment. "Last I saw, chicken nuggets.

And robot toys. Took me almost a year to find working batteries for the robot dog he got one Christmas."

Kyrie laughed. "Isaac sounds wonderful." Her hand returned to my arm, and we were now facing each other, standing much closer. "And despite the difficult situation, it sounds like you're trying your best, Dyno."

My hands found placement on her back, her waist held snugly between my forearms. Her hands floated up to rest on my shoulders in such a natural, light movement, like we were meant to hold each other this way.

"You really want all of us?" I asked. "And all the baggage we'll bring along? Because there's no separating us from that."

"Yes, I do." Kyrie's hands cupped the sides of my neck, her face earnest but still a little wounded. "Is that so hard to believe? Just because Isaac's mom didn't support your relationship with the other guys?"

"It's not just her," I admitted. "Women tend to see us as fun and not something that could be serious."

"Why?"

"Because we have the audacity to be attracted to men too."

Kyrie huffed out a breath. "I guess I'm just attracted to men who also like men."

I laughed, hands running up her back to bring her closer. "We thought four years ago you might be perfect for us, and you just keep proving us right."

"Ever since you all brought me back home, and my father lectured me about safety," her thumb traced along my jaw, "I thought about you three, because I was safe the whole time I was with you guys. At home, I was just...stifled."

I reached for her hand, taking it reluctantly from my face. "There's more you should know."

Her fingers curled around mine, much like when we'd danced together. "Okay, I'm listening."

"My son's mother sometimes keeps me from seeing him because," I clenched my jaw, trying to keep the flash of anger at bay, "I made the mistake of telling her my father had abused me."

Kyrie's face crumpled. "Oh, Dylan…"

"Abused kids often grow up to be abusers," I went on. "Because it's all they know. I could have turned out just like my old man if I hadn't run away to the Hopi reservation when I was sixteen. I met my birth mother for the first time, learned the ways of her people. She was already sick though, and she passed away a few years later."

Kyrie's hand returned to my face, knuckle sweeping over my cheek. "I'm so sorry."

"It's alright. She's still here, just in a different form. And meeting her changed the course of my life." I met Kyrie's gaze, determined. "Because of her, I'd never hurt a child or a woman."

"I know that." Kyrie said it as if it were obvious. "I knew it the minute you saved me from someone who wouldn't hesitate to hurt me."

She was practically against my chest now, only her forearms between us while she caressed my face and neck, soothing me like some wounded beast.

"I don't know if Lacey actually believes I'll hurt Isaac or if she's just using that as an excuse to be manipulative, but…"

"It hurt you." Kyrie's touch swept over my brow, whispering the words I couldn't bring myself to say. "Whatever she believes, it's not true, Dylan."

I huffed out a laugh despite the heavy conversation. "I love it when you say my name."

"Dylan," she crooned again. "If you need my help in getting your son back, just say the word and I'll be there."

I breathed in her sweet scent, pulling her tighter against me. She might be more than what I deserved, but fuck if I was ever going to let her go. "I'm sorry for what I said before I left."

"Hm, you weren't wrong." She dragged a finger along the shaved side of my head. "But I don't care who knows about us or what this will do to me politically."

"Me either, but I needed to know." I gripped the back of her neck, holding her in place with my lips hovering just above hers. "If you were serious about us or just wanted to play."

Kyrie's lips pursed, playfully defiant. "Are you satisfied with what you learned?"

I kissed her in answer, holding nothing back. She stumbled under the force of it but quickly recovered, held up by my grip on her. Maybe T-Bone was gentle with her, but if she was going to be with the three of us, she needed to handle our rough style of love. She took my kiss in stride, meeting each lash of my tongue and holding the back of my head to pull me deeper. When she bit down on my bottom lip and sucked hard, a deep groan of satisfaction left my chest.

She was perfect, *so* perfect.

Who would have known pretty and sweet Kyrie Vance was made for tumbling with roughneck bikers?

"Please," she begged sweetly on a breath before I devoured her lips again.

"Please what?" I ran one hand down her back until I cupped her ass, the sexy globe filling my palm with a satisfying weight as I kneaded it. "Tell me what you want, Miss Ambassador."

She laughed, bringing a finger against my lips to stop my next kiss. I just sucked it into my mouth and waited for her to speak.

"First, don't call me that."

"Hm." I bit lightly on her fingertip in response.

"Second." Kyrie paused, licking her lips. "I want to go back inside," she whispered. "To be with all of you."

The look she gave me was ravenous, so openly wanting. She didn't just accept the idea of being shared, she *craved* it. She wanted it as badly as my cock ached for her right then. And somehow, I was one of three lucky bastards in the world who had the privilege of her want, of her *trust*. Because I knew for her, the two were intrinsically linked.

"You want all of us?" I repeated, just to make sure this wasn't some kind of fever dream. "Right now?"

Kyrie pulled out of my arms then until only our hands connected. Her fingers clasped around mine and tugged me toward the door. "Right now, Dylan. I'm tired of waiting."

I trailed behind her with our hands linked until we reached the top stair landing. Then I picked my woman up, hauled her over my shoulder, and raced down the stairs to the shrieks of her laughter.

CHAPTER 28

T-BONE

"This is abnormally fast healing." The center's doctor, Priya, leaned in to inspect Grudge's eyes again. "I've never seen anything like this."

Most of the cuts around his eyes and brow ridge had closed up without the need for stitches, and the swelling had gone down. He still had broken blood vessels in one eye, which made it look completely red and creepy, but was otherwise fine.

Another perk of being favored by the gods? We healed from injuries in a fraction of the time. But the good doctor didn't need to know that.

"He's just a really healthy guy," I said, running my fingers through Grudge's short hair again. Kyrie really sexed him up with the haircut, and I couldn't stop myself from touching him. "Good immune system, you know."

The doctor gave me an *uh-huh, sure* look before packing up her things. "Well, if things get any worse instead of better, let me know."

"Sure thing, doc. Thanks again."

She left the room just as a series of rapid thumps shook the walls and rafters above us.

"Huh?" Grudge blinked, still unaccustomed to having vision again, and pointed at his ear.

"Yeah, I hear it too. What the fuck—"

A huffing Dyno then sprinted in through our open door with Kyrie's petite form thrown over his shoulder like he was a caveman. He came to a stop in front of us and set her carefully on her feet, arms wrapped around her legs in a way that hit directly in *my* caveman brain.

"Hey, guys," I said. "Have a good talk—"

Kyrie spun and ran for me, taking a leap that prompted me to catch her with my palms under her ass. Her legs wrapped around my waist, and she planted a kiss on me before my brain had fully processed what was happening.

"We had a great talk." She smiled against my lips before kissing me again, tongue probing and soft lips sipping at me like I was water in the desert.

"Uh, good," I groaned out. With another kiss, I bounced her up higher into a more comfortable position. Her arms and legs squeezed around me in a full-body hug that I never wanted to break. She was so small and light, I was certain I could hold her like this forever.

"I would like to explore some more," she said, pulling back slightly, like she was still shy. "More than what we did before."

"Is that so?" My chest warmed with delight. "I think that can be arranged, little lady."

"With all of you," she added, sweeping her gaze over to Dyno and Grudge, who'd been watching us intently.

Dyno was already sporting a tent in his jeans, so they must have made up nicely already.

"If that's okay," Kyrie added, hesitation creeping into her expression.

"Little lady." I nuzzled a kiss into her neck, eager to put her anxieties at ease. Group fun could be overwhelming in the best ways, and she was still so new to sex in general. Even if she enjoyed herself, she had to be handled delicately. "It's beyond just *okay.* You're more than anything we've ever dreamed of."

"We only want you to be pleased," Dyno added, already palming his thick erection. None of us missed how Kyrie's eyes followed his hand.

I patted Kyrie's ass, bringing her attention back to me. "Let me lay you down, and we'll just see what happens, alright? You can say no to anything we do, at any time."

"Okay."

I kissed her nervous smile away, moving toward the bed. She clung to me until her back hit the mattress, and then she absolutely melted into the soft surface beneath her. That was a good sign—she was relaxed. Her legs remained locked around my waist, but her hands moved over me in light caresses. Fuck, her touch was so soft, almost tickling. Until her, I'd forgotten how different women were from men in bed.

When her small fingers crept under the hem of my shirt, I lifted away to pull it off for her. An idea struck me then at the sight of the other two hovering near, hungry gazes locked onto her.

"Grudge," I said. "Come here."

He came up to my side, kneeling on the bed next to me. He had pants on, to be decent for the doctor's visit, but was shirtless like me, and I'd gotten the sense that Kyrie enjoyed a bit of voyeurism. I grabbed a scruff of hair at the back of his head and brought his mouth to mine in a bruising kiss. Grudge moaned and returned the kiss just as good as I gave it, his hand dragging possessively down my chest.

Kyrie's little gasps and harsher breaths just encouraged us. My free hand caressed her body, memorizing her sweet curves, while I tongue-fucked Grudge's mouth. Imagine my surprise when the shy little lady grabbed my hand and moved it lower.

I moaned low and guttural, letting her guide my fingers to her clit, that sweet spot that made her unravel so beautifully when we were alone together. But I wasn't about to get her off the same way today. She wanted more, so I'd give her more.

I broke off a kiss from Grudge, leaning my head back to let him drag that mouth down my neck. "Take those off," I said to Kyrie, gesturing at her leggings. "Fuck it, take it all off."

"I got it." Dyno lined his body up next to hers, leaning down to kiss her while he traced the luscious curve of her hip and waist. He bunched fabric in his fist, pulling it down slowly over her hip and the long journey down her legs.

"Look, Grudge," I grunted at the man still sucking my neck. "Look at her."

He leaned his forehead on my cheek, hands still trailing over me as we watched Dyno unwrap Kyrie from her clothes like the prettiest gift. Her knees were bent with her legs closed now, arms across her chest. I couldn't see all of her expression over Dyno's shoulder, but he was smoothing hair away from her forehead, peppering kisses over her lips, cheeks, and nose.

"Don't cover yourself, you're beautiful," he murmured.

"*So* fucking beautiful. You're making us ache for you, Ambassador."

She laughed at the nickname, some of the tension draining from her body.

I touched her knee until she looked at Grudge and me again. "Want to keep watching us, little lady?"

"Yes." She nodded, her voice a little breathless.

Dyno smirked at that. "Hm, you can try." He reached across to grab the far side of her neck, then dragged her into him to kiss and suck the soft flesh closer to him.

"Oh, fuck!" Kyrie's eyes widened before they rolled back, her lids closing to the decadence of Dyno's mouth on her neck and shoulder.

As much as I wanted to give him shit for distracting her, she was relaxing again. Her body went languid, knees parting slightly as she became too turned on to be nervous about being naked.

For a few moments, I was the voyeur in this scenario. I watched her writhe under Dyno's skilled mouth, her hips and waist swaying on the bed with the pent-up need for something between her legs. *Soon, little lady.* I released a groan with the thought as Grudge ran a hand down my stomach, reaching into my pants to squeeze my cock which was already solid as iron.

I turned my head to him, nipping at his jaw. "You tryin' to be a distraction too, huh?"

"Heh," he scoffed, grinning knowingly as he gave me a good, long stroke.

"Oh, fuck. Take it out, Grudge. Let's show Kyrie how hard she makes us." We worked in tandem to get each other out of our pants. Within moments, we were stroking each other, kissing and groping roughly while keeping an eye open to the side to watch our girl. "Dyno, stop for a second. She can't see us."

"Mm." Dyno was shirtless now and halfway on top of her, their mouths locked in a deep kiss. He only paused in rolling her breast to hold up his middle finger in my direction.

"Yeah, you'll stick that finger somewhere in a minute."

"Wait, what? I thought I heard my name." Oh, fuck me, she sounded so breathless and husky. I wanted that mouth on my cock so bad.

Dyno chuckled and rolled to his side, giving her a clear view of Grudge and me. Kyrie's perfect mouth dropped open at the sight of us, then closed. Her teeth sunk into her lip, and her round eyes were glued to our hands sliding up each other's cocks.

"Like it?" Dyno propped himself on his elbow and brushed his knuckle against her cheek. "You like watching them touch each other?"

"Mm-hm." She was barely paying attention to him, and it stroked the fuck out of my ego now.

"You can tell them what to do if you want." His hand trailed down her neck to stroke over her chest. "Tell one to suck or fuck the other. They'll do anything you say, beautiful."

"Um…" The shy smile returned, a flush darkening her chest and neck. "You guys can, I dunno, kiss again."

I grinned. The sexy bossy side of her would come out eventually with time and practice. "I'll do you one better, little lady." I grabbed Grudge's ass to pull him closer until the length of his cock nudged against mine. With one hand wrapped around both of our cocks, I grabbed his jaw and kissed him, as she requested.

Grudge moaned and jerked in my hand, his hot length

gliding against mine. I stroked us both and heard Kyrie's escaped moan too. Her toes brushed against my knee, and I released Grudge's face to drag a light touch along her leg. She wasn't all the way open yet but getting there as my fingers skimmed up past her knee and to her inner thighs.

Her skin was so hot, burning up my palm as my touch grew bolder, inching higher. The softness of her contrasted with the hardness gripped in my other fist. My touches were different for each of my lovers too. I jerked Grudge and myself with a practiced confidence—I knew him so well, I could jerk him off in my sleep. But with Kyrie, I still had so much to learn. I had to keep her comfortable and relaxed, ease into what she wanted. She'd never question her own wants with us, ever.

"Guys?" she piped up after a few moments.

Grudge and I broke away mid-kiss, looking to her eagerly. "Yes, gorgeous?"

Her pupils were blown wide, eyes darkened with lust and a *need* I hadn't seen there earlier. "Grudge, can you… suck T-Bone?"

"Oh, that's our girl." Dyno hummed with approval at her side, kissing her cheek while smoothing a hand over her belly. "It's so sexy when you ask for what you want."

Kyrie looked at him next. "And can I…touch you?"

"Beautiful, you can smother me in green chile sauce, and I will happily oblige."

Kyrie's giggle was contagious. Even Grudge laughed as he kissed a path down my stomach for her request. Dyno wasn't usually the goofball in the bedroom, but I knew he was doing it with what we all had in mind. Make her feel at ease. Comfortable. Relaxed. *Safe.*

Grudge's lips slid over me, and I tipped my head back with a groan, my fingers finding purchase in his dark hair.

"Mm, I really fucking like this haircut," I grunted, moving my hips to fuck Grudge's mouth. "Makes you nice and easy to grab while you suck my cock."

"Oh my God..." Kyrie's little gasp brought my focus back to her, but Dyno wasn't doing anything especially titillating. She returned my gaze, the shy smile growing wider. "I'm just not used to hearing you talk like that."

"You get used to it." Dyno turned her face back to his for another kiss. "And then you start talking dirty until it feels natural. Like this." He took her hand, dragging it down his body, then wrapped her slender fingers around the erection in his jeans. "Do you want to stroke my cock, beautiful?"

"Yes," she whispered.

"Yes, what?"

"Yes, I want to..." she trailed off, covering her eyes as another nervous giggle escaped her mouth.

"Nope. None of that." I lightly smacked the skin of her thigh, just hard enough to get her attention. "Use your words, little lady. Communicate. That's how this works."

Kyrie's legs clamped shut with my hand between them. She rubbed them together, desperate for more sensation, which I'd be happy to give her as soon as she spoke up.

"I...would like to touch your cock," she told Dyno with a lick of her lips. "And maybe even taste it."

"Oh, good girl," he praised her, peppering her face with kisses. "Go ahead and unzip me. I'll show you how to touch it."

She absolutely glowed under his praise and worked to free him with both hands. I couldn't make it that easy on her, so my hand slid a few inches higher to reach home— that gorgeous cunt.

"Oh, fuck!" Kyrie's hips kicked off the bed when I

pressed between her legs, no clothing in the way now. Just my palm against hot, slick folds.

"That's perfect, just like that." Dyno guided her fist up and down his shaft. "Ignore T-Bone, pretend he's not there."

"Fuck you. Little lady, pretend *he's* not there. Make your hand all limp and just watch Grudge suck me."

"Shut up." Dyno grinned at me, his hand running down the side of her body, inching toward her thighs where I was. "Gonna share some of that pussy?"

"Maybe if you're nice," I teased. "Kiss me and tell me you're sorry."

"I'll kiss you, but I ain't sorry for shit." He rose up to kneeling, coming closer to me while still giving Kyrie enough room to stroke him.

"You will be when I'm deep in your ass but won't let you come." I grabbed the back of his neck before he could escape and pulled him in for a hard kiss that nearly sent us tumbling from the momentum.

Once we righted ourselves, Dyno's hands roamed over Grudge, who was still teasing me with his fist and mouth. And Kyrie, bless her, rolled up to suck the tip of Dyno's cock into her mouth.

He let out a string of Hopi, English, and nonsensical curses, which only seemed to fuel her confidence. She was hesitant at first, then started sucking him with gusto. Her tongue caressed over his stiff cock, cheeks hollowing as she drew him in with those pretty lips, her hand working in tandem with her mouth.

My palm against her pussy was soaked with her juices, and I nudged my thumb over her clit just to see her hips buck again. "Do you want more, little lady?"

She nodded eagerly, lips sliding over Dyno's blunt head to breathily say, "Yes, please."

I didn't bother telling her to be more specific—I wanted more too.

"Grudge," I grunted out, cupping his face to ease him off my aching cock. "Play with my ass, I want you to fuck me in a bit."

"Mmm." He hummed agreeably before moving behind me.

With him back there, I lowered to my elbows, easing myself down between Kyrie's legs. Her sexy slurps on Dyno were like music to my ears, punctuated by her soft moans and his rough voice whispering praise and encouragement.

I kissed her thighs as I made my way to her center, my fingers stroking through her folds as I teased her opening. She was soaking wet and so ready, but I still wanted to be careful with her.

"Tell me if I hurt you," I said, my mouth hovering inches away from this delectable pussy I was just dying to taste.

"Mm-hm," was the response I got.

So I pressed one slick finger through her opening. She was snug around me, but I only heard moaning, felt her hips rolling up like she wanted more. I pressed my middle finger inside her and felt her freeze, along with a small bit of resistance.

Enough for now, I thought, just as Grudge hooked two fingers inside me and sent a fresh jolt of pleasure through my cock.

I lowered a kiss to Kyrie's clit, licking and nuzzling the sensitive bud as I stroked my fingers through her as gently as I could muster. Grudge was being much rougher with me, though not in any way I didn't like or couldn't handle. I wanted to stroke myself but at the same time not lose any point of contact with Kyrie.

"Are you okay?" Dyno cooed to her gently. "You're so fucking beautiful and sexy. So amazing. You're close to coming, aren't you, good girl?"

His hand gripped her thigh next to my face, massaging the sensitive flesh. Her juices and sweet scent coated my beard and tongue, and I couldn't get enough. I could feel her orgasm building as she drove her hips up into my face, heard it in her moans as they grew more high-pitched and desperate.

Her body finally relaxed around my fingers but before I could insert another, Dyno was right there. He slid a finger inside her alongside mine, and we fucked her together while my tongue lashed at her clit. I don't think she realized it right away, but the moment she did, she moaned wildly, and we felt her orgasm clench around us both.

CHAPTER 29

KYRIE

I was stuffed so full and somehow still craved more. Dyno—his cock—barely fit in my mouth. He was fascinating to taste though—smooth, velvety skin over rigid muscle that jumped and twitched when I touched it in certain ways. I was probably clumsy and not rocking his world or anything, but he moaned and stroked my face while praising me. I put forth my best effort just in the hopes of hearing him call me *good girl* again.

A stretching, pinching between my legs made me gasp. It wasn't painful but intense. Something I hadn't felt yet in my explorations with these men. The next thing I felt was T-Bone's mouth on my clit, his tongue darting out to smother the greedy bundle of nerves in toe-curling sensation. His fingers rocked gently through my pussy, and like magic, the pinching feeling eased away, and I only wanted more.

I pulled off of Dyno to take a breath and look at the obscene but incredibly hot sight before me.

T-Bone between my legs, my thighs splayed over his biceps and his large hand clamped around my hip. His other hand stroked through my channel, making sure I felt every drag of his fingers against my walls while his mouth played my clit like an instrument.

Grudge knelt behind T-Bone with one hand on his back, the other making very similar motions as T-Bone was doing to me. It dawned on me then why T-Bone was moaning, his hips making small thrusts back toward Grudge. He'd told Grudge to fuck him, and he really meant...

"Oh God!" My hips bucked into T-Bone's face, and he let out a pleased hum with my clit between his lips. I was nearing that point again, desperate for that insatiable itch to be scratched, pressure building beneath my skin.

"You're close to coming, aren't you, good girl?" Dyno ran an indulgent hand down my body, pausing to squeeze the flesh of my trembling, spread-open thigh.

I could hardly breathe because *yes*, I was so fucking close. Every hammer of my pulse and rock of my hips was a cry out for more, just a little more to send me over the edge. Dyno's touch crept closer, heading toward my center where T-Bone's fingers pistoned through me. There was a stretching, a tightening, *oh fuck!*

My crashing release came from the spark of knowledge that they were *both* fingering me. I thrashed from the onslaught of pleasure, my body clamping around both of them as if to never let go. Chasing my breath as I floated from bliss, I wanted to cry out in protest when they withdrew from me. What I thought was too much was now exactly what I needed as my body pulsed around nothing.

"How did that feel?" T-Bone leaned his head against

my thigh. His beard, glossy with my wetness, shined almost as brightly as the smugness in his grin.

I wanted to smack him just as badly as I wanted to kiss. But I was still noodly, so I settled for reaching down and raking my fingers through his hair. "You know damn well how I feel."

His dark chuckle morphed into a strangled groan, eyes shutting tight as his fingers curled into my thighs. "Oh, fuck yeah, Grudge," he grunted out. "Just like that, more."

Both of Grudge's hands were on his back now, the silent man's hips moving in slow rolls behind T-Bone's ass. The smug, dirty-talking president was now at Grudge's mercy, squirming and babbling while another man's cock moved through him.

"Does it feel good?" I asked before any bashfulness could stop me. "Feeling Grudge fuck you?"

"Ugh...so good." His whiskey eyes slitted open, the lids heavy as he smiled and sucked a hard kiss on my thigh. "It'll feel even better when I feel your sweet pussy come around my cock."

Jesus fucking Christ, the mouth on that man. How could something so vulgar also sound incredibly sweet?

"Let's hold off on a cock train for now," Dyno suggested, still at my side and caressing me reverently. "It's not a first-time type of event."

T-Bone made a small noise of disappointment but shrugged before he pressed up to his hands and then leaned back toward Grudge. I couldn't tear my eyes away from the two men, strong limbs grasping at each other, jaws moving in hard, demanding kisses. Grudge held onto T-Bone's hips as he continued thrusting, his hands framing the thick cock jutting out straight toward me. A shame I couldn't have it today, couldn't feel the force of Grudge's thrusts pushing T-Bone into me.

Wait. Grudge hadn't touched me at all since we'd started. Was there a reason for that?

A warm hand cradling the back of my neck distracted me from the thought. "Do you want to sit back and watch them?" Dyno asked warmly, lying down next to me. "Or do you want more?"

"More," I answered without thinking, rolling toward him. Then, remembering to be specific, I added, "I want you inside me. Not just fingers but...but your cock."

Dyno smiled as he held my chin and kissed me, his tongue flicking playfully. "I have to ask, Kyrie," he murmured. "Are you on any birth control?"

Aw, shit. Of all the things I could have forgotten about, it had to be that.

"Oh. Um, no."

"That's alright," he assured before pecking me quickly on the lips. "Be right back."

He rose from the bed, and I took the moment to appreciate the full view of him naked. Tall with lithe, lean muscles like a dancer. He was covered in warm, brown skin and dark tattoos. Dyno had no tan lines and little body hair for a man in his late thirties. In a word, he was just beautiful.

"What're you looking for?" T-Bone groaned. He was nearly flat on the bed now, face and chest against the sheets while his hips lifted higher, arching to take more of Grudge.

"Condoms," Dyno answered, his back muscles bunching while he rifled through saddle bags.

"Mm fuck, uh, my bag. Foot of the bed," T-Bone panted. "Should be some stashed near the bottom."

"Can you tell we haven't used these in a while?" Dyno asked sheepishly while he dug through T-Bone's things.

I wanted to bite my tongue, but the question was burning in my mouth. "Because you haven't been with a woman recently or…?"

"No other men either. It's just been us for the last year or so."

I felt a bit of smug pride at that. And at the knowledge that I was not just some hookup. I meant something to these men, just as they did to me.

"Got it." Dyno was on me again in a flash, rolling me flat to my back and pinning me down with a kiss. Pinched between his fingers was a square, foil packet. He broke the kiss to stare at me intently. "You're sure, Kyrie?"

"Yes," I breathed, adding, "please." There were so many things I was unsure about. But this, with *these* men, was not one of them.

Dyno kissed me once more, then pushed up to kneeling and ripped the packet open. "Come here next to us, guys," he said to Grudge and T-Bone. "I'm sure she'll still want to watch."

T-Bone crawled up on his elbows and knees until he was alongside me, Grudge following after him with his hips still nudged firmly against T-Bone's ass. With a content sigh, T-Bone's head and neck flopped down to the bed, facing me with a blissed-out smile and his ass high in the air.

"Come closer." I crooked my finger at him. "I still want to kiss you."

"You'll never see me turn that down," he murmured, sliding over until his hand cradled my cheek, and his mouth devoured me.

Something wide, solid, and round pressed against my

folds. My body seemed to hollow out, my flesh parting to accept what was being given. I broke the kiss and looked up to see Dyno kneeling between my legs, my thighs over his, and his cock notched at my entrance.

"Keep kissing him," he said, teasing my entrance by sliding his head through my wet lips. "It might hurt a little. It's better if you're relaxed and not waiting for it."

"D will take care of you." T-Bone's rough beard scratched my cheek as he ghosted kisses over my face. "Trust him. He'll make sure you're pleased, little lady."

"I already am pleased." My lips found his again, locking into a devouring kiss while tilting my hips higher toward Dyno. I was ready, beyond ready, even. And shamelessly so. I was done waiting for a loveless, arranged marriage with some man who wouldn't put a fraction of effort into pleasing me as these men did.

T-Bone groaned low like a beast, his tongue stroking inside my mouth like he'd done between my legs minutes ago. A hand swept over my breast, fingers closing around the peaked nipple. I whimpered at the small pinch of pain, then felt something similar between my legs before—*oh, fuck yes…*

"Okay, beautiful?" Dyno's roughened voice hovered above me before I felt his kiss on my neck. "Tell me."

"Mm-hm!" I broke away from T-Bone, my turn to babble incessantly at the feeling of a cock moving through me. "I'm okay, it's good! Ah, don't stop—oh! Maybe not too fast…"

"Easy," someone told me. I wasn't sure who, but someone was playing with my clit again. Slow, circular movements of a thumb matched the steady drags of Dyno's cock through my body.

It was *so* much, so intense, and yet I craved the fullness

of him every time he pulled back. With every thrust inside, the intensity grew more manageable and the pinching ache subsided.

"Oh, she's taking all of me," Dyno hissed out through gritted teeth. "Such a good girl. You're so wet, and you want this so bad."

"Yes," I whimpered when he filled me again. "Oh, yes!"

"Yes," T-Bone grunted out, dragging his mouth to my shoulder. His whole body started to rock as Grudge picked up the pace again, slamming into him much harder than Dyno was to me. "Oh, fuck yeah!"

"You feel incredible, Kyrie." Dyno sank into me deeper, his width stretching and caressing my inner walls. "Like you're made for us."

"I want to feel all of you," I blurted out, not fully knowing if I was talking just to Dyno or all of the guys. I was drunk on pleasure and just saying whatever came to mind.

"Oh, you will," T-Bone promised darkly, turning my head to kiss me again. "You may be our property, but you own us, little lady."

He held me in place with a hand on my neck, his kisses both affectionate and demanding. They were punctuated by his soft moans and grunts as Grudge drove into him from behind. I couldn't get enough of those hot sounds and wanted more. I wanted to know what drove this sweet, sexually-deviant man absolutely wild.

My hand dragged down his body, exploring and groping the hard planes of muscle more boldly now, until my fingers brushed the tip of his cock which jumped at the contact.

"Oh fucking gods, Kyrie," he growled. Then softer, "Please touch me again."

I circled his blunt head with one finger as if considering it. He was so stiff and heavy, desperate for stimulation, for relief.

"Don't call me Kyrie in bed." I meant it as a joke, but it came out more serious than I intended. Sex made everything more intense, even the words I spoke.

T-Bone was quick to heel. "Little lady, please touch my cock again. I *need* you to touch me. *Please*, my little lady..." This massive man, who could pick me up and throw me onto his bike with no effort, was complete putty in my hands. *Begging* me.

It made me feel powerful, sexier, and more desired than I ever imagined. But most of all, I could not get over how hot it was to hear this man beg for my touch.

So I wrapped my hand around him, stroking up the long, stiff length to squeeze around the head. His hips kicked, thrusting through my fist with a deep bellow from his chest. Grudge moaned too, his breaths ragged and fingers digging into the flesh of T-Bone's ass. He took control of the movement, rocking T-Bone back and forth through my hand as he drove into his ass. My gaze bounced everywhere, from T-Bone's red face twisted into a grimace of pleasure, the hypnotic rhythm of Grudge fucking him, to his cock pulsing in my hand.

A warm hand smoothing up my chest, then fingers pulling at my nipple, forced my attention back to Dyno. "Forget about me?" he teased, still gliding in and out of me at a slow, controlled pace.

"No, never." I grinned sheepishly, then hummed with delight at the fullness of him inside me. It didn't hurt at all anymore. "There's just a lot going on."

"Too much going on?" He lifted an eyebrow, dark gaze piercing.

"Not at all." I loved all of it. Being at the center of their attention and yet, not overwhelmed by it. Watching them together, while also enjoying them for myself.

Dyno leaned down, lips hovering over mine in a ghost of a kiss. "Do you want more?"

"Yes," I answered without thought. I was insatiable with wanting to know more, to see what else they liked and more ways pleasure could be achieved.

Dyno brought his index finger to my lips. "Suck," he ordered. I did as he said, and a fresh rush of pleasure filled me at his resulting groan. "Good girl."

He withdrew the digit from my mouth and brought it between my legs. I thought he would slide it over my clit, but he dragged it lower, venturing below his cock seated inside me, and pressed it against my *other* hole.

My eyes widened with a gasp. *There?*

Dyno paused, watching my reaction. "Trust me?"

I nodded slowly. That was where Grudge was fucking T-Bone, right? T-Bone, who was moaning facedown in the sheets and delirious with pleasure right at this moment. He wouldn't be such a mess if it didn't feel good.

Dyno pressed in, and I hissed in a sharp breath.

"Relax," he said, bringing his other hand to my clit and nudging his cock through me. "Don't clench. Breathe, beautiful. Trust us to take care of you."

He lubricated his finger some more and did a wonderful job of distracting me while I acclimated to the sensation. It wasn't awful, just strange. But it made his cock feel even bigger, fuller inside my pussy. The drag of him hit my nerve endings differently, sharper as he began to fuck me harder, finally leaving that slow pace behind.

"Oh, look at you," T-Bone rasped, his cheek pressed to the mattress as he watched me. "You're a fucking vision. Look at you getting fucked so pretty."

"Look at *you* getting fucked," I shot back with a saucy grin.

His laughter cut off with a strangled moan as I squeezed harder around his cock, stroking him faster. I was dying to see him lose control and come like a geyser. I wondered what he tasted like…

His face nudged closer to mine for more kisses and strokes through my hair. "You're ours," he whispered. "We're never fucking letting you go, little lady."

"Don't you ever," I whispered back. "Promise me."

T-Bone groaned through a long kiss, rough hands smoothing over my cheeks and hair as we both got pounded. "Can't promise you much, except for this—we are yours, completely."

My skin felt too tight, there was so much building inside me that I wanted to burst. Another orgasm, yes, but more than that. Tears pricked at my eyes, a small release of how much I *felt* for these men. Not just physically.

Dyno started massaging my clit roughly, the strikes of pleasure almost painful from his ministrations. I looked in his direction to find him and Grudge locked in a fierce kiss. It was erotic beyond words, two gorgeous men kissing while their hips bucked and fucked the people in front of them.

And they were all mine.

I could have this whenever I wanted.

The realization was a heady one, so much so that I tightened my grip on T-Bone's solid cock and kissed his neck while he babbled about being so close to coming. I pressed my feet into the bed and arched my hips higher to receive more of Dyno, in my ass and my cunt. He moaned through a kiss with Grudge and started fucking me wildly, losing all finesse to his measured thrusts, and that was just the erotic cherry on top.

I was truly reaching my limit now, my body stuffed full while every touch lit up sparks in me like an electric current—the fuse to set off a bomb.

"Fuck, ohfuckohfuck, gonna come," T-Bone bellowed into my neck.

My arm ached, but I never stopped, only slowed down my strokes as he painted my hand and the sheets underneath him. Grudge kept driving into him, and I swore it prolonged T-Bone's orgasm. His cock pulsed steadily, spilling more cum with each convulsion. All at once, Grudge's thrusts halted, his hips glued to T-Bone's ass and his head thrown back. A throaty moan escaped, reaching the ceiling as his body stiffened and then shuddered with release. The two of them separated after a few seconds of stillness, and T-Bone collapsed into a sweaty, panting heap on the bed.

"How did that feel?" I couldn't help but ask him, chasing my breath as I neared my own peak.

T-Bone smiled wearily at me but didn't answer. His brain was probably too scrambled. Mine would be too if I orgasmed for almost a full minute straight.

Grudge and Dyno returned to kissing, their passion and intensity nearly violent as they bit and pulled at each others' lips. Grudge slid a touch down Dyno's back and when the man fucking me growled and pressed deeper into me than he had yet, I knew exactly where Grudge's hand went.

Dyno's cock struck a new place inside me, made even more intense by the added pressure of his finger in my ass. With his rough handling of my clit and the sight of him and Grudge devouring each other, I was racing toward my finish, and nothing could stop me.

T-Bone slid a hand over my neck, thumb brushing over my achingly sensitive lips as he sucked my earlobe.

"Come for us, little lady," he said. "Come for your men."

That final command did me in, hurtling me into space.

The shockwaves ran through me, and I lost control of my body. I couldn't even feel the bed underneath me anymore. I closed around Dyno in both places he was inside me and felt him convulse in return, then more lightning struck me. I felt like I'd run a marathon, yet so languid and weightless that I could fall asleep instantly.

In fact, I think I did.

I roused to gentle pets of my hair, kisses on my forehead, and the sound of water running. My pillow was a broad chest, covered in a large raven tattoo. T-Bone's arms were my blankets, keeping me warm and secure.

"She lives," he chuckled, kissing my nose.

"Mm, how long was I out?"

"A few minutes. We were all pretty wiped out." His knuckles brushed over my cheek, whiskey-brown eyes warm and loving. "Gonna get cleaned up with us or run off to your room?"

I curled up smaller, placing a kiss over his heart. "You might have to carry me, but I'm not going anywhere."

He didn't answer with words, but the tightening of his arms and the pleased hum from his chest was enough.

CHAPTER 30

GRUDGE

*A*lone at last.

The thought felt bitter, unpleasant all the way to my stomach. Who was I kidding? I never enjoyed being alone. Dyno complained about T-Bone being clingy, but to me, nothing felt better than someone needing me.

After having Kyrie in bed with us though, something felt...*off,* and I needed this ride to clear my head. She and I never touched while it was happening, and I didn't know how to feel about that.

The sun was just peeking over the mountains, and I squinted at the oncoming brightness. The doctor said I might have light sensitivity as my eyes healed. I could have waited until later to do this, but I *needed* to get out of that bed. After that session in the morning, the four of us hardly left it for the remainder of the day. And then Kyrie stayed with us during the night.

Aside from a brushing of limbs now and again, Kyrie and I never touched. Except for when T-Bone and I had switched places at some point during the night and I found myself curled up around *her,* naked. I made off before Kyrie woke up, but it was damn difficult with how soft and warm she was.

I turned my bike sharply, veering off the dirt road into the wilderness. Later on, it would get windy enough to cover my tire tracks. No one ever came out this way, but we could never be too careful. I knew the way to my destination by heart and drove on autopilot, turning at the landmarks that only the Sons of Odin and the Steel Demons knew. A cactus with a broken arm. A boulder striped with layers of red.

I barely took notice of these markers, my focus fully on the sight of Kyrie from last night. Flushed and panting. Shy at first, then wanton and shameless. I could see the relief on Dyno's face when they came back to the room together. T-Bone was sure of her since the beginning, he was just afraid to admit it to himself. Dyno had some lingering doubts, but those were clearly erased from their rooftop conversation. The guys were thrilled to have their wildest dreams confirmed—she fit with us, and it felt right.

But me?

I adored that woman beyond measure, and I had been aching to touch her in earnest. But I wasn't like T-Bone and Dyno. She might fit perfectly with them, but I couldn't shake the feeling that I was too fucked up for her.

It took me a long time to come around to kissing, and I only ever trusted the guys with that. When we had hooked up with others in the past, well, it usually went about the same as yesterday morning.

I was the weird, quiet one with hang-ups about kissing and women, especially. The guys never ignored me in group situations but added partners usually did.

Kyrie though...she didn't ignore me. Her eyes had been on me even as the other two pleased her. If I'd been in a position to touch her, would she have wanted that from me?

I released one of the bike handles to run a hand through my hair. The blunt, shorter ends still felt strange but freeing. I recalled her hands on my head and on my face when she trimmed my beard. I couldn't see her then, but I *felt* her care in how she touched me. She wanted to do a good job. She said I looked handsome.

She's nice, I reminded myself. *She would do that to anyone.*

I sighed into the wind whipping past me and hit the throttle to go harder. How pathetic did I have to be, thinking back to all her sweet gestures to convince myself that she liked me as much as them? She was friendly, kind, and made T-Bone and Dyno wildly happy. That was enough. I should be satisfied with that.

My thoughts were so consumed by her, I almost drove past the drop-off point and had to double-back. I kept my bike idling when I parked it, checking my gun inside my cut and my surroundings while I made my way to the inconspicuous boulder near a cluster of bushes.

I knelt behind the rock and stuck my hand in the little groove on the underside. I felt a piece of paper that had been folded and wedged between the rock and the ground. Once I retrieved the note, I took another cautious glance all around before opening it.

DELIVERED YOUR MESSAGE. *We need to meet urgently. Sunset at the bluffs.* —S

• • •

I TORE the paper into tiny pieces and scattered them in different directions. The wind would do the rest of the work before long. Then I returned to my bike and high-tailed it back to the service center.

THE THREE OF them were recently awake by the time I returned to the room. I opened the door to the sound of soft laughter and murmured conversation. They were still in bed, the freshly changed sheets rumpled and doing a poor job of covering everyone up.

Dyno sat with his back against the headboard and Kyrie snuggled into his side, his arm around her shoulders and fingers tracing lightly over her skin. T-Bone was scooted lower, his feet dangling off the edge of the bed and his head resting on Kyrie's hip. They all looked perfect together, just as they were.

"What's up, Grudgie?" T-Bone asked, hugging a thick arm around Kyrie's legs.

"I got a reply from Shadow. He wants to meet us at—"

"Whoa, hold up." Dyno raised a hand toward me. "Dude, you're *signing.*"

"Huh?" I blinked and sure enough, my hands were making gestures to communicate. I hadn't even realized I'd done it, didn't even think about reaching for a piece of paper.

"It's muscle memory," Kyrie said, lifting her head from Dyno's chest. "You had to sign for almost two full days while your eyes were bandaged."

It made sense, but I didn't like how she was looking at me now, scrutinizing, like I'd been caught in a lie.

Which I suppose was technically true.

"You weren't finger-spelling just now though," Kyrie went on. "That was *actual* sign language."

"Yeah," I mouthed and then signed, *"Sorry."*

A heavy silence fell over the room, increasingly uncomfortable with every passing second.

"He's not fluent," T-Bone said softly. "He just…doesn't like to use it."

"I gathered that." Kyrie spoke quietly, a coolness in her tone that was a shocking contrast to the warmth she usually exuded. "But it seems that's changed now?"

Everyone's eyes were on me, imploring and curious. Just the weight of their stares made me itch for a pen and paper. The written medium let me present my thoughts a certain way, made it easy for everyone to understand, even if it would never be second-nature to me like body language.

Signing used to dredge up memories of the one who'd taught me and the following events that happened because of me. Speaking with my hands felt like I was mocking her after what happened, so I refused to do it except for small hand signals here and there. Dyno and T-Bone respected my choice, and we'd all adjusted. It had never been an issue before.

Then I had to lose my eyesight for two days and feel Kyrie finger-spelling into my palm. I never realized how instinctual it was to speak using my hands. And now I slipped back into it without the sickening dread or memories that usually came along.

Everything was still there. I felt the dread and terror in my stomach now as I thought of it, seeing my only friend ripped away while my ruined mouth prevented me from helping her.

That moment would haunt me forever, but why it didn't consume me this time while I signed, I didn't know. The only difference in my life was Kyrie.

"I think I'll manage," I signed in response to her question. The guys immediately looked at her to translate, but her focus was on me.

And a huge weight lifted off my shoulders when her warmth and smile returned. "I'm glad," she said, using her mouth and hands. "What were you saying before, Grudge? Shadow wants to meet where?"

Shit, I didn't know the sign for bluffs, so I spelled it out and made a vague gesture with a cliff.

"The bluffs," Kyrie confirmed, her gaze shifting between Dyno and T-Bone. "You guys know where that is?"

"It's a few hours' ride." T-Bone scratched the beard on his chin. "Did he say when?"

"Sunset," I reported. *"He said it's urgent."*

Kyrie relayed this to them, both of whom groaned and held onto her tighter, as if she might slip away.

"So much for another relaxing day in bed." T-Bone sighed and kissed Kyrie's waist as he pressed up from the bed. "We should get going if we want to make it on time."

"Should we get Chris and Tiff up?" Dyno asked, his head leaning against Kyrie's.

"Yeah. Depending on what Shadow says, we might not be coming back here. Pack it all up."

They peeled out of bed slowly, pulling on clothes with half-hearted effort. Most of my stuff was still packed away, so I turned to give Kyrie some privacy, just in case it mattered.

"Hey, Grudge?" she called.

"Hm?" I took a cautious glance over my shoulder.

She had the sheet over her chest, though it draped loosely, like she wasn't too concerned about me seeing her.

Her smile was still shy but no less breathtaking as she carefully signed a question. "Can I ride with you?"

"Mm-hm." I jerked my chin in a nod and returned to looking away.

As if I could ever tell her no.

EVEN THOUGH THE ride took most of the day, it was too short with Kyrie wrapped around me.

I tried not to read into how easily she leaned into me on the turns, how her fingers tightened and her thighs squeezed around me. She loved riding and took to it like a natural, that was all. There was no intimacy here, and I had to stop searching for it in mundane things like this.

She asked to ride with you *though.*

Obviously, she likes variety. It still doesn't mean anything.

My trite arguments with myself dissipated at the sight of a tall figure leaning against a motorcycle up ahead. He looked to be standing at the edge of the world. Just beyond him, a sheer cliff face dropped to a river below. The sun had just set, and the fading colors sharply outlined his dark silhouette.

Excitement drove me forward, and I pulled up ahead of T-Bone so I could be the first to greet my half-brother.

Shadow, the Steel Demons MC assassin.

He leaned off his bike seat, straightening to his full imposing height when I parked next to him. Dressed in riding leather from the neck down, only his facial scar was visible, a slash through his left eye and nearly half of his face.

The injury had turned that eye white, and his odd-eyed gaze would have been unnerving if he didn't look so fucking happy.

"Grudge." He held his arms out, his grin almost jovial.

I allowed Kyrie off first, the laughter already escaping me as I went to embrace the big man. Our arms clasped violently around each other, and I sent him staggering back a few feet.

We had only met a few years ago, but he and I understood each other in ways few others did. T-Bone and Dyno knew how I turned out this way, but Shadow was the only person who had lived a similar existence.

I had my tongue removed and was forced to witness something that would haunt me until my last breath. Shadow nearly lost an eye and was covered in a hundred lifetime's worth of scars. And that was only the physical damage done to us.

Miraculously, we both crawled our way out of that hellish existence and found the people who healed what was left of our bruised, battered souls.

"It's been too long, brother." Shadow playfully slapped the sides of my head. "You need to come meet your niece and nephew. Mari will lose her shit when she sees you."

"Mm-hm!" I tapped his chest and nodded. Aside from Dyno's son and Bash's kids, I'd never been around children much. The Steel Demons were extended family, and I hoped we got a chance to meet their twins.

"Kyrie." Shadow stepped away from me and smiled at her warmly. "You look well. The Sons have been taking care of you?"

There was a hint of teasing in his question, and Kyrie

didn't miss it, blushing furiously. "Hi, Shadow. It's good to see you too. And...I guess you could say that."

He laughed heartily while the others pulled up and dismounted.

"Shadow!" T-Bone shouted, raising his arms in the air as he approached. "Looking good, big daddy. Damn, congratulations on putting twins inside of Mari. How about them super sperm—"

"Uh." Shadow cut him off with a hand against his mouth. "I'm pretty sure it wasn't *just* my sperm. Our daughter is most likely Gunner's, but thank you. We're all very happy. Sleep-deprived, but happy."

"Leave it to Travis to make it weird," Dyno laughed, coming in next for his hug. "Congratulations, Shadow."

T-Bone introduced Chris and Tiff before getting into the business at hand. "So what calls for the emergency meeting, big daddy?"

Shadow sobered then, his smile fading as he glanced at Kyrie. "I relayed your message to General Bray, who then informed Governor Vance. The governor then called me in himself, demanding to know where Kyrie was and who she was with."

"Did you crack?" Chris asked, arms crossed in front of his chest.

"Of course I didn't," Shadow said. "General Bray is basically a father to me, so he backed me up, but none of it mattered. Vance wasn't satisfied, no matter how much we tried to assure him that Kyrie was in safe hands. He wanted either names and a location or to see his daughter himself."

Shadow blew out a breath and scanned his gaze over all of us. "So he's mobilizing. He's sending troops into Sevier to search for her."

"What?" Kyrie shrieked. "He knows about the uprising, right? Who knows who's trying to take over now? If he sends troops, they're going to be caught up in the fighting there. He's risking lives for no reason!"

"I don't think he cares," Shadow said apologetically. "It's your last known location, so that's where he's headed. He's panicking and doesn't know what else to do but find you."

Kyrie slapped her hands to her face and groaned with frustration. "Why can't he just believe that I'm okay?" When her hands dropped away, her expression was suddenly calm. Almost eerily so. "I have to go see him myself then."

T-Bone, Dyno, and I all held a collective breath, thinking the same thing. If she went into that territory, there was a chance she would never be allowed to leave. A pang hit me hard in the chest. Just the thought of never seeing her again was unbearable.

"What will you tell him?" T-Bone asked her.

She raked a hand through her long hair. "That I've been with you guys, I guess."

Dyno swallowed. "Platonically or...?"

Kyrie chewed on a fingernail. "I...I don't know."

"What if Chris and I escorted you in?" Tiff suggested. "Make a buffer between you and them three in case any shit goes down."

Kyrie shook her head. "Thank you, but no. I think it'll be worse if my dad and his people don't know you. They might hold you for interrogations or something."

T-Bone approached her, cupping her shoulders as he lowered his forehead to hers. "We'll support whatever you think is best," he said. "But we need a plan, little lady."

Her eyes squeezed shut, the obvious distress on her face

making my chest ache. "I don't know! He's probably freaking out because he thinks I'm dead or a prisoner, and I don't know what that means for you guys if he finds out we…" She took a deep, shuddering breath. "I should go alone."

"No." T-Bone's grip tightened on her shoulders. "We're not leaving you unguarded. Either we all go or we find another way."

"Travis." Kyrie breathed his given name as she blinked up at him. "If you all come with me, we can't act like…he can't know that we…"

"Sweetheart, that cat's going to come out of the bag eventually. It'll be worse if he finds out later that we were hiding it."

"You're not a liar anyway, Kyrie," Dyno added. "Don't take on that burden to protect us."

"I will if it keeps you from being treated like criminals!"

"Been there, done that, got the T-shirt," T-Bone chuckled. "Whatever happens, we can handle it, little lady."

Shadow cleared his throat. "I don't mean to insert myself into your situation, but is it at all possible the governor would *support* your relationship? Why go in assuming he won't approve?"

Everyone went quiet, looking at Kyrie while she thought on that notion. "It's…possible, I guess," she relented. "Not very likely. I mean, don't get me wrong, Shadow. He has no problem that you share a wife with three other men. But I'm certain he's never imagined such a thing for *me.*"

"And with bikers, no less," Shadow added with a small smile.

Chris puffed out his chest. "There is an understandable allure to us, no denying that."

Tiff snorted and smacked his arm. "If you're lookin' to share me, you're out of luck. My hands are full enough with just you."

"Exactly how I like it," the VP purred, leaning into her.

Their banter broke the tension a little, and even Kyrie cracked a smile. "I should just go in and be honest, I guess."

"That's usually the best way to handle things," Shadow said gently.

Kyrie turned to me, signing as she spoke. "Grudge, are you okay with this?"

I just nodded and made an *okay* sign. Wherever T-Bone and Dyno went, I would go. No matter what, I would still guard her vigilantly.

"So that settles it," T-Bone said. "We go right up to the governor and put it all out there."

"Good luck," Shadow said. "The Demons will watch out for you if anything goes south."

"Thanks, Shadow." T-Bone turned to him and the two of them clasped fists. "Hopefully, we don't need our asses saved, but we appreciate knowing you'll be there if we do."

"It's nothing you wouldn't do for us." Shadow released his fist and clapped a hand down on my shoulder. "Happy for you, brother," he said low near my ear. "She's a gem."

I didn't know how to tell him there was nothing to be happy for.

CHAPTER 31

KYRIE

I thought I might throw up the whole ride to Four Corners. With all the twists and turns through the desert, it was a small miracle that I didn't.

We decided not to drag out the inevitable any longer and headed to my home territory that night. I curled around T-Bone's back, my cheek on his shoulder blade and hands stroking his chest as we rode. He was a pillar of strength and comfort, as I knew he would be. He kissed my fingers and rubbed my legs, which pressed tightly against the outside of his own. If I shut my eyes and held on to him hard enough, I could pretend he was carrying me away. Back to freedom, the service center, their clubhouse, I didn't care. Anywhere but the prison we were riding to.

Again.

The bikes gradually slowed to a stop, and I heard voices over the idle rumbling which meant we must have reached the Four Corners entry point. Dad was strict about who came in and out of the territory and kept soldiers posted at all the entrances twenty-four-seven. He'd know we were here before seeing us.

T-Bone's hand lifted away from my thigh, returning to the handlebars as a soldier approached.

"T-Bone, is that you? Long time no see." The soldier greeted him jovially with a fist bump. "You're looking good."

"Not as good as you, Dixon," he greeted back with his usual flirtatiousness. "You been working out?"

"Oh, you know. Comes with the job." I felt Dixon's eyes on me, though I averted my gaze. I was wearing Dyno's jacket with the hood up, so I wasn't immediately recognizable. "Who's this with you?"

T-Bone straightened, nudging me gently to answer. I pulled my hood back reluctantly and stared dead-eyed at the soldier that I recognized but wasn't acquainted with. He knew exactly who I was though, and his eyes widened.

"Miss Vance," he breathed. "Welcome home. Your father will be overjoyed to know you're safe."

"I'm sure," I said flatly.

This was a terrible fucking idea. The pit in my stomach felt worse with each passing minute. We were fools to think this could have a positive outcome.

Dixon turned to face his fellow soldiers at the gate and waved his arm. "Let them through! It's Kyrie Vance!" He gave us a curt nod as T-Bone rolled the bike forward. "Welcome home to all of you."

"Yeah. We'll see about that," T-Bone said before picking up speed.

I did love Four Corners and remembered why as we drove through the streets. While it was getting late and most areas were quiet, I heard laughter and music from a bar we passed. People chatted amongst each other as they waited for food from an outdoor vendor. Two teenagers talked on a street corner while their dogs sniffed each other.

People were happy here, genuinely so. It wasn't a wealthy territory, flaunting riches like Blakeworth. But no one's child had to sit in the middle of the road to beg for food. Life wasn't perfect, but people were content enough to not start an uprising.

My father provided so well for these people, giving them basic freedoms that he struggled to give me, his own daughter. He'd never let me go out alone after dark to grab a bite to eat. Maybe that was the core of my resentment, the hypocrisy of it.

T-Bone's hand returned to my thigh, giving it a gentle squeeze when we came to a stop sign. "City Hall or his residence?" he asked me.

"City Hall," I answered. "He'll still be working at this hour."

His hand lifted away to drive, and it was all I could not to put it back, not to latch onto him permanently and beg him to turn around. To leave the territory and return to that bedroom where we could do more exploring. I wanted to feel him inside me next or maybe Grudge.

A heavy sigh escaped me while thinking of the silent man. *Oh, Grudge...*

He never touched me while all four of us were together, and I wondered if that was by accident or by design. While I made big strides in getting closer to T-Bone and Dyno, it still felt like a gaping canyon between Grudge and me. I had hoped for some closeness while riding with him to see Shadow today, but it had felt like holding on to a block of ice.

I was surprised by his proficiency with sign language,

but I wasn't angry at him for keeping it from me. I just wanted to understand him. If he didn't want to kiss me or speak to me with his hands, I wanted to learn how we *could* connect. How we could learn about each other and be intimate in other ways. Whatever made him feel comfortable and willing to trust me, I would do.

Because what T-Bone had said also held true for me. These men were mine, and I would never let them go.

We pulled up to City Hall far too soon. I remained wrapped around T-Bone even after his boots hit the ground and he shut the bike off. Dyno and Grudge pulled up alongside us while Shadow broke away and continued on the road with Chris and Tiff. Shadow offered to host them at his house while we figured out our personal business with my father.

T-Bone turned in his seat to face me, holding my chin as he planted a scorching kiss on my mouth. "You can do this, little lady." His thumb dragged over my lip, nose nudging against mine. "You belong to the Sons of Odin, and you can do any-fuckin'-thing."

A mirthless laugh escaped me. "I don't think anyone's ever told me that."

Maybe it was weird to think about, but all I could recall was my father telling me everything I *couldn't* do. I wasn't allowed. It was too dangerous. It was improper for a governor's daughter.

Yeah, spending a whole day in bed with three bikers definitely fell under that last one.

"Well, that's a fuckin' shame," T-Bone said. "Because ever since I met you, I've been amazed by all you've been able to do." He kissed me again through a smile. "And I'm not just talking about the way you stroke my cock."

I laughed with a little more humor this time but was

quickly overcome by sadness. "Why does this feel like we're saying goodbye?"

"We're not," he insisted.

"How do you know?"

Someone else's hand cupped the nape of my neck, fingers working in a gentle massage. "Because nothing can keep you away from us," Dyno said. "If he locks you up, we'll break you free. If he locks *us* up, well…" he smiled devilishly. "Remember how I got my road name."

A tiny spark of hope dared to light in my chest when he said that. Maybe everything would turn out okay.

I climbed off the bike and locked gazes with Grudge standing a few feet away. I couldn't read his expression and didn't know what he saw in mine, but we started toward each other and met in the middle in a tight, desperate hug.

"Grudge, I don't know what's going to happen. Hopefully nothing, but I want you to know," I drew in a shaky breath and his arm tightened around my lower back, "I'm never letting you go. You're just as much mine as they are. Whatever you need from me, I will give you. Just name it."

He drew away from me so slowly, brows drawn tight and mouth frowning as if it physically pained him to separate. His thumbs caressed my cheekbones, fingers skimming gently over my face. Then he cupped my face and pressed his lips to my forehead. My eyes closed while I just inhaled the scent of him—leather, ink, and paper.

When he stepped away, he signed a brief sentence. *"I only need you."*

I wanted to cry and jump for joy at the same time. "I feel the same," I answered. "You're perfect as you are."

Grudge blinked, then his eyes widened as if he came to a sudden realization. He started to reach for me again when T-Bone said, "We should get this over with. Then we'll celebrate like a happy quadruple later."

"That's a stupid word," Dyno muttered, heading for the city hall entrance.

T-Bone followed. "Yeah well, you got a better one? How about love-rectangle?"

"Ugh, that's even worse."

Grudge's hand slid into mine, fingers interlacing as he tugged me after them. The warmth had returned to his dark eyes, and I swore even he was smiling.

"I suppose your president's right," I said, the spark of hope glowing even brighter. The guys were relaxed and cracking jokes. If they weren't worried, why should I be?

Once inside the building, we didn't have to go far. Across the long foyer, I saw a small crowd of soldiers, General Bray among them, moving quickly toward us. The general's eyebrows lifted in surprise, regarding the Sons and I cautiously.

"It's true, Governor," he said, stepping aside. "She's home."

The soldiers spread out to reveal my father, Governor of Four Corners, Martin Vance, in the middle.

He looked exhausted and thin. When did the uprising happen, three or four days ago? He looked almost as bad as when I'd been held in Blakeworth for over a week.

"Kyrie." He choked out my name with such immense relief, his posture sagging like he barely had the strength to stand upright. "My girl. Oh, my sweet daughter, you're alive."

"I'm okay, dad." I came forward to accept his hug, smiling to reassure him. "I've been okay the whole time. I was never in danger."

Dad clutched me to his chest tightly, his breaths fluttering my hair. I felt his hands lock together around my back and that made me stiffen, like he was already caging me again.

"Never again," he murmured in my hairline. "It was a mistake to let you live in another territory. I'm never letting you out of my sight again."

Fuck. That was exactly what I was afraid of.

I wrestled out of his hug to put some distance between us. There was still so much to say, and this already wasn't looking good.

"Dad," I said in my sweetest tone, still smiling at him. "Everything turned out okay. No one could have predicted the uprising, but the Sons did their job phenomenally and kept me safe."

Still keeping a tight clutch on my arms, he looked past me to the Sons, as if noticing them for the first time. "That is wonderful to hear, darling. Thank you, gentlemen, for fulfilling your duties, as you always do. I know we've had our disagreements, but you have my deepest gratitude."

None of the Sons spoke but gave him tight-lipped nods in response. My dad's thanks sounded like empty lip service, and it soured my stomach. Even General Bray noticed, his head tilting curiously at the words.

"You will be paid handsomely for my daughter's safe return and, of course, you may stay in Four Corners for as long as you like, as my esteemed guests," dad went on. "Now that Kyrie is back, your services are no longer needed, so enjoy your free time—"

"Dad." I cut him off sharply. "There's more you need to know."

He gave me a puzzled look, clearly displeased at his polite, agreeable daughter speaking out of turn. "What is it, dear?"

"Don't you want to know where we've been? What we've been doing?" I almost got a sick, perverse pleasure from goading him like this. I was about to blow the top off his carefully curated image of me. His innocent, mild-mannered daughter was an illusion, and I was fucking sick of playing the part.

I thought I needed to steer this conversation carefully, to be mindful of my father's sensibilities. But all that changed just now with that dismissive attitude toward *my* men. Ordering them away like fucking servants? No. I wouldn't give him the truth gently. I wanted to crash it over his head like the Sons had into my heart.

"Of course I do, dear. But you must be exhausted. Why don't tell me all about it after you've had some sleep and—"

"No." I wasn't going to my rooms, not when I knew he'd lock me in. When he'd have me watched and escorted everywhere *again.*

Dad's eyes narrowed, the suspicion of something finally creeping in. "Kyrie, what's going on?"

"I've been with the Sons this whole time, dad." I willed my voice not to shake, forcing my spine to remain upright. "Not just under their protection but *with* them."

The guys were silent behind me. I could only guess at the expressions on their faces or what was running through their minds.

"What do you mean?" Behind my dad's confused look, I saw some of the soldiers exchanging glances with each other. Some of them got it, even though I had to spell it out for him.

"I mean physically, dad. We've been intimate."

He still looked confused for a second or two, then the

color drained away from his face, his jaw dropping. "You've…*what?*"

"It's true," I said softly. "We've gotten closer since working together in Sevier and—"

"You got involved with a *biker?* Which one?"

My silence was enough of an answer, and he sputtered out the next question like it was choking him.

"Are you telling me you've had…relations with these men? With *all* of them?!"

He probably wouldn't care to hear the technicality that Grudge and I hadn't done anything yet, so I said, "Yes, dad."

"Kyrie, please." Dad turned green, like he was feeling ill. "Please tell me this is some sick joke."

T-Bone spoke up next. "Why would it be a joke?"

My father's eyes snapped to him, and I'd never seen such hateful rage in his expression before. My father was not quick-tempered, just the opposite, really. I rarely saw him angry and never aggressive. If anything, I'd heard criticism that he was too soft as a leader. But he looked like he wanted to tackle my bikers right then.

"Because my daughter would never debase herself with men like *you!*"

"Don't say that!" I snapped.

"Nice to know how you really feel, Vance," Dyno scoffed. "After we've spent years jumping when you called, running around as your hired muscle? After we've bled for your territory *and* saved your daughter? Twice, I might add."

"You *touched* her!" my father roared, shocking everyone. "You—you took advantage of a young girl—"

"They did *not!*" I yelled. "I can make my own decisions!

I chose them, dad. I *wanted* to be with them! For fuck's sake, I *love* them!"

Everyone in the foyer froze. No one even breathed for several long seconds. T-Bone was the first to break the silence.

"Kyrie, I think we should leave."

That snapped my dad back into action. "She is not going anywhere with you! General Bray, arrest these men."

"What? No!" I started back toward the guys, but my father grabbed my arm roughly and pulled me toward him. He wasn't anywhere near as powerfully built as my men, but he was still much stronger than me. My panic grew as the soldiers surrounded my bikers, taking their hands behind their backs and binding their wrists with zip-ties.

I struggled harder against my father's hold and stared in disbelief at General Bray. "They've done nothing wrong! How can you allow this?"

The general inclined his head toward me, the gesture almost apologetic. "They're not formally under arrest, Miss Vance. We'll just detain them for a bit until we come to a solution."

"I'm sure we can find a crime or two in their colorful history to convict them with," my dad said with such a vindictive tone that I didn't recognize it.

"Typical," T-Bone scoffed as the soldiers led them away. They didn't struggle, didn't yell, didn't even seem angry or surprised.

Me on the other hand, I was seething.

"You fucking bastard!" My screams echoed as I fought with all my strength, fought for my men and unleashed my fury at all the unfairness they'd been treated with. "I never should have come back. I fucking knew you would do this! You can't treat people like this, you fucking asshole!"

All my obscenities fell on deaf ears as my father passed me off to the remaining soldiers. "Take her to her room. Make sure the locks are secure, and guard all the doors and windows."

Two men took hold of my arms now, all my thrashing clamped down between them as they led me down the corridor. Where was my valkyrie now? Why didn't she possess me so I could bash a shield over these mens heads?

"I'm not a fucking animal, Governor Vance!" I continued to yell, trying to twist to look at my father behind me. "You can't lock up your adult daughter in her room, you fucking psycho! You can't *fucking* do this to me!"

"Miss Vance," the soldier to my right muttered. "Please stop struggling. We don't want to hurt you." He sounded young, if even sweet. "Sorry," he added. "I agree that it's not right what's happening."

Something about his gentle urging made all the strength leave my body, and I sagged heavily against my escorts. It wasn't their fault, they were just doing as they were told. It was my father's fault. And mine, for bringing myself and the Sons back here when I *knew* what would happen.

The soldiers deposited me in my bedroom without a fight. I sagged onto my bed like a rag doll, limp and lifeless until they left and the lock clicked behind them. That sound re-awoke my rage. That fucking *click* that I heard every single night for four years straight. Shut in my room like a petulant child.

Well, if my dad wanted to treat me like a child, then I'd act like one.

I grabbed the first heavy object I saw, a paperweight on the nightstand, and flung it with all my strength at the mirror on the adjacent wall.

CHAPTER 32

KYRIE

I slept like shit, and not just because of the pieces of my trashed bedroom surrounding me. Every time I started to drift, I remembered my men were spending the night in a cell, and the blinding rage at my father flooded my system.

Morning came and a maid, escorted by two soldiers so I wouldn't escape, brought me breakfast on a tray.

"I'm not eating," I informed them, my voice raw from all the screaming and crying. "Not until my father frees them."

The maid stared at me while the soldiers eyed my trashed bedroom before they put the food on my dresser and left. I stuck to my word and didn't touch the food, choosing instead to inspect the walls and air vents in my room.

Maybe I could escape through an air duct or hide in a hole in the wall, make my escape that way. What I would give to have an axe in my hands now.

I whipped around in a circle, furiously trying to find the valkyrie hiding in the corners of my vision.

"Where were you?" I demanded. "I *needed* you then. Your strength, your weapons. They took my men away, and I couldn't stop them on my own. So where the fuck were you?!"

I screamed at the walls like a madwoman and kept spinning until I was dizzy. No matter how quickly I turned, I could never see the valkyrie head-on. She never answered, and I kept trying to find her, to confront her and demand her help. One axe swing could break the lock on the door. She could get me past the guard outside and out to the jail to free my men.

With an exasperated cry, I collapsed to the floor. My vision spun and my empty stomach roiled. I threw the first thing I saw, a jewelry box that I had already broken last night.

"If you're really my mother, then *help me!*"

She only stood there, as useless and silent as my guards, taunting me.

I didn't know how much time passed, hours probably. My stomach growled, but I only took a few sips of water for my parched throat. Part of me wanted to clean the room out of sympathy for the maids, but there was a twisted satisfaction at seeing the destruction too. I'd kept everything bottled up until last night, and it was strangely freeing.

That feeling would only last so long though, the longer I stayed here.

My bedroom door unlocked with a click at some point, and the person coming through was the last one I expected to see.

"Mari?" I gasped, scrambling off my bed. The trashed

room was embarrassing now, something I didn't want my friend to see.

"Hey, Kyrie." She smiled at me before turning to the soldier who had escorted her in. "It's alright, I'd like to talk to her alone."

"But…"

"You can double-check with General Bray, if you'd like. He won't object to it."

If I was in a better mood, I'd snicker at that. The general was her father-in-law. Once the door closed again, we rushed forward to wrap each other in a hug. Mari had been there at my Blakeworth rescue with the Sons. Her four husbands were the highest-ranking officers of the Steel Demons MC and close allies of the Sons.

"What are you doing here?" I asked. "Shouldn't you be nursing twin babies or something?"

"That's what breast pumps and four daddies are for," she laughed, rubbing my back. "Anyway, Chris and Tiff are having a ball with the twins. They'll survive without Mommy for an hour or two." She pulled back to look at me, genuine concern in her features. "We heard what happened. You doing okay?"

"Uh, no. I'm pretty far from okay." A mirthless, exhausted laugh escaped me while I gestured around to my trashed room. "Pretty much the worst case scenario happened, as I thought it would."

"Your dad won't condemn them, as much as he would like to," Mari said. "Reap and Gun are in his ear right now. They figure he just has to cool off on the realization that his daughter had sex, and then he'll let them go."

"No offense, Mari, but if that's what they think, they don't know my father at all." I sighed and sank down on the one spot on my bed that wasn't covered in broken stuff. "No one knows the side of him that I do, really."

Mari frowned, then pushed aside some debris to sit next to me. "What do you mean?"

I told her everything in broad strokes, because the individual stories were too many to tell in one sitting. My father was overprotective to the point of paranoia. He valued my safety over my growth and even my happiness. I even told her I didn't know the Collapse had happened until a week later, because he wanted to protect me from that information. He thought I was safest within these walls, but Malcolm Blake successfully lured me out of here because no one gave him a second glance. All because he was the son of a governor. But T-Bone, Dyno, and Grudge were thrown in a cell when they did nothing but care for me.

Mari listened without interruption. We weren't especially close, but I'd never had a girlfriend I could just vent to. And bless her, she let me air it all out.

"It's funny that you mention paranoia," she said after I'd finished. "The official reason I'm here is because your dad put it out to the hospital that he wanted you to have a mental health evaluation."

"Ugh, of course he did," I groaned. "I wanted to fuck the three hot guys *he* assigned to guard me. That can only mean I have some loose screws."

Mari chuckled at that. "He clearly doesn't understand women."

"Nope. My mom's been gone too long."

Mari gave a gentle squeeze of my knee. "That kind of explains why he's so protective of you."

"I guess it's better than him resenting me for her death."

"That still doesn't make it okay for him to treat you like this."

I sighed, tilting my head until it landed on her shoulder. "What do I do, Mari?"

She took a deep sigh of her own, leaning the side of her head against mine. "In my experience, there's only one thing you can do when you're stuck between a wall and a man who won't listen."

"And that is?"

"You *make* him listen." She rubbed across my upper back, soothing as well as encouraging. "It's never easy, but your choices are either folding to his demands or sticking to your guns. There is no middle ground at this point."

I knew what she was saying, but it still took me a while to voice it. "If I ever find a way out of here and want to be happy, I might never speak to him again."

Mari squeezed my shoulder. "It's hard to draw that line in the sand. Especially with family, the people you love. But if you want to live *your* life with the men you love, you have to maintain that line."

"You're right. I know you're right."

She hugged me from the side before releasing me and scooting away. "I'll tell your father everything came up normal in your mental health evaluation. He'll probably be ready to talk to you after."

"Thanks, Mari." I smiled weakly at her. "It was good to see you."

"You too, Kyrie. Hopefully it's not the last time." She went to the door, then paused to look back at me. "Not now, but when you're ready, I know a good tactic for opening a line of communication again. On your terms, of course."

"What's that?"

"Grandbabies." She smirked before slipping out the door.

MY FATHER SUMMONED me the next day for lunch. After Mari left, I spent the following afternoon and morning cleaning up my bedroom, only because I felt bad for the maids. I slept just as restlessly as the night before and was now convinced I could only truly rest with warm bodies pressed to me on all sides. With a heartbeat under my ear and muscular arms draped over me.

It had been just over a day, and I missed them with a gnawing ache that threatened to swallow me whole.

I dressed for lunch, and my soldier escorts led me to my father's office. Governor Vance sat behind his large wooden desk, a hand on his forehead as he poured over some documents. "Thank you, gentlemen," he said, barely glancing up when we arrived.

My guards left, and I stood where they deposited me, trying to keep from glancing at the spread of sandwiches, salads, cheese, olives, and more on a buffet table near the large window. I still hadn't eaten anything and wasn't about to break my hunger strike now.

Dad finally glanced up, looking at me cautiously, as if the soldiers had brought a wild animal to his office. "How are you feeling, dear?"

"Are you going to let them go?" I asked in reply.

His lips pressed into a thin line. "If I don't?"

"Then I'll never forgive you." I held up an index finger as he started to let out an exasperated sigh. "Before you write me off as being a spoiled, dramatic little girl, let me assure you that I am not exaggerating. I'm tired of this, dad. I've had enough."

He started to rise from behind his desk. "Let's have some lunch and talk this over—"

"No, we're not doing that." My stomach rippled with hunger the moment he said *lunch*, but I clenched my fists, standing as firmly as I could.

My skin erupted in goosebumps as I sensed the valkyrie approach me then. She stood just behind me, a tangible presence despite being invisible to my father. If I leaned back, I was certain I'd feel her shield press against my shoulder blades.

It dawned on me that *this* was the moment she was waiting for. Now was the time I needed her support, when it was just my father and me. I latched onto her visage for the strength and power she exuded. My heartbeat was the axe against her shield, beating out a war cry.

"Every time I do something you don't like, we sit down over lunch, and you *lecture* me," I said to my father. "You just talk at me and scold me, listing out all the reasons why I shouldn't have ditched my guards, stuck my head out of a car window, or taken *one* puff of a cigar. And you *never* let me talk. You. Never. Listen."

The side of my fist came down on an end table next to me. It wasn't an axe on a shield, but it would do. The thump against the wood was satisfying, strengthening my resolve. I heard the subtle clank of armor as my valkyrie shifted. In my mind's eye, I saw her tilt her head, a slight smile forming on her lips.

"I've had enough of being treated like a child, dad. I'm my own person, capable of making my own decisions. And I won't let you punish innocent men because of what *I* chose to do with them."

"Darling, I…" Dad slouched over his desk, rubbing the heels of his palms into his eyes. "It just doesn't make any sense to me. Why would you get involved with a biker gang? I raised you to be modest and gentle. To have self-respect."

"I *have* self-respect!" My fist crashed down on the end table again, and the valkyrie's chin dipped in an approving nod. "*They* have been respectful of me. You know who doesn't respect me? *You.*"

The word dropped from my mouth, heavy and cutting like an axe swing. "You know who else didn't? Malcolm Blake. Nathan Perry. Governor Perry and all his cabinet members. The only men you want me to be around think of me as some bimbo arm candy. They get married and see their wives as sex dolls. The Sons *never* saw me that way. They saw *me*, the person! But you never respected them either, did you?"

My father was quiet for a long time. During that heavy silence, I was starting to think he might have actually heard me. Actually listened.

"Sweetheart," he began tentatively. "I'm so sorry you feel that way. I never—"

My well of sympathy empty, I cut my palm through the air to silence him. "Please, don't. I know you have justifications for everything. I don't want to hear them." He was good at feigning ignorance, I'd give him that. But he couldn't use that on me anymore. He knew exactly what he was doing.

"Since what *I* want doesn't matter to you, how do you think the Steel Demons will react to you imprisoning their friends?" I peered at him curiously. He had to have thought of that. Maintaining his image was everything, and the Steel Demons were heroes in Four Corners.

Pissing them off would turn the whole territory against him.

"I've already heard their case," dad admitted gruffly. "General Bray is Reaper's father, as you know. I got an earful from him as well."

When it came to his general and other advisors, my dad was actually a great listener. It was ultimately what made him a good leader, that he took advice from people he respected.

It hurt, more than I wanted to admit, that I wasn't included among those people. And neither were the Sons.

"Tell me this," he said, drumming his fingers on the desk. "What if my instincts are right? That those men will just use you and then discard you when they're done?"

I bristled at his speculation. Malcolm Blake had all but promised me he would do just that while he held me captive. He would use me, never be a faithful husband, and only parade me around on his arm when he needed me. A governor's son, privileged and well-reared, like me.

As tempting as it was to spit out those thoughts, I responded, "Then I will learn from the experience and do my best not to repeat it."

My father snorted, dismissive of me *again*, and the valkyrie within me beat a louder drum beat against her shield.

"Have you ever considered you might be wrong?" My temper flared, the embers of it still hot despite burning off most of my rage the night we arrived. "Did you ever think that they could be good to me? That they treat me better than every politician's son or nephew you've introduced me to? Is it *so* hard to believe that they're actually wonderful, and they make me happy?"

"Even if that were true, Kyrie." My father grimaced. "All *three* of them? People might think that you're—"

"What, like Mari?" I shot back. "The most loved and respected medic in the territory? Who has two perfect babies and *four* adoring husbands? Geez, dad, you're right. Why would I want to be anything like her?"

"Even you must realize Mari's situation is the exception, not the rule. It's not even the same thing, because her men don't…"

The realization dawned on me like a light bulb clicking on. A harsh laugh burst from my chest as I pressed a palm to my forehead. How could I not have seen this sooner?

Holy shit, Dyno. You were right.

"It all makes sense now," I said. "Everything, going all the way back to the beginning. You've never given the Sons the credit they're due because it grosses you out that they have sex with each other."

"Kyrie, please." Dad raised his hand in protest, the disgust clear on his face.

"You gave them just enough to keep them on the hook," I went on. "Paid them well enough, let them stay in town for as long as they wanted. But you never gave them a home, not even after their clubhouse burned down and they lost so many members. Not just club members, but *family* members! And the three that remained finally caught on and said, 'Fuck you, Four Corners.'"

"Kyrie, please don't use that language."

"That's why they left and never came back. Now your daughter's all wrapped up in not just bikers, but *queer* bikers." I emphasized the word to make him even more uncomfortable, and it worked. "Seems like leaving was the right idea."

I turned to the door, only pausing at my father's desperate, "Sweetheart, wait. Please don't leave."

I looked at him over my shoulder. "Are you going to force me to stay?" I had a strong hunch that Mari would let it slip to the public if he did, and he'd be in hot water for that too.

Dad's shoulders slumped with a heavy sigh. "No. I… just, I'm asking you not to go. Not so soon after you got back."

My hand went to the doorknob, bitterness rising in my throat. "You'll release them?"

He sighed again. "Yes…I have no reason to hold them, so I must."

I closed my fingers around the knob. "Will you ever support me being with them?"

It took a long time for an answer to come. "I'm sorry, sweetheart, but no. I can't support it."

I turned the knob and left my father's office.

CHAPTER 33
DYNO

"Give it a rest, T." I leaned my head back against the brick wall, closing my eyes to the sight of T-Bone inspecting the bars of his cell again.

"Shut your fucking mouth, D," he growled back. "You wanna sit here while I get our girl back, you keep that to yourself."

"It's not that I *want* to be here. You're just driving yourself nuts looking for a crack in those bars. Take a step back, that's all I'm saying."

He ignored me, as expected. Once T-Bone set his mind to something, there was no changing it. The governor's soldiers had stripped us of all our weapons, even my mini Molotovs, so we were sitting ducks in our jail cells. And with someone as precious as Kyrie taken away from us, T-Bone was only more determined to break out. So I looked away, leaving him to scrutinize the joints in the metal bars and turned my attention to Grudge.

He'd requested a pen and several sheets of paper from

the soldiers who tossed us in here. They'd granted him the materials without protest. We'd been in here over twenty-four hours by my estimate, and Grudge had been writing nonstop. He had paused in his furious scribbling when I looked over, now leafing through the sheets as he read them. We had been placed in separate cells, and he was sitting on the bench in his, one leg stretched out, the other on the floor as he scanned his writing with a furrowed brow.

"What've you been working on over there?" I called. "Your autobiography?"

To my surprise, he nodded and said, "Mm-hm." He wrote something at the top of one page and held it up to show me that it said, *For Kyrie.*

"Grudge..."

T-Bone even stopped pushing on his cell bars to look over. His hands dropped away, limp at his sides when he realized what Grudge had been doing.

"Grudgie, come here," he ordered softly.

Grudge stood and moved to the wall of bars that bordered his cell and T-Bone's. Our president reached through, tugging the other man closer until they were both pressed up against the bars.

"You didn't have to do that again," T-Bone whispered. "You heard what she said and you know she meant it. You're perfect, and she...she *loves* us. She wouldn't make you—"

"Hm!" Grudge jerked his head down with a sharp huff to cut T-Bone off, then he stabbed at her name at the top of the paper with a finger.

"But he did have to," I said, voicing my interpretation of Grudge's body language. "It's because of how much she means to us that he had to write it all down again. Because she deserves to know. Right, Grudge?"

He nodded, determination taking over his expression. Grudge pointed at T-Bone's chest, then at me, before gesturing to himself with his palms open.

With a sigh, T-Bone reached through the bars to cup the back of Grudge's head, fingers stroking his neck and hair. "I get it, man. She knows my and Dyno's baggage. She deserves to know yours too."

Grudge leaned his forehead on T-Bone's, releasing a soft sigh as he traced the other man's lips and then his own. T-Bone smiled at the gesture. "You want to kiss her, just do it. I promise you she won't care. She just wants you like Dyno and I do."

Grudge shook his head and waved the papers in his other hand.

"Nothing you've written down will make her want you any less," I said, rising to my feet to stretch. "She's already part of us, Grudge. It's just a matter of getting her back."

"Hm." Grudge looked less convinced of that until T-Bone tightened his grip on the back of his neck.

"Don't start doubting yourself now. You have us *and* a beautiful woman who wants you just as you are. Do I have to suck your cock right now to prove it?" He trailed a hand down Grudge's torso, cupping through his jeans while keeping his grip tight on the silent man's neck. "If I told Kyrie to suck you, you know she would."

Grudge groaned and squirmed in his grip, but T-Bone didn't let go.

"She does it so well," I chimed in, reminiscing on our time in bed together. "You can tell she genuinely enjoys it and wants to please. Oh, and the way she looked up at me with my cock stuffed in her mouth, like she wanted to make sure I liked it. Fuck, it didn't even matter that she'd never done it before. Her eagerness was just everything."

The two of them were groaning now, and it looked like Grudge was returning some of T-Bone's groping.

"Trying to make us jealous over there?" T-Bone asked.

"Maybe," I supplied.

He leaned his forehead against Grudge's with a decadent sigh before reluctantly untangling from the other man. "Fuck, we've got to get her back and get the fuck out of here."

"It'll never be soon enough." I started to pace my cell, restlessness getting the better of me. "Fuck, I hope she's okay."

The next few hours passed with only the sounds of my boots on the floor and Grudge shuffling papers. Long after I reclined on my bench and he folded the pages of his life story to tuck them into his cut, the jail's door creaked open and sharp, booted footsteps approached us.

"Good news, gentlemen," came the voice of General Bray, head of the Four Corners' army.

"It must be great news if the general himself is coming to deliver it," T-Bone said, barely containing his sneer.

Bray ignored the remark. "You boys are to be released." He withdrew a set of keys from his pocket, the sound crisp and musical. "Effective immediately."

"And Kyrie?" T-Bone asked.

A smile pulled at the general's lips as he moved through to unlock our cells. "She is also no longer a prisoner and has refused to be guarded by my soldiers. Your two cohorts are with her in the dining hall."

Bray stepped aside when he opened my door, but I remained standing in place with my arms crossed. "Anything else you'd like to release, General?"

He swept his arm toward the hallway leading out of the jail. "Your weapons are just outside."

"If anything's been tampered with..."

"Nothing has been, I assure you." Bray inclined his head. "I apologize on the behalf of the governor for this whole ordeal."

T-Bone let out an indignant snort. "No offense, General. You're not a bad guy, but your apologies are too little, too fucking late." He walked out of his cell, striding toward the exit. "We done here, guys?"

"Yeah." I followed after him with Grudge on my heels.

He wasn't my favorite person in the room, but I didn't have beef with the general. We were friends of his family, but he still had a job to do and couldn't override the governor on everything. Grudge's hostage situation a few years back was a sore spot, but that wasn't the general's fault. He negotiated Grudge's return to us as best he could.

Regardless, none of that changed the fact that this territory left a foul taste in my mouth, and I was dying to leave.

Just as soon as we get our girl, I thought, the anticipation hurrying my movements as I re-armed myself with my guns, knives, and mini Molotovs.

Once we were all suited up, the three of us walked freely through the main floor of the city hall building. Soldiers and employees steered clear of us, as though not wanting to risk our ire.

We found Kyrie, Chris, and Tiff in the dining hall where the governor had hosted many dinner parties. Some of which we'd been invited to, some not.

"There they are," Chris called from the head of the long table in the middle of the room.

"About time," Tiff chimed in, sitting to his right.

Across from her, Kyrie was bent over a plate of food. Her cheeks were puffed out when she looked up, jaw moving furiously to chew and swallow everything she'd shoved in there.

"Little lady," T-Bone laughed as he approached her. "Did they not feed you in here? We're leavin', you don't gotta store everything in your face like a chipmunk."

"This girl went on hunger strike for your asses." Chris stared at her with a mixture of awe and disbelief. "Refused to eat until she knew you'd be let out."

"What? Kyrie!" All the humor dropped from T-Bone's expression as he stepped back to let her chug some water. "Why would you do that?"

"I'll tell you right now," I said, nudging my way up next to him. "No man on earth is worth skipping meals for."

"Mm-hm." Grudge shook his head in agreement, coming up to T-Bone's other side.

Chris' eyes slid to his wife. "Would you go on hunger strike to get me out of jail?"

Tiff rolled her eyes. "Does a fish walk on land?"

Kyrie finally swallowed her food and looked at the three of us with so much relief, it made my chest ache. "You guys are okay?"

I swept her up in a hug that lifted her off the ground, catching her mouth in a kiss before settling her back down to earth. "We're fine, beautiful. Never been better."

"You're sure?" Her hand remained wrapped around my shoulder as she reached for T-Bone.

"We'll be better once we're out of this fucking territory." He caught her hand and kissed her wrist before letting her palm reach his face. "Anywhere you'd like to go?"

Kyrie released me, her hand trailing down my arm as

she kissed T-Bone with a laugh. "You're leaving it up to me?"

Meeting T-Bone's eyes over her head, I shrugged. "Fuck it, why not? We go where the road takes us."

Kyrie went to embrace Grudge while Chris and Tiff rose from the table. "While this has been fun, we'll head straight to the clubhouse," Chris said. "Enjoy your honeymoon or whatever you do. We have prospects to find."

Tiff nudged him with an elbow. "And business to do."

"We'll be back before long," T-Bone assured them. "Thank you both for backing us up on this ride."

We said our goodbyes, then Grudge said something to Kyrie in sign language. She smiled, then turned to speak to all of us as she signed a reply.

"Honestly, I'd just like to go back to the clubhouse too," she admitted, hands flying gracefully through the air. "These last few weeks have been nonstop, and I'd like some time to rest. Obviously I'm not an ambassador anymore, so I'd like to figure out what's next for me."

T-Bone stroked a hand along her cheek, his gaze warm and affectionate. "So, that's it? You and your dad...?"

Kyrie shook her head, her lip wobbling for a moment before she steeled herself. "He doesn't support me being with you, so this is how it has to be."

I took one of her hands and leaned down to place a kiss on her forehead. "I'm sorry, gorgeous. We all know what it feels like to have family not support you."

"Hm." Grudge wrapped an arm around her waist, holding her against his chest while he gestured to all of us.

"Exactly, you have all of us," T-Bone elaborated. "And we'll support whatever endeavor you choose." He leaned down, lips hovering over hers. "As long as you remember you're *our* property."

Damn, that turned *me* on. Kyrie shivered before slapping a playful hand to his chest, her cheeks flushing. "Like you'll ever let me forget."

T-Bone chuckled darkly, then kissed her before straightening. "Going home sounds great." His eyes met mine. "Maybe we'll take the scenic route."

The groan left my chest before I could stop it. "Oh, you dirty dog."

T-Bone and Grudge shared a grin while Kyrie spun in a circle to stare at all of us. "Okay, what does that mean? You guys are talking in code."

T-Bone turned her toward the exit, then swatted her ass. "Ride with me and find out, little lady."

WE ONLY RODE two hours out of Four Corners before T-Bone couldn't wait any longer. He pulled to the side of the road with Kyrie clinging to his back. Grudge and I pulled up behind them, the air already surging with our anticipation.

It *was* a scenic area, to be fair. This road was a remote mountain pass, rarely used despite how beautiful the views were, probably because it wasn't a direct route to anywhere. We used it hundreds of times to avoid detection on the main roads to and from Four Corners. Over the years, we'd made many memories here, and we were about to make some more.

T-Bone dismounted his bike and hoisted Kyrie off, only to place her facing backwards on the seat. He stood between her thighs at the rear end of his bike and kissed her fiercely, hands holding firm to her slim waist.

"T-Bone, what are you doing?" She was breathless from his kiss as Grudge and I came up on either side.

"You." He grinned against her mouth, fingers creeping under the hem of her shirt. "I've never seen a more gorgeous view in my life." She turned her head, glancing at me for a moment before T-Bone dragged his mouth to her neck. Then her eyelids fell and a decadent sigh left her mouth. "What if someone drives by and sees us?"

"You don't sound that worried." I cradled the back of her head and kissed her waiting mouth, loving that I could taste T-Bone on her soft lips. "Not many people come this way. And if they do, well…" I kissed her again, palming her breast until she moaned into my mouth. "Then they'll be lucky to see such a beautiful view with us."

Kyrie turned to look at Grudge while her hips lifted in T-Bone's grip. He peeled our girl's leggings down while she reached for our silent lover.

"Grudge, can I kiss you?" Her breath was coming in small pants already. "Not on your mouth, I know. But other places—oh!"

He had turned her head with a gentle grip on her jaw and sucked her earlobe with those incredible lips of his.

"That's a yes," I whispered into her other ear, tracing the shell with my teeth.

She had no idea what she was in for, especially once Grudge did move on to kissing and then oral. It might not happen today, but her mind would be blown once it did.

With her lower half bare, T-Bone resumed his position between her legs, running his hands sensually up her thighs to the delicious flare of her hips. "So beautiful," he murmured in awe.

Kyrie reached for him, gripping the edge of his T-shirt

in her tiny fist while Grudge and I made her squirm with attention to her ears and neck.

"I need you," she whimpered, dragging him forward until he was pressed flush to her.

"Little lady, I've never needed anything more than I need you right now," he answered roughly.

Their mouths met in a hard kiss and a tangle of limbs that removed his shirt and hers. My cock swelled in my jeans, and I couldn't stop touching her, stroking her hair and kissing her neck while Grudge did the same to her other side. She was truly the center of us, the one person we all wanted to please and care for.

When T-Bone started kissing lower down her body, I stopped him with a hand on his shoulder. "I haven't tasted her yet," I said to his questioning glance.

"And I haven't been inside her yet," he growled with a rare possessiveness. "Don't be trying to take my spot."

"Who says I'd take it from you?" I grinned, running a hand up Kyrie's thigh toward her spread-open center. "Maybe we could share that too."

"What?" Kyrie went wide-eyed at the suggestion.

T-Bone laughed darkly and came up to give me a biting kiss. "And you call *me* a dirty dog." To Kyrie he said, "We'll save that for another day. Right now, it looks like your dance partner wants to cut in on my fun."

"Oh, I'm sure you can still make yourself useful." I nudged my way next to him, making Kyrie's legs even wider as they anchored to my and T-Bone's outer hips.

Her balance teetered for a moment on the bike seat until Grudge slid in behind her, supporting her back with his chest. Kyrie grasped his thighs on either side of her, leaning her weight back until her head rested on his shoulder. He kissed her temple, arms wrapping around her middle so that she was even more secure. Safe.

I leaned in, eager for one more taste of that mouth before I kissed her down below. Kyrie blew a soft sigh over my lips, the sound content and relaxed, and I let my smile linger on hers. "You good?"

"So good." She teased my lips with a small bite. "Could be better though."

"Is that so?" I dragged a slow touch down her body, watching the anticipation build in her face. When I bent to let my mouth follow, one of Grudge's hands pushed my head down further.

T-Bone chuckled lightly. "Grudgie wants to watch you eat our girl." I felt him wind my braided hair in his fist. "So do I, for that matter."

I heard kissing noises above me but didn't stray from my task. Kyrie wriggled underneath me as I kissed her hip bone, making my way down to her center. I moved her leg to my shoulder, dragging a kiss down until I enveloped her whole pussy in my mouth.

Her cry of pleasure and the buck of her hips against my face was the most satisfying thing. My tongue parted her lips and took a long, decadent lick from her opening to her clit. Her sweet, musky taste flooded my mouth, and I couldn't hold back the indulgent moan. She was ambrosia on my tongue, driving me wild with the need to fill her.

Someone unzipped me and freed my cock, thank fuck. I felt T-Bone stroking a moment later, easing some of the ache. His sliding grip on my length matched my tongue thrusts into Kyrie's pussy, the two sensations contrasting but equally pleasurable.

T-Bone only allowed me another moment of feasting on her before yanking me upright by my hair. "I want to taste her on you," he growled before attacking my mouth in a rough kiss.

I stroked my tongue into his mouth, much like I was doing to her cunt moments before. The moan he let out was feral, his tongue surging for more as I fumbled blindly for his cock. My other hand remained on Kyrie, finding the hard swell of her clit and the rolling of her body underneath as I rubbed that spot. When I peeked one eye open to see how Grudge was faring, well, I had not a damn thing to worry about.

Kyrie had one arm up and wrapped around the back of his head. Her other hand linked with his as it moved reverently over her body. Like a work of art, they were beautiful to look at, almost painfully so. Grudge dwarfed her with his bulk—all muscle, tattoos, and scars, while she—fragile and soft with unblemished skin, directed where his hand moved. His eyes were rapt on hers, entranced, like he was under a spell. Their faces were close, nuzzling but not kissing. Not until he dropped a kiss to her shoulder, then ran his mouth up to the sensitive part of her neck.

Kyrie's soft whimper reminded me of my task—making her come with my mouth.

Turning away from T-Bone and back to her, I pushed her legs up higher, knees nearly to her chest as I sank down and devoured her. I loved sucking as much of her lips into my mouth as I could, running my tongue over her folds and flicking her clit until she cried out. As I felt T-Bone lean in next to me, it was clear I wasn't the only one obsessed with her taste.

"Give me some of that," he groaned before diving down.

"Oh my, what are you…fuck, what?" Kyrie's moans

and babbles were ragged, mouth open and eyes hooded while she watched us both go down on her.

We held her legs high and secure, probably with Grudge's help, and messily alternated sucking her clit, her folds, kissing and licking her beautiful flesh.

"How did…did you guys plan this?" Her voice was high, her breaths tight.

We didn't plan anything, she was just that addicting. Come to think of it, I'd never tag-teamed going down on a woman like this before. I was pretty sure T-Bone hadn't either. The thrill of sharing something new with them sent a fresh surge of pleasure through me and I palmed my cock, aching for another hand or a mouth on me.

Eating pussy with a partner was messy, clumsy, and too fucking hot to comprehend. Our tongues frequently ran into each other, turning into greedy kisses to share her taste before we turned attention back to her. Kyrie's orgasm came on faster than we all expected, surprising even her. A few tongue swipes of her clit had her shaking, shivering, and whining for release. I latched on to that bundle of nerves and sucked until the release shuddered through her and she pushed us away.

T-Bone and I wore matching grins as we came upright, her juices shining in his beard. "I take it you enjoyed the show, little lady?"

Kyrie still couldn't talk. Her chest heaved with ragged breaths, eyes unfocused and lids heavy as she floated back down from her high. "Uh-huh. Really hot."

"So are you." I stepped away so her legs could come down and wrap around T-Bone, fitting snugly around his waist. She was far from done, and the look she pinned him with was hungry. Because I couldn't resist being a distraction, I grabbed her neck and pressed a quick kiss to her mouth. "Grudge," I said, releasing Kyrie to kiss the man sitting behind her. "You good, or do you want to change positions?"

"Hm." He shook his head and tightened his arm that was wrapped protectively around Kyrie's stomach.

"You sure?" I smirked at him, idly stroking myself while enjoying the sight of him acting so possessive over her. "Kinda hard to reach your cock with you sitting behind her."

"Mm-hm." He shrugged like it was no big deal. He knew someone would take care of him before we were all done.

"Suit yourself. Guess I'm a free agent." I walked in a circle around the motorcycle and my three lovers, letting my hand run indulgently over each person. "None of you are off-limits to me."

CHAPTER 34

KYRIE

Dyno's expression was a mixture of playful and predatory as he walked around us, one hand trailing over our skin, the other stroking his cock. "None of you are off-limits to me," he said with a thrilling kind of glee.

Oh Lord. As if him and T-Bone going down on me at the same time wasn't crazy enough. Who knew what he was about to do?

In front of me, T-Bone's gaze was heated, glued to my spread-open center. His calloused fingers dug into my hips, erect cock rubbing over where he and Dyno had just devoured me. My flesh was still sensitive from my orgasm, pulsing under his heavy length.

Behind me, I felt Grudge's solid chest against my back. He held me up, stable and supportive as a castle wall. His erection pressed against me through his jeans, though he made no move to take it out.

I wanted him too, this big, quiet man I still had so much to learn about. He seemed content to just hold me though, touching me with such care and affection. Every second was a battle to not kiss him.

He kissed me though. Sometimes gently, sometimes with teeth and rough pulls on my neck and earlobe. I never knew what was coming, always at his mercy and gasping at the explosion of sensitivity along my skin. Part of me wanted to flip around and face him, to see his face as I took his length in my hand and rode him. The other part was content to stay right here on my back, spread between these men to do what they wanted with me.

"Fuck, little lady," T-Bone said in a rough whisper, hips pulling back to notch his head at my entrance.

"Big gentleman." I laughed at how silly the words sounded.

He huffed out a laugh, pressing forward just an inch before pinning me with a dark stare. "I'm the furthest fucking thing from a gentleman right now."

"Prove it," I challenged him.

T-Bone was so sweet, a giant teddy bear of a man who was always respectful and protective of me. I'd seen glimpses of his darker side and knew he was capable of unspeakable violence. He wouldn't be an MC president if he wasn't.

I wanted some of that darkness now. I didn't want my warm, kind protector. I wanted him to defile me.

T-Bone answered my challenge with a growl and a surge of his hips that pulled a cry from my throat. He was fully inside in a single thrust, and I felt split in half in the best possible way.

"Be careful what you ask for, little lady." He held my waist in a bruising grip, hands clamping down as he dragged the full length of his cock from me before slamming it back in.

"Fuck!" I screamed, hands scrambling for Grudge, the bike, anything to keep me on solid ground.

T-Bone fucked me with a few more punishing thrusts, each deep drive of his cock into me feeling like it was pushing the air out of my lungs. Then he slowed, studying me while his hips rolled fluidly. "Too much?"

"No," I panted, grasping at his muscular forearms. "Don't stop. Please."

The corner of his mouth ticked up as he slammed home, grunting in satisfaction at the resulting scream he pulled from me. "That's my girl. She can take all of me." His head threw back as he picked up the pace, and I wished I could bite the sexy column of his throat.

Grudge's hands held my breasts, teasing my nipples into hard peaks and countering the rough rocking and slamming as T-Bone fucked me. It was all I could do just to hold on, just to take and feel and relish in one of my men using my body.

I didn't see Dyno at my side until he cupped my jaw, turning my head to look at him. "Your mouth is hanging open," he teased, running his thumb along my lip. "Would you like me to put something in it?"

"Yes!" I cried, tongue already out and seeking him. My lips had sealed around the silky head of his cock by the time T-Bone slammed into me again, and my scream was muffled by a full mouth.

"Ohh, yes. You are incredible." Dyno cupped a hand around the back of my head, and I melted at the praise. He made me feel so confident and sexy, any nervousness I had was gone the first time we were together.

Dyno's other hand smoothed down my body, reaching between my legs to where T-Bone continued to destroy me in the best way. His fingers spread, stroking my lips and the sides of T-Bone's cock as he glided through me.

"Oh fuck, D. No, don't. Don't touch me yet," T-Bone grunted over the smacks of his hips against my thighs. "It's too fucking good, I don't want to come yet."

"Suit yourself," Dyno chuckled. His hand inched higher until his fingers skimmed over my clit. He pressed down, making small circles on my slick flesh while I bucked and moaned.

"Do you like that, sweet girl?" His voice came from above me, teasing and musical, like a filthy angel.

I took more of him down my throat in reply, addicted to the length of solid muscle and smooth skin, how it twitched and pulsed on my tongue. Why did it turn *me* on so much to please him with my mouth? Or maybe it was the combination of everything—the delicious, rough fucking, a hand on my clit, more hands on my body, and a man's cock in my mouth.

I felt like a filthy whore, and I *loved* it. If my father knew what I was doing now, he would die on the spot and then spin a few dozen times in his grave.

But he was the furthest thing from my mind as T-Bone's cock hit me in a spot again and again that sent pleasure lighting me up from the inside. Dyno's ministrations on my clit built upon that sensation, sending it to my nipples, my fingers, my toes. Everything started spasming as I climbed toward orgasm. Even T-Bone's furious rhythm stuttered as I squeezed around him.

"Oh goddamn it, fuck. She's so close to coming," he hissed through his teeth, staring at me hungrily. "Little lady, you will be the death of me."

I couldn't answer with my mouth full of cock, so I moaned louder, squeezing around his waist with my thighs to pull him forward. He was inside me, fucking me so hard that the slaps of our bodies echoed across the desert, and I still needed more.

"She's gonna make me come too," Dyno groaned. His supportive hand on the back of my head turned into a fist, sending tingles along my scalp as he swelled in my mouth.

Oh yes, yes! I sucked him even more vigorously, my free hand finding his balls and massaging the heavy sac. The animalistic moan he let out was such a sexy rumble, I swore I felt it vibrate over my clit.

"If you're trying to get me off first, gorgeous," he rasped, "it won't work."

He changed…something about how he was rubbing my clit, but I couldn't tell what. All I knew was that the waves of pleasure *soared* in intensity. What was, at first, a gradual climb had turned into a hurtling race to a peak. There was no stopping the momentum, and I shattered with the full force of my release. I lost all control of my body and let the pleasure ride me like a woman possessed.

I could barely hear the grunts and curses of my men over the rush of blood to my ears. T-Bone's length remained inside me, so deliciously solid and hot for my body to grasp and squeeze. Dyno, on the other hand, spilled his release over my tongue just as I saw the other side of the peak. I swore the jerks of his cock and the salty taste of him stretched my orgasm out even longer.

I was breathless, heart racing, achingly sensitive, and covered in sweat. My men didn't fare much better. Dyno staggered as he withdrew from my mouth, clutching one of the bike's handlebars for support.

And still, I wanted more.

"I have no fuckin' idea how I'm still alive right now," T-Bone muttered, leaning to brush a kiss over my lips.

I indulged his kiss briefly before pressing a palm to his chest. "Back up for a second."

His amber eyes flashed with concern as he pulled from my body, cock stiff and coated in my wetness. "You okay, Kyrie?"

I slid down the back of the bike until my feet touched the ground, then promptly flipped over, presenting my ass to T-Bone's cock.

And my face to Grudge's.

Now in front of me, the quiet man stared wide-eyed as I straddled the back of the bike, my toes barely touching the ground as I leaned my stomach down over the seat between Grudge's legs.

"Jesus…" The whispered word came from T-Bone, followed by an appreciative hand roaming over my backside.

"Grudge." I braced a hand on his thick thigh, reaching tentatively for his zipper with the other. "Will you let me?"

His face held an expression I couldn't read, but his palm came to my face, thumb stroking tenderly over my cheekbone. It wasn't a clear yes or no, so I hesitated, waiting for any other sign.

Dyno came up to his side and grabbed the back of his neck roughly, leaning to give Grudge a hard, sucking kiss on his neck. "Tell her yes," Dyno urged directly into his ear. "She wants you *now*. She wants us, and she's *our* woman. Don't try to convince yourself that she's not."

"He's right, Grudge," I said, running a touch up and down his thigh. "I've always wanted you. Ever since *you* saved me, I've wanted you."

Every breath of it was true. Grudge was the first of the Sons to pull me to my feet, to check over me for injuries as his first concern.

He was the first to tell me I was safe with them.

Neither of us knew it back then, but in that moment, he became mine.

"I want to please you." My voice took on a whine as I rubbed the thick erection in his jeans. "I want to do this for you. Please, Grudge."

His head tilted back with a thick groan, and *finally* he unsnapped the top button and pulled the zipper down. I eagerly went to help, and it felt like I was unwrapping a Christmas present. But I was not prepared.

"Oh my…"

I'd seen his dick the first time we all got together but not this close. For some reason, I didn't expect it to be *this* enormous. I stared at it in wonder as I gave him an experimental stroke from base to tip. My fingers didn't even meet when they wrapped around his girth.

A playful slap on my ass broke me out of my trance. "You'll get used to it," T-Bone chuckled. "Take him a little bit at a time." As if I didn't need any more trouble concentrating, he then entered me from behind in one fluid movement.

"Easy for you to say," I choked out, my back in a deep arch as he spread me apart again.

Thankfully, Dyno was there to coach me through it. "He likes it when you suck his head and stroke him with your hand." He leaned over to demonstrate, and I could not even begin to describe the sheer, surreal eroticism of watching one man suck the other's cock while another fucked me from behind.

"Oh, fuck yeah," T-Bone groaned from behind me, hips bouncing off my ass as he drove into me. "Lick Grudge's shaft while D sucks his head."

I happily obeyed, running my tongue up and down his

stiff length, even sucking a few kisses while Grudge moaned and squirmed from our attention.

"Now suck his balls, he loves that."

Dyno returned to stroking up and down his length while I nudged my mouth down lower. T-Bone's instructions made it all hotter, if that was even possible. I wanted to pinch myself every other moment to make sure this was really happening. But I didn't need to, because someone pinched my nipple, slapped my ass, kissed me, or fucked me. I was overwhelmed by incredible sensations and feelings that could never be illusions.

"You handle him now," Dyno said, taking both of my hands and wrapping them around Grudge like he was passing me a baton. "Blow his mind like you did with me, beautiful."

My eyes locked onto Grudge's as I slid my lips over his rounded head. Something about eye contact with him was just so electric. His eyes were deep, expressive, and soulful. They fell closed as I sucked him into my mouth. If I couldn't kiss him, I'd try my damn hardest to please him with my mouth in this area.

He was already slick from Dyno's mouth, the tip of him leaking beads of salty precum that I lapped up greedily. It was no exaggeration that I needed two hands to work him, and I tried twisting my palms in opposite directions as they slid up and down.

The results came instantly—a rough moan dragged from deep in his chest, and his whole body shuddered.

"Good?" I asked, the eagerness clear in my voice.

"Hmmm..." It sounded like a long contented sigh, and the bliss on his face made me turn to jelly. But it was the way he touched my cheek again, letting that hand skim down my neck, then my shoulder and arm, that made me absolutely melt.

"I love making you feel good like this." My tongue flicked the sensitive underside of his head before sucking him down again. I slid my mouth on him up and down a few times as far as I could go, then released him with a pop of my lips to rest my aching jaw. "You taste so good, Grudge. I never want to stop sucking you."

Maybe I wasn't on T-Bone dirty-talking level yet, but talking to Grudge felt natural, less awkward for some reason. And I had a feeling I wasn't the only one who felt reassured by praise during the act.

His jaw and fists clenched, every muscle tight like he was trying to hold onto some thin semblance of control. I swore his hands shook as he lifted them to sign to me. *"I don't deserve you."*

"You're right," I said. "You deserve more than me. That's why you have these two."

I looked over my shoulder to see Dyno and T-Bone kissing fiercely. A kiss was always a battle between these men, a fight for dominance with rough sucks and bites. T-Bone's hips continued to snap against my ass, his thumb circling my other hole where Dyno had fingered me the first time.

A thrill raced through me as I returned to face Grudge. I wasn't prepared for him to cup my face with both hands, nor for him to lean down and slide his lips against mine.

The motion shocked me into stillness, but I recovered the moment I felt him pull away. I would *not* make him regret this leap of courage with me. His beard was rough under my palm as I pulled him back, pressing my mouth to his with all of my pent-up need.

Grudge's lips parted and he took a small, tentative suck

on my bottom lip. I sealed my lips over his, closed my eyes, and just savored the taste of him. His lips were soft and full, so plush as they sipped on mine. As he began relaxing into me, I realized how intuitive of a kisser he was. He treated it like a dance, alternating between firmness and softness, but always exactly what I needed in that moment and leaving me breathless.

"Look at them…"

I heard the soft murmurings of the guys behind me, and it only spurred me to kiss Grudge harder. My tongue surged into his mouth, reaching for his and finding nothing before I remembered.

I pulled away, lowering my chin ashamedly. "Shit, I'm sorry. I forgot."

He only let out a dismissive huff and touched my jaw to kiss me again. When he pulled back, he smirked and signed, *I like your tongue.*

"Oh, you do?" I giggled, leaning into his chest like we were the only two people in the world. "I like all of you." I stroked up his length to illustrate this, loving that he was still hard despite us getting sidetracked.

"Mm, Kah," he said softly, resting his forehead on mine as he caressed my face.

"Grudge," I answered back.

He caught my mouth in another kiss, this one charged with heat and desire that I felt all the way to my pussy.

"Oh fuck, I felt that," T-Bone said, his voice rough. He stilled while fully sheathed inside me, hands smoothing up my back and then back down, thumb resting over my ass again. "Did you like it when Dyno played with you here?" he asked, his expression wicked.

"Yes." I lowered to Grudge's cock again, flattening myself along the bike seat. "Please."

T-Bone needed no further begging from me. I watched his thumb go to his mouth, hypnotized by the motion, and was completely caught off-guard by Dyno leaning over and using his *tongue* to tease me there.

"Oh my God!" He was just as enthusiastic back there as he was with my pussy, licking and sucking with abandon. As the shock wore off, I realized it actually felt *good.*

Dyno stopped before I could explore the feeling for too long though, and T-Bone's slick finger pressed through the ring of muscles. It was easier this time, with less of the uncomfortable stretching from before.

With Grudge's cock back in my mouth, I got a rush up my spine with the knowledge that I was filled in every hole and loved every hot, pulsing, intense second of it.

"I'm not gonna last." T-Bone's groan almost sounded pained, though his strokes never faltered as he moved through me.

"Hmmm…" Grudge sounded like he was agreeing, large hands gathering my hair out of my face as he thrust through the circles of my palms.

Dyno walked around to the side of the bike, a casual, naked observer as he pulled a water bottle from a saddlebag to wash his face and mouth. "Damn, I wish you three could see yourselves right now. This is just the hottest thing I've ever seen in my life."

His words had an effect on all of us. I sucked Grudge like I needed him to live, while he pistoned up to tap the back of my throat again and again. T-Bone's cock swelled inside me, the impact of his thrusts reaching a new height of punishment, and I swore he slid another finger into my ass to make me feel even more of him.

I couldn't tell who came first, only that it was a chain reaction. Grudge exploded in my mouth as I shattered, the taste of him dragging out my orgasm convulsing around T-Bone's cock and fingers. T-Bone pulled out of me all too soon and sprayed his hot release over my back.

Who knew how long we stayed like that, just piled into a heap of skin, sweat, and cum, trying to catch our breaths.

At some point, Dyno, with his pants back in place, slapped T-Bone's ass as he headed back to his bike. "Let's get cleaned up," he called as he mounted his vehicle. "I know a hot spring nearby. Then we can go home."

Home, what a concept.

A sense of lightness and contentment settled over me. Four Corners was never my home, despite having been born and grown up there. I never felt at home until I jumped on the back of the motorcycle and held onto the man in front of me.

"Careful, little lady." T-bone gingerly lifted me up from the bike seat, brushing a kiss over my shoulder. "Can you stand?" he added with a chuckle.

"Mm, I think I can manage." I shot him a teasing grin over my shoulder. "Does that bruise your ego?"

"Not at all, darlin'." He kissed me, our matching grins touching. "They heard you screaming across the Grand Canyon, so my ego is very much intact."

I smacked his chest and he laughed, helping me off the bike so I could get dressed.

Yes, that solidified it. The only home I needed was with these men.

CHAPTER 35

T-BONE

Fuck me, I couldn't remember the last time a ride felt so good. Freshly washed, freshly fucked, and now with my steed between my legs and home on the horizon, what could be better?

I glanced at my mirror, catching sight of Kyrie wrapped around Grudge in the back of our little pack. She had an arm thrown over his shoulder, hand splayed on his chest, and his fingers curled around hers. Her mouth pressed to his ear, either talking to him over the wind or just teasing him with that little pink tongue. Whichever it was, Grudge was grinning like I'd never seen him do before. It looked like how mine felt after we finished that epic fuckfest by the side of the road.

Grudge, Dyno, and I had been happy together for years. Our bonds were strong, forged by spending our lives as misunderstood outcasts. But Kyrie elevated that to something new. What she brought to us was deeper than the day-to-day surface-level happiness. If the guys and I were brought together by pain and sacrifice, she came to us with the force of healing.

Healing came with its own type of pain though, the kind we were a lot less familiar with. Leaning into that was, in some ways, harder than riding out to battle, guns blazing. But I knew it had to be done, all of us did. I'd never be able to love her like she deserved until I found closure from losing Bash. Dyno had to let his guard down and be honest with her about his kid. And Grudge?

My gaze flicked to my mirror again. Kyrie's cheek rested on the back of his shoulder, and he held her thigh in a possessive grip as he drove with the other hand.

Being able to kiss her was a huge breakthrough for him, but that only scratched the surface. The rest of it was written on those pages, folded and tucked into his cut inches away from where her hand rested. He might give it to her to read the moment we got home, or he might not be ready for weeks or months.

But healing took time, and none of us were unfamiliar with patience. Kyrie still wanted us after waiting four years, after all. I had no doubt that when Grudge was ready to let that final barrier down, she'd still find him as perfect as we all did.

My chest sparked with *something* at the thought of all four of us at home, together. It expanded uncontrollably, reaching my face until I wore a big stupid grin for the hundredth time that day.

I never gave much thought to the future. MC life forced me to live day-to-day, sometimes even hour to hour. But with Kyrie with us, I wanted to live through the year, maybe even the next several years. I couldn't wait for when our time before her was just a distant memory, when it would feel like she'd always been a part of us. I wanted to see her grow wise with all that life had to offer. I wanted to tease her about her first wrinkles and her first gray hair. And if she got down on herself about that shit, I wanted to remind her how beautiful she was. I wanted to see her with Dyno's son and maybe round with a baby from one of us.

For the first time in my life, surviving beyond the next day or week mattered to me. I wanted it all, a future with her and them.

Should I ask her to marry me? Marry us? I scratched my beard at the thought. Traditional relationships were not my forte. I'd never had one in my life and had no idea how they worked. Kyrie might appreciate something like that, but did it matter if she was already with the three of us?

I'd have to ask her once we were settled in at home. We could easily pitch in three ways on a ring for her. She'd wear a rock fit for a princess. She needed a property jacket too, so that everyone knew she was ours. Maybe even a tattoo. Shit, that'd be hot.

Much to my annoyance, Munin found this to be a perfect time to tug at me. He was in the sky somewhere but pulled insistently on my consciousness like he wanted me to use his eyes right fucking then.

"I'm driving, bird. What the fuck?" I glanced at the sky and only heard a caw and a faint metallic sound before it all went fucked.

There was no time to brake for the length of chain that pulled taut across my path. It caught the front of my bike, and I went flying.

Sandy ground rushed underneath me before I landed hard. Pain rocked up to my shoulders and my teeth. I tried to roll to absorb some of the impact, but the damage had been done. I was rattled, my brain still catching up to the fact that someone had laid a trap for us. Whoever did this wanted the element of surprise, and they succeeded. Not even Munin saw it until it was too late.

I rolled to my feet and ran back toward the chain and my bike, ignoring how the ground swung unsteadily beneath my feet. Kyrie and the guys were back there.

I drew both of my handguns, adrenaline and a fresh wave of rage fueling me now. Yeah, I was the most emotional of us, in all aspects. To lovers, I was passionate and moved worlds to please them. My enemies? They experienced a world of pain before they died.

Our would-be attackers started coming out of the woodwork, pointing long rifles at us from behind bushes and large clusters of boulders. I fired at them without hesitation, forcing them to pull back and seek cover.

Cowardly bunch of limp-dicks.

"You alright?" Dyno called to me. He and Grudge were able to brake before reaching the chain. They had weapons drawn and were off their bikes, protecting Kyrie between them.

"Fuckin' peachy," I yelled back. "These fuckers seem a little shy, D. Why don't you flush 'em out?"

"Thought you'd never ask."

He holstered one gun and grabbed one of the mini Molotovs on his belt. In one smooth motion, he lit the fuse and tossed the small bottle over his head toward a cluster of bushes. The tiny but powerful bomb exploded just before impact and rained fire down on the assholes who wanted to fuck with us for whatever reason.

It was beautiful.

They flushed out all right, but it wasn't screaming in terror like I'd hoped. A leader jumped out first, signaling to the others to come straight for us. They fanned out, the first wave holding long shields as they encircled us. I took a couple test shots at the shields. Yup, bullet proof.

"Hold your fire!" the leader yelled at me. He and everyone else wore helmets with dark visors obscuring their faces.

"How 'bout you hold my dick, how does that sound?"

"T-Bone..." someone hissed behind me.

I turned to see the shielded assholes had almost completely surrounded the others. Through the gaps between shields, rifle barrels pointed inches away from Kyrie, Dyno, and Grudge.

Shit. There were a lot more of them than I realized.

"We don't want to hurt anyone," the leader said. "We just want you to come with us and have a talk."

I turned, pointing my weapon straight at him. "Yeah? Well you could have asked fucking nicely instead of throwing me off my bike. So, sorry, but we don't want to talk to you."

I fired at him without warning, narrowly missing his head, but got him in the shoulder. He went down, hissing and clutching at it. I was pretty sure I heard a metallic *plonk* on impact, which most likely meant he was armored and the wound wasn't fatal.

That was disappointing. But whatever, fuck him.

A shot at my feet kicked up a small dust cloud, and I turned in the direction of the shooter, clicking my tongue.

"You need to work on your aim, soldier." I returned fire with a single shot, hitting him in the leg. His cry of pain was musical as he went down.

"Stop shooting immediately!" another one of them yelled.

"I'll stop shooting when you fuck off, and let us be on our way!"

The shielded ones were closing in on the others, and I could barely see them over the crowd of black helmets. Dyno's arm went up as he released another Molotov, and that prompted them to scatter.

In their panic to escape the bomb, they turned their backs on us. Fucking amateurs. Grudge, Dyno, and I let loose, opening fire at their exposed backs. Normally we weren't the type to shoot in the back, but all the rules went out the window the moment these micro-dicks pulled up on us.

A few of them fell, both from our shots and the explosion that popped off, but the shitbags were well-trained and had a one-track mind. The rest recovered quickly, spinning back around to protect themselves with their shields. Dyno, Grudge, and I formed a tight circle now, guns pointing out while we protected Kyrie in the center of us.

"This is your last warning," one of the shielded fucks bellowed. "If you do not come peacefully, we will take you by force."

I let out a laugh that sounded maniacal even to my ears. "What gave you the impression that we would ever go peacefully?" I aimed my gun straight at his eyes through the small window in his shield. "I must not have made myself clear. Leave us alone or fucking die."

Fear flashed through the eyes on the other side of that shield. I didn't know what these guys were expecting, but it sure as fuck wasn't my level of crazy.

Sure, we were outnumbered. They would probably succeed in capturing us. But they also seemed hellbent on not hurting us. Any other army would have gunned us down the moment Dyno's first bomb exploded. For whatever reason, these people badly wanted us alive.

And because they pissed me the fuck off, I wanted to make them regret that decision.

I fired at the coward with the scared eyes, the bullet cracking the protective glass in his little shield window, and then chaos erupted.

With a single command, the shields rushed, pressing in on us on all sides. I felt Kyrie's hands on my back, heard her small whimper of fear, and tried to make myself as broad as possible to protect her. The guys and I threw our elbows out, pushing and kicking against the shields crowding in, but it was no use. We were just banging ourselves up.

Dyno's arm lifted to throw another bomb, but someone grabbed his elbow and wrenched it from his hand. They threw it far away from everyone, the explosion quiet and distant compared to the others.

Another arm reached between shields through the gap between my and Grudge's shoulders and grabbed Kyrie's wrist.

She screamed, pulling back against the soldier who tried to drag her out of our protective circle. I broke his hold on her and pulled him directly in front of me. My other arm went wide, going around his shield to press the barrel of my gun directly to his soft, unprotected neck.

"Touch her and die," I said, then pulled the trigger.

His head jerked from the impact before he fell to the ground, dead before he crumpled into a heap. Blood droplets covered my arm as I ushered Kyrie behind me. The death of their fallen comrade only made the soldiers rush forward even more insistently, instead of having the opposite effect as I'd hoped.

Dozens of arms grabbed at us, trying to break up our circle and pull away our weapons. Someone was able to grab Grudge's shotgun, so he started throwing punches. The motion created more room for the soldiers to reach between us, and someone else grabbed Kyrie's arm and started pulling her.

"Don't let them fucking take her!" I roared, rushing toward that mane of blonde hair like a bull after a red flag.

Our protective circle was fucking broken, and now it was just a mad scramble to get her back. The soldiers immediately formed a line of shields to block us, but we jumped and threw our shoulders at those motherfuckers. They must not have expected us to go so hard because we broke through easily.

Get her back. Protect her. Keep her safe. Those were my only thoughts as I fought against a wave of armored bodies, keeping my eyes on her hair, shining like sunlight. She was getting further away. I was moving too slow, I had to pick up the pace.

Something tripped me, and I landed facedown in the dirt. Before I could push up, something heavy and dense landed on my back and knocked the wind from my lungs. More weight fell to my arms and legs, pinning me to the ground.

"We have him secure," someone said.

I coughed out a mouthful of dust. "Like fuck you do."

"Should we sedate them?" the same person asked.

"If you're not a dumbass," I advised.

"No. We're to take them to Langley immediately, and they need to be of sound mind. All of them."

"You're gonna regret that." I hissed against the bite of a zip-tie cutting into my wrists.

"Different van then?"

"Nah, same one. If they can see she's unharmed, maybe they'll be more cooperative."

"Fat chance, pencil dick," I chimed in.

They all ignored me and grabbed my biceps to pull me upright. Ahead of me, I saw a large van painted completely black with the back doors open. Kyrie sat inside, her wrists bound in front of her and her face wrought with worry, but she otherwise looked fine.

"On your feet," one of the dick wipes ordered me.

I stood, and once I did so, swung a leg out to trip one of my escorts and knock him on his ass. "That's for tripping me," I said before spitting out a mouthful of dirt. "Cheap fucking shot."

He scrambled to his feet, all flustered and embarrassed as he took hold of my bicep again and walked me to the back of the van. The two of them stopped me right at the door and patted me down, taking my extra ammo and knives that I didn't get to use.

"Fellas, if you wanted to feel me up so badly, you could have just asked," I said. At their indignant scoffs I added, "The answer would've been no, by the way. You dickchumps wouldn't know how to please a man *or* a woman if they came with step-by-step instructions."

"He's clear, put him in," muttered the insecure manbaby that I tripped. "And put a gag in his fuckin' mouth."

"Oh, *now* we're talkin'." I leaned into his face, just to make him even more uncomfortable. "What other kinks you got, fuck boy?"

The other soldier dragged me into the van, and just like that, all my focus shifted to the gorgeous woman fighting back tears on the small bench next to me.

"Little lady—"

"T-Bone," she whimpered, bringing her bound hands to my face. She touched my eyebrow ridge, and her fingertips came away bloody. I must've hit the ground harder than I thought.

"It's nothing. Are you hurt?"

She shook her head but fuck, her whole body was shaking from fear, and I hated that I could do nothing about it. "Who are these people?"

"Dunno yet, but I know a few things. Hey, come here. Listen to me, Kyrie." I couldn't hold her with my hands zip-tied behind me, so I leaned into her, nuzzling her face and kissing her forehead until her eyes met mine. "They want us alive, which is a good thing. Even better, they don't want us drugged or incapacitated. One of them really wanted to knock my ass out, but his superior nixed that. And third, they're not trying to keep us separated. So this probably isn't your typical hostage situation."

"Then what could it be?" she demanded.

"Still figuring that out. We'll probably know before too long."

I turned to look out the open van doors where Dyno and Grudge were being subjected to their pat-downs. The dipshit I tripped reached into Grudge's cut and pulled out the folded papers he'd stashed there. Grudge's expression remained neutral, but I saw how his arms flexed against the cuffs as the asshole unfolded the sheets for closer inspection.

"For Kyrie?" The soldier turned to face us sitting in the van, a cheeky little smirk coming to his face. "Aw, was this a love letter for her?"

Grudge's jaw clenched in answer, and the soldier walked away with the most private details of Grudge's life in his hands. The moment my hands were free, I was going to divorce all of that that fucker's teeth from his gums.

And I'd bestow the same treatment to whoever ordered our capture.

CHAPTER 36

KYRIE

The four of us were mostly silent as the van drove. Aside from the observations T-Bone had given me, none of us knew what was going on.

The small, square windows in our mobile prison told us little about where we were going, at least for the first few hours. At some point, I saw flashes of black amid the neutral tones of the desert. I shifted in my seat to look out the window behind me, and my blood froze at what I saw.

Burned ruins. Charred husks of what were once businesses and homes, some of which I recognized. They just kept going on and on as we drove.

We had to be back in Sevier. Or at least, what little remained of it.

Everything clicked into place for me right then. The highly organized soldiers in black uniforms, just like the ones that had stayed at the service center before us. The guards after the uprising who wouldn't let Dyno and

Grudge into the territory had also been clad in black and seemed to be a professional unit.

These men were part of the new regime running the territory.

Which meant they had to be working for the new governor, or whatever the new leader called himself. I didn't know whether to feel comforted or more worried about the apparent orders to keep us alive and lucid.

What did they want with me, a former ambassador who no one had listened to, and her bodyguards? Were they rounding up everyone from the old leadership who was still alive? And if so, for what purpose? To make an example out of us? I couldn't shake that this whole situation had a very prisoner-of-war feel.

The worst part had to be knowing that no help would come for us. My father and I were cut off from each other, something I was still reeling from. And the Sons had no way of getting a message to the Steel Demons for help.

We were well and truly on our own.

My valkyrie seemed oddly unconcerned though. She sat on the floor of the van across from us, one leg stretched out leisurely and her forearm resting on her shield. Did she even know what was in store for us? She always seemed to know when I was in danger.

As usual, trying to look straight at her ensured that she disappeared from my vision.

I stared out the van window at the blackened remains of the vacation homes Governor Perry and Nathan had shown me when I first arrived. There was a small sense of vindication that they would no longer lord over the town, flashing their wealth and sense of superiority. Then again, I didn't know if they were still alive, and no one deserved to be gunned down in the street.

Once out of the city center, where the governor's cabinet and their associates had worked and played, it was like we'd entered a brand-new territory.

The burned areas stopped abruptly at the edge of an open field where several people tilled dark soil. Beyond the field, structures stood perfectly intact. Homes and businesses alike appeared to have been untouched by the violent uprising that occurred only a week earlier.

Not only were the buildings undamaged, people milled about fearlessly. There were no armed guards here, just more people farming and walking around carrying armfuls of what appeared to be food and supplies. Construction crews in orange vests and hard hats unloaded lumber from a truck. There were even young children running around and playing.

It looked like Four Corners when my father began rebuilding after the Collapse.

But my father never kidnapped people and forced them into a van, so this new regime wasn't about to score any points with me.

The van eventually stopped in front of a two-story building that looked eerily familiar. I squinted at it, trying to remember, when Dyno cursed under his breath.

"If that old geezer ratted us out, I'm gonna be pissed."

"This is the place you guys took me," I realized. "With the basement bar."

"Looks different in daylight, huh?" T-Bone remarked.

The van stopped abruptly and the tension ramped up, the guys restless and tugging at their bonds. When the doors opened to bright sunlight, the soldiers just outside gestured for us to come out rather than dragging us forcefully.

"Come on out, folks. Any day now," droned the

younger man who had taken sheets of folded paper from Grudge's cut.

Grudge was the first one to leave the van, leaning aggressively to snarl in the soldier's face. The soldier flinched and stumbled back, much to the amusement of his squadron.

"Let's go." The leader rolled his hand for the rest of us, stepping to the side as we made our exit. Dyno went next, and then T-Bone jerked his head, indicating I should follow. The Sons of Odin president felt like a shield at my back as I stepped out. Always protecting me, this man.

The soldiers surrounded us, directing us where to go without actually touching us or forcing us to move. Another odd way to treat prisoners? I glanced at T-Bone over my shoulder, and he just gave a small shrug.

We made our way up the stairs to the main floor where two more soldiers were posted outside the front door. They let us through, and we filed silently inside. Behind the front counter, where T-Bone and the owner had talked in some sort of code last time, was the last person I expected to see.

"*Anita?*" I gasped without thinking.

Her eyes darted up from what looked like blueprints spread over the counter, and her jaw dropped. "Miss Vance! You…you're okay!"

"*You're* okay! And it's Kyrie, damnit." Despite the situation, I couldn't help the laugh that escaped. I was just so immensely relieved that she was alive and well.

She looked better than ever, honestly. The Anita I knew had been timid and constantly worried about stepping out of line. This woman rounded the counter with a laugh and came over to hug me, paying no mind to the men with guns surrounding us. I would have hugged her back if my wrists weren't zip-tied together in front of me.

"Don't worry about anything," she said with a beaming smile. "The territory is in much better hands now."

I could only stare at her. Someone must have body-snatched my former assistant and replaced her with a clone.

"She's to meet with Langley immediately," the soldier reported. "The men are to wait here."

Anita nodded like she'd been expecting that. "We'll talk later," she said with a light squeeze on my arm.

A soldier nudged me to move, and I realized they were leading me to the side door, the one that led to the hidden bar under the basement.

"Wait, where are you taking her?" T-Bone demanded, swinging his shoulders to move away from his own cluster of guards. "She's not going anywhere alone with you chodes."

"Governor Langley has requested a private meeting with Miss Vance," Anita explained, her voice firm and even. Was it only weeks ago that she was visibly intimidated by the sight of my men?

"I don't give a fuck if Odin himself wants a meeting with her. She's not going into a room without us."

"You're not in any position to make demands," said one of the soldiers.

T-Bone turned on him, making the other man step back because of his height and aggressive body language and despite his hands still tied behind him.

"Try me, little bitch. I can get *real* creative with positions."

"T-Bone," I barked, surprised at the authority in my own voice.

He turned to me, his expression and posture immediately softening.

"I'll be alright." My voice was barely above a whisper, but I knew he heard me. "It's okay."

He'd been running hard on adrenaline ever since getting thrown from his bike, and his emotional state wasn't helping. He'd shot people, even killed someone right in front of me. I knew he was only trying to protect me, but this aggressive, loose cannon behavior wasn't helping us at all.

"Listen to her, T," I heard Dyno say behind him. "We don't have our weapons, and we're still outnumbered. You need to chill."

"She won't come to any harm, I promise," Anita added. "You have my word."

T-Bone's eyes remained glued to me, his breaths still ragged for several tense moments. Finally, his shoulders lowered a fraction and he said, "Be careful, little lady."

"I will." The soldiers ushered me along before I could say anything else.

The trip down the hallway was nothing like the first time I'd been here. Back then, I was excited. Fearless and with men I trusted implicitly. Now, I only felt numb as I followed the armed strangers to the second door and down the narrow stairs to the basement. It was like all of my fear had been used up when they ambushed us and forced us into the van. I had none left and didn't know what to think. They captured us and took us here, but took care not to hurt us. Anita was with them, and she was so different. My answer was at the bottom of these stairs, ironically in the room where I all but realized I was in love with the Sons of Odin.

The basement bar looked the same at first glance. The same cozy furniture was spread throughout the space. It still felt warm and inviting with all the dark wood, low ceiling, and dimmed lighting. But instead of people drinking illegally, there was only one man seated down here.

"You."

The word dropped from my mouth in disbelief at the sight of the bodyguard I'd seen while working at the capitol. We never met directly, but I remembered his bushy eyebrows, scowling face, and solid build. When I spoke up in meetings and all of the officials flat-out ignored me, sometimes it seemed like he was the only one listening.

He snorted amusedly when I acknowledged him. "So you do remember me, Ambassador." He set aside a stack of documents he'd been looking at.

"Did you plan the uprising?" The question blurted out of my mouth before I could think. "While *guarding* a cabinet member?"

He nodded casually while gesturing to one of his soldiers. "Ortiz, cut that tie off her wrists, and get her some water, will you?"

The soldier obeyed quickly, holstering his gun to draw a knife. I instinctively backed away, but he took my forearm in a surprisingly gentle grip. "Hold still, please," he muttered.

He cut the tie with a quick flick of the blade and immediately folded the knife away. The next thing I felt was a glass of water being pushed into my hands while my wrists throbbed with soreness.

My dry tongue stuck to the roof of my mouth, but I resisted draining the whole glass and gave the soldier my best glare. "Do I look stupid to you?"

He rolled his eyes but snatched the water from me, took a big gulp, and handed it back. "Satisfied?"

I drank the water greedily then, probably looking feral and *very* unladylike as I poured the liquid down my throat while hardly taking a breath. The glass emptied too soon, and I actually considered asking for another.

"My name is Gerard Langley," said the ex-bodyguard. He gestured to the armchair across the low coffee table from where he sat. "Please have a seat, Miss Vance. I'd like nothing more than to have a civil discussion with you."

"A civil discussion?" I repeated. "That's why you ambushed and kidnapped me and my men?"

"Using non-lethal methods," Gerard acknowledged, like that made it better. "Unlike your man, who fired live rounds and killed one of mine at point-blank range."

"He was protecting me! Your people kept grabbing at me and trying to separate us."

Gerard spread his palms out in a lame gesture of apology. "I'm a man who doesn't wait for things to happen. I *make* things happen. I wanted a meeting with you, so," his hands lifted to gesture to the whole room, "here you are."

"People have the right to say no," I spat back. "You can't just run people off the road, throw them into a van, and expect to have a productive meeting. What makes you think I want anything to do with you?"

"A few weeks ago, you were passionately standing up for the people of this territory. Do you still want them to thrive?"

The question was so out of nowhere, I had to stop and repeat it in my head. "What?"

A smirk pulled at his lips. "The people will most likely elect me as governor. And I want you to be in my cabinet."

CHAPTER 37

KYRIE

"I'm sorry, but…*what?*" And because I was in such utter disbelief I added, "Are you insane?"

Gerard's eyebrows lifted as he let out an amused huff. "Did you ask the former leaders that same question when they gave you a tour of their vacation homes?"

"I—"

"How about when they showed you the burned vineyards?" he asked. "Did you know there were still workers in those fields when they set fire to them?" Before I could answer, he pulled down the collar of his shirt to reveal extensive scarring along his collarbones and the top of his chest. The flesh was raised, shiny, and pink. He covered the burn scars quickly, leaning back in his chair. "I was one of the lucky ones."

"I'm…sorry." I whispered the sentiment weakly, with a heavy swallow. A soldier pushed another water glass into my hands, and I drank it down with a small thanks.

"So do you understand, Miss Vance?" Gerard asked,

gesturing again to the chair across from him. "Why I planned the uprising? Why I'm not willing to wait around for other people to do the right thing? They never will, not until they are directly affected. Unless," he swept his hand toward me, "a rare person like you comes around."

Cautiously, I approached the armchair across from him while still making an effort to not get too close. "What's so rare about me?"

"You actually care about those who were born with less than you." Gerard sat back, seemingly pleased that I'd sat across from him. "Not only that, you're smart and tenacious enough to fight for them." He grinned, rubbing his jaw. "My favorite part of the day was watching you argue with those capital men. You don't come off as intimidating, but you're a force to be reckoned with, Miss Vance."

I wasn't sure if that was a backhanded compliment or what, but I pushed the thought aside to address the biggest elephant in the room.

"I'm sorry for what happened to you," I began. "For your and everyone's suffering under the last government. But," I pulled in a breath to steel myself, "that doesn't excuse sealing off exits in a building and *bombing* it. I can't align myself with someone who would do such a thing."

Gerard gave me a hard look. "Every politician in that building had blood on their hands. You must know that none of them were innocent."

"*I* was!" I shot back. "I passed out from smoke inhalation. T-Bone fucked up his shoulder to get us out. We could have died alongside everyone else!"

"But you didn't," Gerard helpfully pointed out. "And most of the people at the Sevier Day Ball survived, thanks to your men."

"They…what?" I was all fired up to argue some more, but those last two words had me stuttering.

"They didn't tell you?" Gerard tilted his head amusedly. "Interesting."

"Tell me what?" I demanded.

"The other two, the one with the long hair and the silent one. They bombed one of our barricaded exits to let people escape."

I brought a hand to my chest, as if I could control the wild beating of my heart for these men. None of them said a word. Maybe they'd been looking for me and T-Bone, but even so, they saved the lives of people who probably wouldn't have done the same for them.

"We also evacuated the servers, cleaners, and assistants before our little show," Gerard went on. "I don't know if you overheard the complaints about no champagne being served before things got interesting. We could hear the bitching from outside."

Nope, I had been too busy making out with T-Bone in the corridor.

"That was how Anita survived," I said, to which he nodded. "Do you take credit for her attitude adjustment too?"

His eyes narrowed. "Do you prefer her cowering and subservient?"

"Of course not. I just—"

"She no longer has to worry about anyone harassing her at work or abusing her if she does something wrong. You may not have mistreated her, but she had no power as your assistant. No one to advocate for her if her boss or someone else tried to abuse the authority they have over her."

"I'm glad for that, I really am. It just concerns me

because no one's personality radically changes like that in just a week."

"Really? Did you bother to get to know her outside of work?" Gerard challenged. "You became so close to her that you would know what a sudden personality shift looks like?"

"I…no, I guess not." My eyes dropped, embarrassed at my presumption.

"That woman out there is one who feels empowered and safe." Gerard pointed toward the stairs I came down. "I want to rebuild this territory into one where every woman, child, and man can live without fear. Where they feel like they matter, not like they're cogs in a machine for the rich."

"That's admirable," I said cautiously. "But how will you be different from every other governor who claims power after an uprising?"

"I haven't claimed anything," he answered quickly. "Once everyone has their basic needs met and there are no other immediate worries, we'll hold elections." His hands folded in his lap. "And there will be a vote."

"But you expect to win."

He shrugged. "I do, yes. The people see me as their leader. But here's the thing, Miss Vance." He leaned forward. "Political games sicken me. I'm a doer, not a puppet-master behind a curtain. I'd rather be out there, building houses and cooking food for those who have noth-ing, because I've *been* there." He leaned back again with a hand to his chest. "I understand that laws and legislation are needed, but I refuse to let my home be run by self-inflated buffoons again. I need people who care about what matters, who know how the game is played, and who are tough enough to get it done." Gerard inclined his head toward me as he also extended his hand in my direction. "Even better, you grew up in a territory that has successfully cared for its citizens and maintained peace. You are exactly what I'm looking for, Kyrie Vance."

He's fucking serious, I realized. I couldn't figure this guy out. He wasn't afraid of using violence, clearly, but he also didn't seem completely unhinged either. I found his passion admirable and what he'd been through heartbreaking. But I still didn't *know* him. He was capable of executing an uprising that toppled a government, so he was no stranger to complex plans and strategies. What if this was all just an elaborate ruse to set up a dictatorship?

I so badly wished that my guys were here to give me a different perspective. My gut was silent, my thoughts pulled in all different directions. He could be trying to establish a strong but peaceful territory like my father's, but he could also be full of shit. I didn't know what to trust.

My valkyrie stood silently in a corner of the room, invisible to Gerard and his soldiers. She gave nothing away, just stood there like a fourth bodyguard. Fuck, I wish she'd tap out a message on her shield or *something.* But I got nothing from her.

The only thing I could think of was to find out as much information as possible, and for that, I had to keep talking to Gerard.

"You saw how they treated me in those meetings," I said after a long silence. "Everything I said fell on deaf ears. What makes you think anyone will treat me differently this time?"

"Because you'll be working for me," he said easily. "My people trust my judgment. Once they see I've appointed you, they will listen to you." He picked up a tumbler of whiskey, which I hadn't noticed until now, and took a small sip. "Of course, you will have to work hard and prove yourself. Your accomplishments will solidify people's trust in you." He smiled behind his drink. "Maybe you'll be elected as the next governor."

I couldn't hold back the snort. A female governor, in this day and age? It was a pipe dream.

"And what if I tell you no?" I said, folding my hands in my lap. "That I want nothing to do with running a territory anymore and just want to be an old lady to my biker men?"

Gerard shrugged, but he wore a little smirk that said he didn't believe me. "I have no interest in keeping prisoners. You and your men will be free to go."

"Really? So you just kidnap people when you want to have meetings but you don't keep them?"

His smile only grew wider. "Did we harm you? Injure you or make threats to do so?" He gestured to my empty water glass on the coffee. "Or did I remove your restraints and give you something to drink like a hospitable host?"

"Your soldiers put the restraints there in the first place!" Was he trying to make me feel crazy? It seemed like he was going for some kind of Stockholm Syndrome effect.

"I wanted to make sure you heard my offer. Now that you have," he shrugged again, "you are free to make your own decision with that information." With another sip of whiskey he added, "I don't think you want to say no though."

"You're not making a great case for yourself as a boss," I threw back. "Maybe you know how to overthrow a government, good for you. But you've told me nothing that would make me trust you to run one."

Gerard stared at me pensively for a long time before setting his whiskey down. "I give you my word that once you leave this territory, you won't see me or my army again. We won't be expanding our borders or invading other territories. All we want is our home and our rights back."

"I'll believe it when I see it," I snorted.

"You will," he said lightly, like it was inevitable. "And sooner, if you work with me."

The balls on this guy were something else. Didn't he know how many territories had risen and fallen since the Collapse? My father's cartographers were constantly redrawing maps because borders and names were always changing.

"I'll admit one other thing to you, Miss Vance." Gerard's face hardened. "The real reason I captured you and your men using my best units was to send a message to your father."

"My father?" I blinked at him in confusion.

"Him and all his political allies." Gerard's face relaxed again as quickly as flipping a light switch. "Four Corners has never caused us any direct trouble, but I know they had agreements with the previous administration." He leaned back, bringing the drink to his lips. "You may tell your father how we captured you. And if they choose to bring violence here in response," his eyes flashed as he took a small sip of liquor, "we'll be prepared."

I kept my face blank, trying not to betray how badly I wanted to burst out laughing. *Ha, joke's on you! My father and I are probably never speaking again, and I don't have sway over him anymore, dickbag.*

Instead, I tried my best to look intimidated as I said, "Understood."

I BLINKED and shielded my eyes when the soldier in front of me opened the door to the main room. I hadn't realized how dark it was in that basement, and my eyes were still adjusting when I heard T-Bone demanding, "Where is she? What the fuck happened?"

"I'm here, guys." I stepped out from behind the soldier and rushed to hug T-Bone.

"Thank fuck." He couldn't hug back with his hands still behind his back but rested his cheek on the top of my head. "Are you okay, little lady? Please tell me he put hands on you because I swear to fuck—"

"No, he didn't. And yes, I'm okay." I looked over my shoulder at the soldiers just standing around. "Are you going to cut their ties off or what?"

My mens' hands were free in the next few seconds, but I wanted to scream at the sight of their bloody, red wrists. Maybe none of us were badly injured, but I hated that they were hurt at all.

"Oh my God, you're *all* bleeding!" I grabbed for their wrists like I could do something about it.

"Sweetness, we're fine. It's nothing." Dyno stroked my cheek, dried blood on his thumb, while Grudge came up to sandwich me in a hug between him and T-Bone. "Just tell us what the hell happened down there."

"We're free to go," I said numbly, my cheek against T-Bone's chest. "Let's go home, please."

He loosened his embrace around me to look at my face more clearly. "They're letting us go? Just like that?"

"Just like that."

"What did their leader want to talk to you about?" Dyno demanded.

"I'll tell you all later. Can we just leave?"

The three of them exchanged looks of disbelief while I pulled myself out fully from between them, looking for one soldier in particular.

"Hey, you!" I called, pointing when I spotted him. "You have something that doesn't belong to you." I held my palm out. "Give it back."

The soldier, probably no older than me, turned beet red while his fellow soldiers snickered. Finally, he pulled the stack of folded papers from under his tactical vest, and I snatched them from his hand.

"Here you go, love." I spun, holding the papers out to Grudge, whose face was a mixture of shock and amusement.

But he refused to take them, holding his palm out and shaking his head before pointing at me. *"For you"*, he signed.

"Grudge…" I whispered, wishing we didn't have an audience. I didn't know exactly what he'd written, but knew it was significant to him. And intensely private.

"You heard the man, little lady." T-Bone came to stand next to me to address the soldiers. "If we're really free to go, we'd appreciate all our weapons back too. And a ride back out to our bikes would be the absolute *least* you can do," he added snidely.

"Your motorcycles were brought here on a separate truck," one of them reported. "We'll return your weapons once you're outside of our borders."

"Oh, we're being escorted, how nice," Dyno drolled. "Can you at least put gas in our bikes then? For the inconvenience?"

"We can probably arrange that," the lead soldier said, much to everyone's surprise.

"Well." T-Bone clapped his hands once. "Let's get fuckin' to it then."

I found myself pressed to Grudge's chest while the other two watched the soldiers like hawks. His arms wrapped around me like my valkyrie's shield, hands moving in soothing, protecting passes over my back.

The folded papers poked me in the chest, pressed between me and him. I'd read them with him present and no sooner. Once we were home, safe. When I wasn't so exhausted, drained, and when my head wasn't spinning with the events of the last twenty-four hours.

CHAPTER 38
GRUDGE

For once, I couldn't wait for a ride to be over. Even with Kyrie wrapped around me, her lips on my neck and her fingers curled into my shirt, I wanted us off the road and somewhere quiet. Somewhere we could just rest and process.

Chris and Tiff were full of questions when we arrived home, but T-Bone was still too bloodthirsty to talk. He stormed off to our room, and I heard the shower turn on a moment later. Ice cold, no doubt.

Ever the level-headed one, Dyno pulled our VP and treasurer aside to fill them in on what happened. None of us pressed Kyrie about what was discussed in that basement, and I was ready to go feral myself if anyone did.

She stuck close to me and seemed to forget all about the sheets of paper still folded and tucked into the front of her shirt. I wasn't upset about that. She probably had enough to think about.

Once Tiff stopped fussing over her and followed Chris

and Dyno, I pressed a palm to Kyrie's cheek until her eyes met mine.

"Shower?" I asked, making the sign for it. *"Food? Sleep?"*

Kyrie smiled wearily, but it eased the ache in my chest all the same. "Shower sounds good. I have no appetite, but sleeping for a long time sounds good after that."

I nodded and led her to the spare bedroom where she'd first spent the night. She'd be spending the nights with us from now on—that is, if reading my confession didn't make her change her mind, but T-Bone would be icing his blood in our shower for at least the next twenty minutes.

I turned the water on for her and grabbed a clean towel, then kissed her forehead and turned to leave, when her hand shot out and grabbed my forearm.

"Stay with me, Grudge," she whispered, adding, "Please?"

How could I say no? Her eyes were sad and pleading, and she needed me.

I turned back to face her, cupping her shoulders as I leaned down. And like a fucking pussy, I hesitated an inch away from her lips.

Like she hadn't told me with her own mouth that she wanted me. Like she hadn't clung to me, already kissed me, or stroked me while T-Bone railed her. The proof was all there, and still I held on to doubt that it was true.

"Grudge." She said my name with a cute little growl before closing the distance, reaching on her tiptoes to smash her mouth on mine.

Steam from the shower filled the small room as I caught her by the waist, holding her tight against me while those soft lips moved against mine. I'd never kissed a woman before her, and it was like sinking into a soft bed.

Everything she did, I mapped in my head and saved it to

remember. She'd been a wild thing earlier on that bike, biting and devouring me. Those were the kinds of kisses I was used to. She was sensual now, all soft presses and sweet sighs. I wanted to savor them like precious sips of water, because this woman made me feel more alive than ever before.

We undressed each other, our kisses pausing only when a scrap of clothing got in the way. I was half hard once we stripped down, but she didn't touch me there. Instead, she led me by the hand into the shower, pulling me under the hot spray with her.

The water ran dark with dried blood from our wrists, and we gently washed our raw, irritated skin with soap. Kyrie hissed with pain when I rinsed around her cuts, and I pulled her closer with a kiss on her temple. Her pain was my pain, and I wanted all of it washed away.

We washed each other, making soft passes over the other's skin with hands and a small bar of soap. Kisses falling wherever they reached. My life and instincts forced me to be hypervigilant of my surroundings, but right then, my whole awareness was this.

This was the quietness I wanted. The intimacy and alone time with her that I'd been craving, and I never wanted it to end.

But the water did run cold, and I shut it off the moment Kyrie started shivering. I wrapped her up in the biggest towel we had and carried her to the bed like that.

"You're dripping water everywhere," she told me with a soft laugh.

"Eh." I shrugged and continued to pile blankets and pillows around her until she was thoroughly cocooned. Only then did I grab a towel for myself and swipe it over my skin and hair.

"I'm missing my favorite pillow." Kyrie stuck an arm out, reaching for me.

How? Just how did she know how to make my chest feel like I swallowed the sun? I loved the guys, but this was different. She made me feel like she needed me, and I ate it up like T-Bone ate cinnamon rolls.

I finished drying off, then grabbed her hand and kissed it before sliding in next to her. She was already warm like a small furnace and squeaked when I put my cold hand on her belly.

"Not your feet! No, not your feet!"

Too late. I put my icy foot on Kyrie's calf until she howled and held her close when she tried to squirm away. Glaring, she touched her nose to mine and then licked it. I pulled back, stared at her intently for a moment, and then crossed my eyes. The cackle she let out was my favorite sound in the whole world.

"Forgetting everything is exactly what I need right now," she said, snuggling into my chest. "And you're the best at doing that. Thank you, Grudge."

I tapped her shoulder until I was sure she was watching my hands. *"Sorry about your dad,"* I signed.

She let out a sigh that seemed to deflate her whole body. "I was expecting it, to be honest. I had hope for a better outcome, but I think deep down, I knew he would never support us."

"Maybe one day," I offered with a shrug.

"Maybe, but I won't hold my breath. I've made my choice." She planted a kiss on my chest. "And if I had to do it over again, I'd choose you every single time."

I stilled beneath her. Even my hand that had been stroking her back had paused, and she noticed.

"You think that letter is going to change my mind about you?" Kyrie said.

"I don't know," I signed, then reached for a pen and paper on the nightstand to elaborate. *If you're going to choose us, that should be an informed decision.*

"I've already chosen," she said more firmly. "Based on enough information for me. But if it's important to you that I read the letter, I will."

You deserve to know what it says, so yes, I wrote. *T and D are the only other ones who know what's in it. If we're all in this together, you shouldn't be the odd one out.* I hesitated before adding, *It might be difficult to read. It's…graphic.*

That only seemed to steel her even more. She gave me a firm nod and said, "Okay then. I'm ready."

I got up to retrieve the folded stack of paper that she'd put aside when we undressed for our shower. After handing them to her, I signed, *"Do you want me to let you read alone?"*

"No, of course not." She patted the space next to her where I'd just been.

Nerves flipped in my stomach, but I returned to the warm space at her side. Kyrie snuggled into me again, relaxing as she unfolded the stack. My arm went around her shoulder, and I could read over the top of her head. Not that I needed to. I knew every word as if they'd been carved into me.

FOR *Kyrie*

I WAS NEVER SUPPOSED *to be born. My mother was barely more than a child herself when she had me. Still, she was brave and sought help to get away from the man who preyed upon her and many others.*

Help came in the form of a community of women who gave her shelter, food, clothing, even diapers and baby things for me. Before moving into the community, she was asked if her infant was a girl, and she told them yes.

For the first twelve years of my life, she kept me hidden away, and I didn't understand why. She told me never to speak or make noise when she went off to work for the day. I overheard other women asking about her "daughter", and my mother would say, "She's sickly. The sunlight is bad for her. She has a poor immune system, and it's not safe for her to be exposed to blood."

I was confused, lonely, upset. And so fucking bored. I started acting out, yelling and fighting with my mother because I was cooped up and bored out of my skull. This devastated her, and she would cry while telling me she was protecting me, that my life depended on it. I should have listened, but I didn't.

I kept fighting with her, and when someone came to investigate the noise, this other woman was stunned to see that I was in fact a son and not a daughter. My mother was beside herself. She begged and cried for the other woman not to tell the elders.

I didn't know why it was so serious. I had no idea.

The other woman was a friend of my mother's and seemed to take pity on her. She agreed not to tell, but issued a warning.

"His voice is going to start changing," the other woman said. "You won't be able to keep him safe forever, unless you silence him for good."

I was sent to bed while the two of them discussed in whispers. I barely slept that night, but I imagine the two of them went into great detail about how to "silence" me, because I woke up with my arms, legs, and forehead strapped down.

· · ·

KYRIE STOPPED READING THEN, her chest heaving with anxious breaths as she looked up at me. "Grudge, I don't know if I can keep reading this. Your own mother…she took away your ability to speak?"

I grabbed the notepad from the nightstand. *It's a painful memory, but I'm not angry at her for it anymore. She did it because she thought it would protect me.*

"Why did she keep you hidden away? This community, it sounds unhinged."

I nodded and released a heavy sigh as I wrote. *It is. You'll see why if you decide to keep reading.*

Kyrie leaned her head back on my shoulder. "Okay, just give me a minute." She looked at me, eyes bright and passionate. "If you went through it, the least I can do is read about it."

I shook my head and scribbled out, *No. I never want pain for you. If it's too much, stop. You have a right to know, but I won't force it on you.*

She kissed my cheek. "You're sweet. That's why you're mine."

I caught her lips with mine, savoring the sweet presses for a few moments before she continued reading.

I'M sure you can gather what happened next. I fell in and out of consciousness, but I remember choking on blood, trying to scream, and thrashing with all my might to escape. When I came to, my mouth felt all wrong. Everything was sore and aching, and at first, I thought I'd had my teeth removed. Then I realized I couldn't call out to my mother.

. . .

A TEAR ROLLED down Kyrie's cheek, and I wiped it away. She sniffed and took a deep breath, but continued to read.

MY MOTHER WAS SOBBING in the corner of the room. There was blood everywhere. She took one look at me and looked away. She kept saying how sorry she was, that she had to.

And I still didn't understand, because even after I started healing, life carried on like normal. I was still hidden away in our room, forbidden from leaving or seeing anyone except her. And now, I couldn't say anything. I couldn't tell my mother I was hungry, thirsty, or that my mouth was hurting again.

As time went on, she barely spoke to or acknowledged me. She'd take one look at me and start crying again. When I tried to get her attention, she would shove me away. All she ever said was that she had to, she did it to keep me safe. Maybe that was true, but I ended up more alone than ever before.

I was fed up with being stuck in the same room, and I no longer trusted my mother. So I snuck out and started exploring. I stayed hidden and mainly watched the community's women doing everyday chores. Cooking, farming, laundry. I never saw a single man.

One day, I ran into a girl about my age. Or rather, she caught me sneaking around. She spoke to me using her hands and over a few months, taught me to communicate in the same way. Her name was Charlie, and she was my first friend.

I was ecstatic. Finally, I had someone to talk to besides my mother. And I could actually talk to her without needing my mouth! I learned ASL as voraciously as I could and practiced the hand gestures in bed at night when my mother was asleep.

KYRIE SMILED as she read about me and Charlie, but

seeing as I knew what happened next, I couldn't share that small joy.

I WAS *voracious for any and all information and peppered Charlie constantly with questions. Why did she speak with her hands? Where were all the men?*

Charlie told me an accident when she was a baby caused her to lose her hearing. Her earliest memory was of her and her mom, who was pregnant, running away from a bad man who had something to do with her hearing loss. They came here, and she learned ASL from another deaf woman in the community.

'Do you have a brother or sister?' I had asked her. 'What about the baby in your mom's belly?'

Charlie got really quiet then and didn't sign anything for a long time. She looked really sad and I got worried. Finally, she said, 'My baby brother is in heaven so he wouldn't become a bad man.' She looked at me and said, 'All boys grow up to be bad men. That's why they're not allowed here.'

'That's not true,' I told her. 'I'm your friend. I'm not bad.'

'No, you're not bad. I like you. The other girls don't like me because I can't join their conversations.'

'We're both different,' I said. 'That's why we're friends.'

That was the last real conversation I had with her.

KYRIE LOWERED the papers to her lap and looked up at me. "It's going to get worse from here, isn't it?"

I nodded and pointed to the notepad where I wrote that she could stop reading.

"No, I'm okay. I think I just need to prepare myself." She picked up the papers again and continued.

. . .

MY MOTHER *actually tried to have a conversation with me that night. She'd probably noticed I had been in a better mood since meeting Charlie, but I was still angry at her for what she did. She kept trying to talk to me, but I didn't want to engage. I kept ignoring her, and she kept getting in my face. I finally snapped and signed, 'Leave me alone!' without thinking.*

She was like a statue, just staring at me before she started scream-ing, "Where did you learn that?! Who taught you that?"

I realized my mistake and refused to give up Charlie's name, but it wasn't hard to figure out. There were only two deaf people in the community—Charlie and the woman she learned from.

My mother was frantic, and her screaming had attracted atten-tion. People came knocking, and she tried to force me to hide. But I was stronger than her at this point and almost as tall. I refused and resisted. I still didn't fully understand, I was just sick of being hidden away like a shameful secret all the time. Charlie accepted me, so why couldn't she?

The women on the other side of the door broke the lock with a small battering ram, and that was when all of our fates were decided. Mine. My mother's. Charlie's. One of the women was the one who helped my mother silence me. She looked just as shocked as everyone else.

They took us both, and that was when I learned the truth.

At twelve years old, I learned that this community was a cult that presented itself as a refuge for abused women and girls. Men were not only forbidden, they were kidnapped and murdered during ritualistic sacrifices. Any boys born from women in the cult were sacrificed as well.

KYRIE'S HANDS began to tremble as she read, and I held her arms to steady her. Her breath shook as well, but her eyes kept moving over the page.

. . .

MY MOTHER WAS GIVEN *a sham of a trial. She begged for forgiveness with all her might, but I could tell immediately that their minds were made up. She laid out all her reasons for keeping me hidden, silencing me, and pointed fingers at her friend who helped. All of it just made her look guiltier in their eyes.*

She was given a long, painful, dishonorable death. I won't recount the details here, but it will haunt me forever. It happened because of me, and they kept me in a cramped dog kennel across the room to watch. I couldn't do anything to stop it, not even yell, 'stop'. Every time I tried to look away, someone jabbed me with a knife. I was bleeding from hundreds of cuts by the time it was over.

At some point during my mother's torture, she revealed that someone had taught me sign language. A small group went off, I assume to look for Charlie. I don't know if they ever found her, and I hope to all the gods they didn't. They never brought anyone else back to that room while I was in there. While my mother died slowly.

KYRIE PUT THE PAPERS ASIDE, gently folding them as she did. "I'm sorry. I don't think I can read any more."

She then turned to me, arms sliding over my shoulders and back. I let her pull me into an embrace, one that trembled from the shock of what she just learned, but she held fast to me like I was the only thing that mattered.

CHAPTER 39

KYRIE

I didn't know how long Grudge and I held each other. Or whether it was truly him comforting me or the other way around.

The contents of that letter made me want to hug the little boy it depicted, the one who was scared and alone and had no one. It wasn't as graphic as I initially feared, but my imagination and Grudge's writing painted everything vividly in my head. It hung over me now like a dark cloud.

I couldn't even imagine how Grudge felt, having lived that nightmare. Having *that* as his childhood. Fuck, I had no room to complain about my life and my father.

Grudge's head rested halfway on my shoulder and the pillow behind us, my fingers running absently through his dark strands of hair. His arms looped around me, one hand resting on my thigh that he'd pulled over his hip. We were still completely nude from the shower, but sex couldn't have been any farther from my mind.

He'd been calm at my side as I read the letter, while I had been in near tears the whole time. Every time I thought of something to ask him, or just pictured him in one of the horrible scenes he wrote about, I wanted to burst into tears again. All because he was a boy. I wanted to find this terrible cult and root them out like a disease.

"How did you get away?" I asked when I finally composed myself enough to speak. He probably wrote it in the last few paragraphs I didn't read, but I couldn't bring myself to touch those papers again.

"Mm." He scratched his beard and made a gesture I didn't understand.

"Lock-picking?" I guessed, making the correct sign for it.

"Mm-hm." He reached for his notepad to explain in more detail. *You won't believe this, or actually, maybe you will.* He chuckled lightly as he wrote. *A raven flew to my cage and brought me strips of metal that were the perfect lock-picking tools.*

"You're kidding!" I laughed, relief washing over me from that small miracle in all his suffering. "Was it Munin?"

Don't know. I never interacted with a raven again until I met T-Bone, years later.

"Was it hard to pick the lock?"

Not really. I was already decent at it from sneaking out of my room while my mother was away. They had left me outside in the cage overnight, I think in their sacrificial area because _everything_ was stained in dry blood.

My stomach roiled at the thought. "Where did you end up next?"

Homeless and living on scraps for a couple of years. I just kept running, because I thought they were after me. Then prison when I was about 15.

"Prison?" I repeated. "For what?"

Probably stealing food, I don't remember. But it was okay. I was fed, clothed, and housed, and surrounded by men, for once. Quite the opposite scenario of the cult. Met a deaf guy, got to practice my signing a little more. But it always reminded me of Charlie and the fact that it was the reason my mom died so horribly. It was still raw back then, so I preferred to communicate by writing.

"It wasn't you signing that got your mom killed," I said. "I'm sorry for what happened to her, but she was in the wrong in so many ways."

She was a victim too, both of the cult and the guy she ran from. I was hurt and angry for so long, but I don't blame her anymore. She was trying to fight the brainwashing they put her through.

I shifted my position, snuggling deeper into his chest, and let out a sigh of contentment at the feel of his arm tightening around my shoulders. "I'm glad you had Charlie. Wherever she is, I hope she's okay."

"Mm-hm." Grudge hummed softly in agreement while planting a kiss on my head.

"Okay, prison." I traced the winged helmet of the valkyrie on his arm. "What happened after that?"

Stayed there for about six years. Got a lot of tattoos, lifted a lot of weights. A prison buddy hooked me up with a job at a garage when we got out. I stayed in the back, just fixing up cars and bikes and didn't interact with people much. Got lonely again, but I kept busy, so it was okay.

I kissed his neck while he wrote, earning a smile and a delighted hum. It was easy to see now why Dyno and T-Bone were so devoted to him. They never held back in their affection and made sure to include him in every conversation. He deserved nothing less.

Did that for about 8 years. Then a bunch of loud bikers rolled through for some maintenance, and this really annoying fucker named Travis caught sight of me and wouldn't leave me alone.

Grudge chuckled as he wrote, and I cackled the moment I saw T-Bone's given name on the page.

"Was it love at first sight?" I asked, giggling as I sank deeper into the blankets and pillows.

Lust for him, maybe. I don't know what he saw in me, but he was fucking persistent. But I… Grudge paused, spinning the pen in his fingers before continuing. *I still had trouble trusting people. Even after I ran from the cult, people figured out that I couldn't talk and tried to manipulate me. Like I was stupid.*

"I'm sorry." I kissed his chest. "People are terrible."

Yeah. I thought T was trying to do the same shit at first. But he kept coming around to see me and…I liked it. I felt seen and wanted and not just because I was different.

"He's good at making you feel that way," I agreed. "Romantic in a dirty-minded sort of way."

"Mm-hm." Grudge chuckled and continued writing. *We started hooking up and…you know how he is. I never knew anyone could be so selfless. He pleased me while taking nothing for himself. He couldn't sign, but he talked to me like a normal person and was cool with me writing out my responses. Then he started bringing me lunch at work.*

"Awww!" My grin stretched from ear-to-ear, and Grudge laughed, blushing as he went on.

After a little while, he introduced me to D, who was all grounded and calming in contrast to T being an overexcited puppy. So that's how the three of us got started.

"Did you join the Sons after that?"

Yes. I prospected under Bash's presidency after T got me fired and I had nowhere else to go.

"He got you fired?!"

A shop customer called me a retard, and T beat the shit out of him. Would have killed him if a bunch of guys hadn't intervened.

"That sounds like something T-Bone would do." I sat up, gently taking his pen and notepad and putting them off to the side. "And after all that, you really thought my opinion of you would change?"

Grudge wore a vulnerable expression. His eyes told me clearly that he'd hoped it did not. Now that I knew, his hesitancy to trust was understandable. More than that, it had been essential to his survival.

Emboldened, I pressed down on his chest and threw a leg over him to straddle his waist. His eyes darkened, hands falling to rest on my knees.

"Kah?" He voiced my name like a question, but there was no question in my mind.

"Just in case it wasn't clear." I leaned down until our noses touched and my lips hovered over his. "You are perfect, and I love you, Grudge."

He hissed in a sharp breath, dark brows pulling together. That was the last thing I saw before his mouth crashed to mine.

His kisses took my breath away. Those lips were so sensuous with light pulling and sucking motions that I didn't know were possible. It felt like he'd developed extra muscles in his lips just for kissing.

I relaxed the whole length of my body on top of him while his hands made long passes up and down my back. Everything he did was intentional, precise. Rough fingers molded to the dip of my waist and traced the edges of my shoulder blades. He held the nape of my neck as he kissed the breath out of me, then brought his thumbs to my cheekbones.

Grudge released me with his hands and mouth to quickly sign, *"I love you too. Sit on me."*

"Sit on you?" I repeated with a giggle. "I already am."

Smirking, he shook his head and tapped his lips.

My brows lifted at the obscene image that popped into my head. Before I could clarify, Grudge slid his arms under my thighs to draw me upward as he slid down.

"Grudge, are you sure—ohhh..."

My knees were on either side of his head. I was spread open right over his face, and he was kissing me down there. And if I thought his kisses on my mouth were amazing, *holy fucking shit*, this was next level.

While he couldn't lick me, that mouth was sucking and kissing me in the most exquisite ways. The pressure of his lips was softer than fingers but firmer than a tongue. And when he dragged a kiss over my clit, the friction had me flailing to stay upright.

"Need an assist over there?"

I looked over my shoulder to see T-Bone and Dyno standing in the doorway, both of them shower-fresh, shirtless, and with devious grins. Dyno's hair was loose instead of in his usual braid. T-Bone still had water droplets on his skin, and both of them looked delicious enough to eat.

"How long were you two eavesdropping?" I asked, panting already. Grudge carried on eating me like they weren't even there.

"We didn't overhear your conversation, just when things started to get fun," Dyno said. "We do have some semblance of privacy."

"And if you prefer this be private between you two, we'll butt out," T-Bone added.

It was sweet of him to offer, but I could tell how much

he wanted to stay. And honestly, having them all in a group was like catnip to me.

"I think I got the hang of this now." I rolled my hips over Grudge's mouth, eliciting a sensual moan from him. "But you know what else I'd love?"

"Tell us," Dyno breathed while T-Bone draped his arms over Dyno's chest, hands smoothing over tattoos and lithe muscles.

"I want to watch you two while I ride Grudge's face." Was that *me* saying those words? I could hardly believe it. "Let's see if you can put on a show hot enough to make me come."

"Is that my little lady speaking with that dirty mouth?" T-Bone came up to the bedside, beaming with pride as he cupped the back of my neck. "We'll give you something worth watching, sweet filthy girl."

His fist curled in my hair, holding me in place while he kissed me, deep and probing with promises of more to come. At the same time, Grudge's lips swept back and forth over my clit in a way that had me grinding into his face for more sensation. That spurred T-Bone to kiss me deeper, and I couldn't get enough of being endlessly caught between these two men.

Eventually, T-Bone was dragged away, and his face tipped to the ceiling with a groan while Dyno cupped his erection. "What do you want to do to our girl when she's done watching us?" Dyno leaned in to kiss T-Bone's neck as he kept rubbing the front of his shorts.

Immediately, I realized my mistake. I told the kinky one and the dirty talker to put on a show.

This wouldn't last long for me.

"I want to watch her bounce on Grudge's cock, then I want to suck the taste of her pussy off of him." Fucking

Christ. T-Bone growled the words out with his fist in Dyno's hair, then pulled the other man away from his neck to kiss him just as hungrily as he did me.

T-Bone broke the kiss just as roughly, leaning his forehead on Dyno's as he continued. "I want to play with her ass while she fucks Grudge, get her nice and ready to take your cock back there. I know you've been dying for it."

"Fuck!" My hips kicked forward as a bolt of pleasure zipped up my body. Grudge just moaned like he was in the happiest place on earth, hands running up my body to tease more pleasure out of my nipples.

"I can't wait to feel her come around my dick in her ass." Dyno picked up where T-Bone left off, the two of them groping and roughly kissing on each other's mouths, necks, and shoulders. "And when Grudge comes outside her pussy, I want to go down on her and taste them both."

"Oh my God..." My hand found itself clenched in Grudge's hair, anchoring him down as I rode his lips with abandon. He only encouraged me, hands clasped on my ass to help drive me forward and back.

"That's it, little lady. Get his beard all wet. I want to taste and smell you when I kiss him." T-Bone now had Dyno's back to his chest, one arm braced around Dyno's torso and the other hand sliding long strokes along his cock, which was thickening by the second. T-Bone's hips also made small thrusting motions, and I could just imagine the length of him gliding along Dyno's smooth backside.

His gaze fixated on me while his mouth pressed to Dyno's ear. He took the lobe between his teeth, sucking on it and making Dyno squirm.

"Aw yeah, thrust that cock through my hand," T-Bone

urged him. "Imagine that's her sweet little ass you're fuckin'."

"Oh God..." I was so close and yet dying for this hollow, empty sensation to be filled. I needed something inside me more than I needed to breathe. Everywhere I looked was a sharp reminder of that need. Grudge below me, his incredible body and poor untouched cock behind me and then those two standing mere feet away. It was all too much and not enough.

"Guys," I pleaded in a high, breathy whine and halted my movement on Grudge, even though I hated to. "I need—"

"What you need is to ride your man's face like a cowgirl until you come." Dyno's words carried sharply, his tone domineering like I'd never heard before. His expression was just as commanding, even as T-Bone sucked the crook of his neck and stroked his cock. Jesus, this man was like a Swiss army knife of kinks, and I never knew which was going to pop up.

That was just one of the things I loved about him and why I immediately slid my pussy along Grudge's mouth again. The sweet man beneath me seemed to sense what I needed, and my head threw back with a decadent sigh when I felt his fingers press inside.

"Yes, oh yes!" I angled my clit toward his mouth while his fingers curled to make delicious friction against my slick walls. "Oh, Grudge, yes! That's perfect, so good..."

"Don't you want to fuck them both so bad?" T-Bone's voice caressed my ear like his mouth was physically against it.

"Mm-hmm." Dyno's answer was just as sensuous. "At the same time, I never want to stop watching. They're beautiful together."

"Fuck yes they are."

They kept talking, but it was getting harder to hear over my own moans and the blood pounding in my ears. Grudge's fingers tapped a spot over and over that made me feel like a bottle of lightning. And his lips...holy shit, those perfect lips wrapped around my clit and sucked like he needed my orgasm to live.

I came to the sight of T-Bone and Dyno locked in a tight embrace and lust-filled kiss. Pleasure rocked through me from a man whose kisses and ministrations were unique, beautiful, and entirely his own. I bowed forward over Grudge's head, my strength temporarily stolen by my orgasm.

His hands rested on my back, rising and falling with my ragged breaths. And as I slowly came down from my high, I felt him draw a heart on my skin with his fingertip.

CHAPTER 40

GRUDGE

So this was the intoxicating taste the other guys couldn't get enough of. I thought I had missed having a tongue before but never truly until now. I would have liked to savor Kyrie on my tongue, feel the full range of her flavor on my taste buds. But I got her off, and that was good enough.

Her thighs, which had been tense and quivering, now relaxed on my chest where she sat. Her knees were still on each side of my head, and I tickled the sensitive backside of one just to see if she'd respond.

Kyrie leaned up and scooted down my body right away. "Sorry, sorry. I wasn't suffocating you, was I?"

A little thing like you? Never. Fuck me, do you have any idea how beautiful you look after you come? You're glowing, you look so happy. All I ever want to do is make you happy. I can't believe you chose me. I'm completely in love with you.

My head was full of thoughts I couldn't adequately express to her. If I reached for pen and paper, I'd have to stop touching her, and I couldn't bear to do that right now. With her help, I'd learn to sign again. Now that Charlie had one more person to remember her, it didn't hurt as badly to speak with my hands. Right then, I settled for shaking my head no and huffing out a soft laugh.

Kyrie pressed up, her expression seductive as she reached behind her and wrapped a delicate fist around my stiff cock. "No one's touched you here yet," she said, her voice almost mournful. But her eyes slid to our viewers, and her lips turned up in a playful smile. "And our audience really thinks I should keep riding you."

"Yes, you should." T-Bone and Dyno approached the bedside, still tangled up in each other while equally focused on us. "Grudge's cock is so fun to ride. His girth is perfect—"

"Oh my God." Kyrie brought a hand to her face, unable to stop her laughter. "Travis, you are too much."

"No, I'm not." He released Dyno to cup her neck, leaning in with a grin. "I'm perfect for you too."

"You are," she admitted in a breathless whisper before taking his rough kiss.

Dyno, meanwhile, climbed onto the bed behind her, sitting on my thighs as he hugged around her waist and dragged kisses along her upper back. Unable to help myself, I rubbed a thumb over her clit, enjoying the view as she squirmed between the three of us.

T-Bone broke his kiss from her with a chuckle, sitting on the edge of the bed as he leaned down towards me. "Now *this* is what I've been dying to taste," he said before taking my mouth.

He moaned the instant he tasted Kyrie on my lips, and how could I blame him? We were all addicted to her.

I felt his fist in my hair, a pleasurable sting of pain as T-Bone's mouth moved on to my ear.

"Proud of you, Grudgie," he whispered, the words meant for me alone. "You were brave to tell her."

Right then, I felt a wet, silky heat envelope the head of my cock, and T-Bone smothered my moan with another kiss. Kyrie's slow descent on me was nothing short of the most blissful torture I'd ever felt. I fisted the sheets at my sides, fighting the urge to snap my hips up. She paused halfway down, rising up again until just the head remained inside. When she lowered again, the most delicious pressure surrounded my cock on all sides, and I could *not* get enough.

"Lean on me. Easy, there you go." Dyno soothed her as she paused again, his hand coming around to stroke her clit, and by extension, my shaft.

"I'm okay," Kyrie panted. "Just still catching my breath."

"You put in some work riding this face." T-Bone gave an affectionate tug on my beard. "Is our little lady ready for an assist yet?" He ran an indulgent hand up her body, rolling his palm over a breast before closing that hand around her throat. He waited for a beat, gauging her response.

Kyrie's mouth parted on a gasp. Her eyes pleaded as her head tilted, lips reaching for contact. T-Bone gave it to her, holding her trapped between him and Dyno while she impaled herself on me.

I watched her hands move, saw the edge of a naughty smile while the guys were distracted with kissing her. Kyrie reached forward and back, taking a cock in each hand and gave them a stroke.

"Fuuuck," the two of them said together.

Our shy girl was getting bolder by the day. Kyrie's pleased grin made it clear that this side of her had been dying to come out. She was *so* right for us, and I felt secure in including myself in that now. This woman deserved the world, and somehow, three fucked up bikers knew exactly how to give her everything she needed.

She started doing a little bounce on me while turning the two of them into putty in her hands. We were all enraptured by her. No one made a sound while she worked the three of us, except for the occasional kiss and our rough breaths.

Dyno was the first to break out of the spell she'd put us under. He grabbed the nape of her neck and turned her head to kiss her forcefully. "I can't fucking take it anymore," he growled before pressing down on her back. "I need to be inside you."

Kyrie's chest pressed to mine as Dyno leaned her down, a smile on her lips as they moved over mine. She was mine to kiss again, mine to stare at and adore. Her kisses were punctuated with soft moans and gasps while Dyno played with her ass. It didn't take long before she got louder, her hips rocking back and forth. She pressed up to her hands and crashed her pelvis down, rocking and grinding as she chased her release.

T-Bone came in from the side, sliding his fingers down her belly to that spot that would set her off. "Come for us like a good girl," he said in her ear.

The result was instant and incredible. Her body locked up with a sharp cry, and she shuddered as the orgasm rippled through her. I saw the whites of her eyes, and the way her pussy convulsed around me threatened to undo me.

Kyrie slumped against my chest again, her skin warm

and dewy with sweat. I ran my hands along her sides and she shivered. When she looked up at me, spent and flushed, I brought my hands in front of my face to sign, *"Good girl."*

Her grin stretched wide and she nuzzled my neck. T-Bone dropped a kiss in the center of her back, then smoothed his hand from her nape to her ass. "That's our good girl."

Kyrie sighed decadently, and I swore she melted over me even more.

"Is your ass ready for me, gorgeous?" Dyno petted her back with one hand, smirking while his other hand continued to play with her. "You look so relaxed."

"Is yours ready for me?" T-Bone asked him, smacking Dyno's ass once before moving to kneel behind him.

"Yeah, should be oil around here somewhere. Check under the bed."

Kyrie burst out laughing at that. "You guys keep lube in the *guest* bedroom?"

"We're three dudes who fuck, we got it stashed everywhere."

T-Bone found it in the nightstand drawer, and the guys returned to their positions. Kyrie remained prone on my chest as Dyno began a careful entry into her backside.

"You tell me if I'm hurting you," he told her sternly. "This should not hurt. Don't feel like you have to muscle through it."

I hugged around Kyrie's back, kissing my way from her shoulder to her neck in hopes of relaxing her. She hummed and sighed out a deep breath, nuzzling into me some more. I felt her smile against my neck as I finger-spelled *relax* against her skin.

"I could feel you sign on me all day," she said dreamily. "I love how you touch me, Grudge."

What I would give to just tell her the same thing, right at that moment. I kissed her instead, hoping it got the meaning across. She seemed to understand, kissing me back just as intently with that sweet tongue sweeping into my mouth. I remembered how it felt on my cock and groaned, rolling my hips up to sink even deeper into her pussy.

I felt the moment Dyno pressed into her ass. Kyrie froze with a sharp gasp, and her slick walls seemed to hug around me even tighter.

"Pain?" Dyno asked.

"Um, no. I don't think so. Just…different."

I stroked her back, her arms, kissing her everywhere I could reach.

"You're doing so good, little lady." T-Bone reached from his place behind Dyno to smack lightly on her ass cheek. "Our girl takes our cocks so well. And she's so fucking sexy when she does it."

The praise did the trick, and she melted over me again. Dyno pressed in a little more before drawing back, and then *I* was the one gasping. Fuck, there were just no words. It was like having my cock stroked while being inside of a woman at the same time. Extra sensation and movement that wasn't from her but from the other man fucking her. The sheer fucking eroticism of it had me grasping Kyrie's hips and fighting every instinct to buck deeper into her.

She noticed how wild it got me, and that only seemed to heighten her enjoyment. "Can you feel Dyno too?" Her grin turned salacious. "Does it feel like he's fucking you?"

Goddamn, she was going to give T-Bone a run for his money with the dirty talk. Speaking of, I heard his low murmuring and the wet sounds of his hand fucking Dyno. We were all about to be cock-deep in someone soon.

Dyno gave a few more thrusts to make sure Kyrie was comfortable before he leaned over her, his chest nearly to her back. "Hey, gorgeous." He greeted her with an ear nibble.

"Hey, yourself. What's going on?"

She got her answer when he bellowed, "Oh, fuck!" and pressed his forehead to her neck. T-Bone entered him in one deep stroke. Kyrie's eyes went wide at the realization and looked behind her.

T-Bone waved at her, grinning from where he knelt. I couldn't see but knew his hips were snug against Dyno's ass, and his cock buried to the hilt. "It's a Kyrie-Dyno sandwich today. Next time I want to be the filling, though."

"You are ridiculous." Kyrie laughed, then stopped abruptly when she looked at me. "Grudge, are we crushing you?"

I shook my head as Dyno said, "He's fine. T will stay upright, and I'll keep my weight off you." He planted his hands on the bed, framing Kyrie and me while he brushed another kiss on her shoulder. "I'll try to, anyway."

"How do *you* feel?" Kyrie twisted slightly to land a kiss on Dyno's mouth. "Being inside me and…him inside you?" She was adorably fascinated by the whole formation.

"It's pretty fuckin' heavenly." He grinned at her, doped up on love and lust in equal measure. "How about you, feeling alright?"

"Yes." Not only did she say it, she rocked backward to take more of his cock and mine.

I grabbed at her thighs, his arms, anywhere I could reach for purchase. The combined sensations of them were just too good. And with that, we all started moving, seeking a rhythm that was uniquely ours.

Kyrie splayed flat on my torso, her head next to mine on the pillow. She couldn't do much but absorb our impact and seemed content with that. Our little cowgirl had done plenty of riding already. Dyno leaned all the way forward, past her shoulder to kiss me, and she seemed to enjoy that too. She teased us both, wiggling her hips as we both surged in and out of her and kissed our necks and ears.

Dyno grabbed her hair in a rough hold and turned her head to kiss her, hips pumping against her ass with the extra force of T-Bone thrusting with him. Her long, graceful neck was right in front of my mouth and I attacked it, pulling the sensitive skin with my lips while I finally gave in to the urge to fuck her with everything I had in me.

What a sight we must have been, the three of us and her.

"Fuck, I can feel you Grudge," Dyno rasped, delirious with the heady rush of pleasure. "Feel you through her, every time. Fuck."

I could feel him too, every inch sliding against me through this incredible pussy that blew my mind on its own. But having them both this way? It was on another level.

"Wish you all could see what I'm seeing." T-Bone's tone was almost reverent. "His hot ass, her sexy ass, and the handsome fucker down at the bottom there, damn." I felt a hand stroke up my thigh. "Hottest group of people I've ever fucked."

"I was about to say the same thing." Kyrie pressed her forehead into my neck with a smile, and I cupped her face. The need to touch her constantly was just too great, even when I was already inside her. Even when we were a sweaty pile of thrusting, groping bodies, I needed constant confirmation that this woman lying on my chest was really here. And that she was mine.

Kyrie mouthed along my bearded jaw until her lips found mine and kissed me like I was the only man with her. Her skin slid against mine with every drive of me and Dyno into her. Through the hot embrace of her pussy, I felt his rhythm falter, his thrusting going wild. He moaned against her back, eyes shut tight and brows furrowed with tension.

"Gonna come for me, D?" T-Bone fucked him as steadily and punishing as ever, hands on Dyno's waist in a bruising grip with each long drive of his cock. "Gonna fill up our girl's sweet little ass?"

"Yeah…fuck…I can't…"

Kyrie and I both felt him swell, and it started a chain reaction. She gripped me tighter as a result, and then *I* was reaching the point of no return. Her hands fisted the sheets and dug into my shoulders. Moans turned into screams, and I got closer and closer with every frenzied, desperate crash into that heavenly pussy.

"Fuck me, are *all* of you coming?"

T-Bone's question would've been funny if I hadn't felt Kyrie's orgasm rippling over me right then. The rhythmic squeezing along the length of my cock was too fucking good, and I couldn't hold back any longer.

I pulled out just in time, lifting her off me as I sprayed white ropes against her clit and her thighs. My pulse roared, pleasure shooting through me with each release until I was drained. Kyrie sagged against Dyno, the only one holding her up after her own orgasm.

I didn't know how he had any strength left, but he laid

her down gently across my thighs, pulled her legs apart, and licked my cum from her skin.

Just as he said he would.

Kyrie shuddered with a soft whimper, likely sensitive and aching, as his tongue traveled over her clit and folds.

"Too much?" He paused, watching her.

"No." She grabbed the back of his head and pressed his mouth directly to her with a laugh. "Perfect."

"Scoot over, D. Grudge, come here." T-Bone was still deep inside Dyno, his body taut with his own imminent release. "You know what I want," he added, eyes dark with lust.

With a little effort of my freshly-fucked limbs, I came to standing on the bed with my cock at T-Bone's mouth level.

"Let me taste our little lady on your fat cock." He took me in his mouth at the same time that he drove a deep thrust into Dyno, who moaned against Kyrie's pussy. She in turn threw her head back, arching deeply as her hands dove into Dyno's hair.

T-Bone's moan around my length reached all the way down to my toes, and I had to put a hand against the wall to steady myself. He sucked me greedily, tongue swirling around to lap up all of Kyrie's taste. I *had* been going soft, and was sensitive for a moment, but seeing all of them from this angle…what a fucking view.

Watching T-Bone's cock disappear into Dyno's ass with a rough crash of flesh. The long, slender muscles of Dyno's back. Dyno's face now buried in Kyrie's pussy like he was trying to take her to another orgasm. And her. Flushed and well-fucked. So beautiful and erotic with her hair and legs spread across the bed. And all of this was happening while one of my favorite mouths sucked my cock.

T-Bone hummed a satisfied, "Mm-hmm," when he noticed me getting hard again. And just like that, we were at it again.

He was the one to start the chain reaction of orgasms this time, slamming into Dyno with a final deep thrust that had him moaning loudly around my cock. Kyrie was next, T-Bone's pleasure becoming hers as she writhed and shook under Dyno's tongue. At the sight of her I was done for, spilling into T-Bone's mouth with a deep groan from my chest.

That second round did us in, and we all collapsed into a heap on the too-small bed.

"Shower. Bed," T-Bone grunted like a caveman, pulling an exhausted Kyrie against his chest. "I mean, our shower and our bed. This isn't your room anymore."

"'Kay." Kyrie's cheek smooshed against his sternum, eyelids drooping. "In a minute."

Dyno flung an arm around me and brought his head to my chest. I drove my hands through his hair, stroking his head and neck while my heartbeat drummed under his ear.

In truth, none of us were ready to leave this messy but perfect little love nest we'd made.

CHAPTER 41

KYRIE

"So what are you gonna do?"

Chris' gaze bore into me across the table, at least until Tiff smacked his arm with a disapproving click of her tongue. "Leave her alone. She can't make that kind of big decision on the spot."

It had been five glorious days of hardly doing anything at the clubhouse. I took naps in the middle of the day, helped myself to snacks, read books, and made love with my three men whenever I wanted to. Every moment was freeing and enjoyable, but as the days passed, I found myself restless.

I wanted to do something meaningful for others. It was like an itch I needed to scratch.

I had told everyone what Gerard and I had discussed in that basement. Everyone agreed that it was foolish to work with someone who had captured and imprisoned us. And yet, I couldn't stop thinking about his offer.

"She's leaning toward yes. I can see that look in her eye," Chris went on, staring at me intently. "It's been mulling around in your head for a while, huh, little lady?"

"Don't call her that!" T-Bone hollered from across the house, his lumbering steps quickly approaching. "Only I can call her my little lady." He bent to kiss my neck on his way past me into the kitchen, and I secretly preened at the possessiveness.

"Glad you aren't losing your hearing, old man," Chris teased. "Even if it is selective."

"What?" T-Bone barked.

"Nothin'!"

I usually loved the guys' banter but right then, it was all background noise to me. My head swam with what-if scenarios. If I didn't work in public service again, what would I do? Just...stay here and be an old lady to my men? Maybe that was appealing to some people, but I wanted to do more. And if I didn't take this offer from Gerard, how else would I get my foot in the door? Now that Dad and I were estranged, I had no other connections.

No one would give me a chance, and that was the best-case scenario. Some territories out there would throw me in a prison just for being female and openly wanting to work in government.

Round and round my thoughts went, until a warm kiss on my cheek pulled me to the here and now. I met Dyno's thoughtful gaze with a sheepish smile. "Hi, sorry. I'm just...thinking."

T-Bone turned to face us at the table, leaning against the kitchen counter. "So you *are* considering saying yes." The surprise was evident in his voice.

"No. I mean, I don't know."

Grudge came in silently, running a hand along my upper back in a show of support. He took the seat next to me and began to sign, his hands moving more fluidly since he'd been practicing. *"Tell us what's on your mind. Let us help you."*

"I do want to work for a territory's government again," I said, using my hands and voice. "It's what I know and what I'm good at. I want to be an advocate for people who need a voice at the top, to give them safety and stability. I'm just not sure I want to work with *him.*"

"You're right to be cautious," Tiff said. "You don't know what this guy's endgame is. What's he trying to accomplish for himself?"

"I should have asked him that," I admitted.

"Maybe you still can," Chris suggested. "If he's willing to keep talking things out with you. Like Tiffy said, it's not an easy decision."

T-Bone rubbed his hand over his beard. "So, I know I kinda went apeshit when his guys captured us and all, but if I'm gonna be perfectly honest, I don't think it was the most unreasonable thing in the world."

The rest of us stared at him like he'd grown an extra head. *"I can't believe what I'm hearing,"* Grudge signed, which I relayed to the others.

"I know, I know. It was the thought of Kyrie getting taken from us that made me lose my shit. But I mean," T-Bone shrugged, "back in our day, we had to apprehend people in a similar way to talk to them. That's just how we did things."

"We're a biker club," Dyno reminded him. "They were trained soldiers under a guy who's trying to become a governor."

"So? He was a bodyguard. He worked in fields. The guy probably grew up a scrappy street kid like us." T-Bone paused, eyes landing on me. "I'll even go as far as saying that if Four Corners was run by a different man than ol' Vance, and those people were struggling, starving, and fed up, shit I probably would've joined an uprising too."

"Bash would have rallied the club to overthrow a piece-of-shit governor," Dyno agreed with a nod. "No doubt in my mind."

"Mm-hmm," Grudge chimed in and signed, *I can understand his reasoning. We would do the same if in that position.*

"But kidnapping people?" I asked. "When they're heading home, just minding their own business?"

"Depends on how important those people are, what kind of leverage we'd get, but sure. We're not above it," T-Bone said, then grinned salaciously, running a hand toward his crotch. "You're giving me kidnapping fantasies, little lady."

"Excuse you, we're still here!" Chris exclaimed.

A peal of laughter burst out of me before I could stop it. "I would have much rather been kidnapped by you than the first guy who stole me away."

Dyno snorted. "Hey, it worked out for Mari and the Demons."

"Alright, we're leaving." Tiff started to get up from the table until I reached over and touched her arm.

"No, please. We'll be serious, and I really want every-one's input on this."

Tiff gave me a skeptical look but sat down and rolled her hand for me to continue. "Alright, keep talking it out. What are your concerns?"

"I hear what you guys are saying, and I might be

willing to let the kidnapping thing go, provided it doesn't happen again. Gerard promised it wouldn't. But that's the thing, I don't know if I can trust him."

"Yeah. Even if he's an effective leader and fights for his people, that doesn't necessarily mean he's a good person," T-Bone mused.

"He could be lying about everything," Grudge said, then reached for a notepad to elaborate. *Even if he's a good governor for years, he could turn around and become a dictator overnight. It just depends on what his goal is. Does he want endless power and wealth? Or is he satisfied with a safe, stable territory?*

"What Grudge says is right," Dyno added. "Dozens of territories have risen and fallen since the Collapse. So many people have suffered from lofty promises spoken through the teeth of a liar. It's a very realistic thing to worry about."

"Oh, trust me, I'm worried about it," I said. "But most of those have been conquered by violent invasions, not with any diplomatic plan in place."

"We already know Gerard isn't shy about using violence," Dyno argued. "They bombed a building with people inside. They burned half a city, Kyrie."

"They also evacuated service staff before the bombing. They told you what was happening so you could get us out. They didn't have to do that."

Grudge snorted and wrote out, *Those aren't very high stan-dards for having allies.*

"I know, love. I'm just thinking out loud."

He melted whenever I used that pet name, and right now was no exception. My quietest man dragged my chair closer and locked his hands around the far side of my waist. I tried to concentrate while he peppered kisses on my neck and shoulder.

"If Gerard genuinely wants to create a fair, stable territory, he wouldn't be opposed to putting limits on his power. Before the Collapse, the old US government had checks and balances so that no single branch could hold too much power."

"Yeah, and look how that turned out," Chris scoffed.

"Well, we have the gift of hindsight now," I answered. "We can see what didn't work before and propose laws to fix that. If he refuses power limits, that's pretty telling in and of itself."

The room went quiet for a while. I waited for more arguments but none came. Eventually, it was T-Bone that said, "Sounds like you've made up your mind, little lady."

I shook my head. "No, far from it. But I think I have some clarity on what I should talk to Gerard about. His answers, or lack thereof, will help me come to a decision."

"So." Dyno tilted his head. "We're going back?"

I looked at him and then everyone else. "You guys are okay with that?"

"*We support you,*" Grudge said.

"There is a chance he's not a total piece of shit, and I think it's worth it to find out." T-Bone's face went stern. "But you are not meeting him alone again. No fucking chance. We're in the room, or it doesn't fucking happen."

"You do realize you're not actually my bodyguards anymore, right?" I rose from the table and went to him, standing on tiptoes to loop my arms around his neck.

"True, we're not." T-Bone drew me against his torso and rested his hands on the small of my back. "But you're our old lady, our property. We don't protect you for a paycheck. We do it because you're the reason our hearts beat." He leaned down, teasing a kiss just out of my reach. "And why our cocks rise."

The laugh burst from my mouth just as my palm slapped to his chest. "You're almost romantic, but then you have to ruin it by being dirty."

"You love me dirty," he chuckled.

"I love you no matter how you are."

He paused, blinked once, then finally gave me that kiss.

CHAPTER 42

KYRIE

"I must admit, I didn't expect to see you again, Miss Vance." Gerard's eyes scanned the table to acknowledge the three men at my sides. "Nor the Sons of Odin."

"Yeah, the feeling is mutual," T-Bone said.

"This isn't an acceptance of your offer," I cut in. "But I wanted more information from you and came up with terms that would have to be met before I say yes."

"Of course." Gerard spread his hands, ever welcoming and diplomatic. "Name your terms."

"I want them in writing," I said, adding a hard edge to my voice. "And signed by a witness that is not you or me."

Gerard tilted his head, regarding me curiously. "You do realize your terms aren't enforceable yet, Miss Vance?"

"I know that. But after we make multiple copies and put them in several secure locations, whoever finds them generations from now will know which side I was on. If I'm betrayed, at least those who come after us will know what *I* stood for."

Gerard wore the look I'd seen often during my brief time as an ambassador. The look of a man who underestimated me.

"Very well," he conceded. "I'll track down someone to transcribe this whole meeting and witnesses to sign your terms. In the meantime, please." He gestured to the spread of untouched food on the table in front of us. "Help yourselves. You've had a long ride and are my guests."

"Fat fuckin' chance," T-Bone muttered as we all watched Gerard leave. He picked up a generously seasoned hard boiled egg and sniffed it.

"I'm pretty confident the food is safe." I swiped a thin cracker through some cheese dip and stuck it in my mouth before I could overthink it.

"Kyrie!" Dyno hissed. "Just because he gave you clean water in that basement does not mean the food is safe *now*."

"It's fine." I chewed the cracker and cheese, then washed it down with the wine provided. "More than fine, it's really good actually." Grudge decided to be brave next, biting into one of the eggs T-Bone had been inspecting.

"Those do look really fuckin' good," the skeptical president muttered.

Munin then hopped down from his shoulder, stepping delicately around plates on the table until he came to a bowl of peanuts. He dove face first into the bowl, making happy little caws and vocalizations at his find.

All of us were digging in by the time Gerard returned with three other people. "I wondered how long it would take you to come around," he remarked with a smile. "Believe it or not, I *want* to be allies and a good host. Let me know if anything is not to your liking."

"It certainly beats getting tied up and thrown in the

back of a truck." I couldn't help but bring that up again. While I understood the reasoning better, thanks to my men's perspective, I still didn't want him to think I had forgiven or forgotten.

"And yet here you are," Gerard returned lightly. "I stand by what I did, Miss Vance. I accomplished what I needed to do, with minimal harm to you and your men." He looked at T-Bone. "If only I could say the same about my own people."

T-Bone noisily gulped down a swallow of wine. "I also stand by what I did," he said. "You attacked us. We defended ourselves. Anyone who lays a hand on our woman deserves death."

I raised a hand to interject. "I am sorry about the soldier you lost. But I think you can agree that our reaction was understandable given the circumstances."

Gerard inclined his head. "I'm willing to put it behind us, if you are."

"I suppose that's what we're here to find out."

"Indeed." A smirk lifted the corner of his mouth before he turned to introduce the three people who'd walked in with him. "This is Renae. She was a court reporter before the Collapse and volunteered to transcribe this meeting for us. Loraine and Riley were both attorneys and have agreed to sign any agreements we make today as witnesses." He inclined his head, lifting an eyebrow. "Does this suit you, Miss Vance?"

"It does, thank you." I nodded to the three of them taking seats further down the long table. "And thank you for joining us."

Renae prepared herself with a small keyboard she'd brought, and then we began the meeting officially.

"The floor is yours, Miss Vance. Name your terms for

accepting my offered position as Lieutenant Governor of the newly formed territory of Gerardson."

My heart skipped a beat, and I thought I didn't hear him correctly. He wanted me for *Lieutenant* Governor? Second-in-command of the whole territory? He didn't mention that in the first meeting.

"Gerardson?" Dyno scoffed. "Naming the territory after yourself?"

The man shrugged. "It's what the people want to call it."

The transcriber tapped on her keyboard without comment. It was the only sound in the room as everyone waited for me to begin. My gaze locked onto Gerard's, whose eyes shined delightedly. He wasn't a stupid man and excelled at scheming. What game was he playing now?

It didn't matter, I'd find out soon enough. And I had tricks up my own sleeve.

"I want all kidnappings and hostage situations criminalized," I began. "This territory will not condone or orchestrate such actions, if I am to be a part of it."

Gerard shrugged. "It wasn't something I ever planned to make a habit of, but sure. Done. What else?"

"Violence will be outlawed, unless it's in self-defense or an act of war," I said. "It doesn't matter if it's your soldiers, citizens, police, with weapons, or without. I will not be part of a territory that uses fear tactics to keep people in line."

"Neither will I," Gerard answered solemnly. "We'll draft an extensive and fair penal code, Miss Vance, I assure you. What else?"

I swallowed and folded my hands together. "If I'm to spend a significant amount of time in this territory, I want the Sons of Odin MC to be able to come and go as they please. We will not tolerate harassment by your soldiers or police."

I felt my men's eyes on me in the silence that followed, but it was their hands squeezing my knees under the table that lit a fire under my skin. If Gerard noticed, he made no mention of it.

"Of course. Your people will have free reign throughout the territory, provided they don't break any laws you yourself agree to set in place."

"I'm not a hypocrite," I retorted.

"Good. We don't want a repeat of the last government, now do we?" I didn't dignify that with an answer, and he didn't wait for one. "Since you mention it, I've considered employing the Sons of Odin to work *with* my units. Gerardson and the surrounding areas will need protection, especially in the early days."

"We don't work for governors anymore," T-Bone said snidely. "Hasn't been very beneficial in our experience." He angled his head toward me. "Well, except for that last time," he amended softly, hand tightening around my thigh.

The touch and his words made me burn even hotter, but I had to concentrate. "The Sons of Odin can decide if they want to work with your units or not at a later date. That's entirely up to them and not pertinent right now."

"Fair enough." Gerard shrugged again. "Anything else?"

I took a moment to steady myself. This was the last piece I needed *and* the most important.

"I need you to agree to limited powers. Checks and balances in whatever governmental structure you create, with no loopholes. I want to see those limits personally before I agree to anything."

Gerard was silent for a long time, though he didn't seem angry. More curious than anything. I could almost hear the gears in his head turning.

"You think I'm hungry for power, Miss Vance?"

"I don't know you well enough to make that judgment. That's why I'm laying out my terms and making sure they're recorded. I would like to trust you, Gerard." I leaned back in my seat and lifted my chin. "But I don't know if I can."

Gerard nodded slowly, then smiled as he huffed out a soft laugh. I didn't understand what was humorous. He seemed...pleased. Like I had done exactly what he wanted, and that made me uneasy.

"I will agree to limited powers," he said finally. "We'll create three branches that each support and limit each other, just like before the Collapse."

"But better."

"But better," he agreed, smiling again. "Anything else?"

I racked my brain for something, anything else that I hadn't mulled over hundreds of times already. Something that would expose any nefarious intentions he had. But he had been agreeable to everything I said, and I had no other terms.

"That's everything." Those two words cut through the air like the final stroke of a pen.

"Excellent. Would you like to look over the transcript before it's signed?"

"Yes, please."

I must have read over that document at least three times before adding my signature to the bottom. The transcriber made several copies for me right then, and our business for the day was done.

"I'll have drafts of limited powers, a constitution, and a

penal code for your approval by the end of the month," Gerard said before lifting an eyebrow. "Unless you'd like to help me write them?"

"I, uh." The reality was sinking in now, my brain swimming with what I'd just done. "I would like to be involved in the process, yes."

"I was hoping you'd say that. How else will we find out if we work well together?" That clever, scheming look was in his eyes again. I knew in my gut there was something he wasn't telling me. "There's also the matter of planning the election."

"Is anyone running against you?" I asked.

"Not yet that I know of." He canted his head to the side. "But an endorsement from your father would still go a long way in gathering the people's confidence."

Ah, here it was. The ace up my sleeve.

I folded my hands in front of me. "Are you committed to having me as your running mate, Gerard?"

"Yes, absolutely."

"Good, because I come with myself and my experience alone. If you were hoping for access to Four Corners' support and resources, I'm afraid I can't help."

His brows knitted together in confusion. "And why not?"

"My father and I had a falling out. We are no longer speaking." I gave him my best innocent smile. "You're known to the people as a righteous man. I hope this doesn't mean you'll have to go back on your word."

"Ah, no." He cleared his throat, seemingly flustered for the first time. "Of course not. I wasn't hinging anything on Four Corners but was just…hopeful." He smiled slowly as he caught on. "You purposely withheld that from me."

"I had to be certain you really wanted me and not just

access to my father. But I'm not the only one withholding things, am I?"

Gerard only laughed as he turned to leave. "I'm truly looking forward to working with you, Miss Vance."

CHAPTER 43

KYRIE

"Jesus, Gerard wasn't kidding about this place." I held on to Dyno's cut as I leaned back, taking in the massive, sweeping lines of architecture in front of us.

"And this place is called a what again?" T-Bone joked, pretending to be dumb, but I humored him with an answer anyway.

"It's a library, sweetheart. Although I've never seen one this big."

We'd ridden to the northeast-most known border of the territory. I wanted to look through some history and legal texts for future legislation, and Gerard had suggested this library.

"It was once the biggest library in the state of Utah, and it almost fell to the Collapse's vandalism. But the citizens protected it, and now it's run by a passionate librarian." He'd smirked at that. "I think you'll like her. I have some things to attend to, but I'll meet you there later."

Is this the hidden Ace card up your sleeve? I wondered. *Who is this librarian?*

Nerves and excitement flipped in my stomach as I slid off the bike seat. I *loved* libraries, and it had been so long since I was in a really grand one.

"We're gonna check out the area." Dyno gestured to himself and T-Bone. "The Blakeworth border isn't far from here."

Grudge cut the engine on his bike and dismounted. Of course my quiet man who owned the Eddas in their native Old Norse would want to see the library with me.

"Be careful." I kissed T-Bone and Dyno, leaning up on their rumbling machines for long, lingering presses, because these guys didn't believe in quick pecks. "We'll be inside."

"Just hope we can find you in there." T-Bone gave one more suspicious look at the massive building before he and Dyno tore off.

Grudge and I approached the entrance together, fingers interlaced as we crossed the threshold.

"Oh, wow!"

"Mm-hmm," he agreed with awe and light amusement as we gazed at the sky-high columns of bookshelves.

Part of the walls and ceiling were glass panes, giving the place an open, airy feel. This was just the entryway, and it felt bigger and grander than my beloved foyer in Four Corners.

A pang hit my chest at the thought of my old home. My dad would have loved this library too. He had plans for a larger, even more accessible public library over the next few years. It was one of my favorite projects of his, and now it saddened me that I wouldn't be able to watch it come to fruition with him.

What awful timing that this was all sinking in now. I'd been so wrapped in my men over the last week that I'd barely stopped to think about what this estrangement meant.

I made the right decision. But it still hurt and made me sad.

Grudge brushed my cheek with his knuckles to get my attention. *"You okay?"* he asked, brows knitted with concern. My mood must have been obvious on my face.

"I will be, love." I kissed his fingers still resting on my cheek. "Just a lot of stuff sinking in right now. My dad and everything."

"None of us would be angry if you wanted to reach out to him again." He paused with a thoughtful expression before signing again. *"Okay, T-Bone may be a little. But only out of protectiveness over you."*

"I know. It might happen eventually, but not yet. I do think it's best that we're not talking right now, it's just an uncomfortable feeling. But I've needed to stand up for myself for a long time, so I'm not about to cave now."

The tension in Grudge's face eased as he smiled at me. *"Don't doubt how strong you are, my sweet valkyrie. Your armor, sword, and shield are here for you."*

I reached on tiptoes to kiss him. "Thank you. Should we browse some bookshelves now?"

"Mm-hm."

We ventured deeper into the expansive building, where the pillars of bookshelves continued. It felt like being a kid in a candy store. My eyes were pulled in all directions, and I didn't know where to begin.

Grudge and I wandered toward the reference desk. When the person behind it turned around, I squeaked in surprise at the familiar face.

"Anita! *You're* the librarian here?"

"Oh, hi, Kyrie! And me? No!" She laughed at that. "My sister is the librarian. I'm just helping her out."

"Oh! I didn't know you had a sister."

"Yeah, it's kind of a crazy story, actually. We couldn't get in contact with each other when the Collapse started and both thought the other was dead." She smiled brightly. "Then Gerard brought us together again."

"Really?" Some pieces were clicking into place now, just not the ones I expected. "You both knew him?"

"No, but my sister Evalyn's boyfriend did. Well," she snorted, "one of her boyfriends, anyway."

"I see."

Anita put down the stack of books she held and leaned her forearms across the desk toward me. "I know you're still unsure about him, Kyrie. He's not the most diplomatic person in the world, and I honestly was scared of him, at first. But then he brought my sister to me and gave her this library to run. And I realized...maybe we need more people like that. People who are abrupt and make things happen instead of hiding behind corruption and generational wealth."

Her eyes slid over to Grudge. "I was so scared your bodyguards would hurt you. I had the same fear about my sister's boyfriends too. You hear a lot about how awful the men in motorcycle clubs are, but what's the truth?"

Grudge made an annoyed huff, and I leaned into him until my head rested on his shoulder. "They might have done some unsavory things, but my men are the best, and I trust them with my life."

"Hmm." Grudge wrapped a possessive arm around my waist and kissed the top of my head.

"My sister would say the same thing." Anita shrugged. "I think it's the same with Gerard."

Her staunch defense of him was curious to me in that context, as was the reddening of her cheeks and expanding pupils when she talked about him.

"I'll keep that in mind," I said, which only made her blush deeper.

"Anyway!" Anita cleared her throat. "Can I help you find anything?"

"I'd actually love to meet your sister, if she's around."

"Oh, of course! I think she's in the law book collection."

"Perfect. That's just what we needed anyway."

It turned out that the library was so huge, Anita had to draw us a map of how to get to that section.

"I should've just brought my bike inside," Grudge joked as we passed through various wings and collections. He had a point. The corridors were plenty wide enough for a vehicle, and there were very few people around. Hopefully having Gerard as governor would get more foot traffic into here.

Some areas were fascinating and off-beat enough that I wished we could stop and browse. Grudge stared especially longingly at a collection all about the history of Scandinavia.

"We'll stop on our way back," I promised him.

The moment we stepped into the law book collection, a rough screeching sound made me jump. Grudge shoved me behind him, spinning in search of what had made that awful noise.

"Huh." He relaxed and pointed to one of the highest bookshelves, which was empty of books but looked to be filled with nesting material such as shredded paper, feathers, and various types of ribbon and string. It took me a second to spot the face staring back at us, two large, dark eyes set in a pale, almost heart-shaped face.

"What is that?" I whispered from behind Grudge's back. "An owl?"

"She's a barn owl with expensive taste. Aren't you, Athena?"

Walking through the stacks toward us was a beautiful woman in her thirties with brown skin and black hair. She smiled cheekily at the still-screeching owl, tossing a long loose braid over her shoulder. "Don't mind her. She thinks this whole place is hers to nest." Returning her attention to us, she said, "I'm Evalyn, the librarian. What can I help you with?"

"Hi, Evalyn. I'm Kyrie Vance, and this is Grudge."

She took us in with a thorough look, eyes lingering on Grudge's cut and patch. "Kyrie Vance, old lady to the Sons of Odin?"

I nodded, trying to observe her as shrewdly as she was doing to me. "Word travels fast, I guess."

"Gerard has told me a lot about you, Miss Vance. And my boyfriends' club is familiar with the Sons."

Grudge signed a question and I relayed it to Evalyn. "He's asking for the name of your boyfriends' club."

"Chasing Death MC."

"Huh!" Grudge let out an exclamation of surprise and signed quickly. *"From back east? They're a sister club from way back in the day. Last time we rode with them was before the Collapse."*

I relayed all of this to Evalyn, who smiled in return. "The very same. Russ is here with me, if you'd like to see him."

Grudge enthusiastically said yes, and the three of us

started walking together. "Congratulations on your nomination to lieutenant governor, Miss Vance," Evalyn said politely. "I take it you wanted to look at some law references while you're here?"

"I would, thank you. I'm most interested in United States laws from before the Collapse."

Evalyn regarded me with a gentle smile. "That would be pretty much everything in the collection."

"Oh, right."

"It's a fair question, actually. Record-keeping has been spotty since the country's fall. Now that there's so much division, it really depends on where you go and who you ask." She gestured toward a desk piled high with binders and folders crammed full of notes, all surrounding a small black screen in front of a keyboard. "I do my best to maintain accurate records, but I'm still only one librarian. I imagine this period in time will be full of blank spots when future generations look back on us."

"How can I help?" The question popped out of my mouth automatically.

Evalyn smiled at me even brighter. "Gerard was right. You are a go-getter. Well, bringing more qualified researchers and archivists to the area would certainly help."

"Do you have colleagues in those fields who would be willing to relocate here? I understand you're from the eastern side of the continent?"

Evalyn's smile wobbled. "You're correct, and I do. And they could be convinced to move here...if the territory was stable and they were able to travel safely." She slid a gaze in Grudge's direction. "Not everyone is lucky enough to be the property of an MC."

"A sentence I never thought I'd believe," I said just as

Grudge stood a little taller, draping a possessive arm over my shoulders. I cast him a smile before looking back at Evalyn. "I'll do what I can. Maybe the MCs can help facilitate safe travel for your colleagues."

She nodded at that. "I'm sure we can work something out."

We reached the far wall of the building's wing where a man in a black leather vest sat at another computer where commands of white text flashed across the dark screen. The back of the man's cut had a skeleton riding a motorcycle, the words Chasing Death MC above and below the design.

"Babe." Evalyn approached him, sliding an arm across his upper back. He startled at the touch, like he was so absorbed in his work that he never heard us coming this way.

"Hi, hon." His arms started to go around her waist before she stopped him with an amused smile.

"We have visitors."

The man turned in his seat. He was cute with brown hair and a clean-shaven face. He looked a few years younger than my guys, and boyish excitement filled his features as he noisily stood from his chair. "Holy shit! Grudge, is that you?"

The man at my side chuckled heartily and held his arms open.

Evalyn's boyfriend threw himself at him, making Grudge stumble as the two men slapped each other's backs affectionately.

"What the fuck, man? How long has it been— ten, twelve years? Where's the rest of the Sons of fuckin' Odin, huh?" His voice echoed up to the tall, slanted ceilings, but Evalyn didn't chastise him for being loud in the library.

Grudge signed an answer, which I relayed to the other man. "He says it's a long story. There's a lot to catch up on."

"No doubt, same here." He looked at me with a smile that would have made me blush if I wasn't already smitten with my three and extended his hand. "Hi, I'm Russ."

"Kyrie." I returned his smile and handshake. "It's nice to meet you."

"Russ is a tech wizard." Evalyn gave him a starry-eyed look as he draped his arm over her shoulders, mirroring her gaze.

"Ah, I'm just a nerd in a cut." He dropped a kiss on her forehead.

"*My* nerd," Evalyn corrected playfully. "A lot of records were computerized and kept on cloud storage before the Collapse, so he's been working on accessing those," she explained.

"Sounds like a project," I observed.

"It is." Russ rubbed his eyes and sighed. "I'll be lucky if I get through ten percent of all the data locked up in the now-defunct cloud systems in my lifetime." He perked up, beaming at us. "It's fun though. Like a digital treasure hunt."

Evalyn kissed his cheek and stepped out from under his arm. "Why don't you boys catch up while I help Kyrie find what she needs?"

"Sure, hon." He flashed another grin at me. "Nice to meet you."

"You too." I followed Evalyn down a side corridor lined with thousands of hardcover texts. "He seems really sweet," I said when we were alone.

"He is." She scanned book spines, lips pulling in a small, private smile. "Until you get on his bad side."

"I know a few like that."

She pulled a few volumes, all about constitutions and penal codes in the last three hundred years, and placed them on a small rolling cart she pulled alongside us.

We had lapsed into a companionable silence after wandering through the stacks for a while, when I decided to broach the biggest issue weighing on my mind. "Can I ask you something?"

Evalyn took a moment to answer, her voice tinged with caution. "Of course you can."

"Do you trust Gerard?"

"Yes," she said quickly, the word clipped and firm. "He served in the US military with Talon, the Chasing Death president. He may not be a club member, but he is family to them. And he brought my sister and I back together. I owe him a lot."

"I'm glad he's a man of integrity, and I'm really happy for you and Anita. But do you think he'll be a good governor?"

"Politics is not my strong suit." She smiled coyly. "That seems to be your arena, Miss Vance."

"We've talked extensively about our platform and plans for the territory. I understand his vision and his goals, but I don't know. I keep feeling like he's hiding something." Maybe expressing my doubts to this woman, of all people, wasn't the wisest move, but my guys already knew my feelings. I needed an outside perspective, and Evalyn seemed like a bit of a kindred spirit.

"He probably is."

I rocked back on my heels. "Well, that wasn't the answer I expected."

"Gerard is clever. And he's sneaky. He's very careful about what he says and who he says things to." She chuckled to herself. "Talon always says he would have been great in Chasing Death, except that they expect full transparency, and Gerard has too many secrets."

"Well, that honestly worries me. If he's keeping some big secret about his plans for the territory, that affects me. If I'm going to be his lieutenant governor, I need to be kept in the loop."

"I'm sure he'll tell you what his plan is when he feels the timing is right."

"That doesn't make me feel any better."

"Kyrie." Evalyn stopped pushing her cart and turned to look at me squarely. "I understand your worry. We're in vastly uncertain times right now, and you're about to be responsible for the welfare of thousands of people. People that Gerard saved. He wouldn't have planned that uprising only to push people back in the dirt again."

"I believe that, but I still don't know—"

"None of us know anything. For all we know, the new territory could fall because of things completely out of Gerard's control."

"But if he doesn't tell me things, I won't be able to help him." It felt like I was talking in circles, and I couldn't hide the frustration in my voice.

Evalyn placed a hand on my arm. "He's not plotting something nefarious behind your back, I can promise you that much."

"I have kind of come around to realize that he doesn't have bad intentions. But the fact that he's so secretive still makes me uneasy."

Her hand around my arm squeezed. "Give him the time to tell you on his own. Have a little faith."

I peered at her, really trying to read the expression on her face. "Do *you* know what he's up to?"

"Not the specifics. Like I said, he's very careful." She returned her hand to the book cart. "But you asked what I think, and given what I *do* know, you don't have anything to worry about."

I sighed, realizing I wasn't going to get any more than that. "Coming from you, that is a little comforting, actually."

Evalyn laughed lightly. "Because I'm a fellow woman?" She tapped a finger on her temple. "A keeper of knowledge?" She then looked over her shoulder, down the long corridor to where our men were catching up. "Or because we have more in common that we haven't even discussed yet?"

"A little of all of the above," I admitted.

She smirked at me and returned to scanning bookshelves.

CHAPTER 44

DYNO

"You nervous, little lady?"

I leveled a look at T-Bone. "Now that you've said it, you're gonna make sure she's nervous. Good job, T."

"It's just a question! And it's a big fuckin' day, everyone's all jumpy."

He was one to talk. Sweat beaded on his forehead, and he could *not* sit still. My six-year-old son Isaac was more calm and collected than him. The kid sat next to Kyrie's full-length mirror, watching her as she turned and straightened the various pieces of her outfit.

"I'm okay," Kyrie answered T-Bone distractedly through the mirror, leaning in to check her lipstick again. "How do I look, Isaac?"

"Pretty," he muttered shyly, unable to look away from her.

"Thank you! You look so handsome, and I'm glad you're here with us."

My son was still getting used to her, but the kid was clearly smitten. Kyrie and I had gone on a solo ride to see him in the hopes that it would sway Lacey into allowing us some extended time together. The moment my son's mother saw me with another woman instead of two men, she practically threw Isaac at us.

"Keep him for the whole summer, if you want," she'd said with a dismissive wave of her hand. "He's been acting out, and I could use a fucking break."

How strange, considering he seemed withdrawn and quiet until we left. Once it was just us and Kyrie, he started opening up, chattering about how much he missed me and the guys. His mom didn't like him talking about us, so I figured he'd bottled it up and acted out with tantrums.

The moment we made it home and Isaac saw T-Bone and Grudge again for the first time in over a year, he started bawling.

"It's okay, we missed you too." T-Bone had shushed and consoled him, holding him tightly while looking directly at me. "You know why? 'Cause you're our son too, little man."

I heard his meaning loud and clear. Once Kyrie was officially lieutenant governor, we could make Isaac ours full-time. If his mother wanted to see him, she would have to put in some effort for a change.

Kyrie made it clear she didn't want to replace Isaac's mother, which was fair. Over the last three months, she had been campaigning with Gerard and essentially rebuilding the territory from the ground up. Her busy schedule allowed for her and Isaac to slowly grow accustomed to each other in small doses.

"Do you love my dad?" my son had asked her over dinner one night.

"Yes, I do," she'd told him with a bright smile. "I love all three of them very much."

That night seemed to be a breakthrough. Ever since then, he asked about her every night she had to work late and seemed to miss her when she wasn't around.

Kyrie was a bundle of nerves on election night, even though they had run unopposed. Isaac held her hand and told her not to worry. She looked at him with such love in that moment that I knew she *was* his mother, even if not by blood.

Now the election results were finalized, and she and Gerard were preparing to address the territory with their acceptance speech. She *was* nervous, and T-Bone bringing it up certainly didn't help.

Grudge came up behind her as she continued to fidget in front of the mirror. He brought his hands in front of her and signed, *"You look beautiful, Lieutenant Governor. You'll knock 'em dead, like you always do."*

Kyrie leaned back against his chest, letting him support her slight weight. "Thank you. I know it'll be fine. It's just…"

"Stop thinking about that flushed piece of shit," T-Bone growled, his choice of words making Isaac snicker. "Your father showed how much he gives a fuck by ignoring the invitation, so don't waste another thought on him."

"I just can't stop hoping he'll surprise me by showing up unexpectedly. And if he's not there, it'll just be disappointing."

"There's thousands of people out there who can't wait to see you lead them," I said. "Who have seen and appreciate all the months of hard work you've put into this. You're changing their lives for the better, Kyrie. Focus on them."

"You're right." She straightened, taking a final look in the mirror. "You're all right. I need to focus on what's important."

"That's our girl." T-Bone beamed at her. His arms crossed over his chest, standing proudly behind her, but I didn't miss the subtle tremble in his fingers at his sides. I suppressed a snort as we filed out of Kyrie's dressing room. Our girl, nervous? She was rock-steady compared to him.

Gerard waited for us in the main backstage room. Only a curtain stood between us and the citizens of this territory, and I could already hear the low murmuring of the waiting crowd.

"Ready?" Gerard asked us, straightening the lapels of his suit.

"Ready when you are, Governor," Kyrie answered him, the perfect image of poised and put together.

His lips twitched into a smirk. "Shall we?"

He and Kyrie walked out together to thunderous applause while the rest of us followed. I held Isaac's hand, keeping him at my side despite his pulling to get closer to Kyrie. Technically speaking, the guys and I were security. But it was well-known that we were Kyrie's family and that being onstage was primarily to support her.

She and Gerard waved, grinning broadly at the cheering masses. It was far from my usual crowd, but even I had to pause and take in all the faces that came to see her. That chose her to lead them. I hoped some of those crusty old fucks from the last administration were out there, stewing in their rage.

Gerard approached the podium and began his speech, while Kyrie stood respectfully to his side. I held Isaac in front of my legs, hands on his shoulders while I half-listened, but mostly I just watched people's faces. It had been a long time since I'd seen genuine hope and optimism in so many expressions in one place. When I glanced at Kyrie, I saw that she was doing the same—scanning every single face that she saw.

I couldn't have been more proud of her and knew how seriously she took this position. She'd put all of herself into bettering people's lives until nothing was left, if she could help it. That was where the guys and I came in. To fill her back up when this job took too much out of her.

She would have long nights ahead, and we'd have long rides. Chris and Tiff were already testing some promising new prospects to be Sons of Odin members. Instead of smuggling illicit goods, our business was turning into smuggling people out of dangerous territories and into ours. There was much work to be done, but the future was bright.

"My first announcement as governor is not something I've discussed with any cabinet members or advisors." Gerard casually turned a page in his speech as Kyrie's head snapped up to look at him. "But it is something I've given a tremendous amount of thought, and I'm certain this decision is the best one for me personally and for the good of the territory."

Everyone on stage froze, and I could feel the waves of adrenaline pouring from Kyrie. She'd been convinced for months, based on a gut feeling, that Gerard had some secret plan he'd been waiting to enact. The guys and I all exchanged looks. It seemed she had been right after all.

"We agreed on four-year term limits for governors and a maximum of two terms to be served," he went on. "However, my place is not up here on this stage. My place is not in an office or holed up in meetings. You all chose me because I acted. I led the charge that drove out the previous regime so all of you could thrive."

The crowd broke out in applause and yells that drowned him out. Some were cheering, others sounded upset or confused because it seemed like he was stepping down. The day after getting elected, no less. Kyrie's chest heaved with ragged breaths as she stared at him. I could only imagine what was going through her mind. And whatever the hell Gerard was doing, what did this mean for her?

"Oh…holy shit." I brought a hand to my mouth in awe. It hit me just as the crowd quieted down.

"I am beyond grateful and flattered that you chose me as your first governor," Gerard continued. "But I believe with all my heart that my place is *beside* all of you, not above you. I'm a man who gets his hands dirty, not one who makes decisions behind closed doors. The truth of the matter is, I'm not made for the political arena. However," he paused, eyes and chin tilting ever so slightly in Kyrie's direction, "I know someone who excels in that area. Someone who is tough and compassionate and who sees all of you. She will not lead you astray."

Kyrie's palm came to her chest, mouth dropping open as his words sank in.

"Is he saying what I think he is?" T-Bone whispered.

"That he's stepping aside so Kyrie can be governor? Yeah, that's what it sounds like." I could hardly believe it myself.

"I will serve as your governor for the first two years of my term." Gerard flipped another page in his speech as calmly as ever. "When we have ironed out all of the intricacies of running a brand-new territory, I will step aside so that my lieutenant governor, Kyrie Vance, can fill the role that she is much more suited to and qualified for than I."

Kyrie was still staring at him in frozen, open-mouthed shock.

"Is this okay?" T-Bone whispered to me again. "She obviously didn't know. And he didn't even ask her."

"She wouldn't have accepted," I said. "She'd never think she was ready or the right person. But she is, and *that's* what he's been holding on to all this time."

"I'll be damned." T-Bone rubbed his beard. "Well, shit, how are we gonna top that?"

"Dunno," I admitted. "Don't want to waste this opportunity, but she probably doesn't need another heart attack right now."

Grudge whacked me in the chest and gestured rapidly.

"Hang on, sign slower," I told him. "Do that again."

"Let's just fucking do it. She doesn't know it yet, but this is the best day of her life. Let's make it even better."

"Agreed," T-Bone said. "Plus, I can't wait any longer. I'm almost jumping out of my fucking skin."

"Really?" I scoffed. "I couldn't tell."

"Fuck off, D. I've never done this before."

"Neither have I, but you don't see me sweating like a whore in church."

Grudge smacked us both to get our attention. *"Focus. When she's done with her speech, we get out there."*

Gerard had stepped away from the podium, and Kyrie walked up to take his place. Her words shook initially, clearly in shock and surprise from what he'd revealed. After a moment, her voice grew stronger and then impassioned. Everyone in attendance was raptly focused on her, like they knew right away that Gerard had made the right choice. This woman was meant to lead them and had the heart, brains, and grit to do the job.

And she was ours. Now and forever.

"Everyone needs allies and loved ones in times of struggle," Kyrie said. "Whether as your governor, lieutenant governor, or just a listening ear, I will be there for you. When I'm facing those struggles myself, I have the three most amazing men to lean on." She turned to look at us, a massive smile on her beautiful face. "Four now," she added to include Isaac, who looked up at me excitedly.

"Yup, she's talking about you, buddy." I patted his shoulder and looked up just in time to see Grudge signaling to all of us. "What? Now?"

He nodded and began striding across the stage with T-Bone on his heels. I hurried after them with Isaac in tow, my stomach clenching and flipping at the same time. Okay, *now* I was nervous.

Kyrie was still smiling, her expression questioning as we walked out. When we all dropped to one knee, it became abundantly clear.

The crowd went absolutely berserk, which was the best outcome we could have hoped for. It was a huge risk, the three of us asking her so publicly like this. But this day was a brand new start for so many people, and we wanted others like us to feel safe to be themselves. And we knew Kyrie would want the same.

She leaned against the podium, tears on the brink of falling, but her grin was as radiant as ever. The audience was cheering too loud for us to hear her, but her lips moved as if to say, "Are you fucking serious?"

"Dead serious, little lady," T-Bone said as the noise ebbed away. "We realize now that we have to share you with the whole territory, but luckily for you, we're good at sharing."

Kyrie laughed, releasing an unladylike snort that was so perfectly her.

"I think we all knew years ago, when we first met, that something was meant to happen between us," I said. "Call it the will of the gods, fate, whatever it may be. You were always meant to be ours, and we were always meant to be yours. I've never been more certain of anything else."

Grudge signed to her, *"We were imperfect, incomplete, until we had you. You are the piece that completes us. I thought I wasn't supposed to exist, but loving you is the reason I exist."*

"Be our old lady." T-Bone's voice was barely above a plea. "Officially, legally, whatever. Will you be our wife in every capacity that matters?"

Soft caws floated through the air, growing louder as the black-feathered bird approached. Thousands of faces watched Munin float down toward the podium until he landed, securing himself with one claw while the other held a small wooden box.

"I don't even need to look at this," Kyrie said, taking the ring box from the bird. "The answer is yes. I love all of you so much, and you complete me too."

"Me too?" Isaac piped up.

Kyrie laughed and rushed to hug him. "Yes, of course you too!"

The five of us forgot about everyone else watching as we embraced and kissed and laughed. My whole world condensed down to these people right here. I kissed T-Bone and Grudge without a single fuck given as to who was watching. This was my family, the people I loved the most.

"At least look at the ring," T-Bone grumbled through

his ecstatic grin. "Tiff sold off a lot of booze to a dry territory so we could buy it."

"I can't believe everything that's happened in a single day," Kyrie laughed, wiping away tears. "I'm shaking so bad, I can't even open it."

Grudge opened the box for her, and I slid the platinum band topped with a two-carat diamond onto her finger.

"There." I pulled her into me, kissing her forehead. "We're here for you in every way, forever."

"Forever," she repeated, sliding her arms around me.

EPILOGUE

KYRIE

TWO YEARS LATER

"Hey, mom, who was Cesar Chavez?"

I looked up in disbelief, my eyes landing on Isaac who had surrounded himself with piles of books in the corner of my office. He was eight years old now, bright and curious. And...I hadn't heard him right, had I?

"What did you say, sweetie?"

"I said, who was Cesar Chavez?" He held up a book. "This book is about him, so he must be important."

My heartbeat settled, and I smiled. I *swore* I heard him call me mom, but of course that wasn't right. He had a mother, although he hadn't seen her in nearly six months.

After Dyno and I went to meet Lacey, they agreed on three-month custody schedules. Isaac would stay with us during the school term, which he badly needed because his homeschooling was seriously lacking, and stay with his mother during breaks from school.

That lasted all of four months.

Isaac was shy with me at first, but we soon became great friends, and I fell in love with the little boy who was a spitting image of his dad. The first three months flew by, and I cried the whole way home after we dropped him off with his mother.

A month after that, she showed up unannounced and practically dumped him on our doorstep. She screamed at us, saying Isaac was acting out and throwing tantrums like never before. He didn't like her food, he missed his friends and his room with us. We'd spoiled him rotten, and she couldn't handle him. I hugged that boy with everything I had, wishing I could shield him from it all while Dyno made Lacey leave.

She hadn't been back since.

While I loved having Isaac full-time, he always called me Kyrie, or *little lady* when he was impersonating T-Bone. Which was fine. I'd been a stranger to him until two years ago. But it still sent a little rush through me when I thought I heard *mom*.

"Cesar Chavez was very important," I said, rising from my desk to take a little stretch. "He helped a lot of people who were being treated unfairly."

"Like you?" It was a genuine question, not flattery. His long, dark eyelashes blinked as he waited for an answer.

"Me?" I said, genuinely surprised.

"Dad always says you help people when others don't help them, and that's why you're the governor."

I just stared at this beautiful boy, stunned and moments away from bursting with how much I loved him and his fathers.

"That's sweet of him," was all I could think to say. "I do try my best."

A knock rapped at my office door and T-Bone swaggered in moments later, heading straight for me.

"What's wrong?" I asked, noting the scowl on his face.

His hands circled my waist and he lowered a smoldering kiss to my mouth until Isaac made gagging sounds.

"Your father's here," he said in a low voice.

I could feel his anger simmering beneath the surface, felt it in his grip at my waist. Even now, he treated my dad like a threat to my happiness, as a malevolent force to protect me from. Grudge probably would have been a more fitting nickname for him than our Grudge.

"Thank you for letting me know." I held T-Bone's cheeks with my palms and kissed him again in an effort to soothe him. "Have Anita send him in."

"Do you want me to stay?"

"No, I'll be alright."

Dad and I hadn't spoken for a year, and then he sent me a letter out of the blue. He spoke casually and didn't mention the Sons at all, so I ignored it. His second letter though, was a long, rambling apology. We'd stayed in sporadic contact after that, but today was our first in-person meeting since I'd left Four Corners.

"Come on, kiddo." T-Bone went to Isaac and ruffled his hair. "Kyrie's got an important meeting."

"Hang on, I'm reading," Isaac grumbled back.

I chuckled, my heart lifting at what a bookworm he was turning out to be. "It's fine, he can stay."

"Oh, *he* can stay," T-Bone teased, kissing me again quickly on his way out. "I'll be right outside if you need me, little lady."

"Thanks, my love."

I leaned against an armchair as I watched him leave, gathering my thoughts and assessing my mental state for this visit. I felt...good. Calm. I used to dread the idea of meeting with my father, because they always centered around me acting out of line and how disappointed he was. He was not an intimidating, scary man, but he used guilt and fear to control me.

Well, now he was in my domain, where I was in control. I wasn't powerless anymore, and he needed to recognize that. My office door opened, and I pushed off the chair to stand.

In my peripheral vision, my armored valkyrie moved into a protective stance, her axe and shield at the ready.

My father was visibly nervous as he entered my office. His eyes latched onto my face and then fell to my stomach, gently rounded with early pregnancy.

"Kyrie—" he began.

"Governor Vance," I said evenly, clasping my fingers over my belly. "How nice of you to visit."

His mouth opened and then closed before a sheepish smile appeared. "Thank you for having me...Governor Vance. Congratulations again, by the way."

"It's my pleasure, and thank you." I gestured toward the two armchairs in front of my desk. "Please, have a seat. Can I get you anything to drink?"

"No, thank you, dear. I'm alright." He shifted uncomfortably in the chair, looking at my belly again as I sat across from him. "Congratulations on your upcoming addition as well."

"Thank you." I ran a protective hand over my belly, careful to keep my face neutral. "We're all very excited."

Dad's eyes darted to my face again. "The father—?"

"All three of my husbands are fathers," I said firmly.

"Yes, yes of course. I didn't mean..."

He trailed off when Isaac climbed onto the arm of my chair and hugged around my neck.

"Are you done reading?" I asked, patting Isaac's back.

"Mm-hm." He hugged me tighter, glancing curiously at my father who looked back at him with equal interest.

"This is Isaac, my stepson," I said.

"Oh. Hello, young man," my dad said politely.

"This is my mom." Before I had time to react, Isaac reached down to pat a gentle hand on my belly. "And this is my baby brother."

"Or sister," I corrected with a soft laugh as I blinked away tears of utter joy.

To further compose myself, I hugged him closer and kissed his messy mop of dark hair. He called me *his mom* so casually, like it was the most natural thing in the world. This precious boy had no idea what that meant to me.

Isaac squirmed in my hug, now embarrassed by the affection. "Can I go see what Dad's doing?" he mumbled.

"Yes," I laughed, kissing him once more on the forehead. "Daddy T-Bone is right outside, go ahead."

My father and I both watched him scamper off, and Dad had a knowing look on his face when his eyes returned to me. "You seem very happy."

Understatement of the century, but I nodded. "I am."

Dad clasped his hands together in front of him. "I'm so proud of you, Kyrie. Truly, I am." He pulled in a deep breath. "I was a fool, I can see that now. And I am so, *so* glad that I didn't succeed with my foolishness. I'm proud that you fought for what you wanted, even if it was against everything I stood for at the time." He nodded to himself, as though trying to believe his own words. "Yes, I'm proud you've done so well for yourself, in spite of how I mistreated you."

"I wasn't the only one mistreated," I reminded him.

He nodded again, hands clasping tighter. "Yes, I know. You're right. Your husbands deserved better. For years, I was unfair to them. They deserve an apology too." His eyes shifted. "If they would like that from me."

I allowed myself to relax, sinking into the cushion of my chair. Our relationship wouldn't be repaired overnight, but we were making progress, and that was better than nothing. He could apologize and grovel all he liked, but it was actions that mattered. And I think we both knew I wouldn't be so quick to forgive him this time.

"If you hadn't given the guys a reason to leave Four Corners, we probably wouldn't have ended up together," I said. "So I guess it wasn't all bad."

Dad looked relieved, but he was smart enough to know he wasn't off the hook entirely. "You are happy and successful. I just wish I had been a more positive force in your life for you to get here." He swallowed, and I saw the shine of tears in his eyes before he quickly wiped them away. "I have many regrets, Kyrie."

My defenses thawed a little more at that, and I reached for his hand. "You know, a wise man named Martin Vance told me that the only way through a difficult time is forward." I squeezed his fingers. "So let's try our best to move in that direction."

He smiled and squeezed back. "I don't know about the wisdom of that man, but it was a very wise woman who said it to him." His gaze cast to the side, looking sad again for a moment. "A warrior of a woman."

He didn't have to say who she was. We both knew.

I released his hand and stood up, then held my arms out for a hug. Dad hung back, adorably careful of my belly while he hugged my upper back. It felt good to hug him, I had to admit. Distancing myself was necessary, but he was still my family, and I had missed him.

"Would you like to have lunch with us?" I asked when we separated.

Dad beamed and offered me his elbow. "I would love nothing more."

"How long are you staying in Gerardson?" I picked up my purse, and together we headed for the office doors.

"That depends." He gave me a cautious smile. "I planned on a brief personal visit, but if the governor of Gerardson wants to discuss business, I'm sure I can rearrange my schedule."

I grinned with a light squeeze on his elbow. "I'm sure we can fit in some productive business meetings, Governor Vance."

"I agree," he paused, "Governor Vance."

Just before we walked out the door, in the corner of my vision, my valkyrie smiled.

The End

Not ready to say goodbye yet?
Join my newsletter for exclusive bonus scenes with Kyrie, the Sons, their children, and the Steel Demons!

Download it at this link:
https://BookHip.com/XHZZTRJ

Curious about Mari and her men in the Steel Demons MC?
Their story begins with Lawless:
http://books2read.com/SDMC1

Acknowledgments

Oh man, this book was a BEAST! Thank you to my office chair, for supporting my butt during the near five months it took to write this story.

I wasn't sure how writing a standalone reverse harem would go, but I am so happy and proud that I could give Kyrie, T-Bone, Dyno, and Grudge their happily ever after. A massive thank you to the Steel Demons MC readers who were rooting for these characters since they first appeared on the page. It was all of you who inspired me to give these characters a love story of their own, and I hope I did them justice.

A huge thank you to Elizabeth and Telisha, who got the first look at this story and eased my nerves about trying something new (I still can't believe I wrote a standalone, LOL).

Thank you to my infinitely patient and supportive husband, Mr. Ash. You asking, "Get your writing done?" and me snarling in response is how we say I love you at this point. Not everyone can hang with a semi-feral author, but you get me.

And if Their Property is your first book by me, thank *you*

for taking a chance on a new author. If you've read this far,
I truly hope you've enjoyed the ride.

See you all in the next book!

-Crystal

Also by Crystal Ash

Harem of Freaks: The Complete Series

Say Your Prayers

Steel Demons MC

Lawless

Powerless

Fearless

Painless

Helpless

Heartless

Senseless

Ruthless

Merciless

Endless

Shifted Mates Trilogy

Unholy Trinity: The Complete Series

For a complete list of books by Crystal Ash, visit her Amazon
page.

About the Author

Crystal Ash is a USA Today Bestselling Author from California. She loves writing steamy, heart-wrenching romance with tortured heroes, especially if they're in a reverse harem. Crystal's other loves include animals, mythology, and well-crafted alcohol, most of which can also be found in her stories.

When she's not writing, she's probably drinking craft beer with her husband or trying to coax her feral cat into accepting affection.

crystalashbooks.com